"For who can rule men... their...

The Grand Inquisitor—The Brothers Kasmirov

"Whatever is exposed by the light becomes revealed, and whatever illuminated by the light becomes the light."

Ephesians 5:13

Dedicated to my wife, Kristie, who makes my life whole.

Thank you, Tracey!

Chapter 1: Pieces

Abigail's sobs cut into Byron's heart as she poured out her pain and fear upon his shoulder. The two of them were safe in the Refuge as the monitors behind Abigail flickered with activity. Enforcers were swarming through all of Axiom. Each monitor showed different levels of assault and intrusion as Figures were rounded up, interrogated, struck down.

All of Byron's associates had gone silent. No one was speaking. No one was reaching out. The very idea of a rebellion to overthrow Lorenzo seemed like an impossible memory. He had complete control over Axiom, and the Lord Protector had broken the barrier of nonviolence. For centuries violence had been a myth of humanity's follies—a forgotten scar which had almost healed. But now, blood ran in Citadel.

The Comande was dead. Byron could still hear the sound of his head splitting as the Lord Protector fired the shot. In one single moment, Lorenzo thwarted Byron's plans. Lorenzo had the upper hand. He had all the resources and power necessary to crush any sort of rebellion.

Abby lifted her head. Her face was red from crying, and her eyes shimmered with tears. She bit her bottom lip until it drew blood.

"We're going to stop him, aren't we?" She pleaded.

Byron didn't have the strength to tell his daughter it was hopeless. He merely nodded and let her plans live on.

"How?" Abby inquired as she wiped her face.

He had no idea. But, she was asking. Byron went to respond when his manipulor flashed. Critical communication was about to be broadcast. Byron flicked his hand towards the wall as an image came into focus.

"Axiom, my beloved Axiom."

At the sound of Lorenzo's voice, Byron's blood boiled.

"Something disastrous has occurred, my children…"

Myra's heart slammed in her chest. Her breath heaved in labored gasps as she carried the wounded man. The smell of charred skin and burnt hair was intoxicating, but she commanded her stomach not to rebel.

Myra could still hear the bomb detonating. She was haunted by the concussive blast which rolled through the mountain, through the tunnels, and had chased after them like hunger. As the fires howled through the tunnels, many hadn't been lucky enough to escape the onslaught. Dozens died immediately. Almost everyone sustained injuries, whether by the flames or the cave-ins which trailed after the detonation.

That was almost a day ago, or so she assumed. In the dark, with hands groping and the sound of moaning, it was hard to know the passing of time. It was always just one step forward, and forward, and forward. If Paul hadn't forced her to leave, more would be dead.

Myra's heart sank. Paul didn't know she was alive. She didn't know if Paul was alive. The idea of a world without him seemed impossible. It was a mountain that offered no freedom. She had no idea what to do next.

How long were the tunnels? Would they die of starvation and exposure before they reached the end? What was she supposed to do once they got out?

Myra didn't know. For now, she could only help the man leaning on her from stumbling and falling.

"Axiom...my beloved Axiom."

Myra stopped in her tracks. Somebody collided with her, and shouts of alarm broke through the tunnel.

"Shhh! Quiet! I thought I heard something," she demanded sharply. Myra inclined her ear. The sound was distant—floating through the tunnels like a whisper—but she knew it was real.

"Something...my children...death has come..."

Hope stirred within her.

They were almost free.

Damien paced in his cell. He was in a room with a cot, metal walls, and a door activated outside by a terminal. A nervous, bubbling energy radiated throughout his body, which prevented him from sitting still. Ever since that moment—the moment when Theo reached out for Damien—everything had changed. Damien didn't have words to describe what he felt and didn't feel.

Damien didn't feel ashamed—the anxiety and bitterness of being alone and vulnerable. It was gone. The moment Theo touched him, it had fled him.

Damien wasn't afraid.

But, what was he supposed to do next? Where did Theo go? Why did he leave Damien locked up? If Damien simply had a couple of minutes to talk to him, he was sure he could convince Theo to agree to his plan—a plan which would reverse all the evil in Axiom.

First, Theo needed to spring Damien out of his cell. Damien didn't have the whole thing figured out, but he assumed if he just called upon Theo's name, then he would hear Damien and appear. Despite feeling a little foolish, Damien closed his eyes and sifted through the words spoken in desperation moments before Theo appeared. He did his best to recreate the concept in his head as words formed on his lips.

"O Great and Powerful Theo. I submit myself unto thee. I need you to appear so that I can impart upon your great brilliance a plan to restore justice and order for all," he said in his most resonant voice.

Damien listened with eyes shut. Nothing happened.

Damien opened one eye to see if anyone appeared.

The cell was empty. His brow furrowed.

"Creator of all things, I call upon your presence." Damien was interrupted as a Com appeared just above his head where there was a wall a second prior.

"Axiom, my beloved Axiom," a voice rumbled grimly. Damien stood beneath the Com and stared into the face of the Lord Protector.

"Something disastrous has occurred, my children…"

Sebastian stirred with a groan. Every muscle in his body felt stiff and heavy. His head was underwater. Slowly, he sat up. Stars danced in front of his eyes as his mind collected itself.

Sebastian remembered arriving at his Quarters. He remembered seeing his father. Remembered pain erupting from his lower abdomen when his father stabbed him. His hand flew to his stomach. He could feel the swollen wound.

It didn't make sense. Why was he alive?

For a second, Sebastian wondered how his father could have tried to kill him. The pain from the betrayal spread through him. How could the man who was supposed to help him understand the world do something so evil? These thoughts made him dizzy. There would be time later to answer them. For now, he needed to escape.

But how? Sebastian couldn't use his manipulor. His father had taken it from him just seconds before Sebastian collapsed. Sebastian was on his own.

A sudden light filled the room, snapping Sebastian out of his growing anxiety as a face materialized on the wall. It was the Lord Protector. Sudden revulsion drenched in fear gathered in his gut. The Lord Protector had known all along about Sebastian's treachery, and when his justice came down upon Sebastian, it had been full. Where could he go where the Lord Protector would not be present?

"Axiom, my beloved Axiom."

Sebastian steadied himself against the wall. His head swam as his legs trembled.

"Something disastrous has occurred, my children. Violence has entered Axiom. Death has come to our perfect society," the Lord Protector stated somberly. Sebastian took an uneasy step towards his bed.

"Who is to blame for this atrocity? It is this Figure."

Sebastian watched the recording of Hydra's destruction. Although he had seen it played in his mind hundreds of times, the sight of it on the Com made his stomach churn.

So many were dead—washed away by a mountain of water. The recording faded, and the Lord Protector's visage returned. Sebastian moved to the door and ran.

"He will be found, and those who helped him will be sought out. They will be destroyed," The Lord Protector promised, as a horrifying reality chased the young man.

Sebastian was a criminal.

Chapter 2: Instability

Damien, Location Unknown

Damien felt disgust accumulate in the back of his throat as the Lord Protector's threat rolled off the tyrant's tongue. Damien wasn't afraid of the man who acted like a god. He'd seen plenty of warlords claim unyielding power. It was the same promise every time. But, Damien knew all kingdoms came to an end, so it was only a matter of time.

But, what was his place in all of it? What was his purpose here? If someone asked him the same questions just a couple of days ago, he would've mocked. His place was out there, in the real world, where he could fend for himself—or so he'd assumed. Now, there was something in him, like a memory, which kept reminding him he was a piece of a much larger puzzle. It was a nudge—gentle, but sure.

What did it all mean? Damien didn't know. The idea of a purposeful life was still a foreign concept. He pushed it out of his thoughts and focused intently on the bigger issue at hand— his escape. Damien needed to get out of his cell, out of whatever Protectorate he was in, and find his way back to Byron—assuming Byron was still alive.

Damien found this unlikely. Rais had known precisely where to find Damien—he was waiting for him and ambushed Damien at the end of the tunnel. The secrecy of the uprising—of Hajj—was undone. In a single moment, all the plans made in the darkness were suddenly, irrevocably brought to the light.

As he weighed this in his mind, the same blunt reality kept standing in his way: he had no idea how to get out of his cell. The only time the door opened was when a slot opened up just wide enough for food on a flimsy plate.

At first, Damien was surprised the door didn't disappear into the wall like all the other doors in Axiom. But, upon analyzing the room, he realized this part of Axiom was older than the rest. There was the hum of electricity in the room. The walls were scuffed and chipped. The air smelled of chemicals, but they weren't strong enough to hide the musk and mildew.

Damien's mind wrestled with his options. He couldn't reach the Com above his head, which meant he couldn't rip it open and use the pieces to construct a weapon. His clothing didn't contain any buttons or laces. The plate they fed him on each day wasn't sturdy enough to sharpen. There were no loose pieces in the wall, cracks in the floor, nor screws in his cot. The room wasn't even big enough for him to build up enough momentum to rush the door.

Damien sat down, defeated. Despite his survival skills and abilities, he was stuck. Exhausted from the mental wrestling, he laid down on the cot and stared at the ceiling. His eyes traced the brush strokes left over from years of faded paint. The hum of electricity grew louder and louder in his thoughts until it itched and clawed into his mind.

Damien bit his lip in frustration and squeezed his eyes shut. His heart pounded in his ears. His breath choked in his throat. He felt helpless, and the feeling was a crushing weight on his chest.

The hum stopped.

Damien waited a second before opening his eyes.

A loud silence was in his cell. He sat upright as he tried to figure out why the hair on the back of his neck was standing.

An invisible force threw Damien to the floor. Dust and debris showered his head as the room shook with violence. Instinctively, he made himself small as the world became unhinged.

Myra, Location Unknown

Myra led the slaves through the tunnels. The voice had stopped speaking, but she pushed onward. There was no way of knowing how far away the origin of the disembodied words was, but she hoped it was not far. She was exhausted, and her burns were beginning to smell of infection. Everyone reeked of body odor and decay.

Her hand slid against the wall. The dirt was soft, like powder. It reminded her of the mountain, of the only home she'd ever possessed. She longed to hide within its embrace. But, the mountain was gone.

That life was over.

There was no Paul to guide her, to reassure her, to teach her. Now, she didn't know where to go. For all she knew, she was leading everyone to their grave.

A strange noise rebounded off the walls. The air smelled funny—stale and heavy.

"Wait," she instructed as she held up her hand. Even though she had gotten used to seeing in the dark, it was still too gloomy to make out what lay ahead.

A breeze, lifeless and warm, stirred her hair as a grinding noise whispered down the tunnel. Her skin crawled. Myra felt the tremors through her feet. At first, she thought her legs were quivering with fatigue as they quaked underneath her. But, the walls started to crack and crumble around her, and she knew something terrible was happening.

"Run!" She yelled as the tunnels behind them dissolved. She could hear the walls breaking and bowing. The sound struck painful fear into her heart. A woman in front of Myra tripped and fell. Myra got caught up in arms and legs and fell, too. People were screaming and shouting, unable to comprehend what was causing the ground to become like water.

Myra stood quickly and reached down to help the woman up. The ceiling above them came crashing down and buried the woman up to her elbow.

Shocked and repulsed, Myra could only stare in horror as a black liquid flowed in the tunnel's darkness. Another violent jolt brought her out of her paralysis as she turned and followed the rest of her group. Fear ate at her mind as tears rolled hotly down her cheeks.

Myra felt a breeze.

Soft and tender.

Like a kiss.

It was coming from her left. As she ran, holding onto the edges of the tunnel as best she could, her hand found emptiness. It was another tunnel. The air coming from it was cool, and moist and she smelled mud and mildew. She couldn't see into the tunnel, though, for it was a deep, lonely darkness.

It had to be the way out.

"Everyone! This way! Follow me!"

Heads and bodies turned in her direction. In the gloom, they could make out her frantic waving. Some continued to run forward, but the majority listened to her and followed her down this new tunnel.

The sound of the earth ripping apart got louder. Myra waited until no one else was coming before she too turned into the longing darkness. As she turned, the tunnel behind her came crashing down.

Sebastian, Industry Protectorate, Station 004

Sebastian felt the terror rise in his chest. The world was shaking with violence he couldn't comprehend.

He ran. No longer was he concerned with remaining hidden in the shadows as his instincts took control. His feet hurried him towards the only place he knew might be safe.

Sebastian stumbled into the Station and found a scene of chaos and confusion. People were staggering around, clutching one another, with fear and terror etched upon their faces. Every manipulor displayed a fiery red. No one was concerned with proximity—not even the Enforcers also caught up in the madness.

Axiom was rebelling against itself. The lights flickered, and the walls quivered. Blue lines darted in all directions like ripples on water.

An earsplitting screech filled the station. Suddenly, the Train hurtled out of the tunnel. Sebastian watched in horror as one of the cars lost its magnetism and careened out of control. Instead of blue lines shooting out of every surface to prevent the car from doing any damage, nothing prohibited it from carving out a path of destruction as it jumped onto the Station.

The car tumbled side over side as it took out columns. Carnage silenced helpless Figures. Sebastian reacted out of instinct as he grabbed the man directly in front of him and pulled him out of harm's way. They stumbled backward, and the air sliced open where the man had been standing.

The train car continued onward until it smashed into the wall. With a violent and final crash, it came to a rest on its side. The ground beneath Sebastian's feet solidified as the shaking ended. Dust and debris choked the air. People were screaming, moaning, and crying out for help.

The man Sebastian saved looked at him with disbelief and fear etched into his face.

"What happened? What did this?"

Sebastian looked at the violence and carnage in front of him and tried to make sense of it all. Never before had this happened in Axiom. But, what was once not possible was now a frightening reality. Like searing steam, a terrifying conclusion penetrated Sebastian's mind.

Axiom was no longer safe.

Chapter 3: Sinking

Myra, Location Unknown

The ground beneath Myra's feet was soft and spongy. Mud oozed into her shoes, and she could feel the soppy dirt working in between her toes. Still, she pushed onward, forcing others to their feet when they fell.

The tunnel was no longer shaking. It seemed whatever had happened was finally over. Myra's heart thundered in her ears, and she wasn't taking the reprieve for granted. They had to find a way out before another shake occurred.

She felt it again.

Wind. It was fresh and light. The exit had to be close.

Myra heard soft cries of alarm from those ahead of her. A few steps later, she felt the shock of cold water reach her knees. It was like ice against her skin. She could hear the hesitation from those in front.

"Keep going! We're almost there."

It was a promise she had no idea was real or not.

The water was up to her waist.

Cold panic accumulated in her chest. What if it was a dead-end? The way behind them was blocked. If this wasn't the way out, then she had led them to their death. Myra bit her lip as the uncertainty weighed upon her. If Paul were here, he'd know what to do.

The water was up to her neck. People were starting to tread in place. She could hear frantic shouting and knew people were losing control.

In front of them was the roof of the tunnel. The tunnel itself disappeared underwater.

"What do we do!?"

"Where do we go!?"

"You led us here!"

"Get off me!"

"I can't breathe!"

"We shouldn't be here! We should've just stayed back in the slave compound! You've killed us!" A harsh voice accused as others joined in agreement.

Myra's head started to swim. The voices filled the little bit of room left in the tunnel. Each fear-laden comment pushed Myra under. The water was now up to her neck as she stood on her tiptoes. She could barely see in the dark, let alone into the murky depths.

"Everyone, quiet!" Myra shouted. Her voice echoed sharply off the walls. Aside from the sound of lapping water, the tunnel was silent.

"Listen to me," she said as sternly as she could muster as she hid her fear and uncertainty. "We are free. Why would we want to go back to slavery?" The question hung in the air, unanswered. "I know the way ahead is uncertain, but we can get there together. I promise." Her words felt heavy, and the promise felt like a weight.

"Now, I'm going to swim ahead. I feel a breeze, and it has to be coming from somewhere. This has to be the way out. Everyone go back wait for me to return."

"Alright. You heard the lady. Let's head back," a young man spoke up. His name was Markus, and he'd been one of Paul's good friends and was like a brother to Myra. Although the same age as Myra, the others respected him.

There were murmurs and snide comments, but the mass of people soon obliged as they headed back to the dry tunnel. As they departed, Myra's mind worked frantically as she pondered what she was about to do—swim into the darkness and hope she found the way out before she ran out of air.

"Markus," Myra said softly. The man turned and swam over to her.

"Yes, My?"

"If I'm not back soon, start uncovering the other end of the tunnel. If you work on one side, it should prevent the whole tunnel from collapsing," Myra declared. In the gloom, she could see his face but couldn't make out his concern.

"Sure thing, Myra. I'll see you in a few."

Myra bit her lip and nodded despite her uncertainty. She waited until Markus swam away before she turned back to the tunnel wall in front of her. She could feel her breath coming in sharp gasps as her fear attempted to take control.

Myra took a steadying, gulping breath and then submerged. Myra held out her hand and found the tunnel ceiling. She kicked and thrust, doing her best to remember what Paul had taught her when she was younger.

The water was silent. Myra could hear her heart pounding faster and faster in her chest. The pressure on her temples mounted the further down she swam. Her hair moved listlessly around her face, like tendrils of seaweed.

She wanted to breathe. She could feel the desire burning in her lungs. Her legs ached, and her body felt heavy and weak. Myra dared to open her eyes and met only darkness.

Panic pounded in her heart.

Myra lost contact with the tunnel ceiling.

Where had it gone!?

Myra sank deeper.

The whisper of death settled into her lungs.

Myra's feet came to rest on the tunnel floor. The silence enveloped her. It was almost peaceful. The light shimmered in the water like droplets of moonlight.

The light!

Myra looked upwards and saw the distant light as it reached down to her. She hadn't lost touch with the tunnel--the tunnel had ended. She had found the way out!

But, it was so far away, and she was too deep.

Would Paul forgive her for failing? Myra hoped so as the last hints of oxygen died in her lungs.

Just as she was about to open her mouth, Myra felt a pair of arms close around her in a watery hug. The person used the ground to propel them both upward. She could feel powerful legs kick and push toward the surface.

Myra breathed in a lungful of water and air as her head came up out of the water. She choked and spat as someone dragged her body towards the water's edge. Myra didn't have the strength to resist whoever was saving her. With finality, the person let go and collapsed in the water next to her.

"You're crazy," Markus stated in between gasps. "A real nutcase." Myra didn't have the strength to disagree. "But, at least you had the guts to get us out," Markus said with a grin.

Chapter 4: Cornered

Damien, Location Unknown

Damien dragged the unconscious guard into his cell and dropped him beside the other two. They were still out cold from where a pipe had fallen on their heads during the earthquake, and Damien knew one of them was severely injured. But, it wasn't his concern. He had to get out of the prison.

Damien's door was open, left ajar after the earthquake. There was no way he wasn't going to take advantage of his change in fortune.

"Preva 1-1-2-2, what's your status?"

For the last ten minutes, the radio on one of the guards had been gargling out the same communication. Damien knew if he didn't hurry, they'd send somebody out to check. Hopefully, he'd escape before they inspected the cells.

"Preva 1-1-2-2, respond!"

Damien snapped the armor on over his body and discovered it automatically fit his muscular physique as the armor shaped his torso. He was grateful for the technology. He once infiltrated a bandit camp near Fenrar's Pass and had to put on armor almost twice his size. A couple of bullets almost penetrated the gaps.

Damien slid the helmet over his head and heard a hiss as it locked in place. Immediately a display appeared in front of his eyes as information collected in the right-hand corner. Most of the symbols, numbers, and words didn't make sense to him, so he ignored it. Maybe he'd have time to figure it out later. For now, he had one goal.

Damien left his cell and glanced down at the keypad. He had no idea what the security code was and improvised with a swift punch, which shattered the screen. The door slid closed. He turned away and stared down the hallway. An intense silence occupied the space.

Where, now?

It was moments like this Damien missed Abby. He doubted she would want to help him, though. They hadn't ended on good terms. It was she who had rendered him unconscious and shipped him off to the slave compound where he couldn't do any more damage.

In retrospect, it was probably for the best. Even though they exiled him, Damien had still managed to mess things up. Because of his actions, he put Myra in danger.

At the thought of Myra, Damien felt a pang of remorse. He hadn't meant to hurt her and endanger her. Damien was trying to save her. But, like always, he had made the wrong choice. He could see that, now. He'd burned so many bridges that he had nowhere to go.

Find Father James.

The idea was so foreign to Damien's self-preservation that he immediately laughed into his helmet. The old man who had been in the cell next to Damien before his transfer was probably dead. Besides, how could he be able to help Damien escape? He'd just slow Damien down.

Find Father James.

It was so clear in his mind. Damien wanted to list all the reasons why it was a foolish idea. But, his tongue held firm, and he became resolute in his next course of action.

Somehow, the best way to escape and claim freedom was to find Father James.

Sebastian, Industry Protectorate, Station 004

The air in the Station was thick with dust and smelled of death and fire. Sebastian's head rang with the sound of the train car crashing through this mind. There was blood everywhere. All he saw was the blood.

Sebastian couldn't look at anything else. He was frozen in his place, impaled by the violence which had shattered the Station. People were running, crawling, lifeless. He heard their pain, muffled and distant. The world was starting to spin.

"Hey!" A man shouted and brought Sebastian out of his reverie. It was the man Sebastian had saved.

"Help me out here!"

Sebastian snapped to attention and ran to help the man. He was shouldering a large section of the ceiling that had fallen on a woman. She was screaming in agony and pinned to the floor from the waist down.

Sebastian dropped to his knees and grabbed the piece. Immediately, his hand felt something warm and sticky. He brought his hand up and saw it saturated in blood. The ringing in his ears returned, and his vision started to tunnel.

"Listen to me," the man shouted in Sebastian's ear. "We're going to pick this up on the count of three, and then I'm going to grab her and pull her out. Ready?"

Sebastian nodded vigorously.

"Alright. One. Two. Three!"

The two men pulled up with all their strength. Pain stabbed into Sebastian's palms as the concrete bit into him. His hands started to slip as he grunted and strained. The woman cried out in pain as the weight of the rock lifted. Swiftly, the man let go of the piece and grabbed the woman by the arm.

Just as Sebastian's strength gave out and the concrete slipped from his grasp, he pulled the woman to safety. The piece came crashing down with a thud as Sebastian's breathing came in sharp gasps.

A hand gripped his shoulder. Panic pricked in his heart.

"Thanks for the help. Up for round two?" Asked the same man. Sebastian looked all around him. There were so many hurting. He knew he should run. He knew he should take advantage of the chaos. But, people were suffering.

Sebastian followed as they moved on to the next victim.

Damien had no idea where he was going. Sure, he had a goal—find Father James—but he still didn't know where he was supposed to go next. Damien tried to access any sort of data the guard was carrying but didn't understand how to operate the armor. So, he went with his always reliable gut.

As he sauntered through the halls, a red light blinked in the left corner of his helmet. Someone was trying to contact him. So far, though, he hadn't encountered any other guards, which meant nobody knew he was missing from his cell.

Damien didn't have a weapon. Or maybe he did somewhere in the armor but didn't know how to access it. Regardless, he was simply a young man in advanced armor who had sharpened fighting skills. Something told him even that wouldn't be enough. Ever since the earthquake had struck, Damien assumed the whole nonviolence in Axiom was no longer the law of the land. Although no stranger to violence, Damien knew this wasn't a good development.

At least it meant he could kill Rais. Slowly. Painfully.

Find Father James.

Damien tried to shake the idea out of his head. It didn't belong to him.

"Preva!" A voice clapped in Damien's direction. Ice cascaded down Damien's spine.

He knew that voice.

Damien turned to face Rais.

Perfect.

The two of them were alone, in the immediate aftermath of an earthquake, without any guards around. How much easier could it have been? Damien waltzed towards Rais, his fists curling into bludgeons as a wicked smile broke open under his visor.

Find Father James.

Damien ignored it as he approached his enemy. Rais deserved what was about to happen to him. He had made Damien suffer, and he concentrated on his hatred.

Find Father James.

Rais was speaking, but Damien couldn't hear a word as his eyes pinpointed all the easiest ways to incapacitate the man. A strike to the throat, perhaps? A jab beneath the rib cage to lower his head, followed by a knee into the face?

Find Father James.

His thirst for vengeance was interrupted by this intrusive thought, and it sliced away at his opportunity to strike.

19

Now, they were too close as Rais hovered a couple of inches above Damien.

"I said, where is the rest of your team, 1-1-2-2?"

Damien had to find a way out, and he had to think fast. He wasn't panicking, but he didn't want to get caught.

"We got separated...sir," he attempted in the gruffest and deepest voice he could muster. Rais's eyes narrowed and he stared at Damien as if he could see through his visor.

"I see. And why weren't you answering your Com? Your team was supposed to secure the prisoners. Where were you headed, anyway?"

Now, Damien felt the prick of panic.

"Umm, I guess I busted my radio during the earthquake. Haven't heard anything from anyone," he lied as he tapped on his helmet.

Damien could tell Rais wasn't buying any of it. For the first time, Damien saw something which made prickly concern start to collect under his skin. Rais had traded out his knife for a gun. It hung on his belt like a totem.

"Earthquake...How did you know it was called that?"

Rais's hand rested on his gun. There would be no way Damien could reach for it before Rais pulled it out. A round this close would probably tear through his armor. Sweat stung his eyes. Damien could hear his heart pounding in his metal shell. He had to think of something fast.

"Lord Byron sent me," Damien blurted. Rais was taken aback and looked at him with confusion.

"Byron? That worm. What for?"

Damien had to be careful. He knew Byron and Rais hated each other. The last time he'd eavesdropped on their conversation, Rais had attempted to stab Byron. Since it was before the laws of nonviolence were altered, the blade had stopped mere centimeters from Byron's neck. But now that things were different, Rais could kill someone who worked for Byron to send a message.

"Before we were hit, he instructed us to go find the old man and deliver him to his Quarters. He wanted to question Father Joshua himself."

Rais was a blank wall. Damien couldn't tell whether or not he had bought it or if he was trying to decide where to shoot Damien first.

"Did he now? Bold move, Byron. Bold move," Rais reflected as he started to pace back and forth in the hallway. "He probably knew the earthquake was coming and I'm sure in the midst of all the chaos, he wanted to take advantage of the confusion and grab all the glory for himself," Rais spoke mostly to himself. Damien was uncertain what to say next. Rais looked down at Damien as if seeing him for the first time and scowled.

"Well, I have a message for Byron that you can deliver yourself. Tell him that if he ever sets foot in my Protectorate, I will kill him. If he sends someone to do his dirty work, I will kill his messenger and then find him and kill him," Rais said gaily.

"Yes, sir. Right away, sir."

Rais gave a hollow laugh and then waved Damien away with a flick of his wrist. Damien readily obliged and walked briskly in the opposite direction. As he was rounding a corner, he heard Rais's radio chirp to life.

"Sir, we got a situation."

Damien could guess what that situation was as he picked up the pace.

"What now?" Rais barked into his manipulor.

"We found the guards. They were in a cell, and someone stripped their armor."

"What about the boy!?" Rais shouted furiously.

"Missing, sir."

Rais turned sharply and looked down the hall, but Damien was long gone.

Sebastian felt weary all over. His hands were blistered and covered in blood where he'd been pulling and lifting heavy pieces of metal and cement off of people. He'd dug at piles of rubble, clawed at twisted bundles of steel, and dared the shards of glass scattered throughout the station. Some people were already dead when he found them.

Sebastian laid the bodies in the hallways leading out of the Station. In the corner, a couple of Enforcers and Caretakers were tending to the wounded. There were few supplies on hand, however. Death was eventual for many of the wounded.

Everyone else walked around in a daze, uncertain about everything they understood. Before now, they'd never seen violence. Never tasted of its carnage. Never felt the weight of its blows. Their minds struggled to grasp what they were seeing all around them as ignorance gave way to reality.

Exhaustion settled into Sebastian like thousands of gallons of water poured into his very bones. Unsteadily, he sat down with his back against the wall and tried not to close his eyes. As he fought sleep, he heard the crunch of debris.

"What's your name?" A man asked gruffly. It was the same man Sebastian had saved earlier and whom he'd worked alongside as they sifted through the rubble. In all the time he'd been right next to the man, Sebastian had not recognized the man's armor.

A jolt of panic struck Sebastian in the chest.

An Enforcer.

"Thomas," Sebastian lied as he swallowed the lump in his throat. Heat rose up his neck. The Enforcer had him pinned. There would be no way Sebastian could get to his feet before the Enforcer was all over him. He could only hope the man didn't recognize him.

"Well, Thomas, I appreciate the help. And for saving my life. Most Figures would've watched it all unfold. But, not you."

It sounded like an accusation.

The Enforcer's hand was on his weapon.

The man had Sebastian pinned as cold dread settled into his gut.

"I'm glad you're not like most Figures," the Enforcer stated as he held out his hand. Sebastian was caught off guard and didn't immediately take it. Eventually, he clasped the hand extended to him and let the Enforcer pull him to his feet.

The Enforcer turned his back to Sebastian and looked out across the station. The air was beginning to thin from the dust and smoke, but a haze lingered.

"Any idea what caused all this?"

Yes.

One person caused this.

Sebastian held his tongue.

"None," Sebastian said hollowly. He felt uneasy. He needed to keep moving. Sebastian's eyes roamed the station as he searched for an escape route, and they locked momentarily upon the face of a woman who was sitting about fifteen feet away. Blood caked her face from a cut above her eye. Sebastian felt uncomfortable as his gaze swiftly moved past her.

"Me neither. There's word it happened all over Axiom, too," the Enforcer reflected.

The woman stood. Her look was one of haunted fury.

"Arrest him!" She shouted as she pointed at Sebastian. The Enforcer stepped forward a couple of steps. Sebastian's heart pounded in his ears.

"What do you mean, F6565? Arrest who?"

More people were on their feet, now, as a crowd gathered. Their murmurs scratched at Sebastian's ears. Their fingers pointed as they spoke in whispers.

"Do you not recognize him? That's him! That's the Figure who blew up Hydra. He did this!" She accused hysterically as she pointed to all the destruction around her. Sebastian took a step back and felt the wall behind him.

He had nowhere to run.

The Enforcer turned slowly. Understanding replaced his confusion as the pieces fell into place. In a single motion, he drew his weapon and pointed at Sebastian's chest.

"Well, Thomas, I think we have a problem," he said coldly. The noise from the crowd was growing louder as they sided with the woman. Sebastian's raised his hands to defend himself as his mind locked in place.

This was it.

He was caught.

Sebastian knew it was going to happen eventually. He knew the Lord Protector would find him. He had just hoped it wasn't so soon.

"Turn around, Sebastian," the Enforcer ordered. Sebastian knew he had no choice. If he ran, the Enforcer would shoot him. With the feeling of hopelessness sinking in his chest, Sebastian turned to face the wall.

"Kill him!" The woman shrieked.

The crowd agreed and cheered the Enforcer on toward the deadly task. Sebastian felt a gloved hand press up against his back. He couldn't breathe, and tears of defeat were brimming in his eyes.

The Enforcer's second hand pressed up against the wall next to Sebastian's head, and the man pushed harder on his back. The Enforcer leaned forward until Sebastian could feel his hot breath on the back of his neck. Sebastian's skin crawled, and terror suffocated him.

"Run!" The Enforcer whispered harshly. Blue lines coursed from the Enforcer's hand as a hole formed.

The Enforcer shoved Sebastian inside.

Chapter 5: Adam

Myra, Location Unknown

Myra felt the weight of exhaustion in her arms and legs as she helped the last person to shore. Everyone was out of the water, now, and drinking in ample helpings of air. Myra crumbled to her knees and did her best to calm her shallow breaths. Meanwhile, Markus was moving amongst everyone, checking on them, making sure they were okay.

Myra watched with envy. Markus possessed natural leadership while she floundered and faltered at any given moment. For all of her false bravado and shouting in the tunnels, all he had to do was put a hand on a shoulder, squeeze someone's arm, look someone in the eye, and then he had their loyalty. Myra shook her head and forced herself to her feet.

"Markus?" The young man detached himself from a woman and made his way over to Myra.

"How are you feeling?" Markus asked genuinely.

"I'm fine, but we have to get everyone moving. There's no telling where we are and whether or not Hob is still looking for us. Hopefully, he assumes we are all dead."

Markus's eyes looked through Myra as if he wasn't paying attention to a word she was saying.

"I think Hob is the least of our worries, My. Look."

Markus pointed past Myra. She turned and looked out over a large body of water. At first, Myra didn't understand what she saw as she recognized thick columns of smoke and vast stretches of fire that danced on the surface.

There was something else on the water.

There were pale, lifeless objects floating on the water alongside debris. All across the lake, piled in islands and gathered in clusters, were bodies.

"Myra?"

Myra felt ice in her veins as the bodies stared emptily in her direction. The fire bounced off of vacant eyes. She'd seen death before, but not the carnage she was witnessing. She fought the urge to vomit as her legs trembled.

Markus stepped forward until he was right next to her. A body came to a rest at the edge of the shore. The water was beginning to rise as it lapped against her feet.

"Where are we?"

Myra's vision began to tunnel, and she felt sick to her stomach. The smell of smoke and decay was thick in the air as she swayed uneasily on her feet.

"Woah, there," Markus said softly as he gripped her shoulder. His rough hands brought steadiness back into her world. Immediately, she felt foolish and weak. She had to pull it together and be strong. The water was still rising, and she needed to get everyone off of the shore and into hiding.

Myra needed to get them back to Paul.

"We need to get moving," Myra said with as much resolve as she could muster. Markus nodded his head. The flames reflected off of his eyes, but otherwise, he seemed unaffected by the surge of death. Myra felt a twinge of resentment, but she ignored the corrosive feeling.

"I'll scout ahead and see if I can find a place for us to hide. In the meantime, could you get everyone on their feet and ready to move?" Myra asked with as much authority as she could conjure. Markus agreed and immediately withdrew as Myra peeled away and headed up the embankment. Her breath came in deep gasps as weariness embraced her lungs.

She'd chosen to scout ahead because she needed to be alone. Her mind roamed over the traumatic events which had unfolded in the last few days. Images of those who died in the initial blast—swallowed up by flames—and the subsequent cave-ins which crushed people she knew and cherished, haunted her. She felt every death shut up in her bones.

If she was honest with herself, she didn't needed to be alone. She needed space to mourn and to grieve. Everything she had learned to trust and find security within—even if it was meager—was gone. All she had was Theo, the only mountain she had left. Now she had the responsibility of leading everyone to safety—to a safety she didn't know how to find.

It wasn't supposed to be like this. Myra and Paul were supposed to be doing this together. Now he was gone. The vacancy of his relationship was a jagged hole.

Myra finally eclipsed the top of the hill, and light burst to life in front of her. For a second, she was caught off guard but then saw similar lights along the ridge, waiting for someone to walk close enough to activate them.

The land before her was a downward slope that ended in a valley. She looked backward at everyone. They were beginning to gather in groups just as Markus had instructed. Where would she be without his help?

She shuddered to think about it as she remembered the pressure of the water closing in around her body just seconds before he grabbed her and pulled her to the surface. Myra knew with Markus at hand, they stood a chance.

As Myra's thoughts consumed her, she didn't hear the footsteps until it was too late. Her stomach plunged as she felt something sharp prod her in her back. With her head still turned, she could smell sweat and dirt. Before she could plead her case, the assailant spoke.

"Who are you, and what are you doing here?"

Myra felt the cold prick of fear in her chest as the tip of the weapon dug deeper. Sweat itched on her forehead as fear condensed in her lungs and weighed down her tongue.

"I asked you a question. Who are you, and why are you here?" The voice asked sternly. Myra finally found her words as another nudge bit into her back.

"My name is Myra. I-I'm lost."

It wasn't a complete lie. But, Myra hoped whoever it was questioning her hadn't seen the rest of the slaves at the bottom of the hill. If so, she had put them all in danger. Again.

"Lost, eh? So, you have nothing to do with what happened to the Dam? Don't know anything about that, right?" Myra tilted her head in confusion. "I asked you a question. Do you know anything about what happened to Hydra?" The voice asked as the tip embedded deeper into her skin. Myra frantically shook her head.

"No. I promise," Myra said with hands raised.

"Turn around so I can see your face," he commanded. The more he spoke, the more Myra could see an image in her head of a young man. She swallowed the lump in her throat and turned around to face her assailant with her hands raised.

Myra was right. The man wasn't a man at all. She surmised he was probably her age. The light illuminated bags under his eyes and uncertainty upon his face. His weapon, which looked like a pitchfork, was leveled at her chest.

"Listen," she began in a hushed tone, "I have nothing to do with this. I'm just as confused as you are...," she said with a tilt of her chin, indicating she wanted to know his name. His weapon lowered slightly as he relaxed.

"AG431. But you can call me Adam. I'm from Agriculture. What Protectorate are you from, Figure?"

The question caught her off-guard. She took an unsteady step back as her mind raced.

"Are you taking a nap up here, or what?" Markus asked as he climbed up the hill and entered the light. He immediately froze and bore a look of confusion when he spotted Adam.

"Who's this!?" Adam shouted as the pitchfork dug into Myra's chest.

"Get away from her," Markus commanded as he advanced one step. His fists curled.

"No!" Myra shouted. Markus stopped with his wrist cocked back. Adam's eyes were narrowed and angry as his gaze moved from Myra to Markus and then back to Myra.

"Listen, Adam, Markus is a friend. You can trust him," she stated surely though every part of her quivered with fear.

"No! You lied to me! I bet you two are Diseased. Just like the other one!"

Markus took another step forward, and Adam bore more weight on the pitchfork.

"Get back! There are no more limits on violence in Axiom. Test me, and I will kill her right here!" Adam threatened.

Myra was finding it hard to breathe as the pain radiated throughout her chest.

"Try it," Markus snapped through gritted teeth.

"And what are you going to do to me? Give me the sickness, too? Get me Extracted!?" Myra heard a genuine fear in the boy's voice. She could see it on his face.

"No, I'm going to beat your face in!" Markus volleyed. The situation was about to explode into jagged pieces.

"Markus, stop!" Myra clapped sharply. It was like a slap to his face as he glared at Adam but maintained his silence. Myra took a deep breath and spoke low, "Adam, I know you're afraid. So am I. I've lost people. People I love. And right now, I'm not your enemy." Adam's gaze returned to Myra's face.

"How do I know you're telling the truth?"

"You won't. But, this is the truth: at the bottom of this hill are the rest of my people," she admitted. Markus sputtered and went to protest, but Myra gave him a scathing stare.

"Your people?"

"Yes, Adam. I am a slave, as is Markus. Or rather, we were slaves until we escaped. We're on the run from a very evil man, so you must understand why I didn't tell you everything up front," she said calmly.

Myra knew she just entered dangerous territory. If Adam worked for Hob, then she'd successfully delivered everyone back over to enslavement. This tension hung in the air as Adam's eyes moved back and forth between her and Markus.

"Are any of you hurt?" Adam asked abruptly. Myra had not expected the question and didn't know how to respond.

"Yes. Some badly," Markus said. His words were terse, but Myra knew he was trying to subdue the situation.

Adam lowered his pitchfork.

"Alright. Gather your people. We need to move," Adam warned. "It's not safe."

Chapter 6: Pouring In

Paul, Slave Compound

Paul stared upward into the warm sunlight as the radiant beams caressed his skin. He breathed in its glow and bathed in its embrace. Paul lingered in the light as it poured in through the wound. The radiance shimmered through the air, bringing dazzling clarity to the dust as the illumination shed itself merrily upon the piles of debris and rubble. The golden threads danced on his skin.

After he had his fill, Paul went back to work as he punched his shovel into the ruins of Hob's mansion. Once the earth started shaking, it was one of the first to crumble. The walls buckled and caved, the ceiling came crashing down, and chaos took up residence.

The slave compound was leveled. The factory was in a state of disrepair, and the chimneys, which once belched black, heavy smoke, were leaning in a haphazard silence. Even the skeletal remains of an ancient city—previously destabilized by time and rot—lay in greater ruin.

But now, the light was breaking through the darkness.

A giant seam had opened in the domed ceiling. Many others—slaves and guards alike—looked upward in wonder at the cracks which glowed with dawn.

Paul grinned as he dumped his load into a wheelbarrow.

"What are you smiling about?" Hob asked haughtily. Immediate revulsion and hatred burned through every lash and every blow healing on Paul's body. His wounds were healing, but his anger towards Hob was furious and full. No matter how hard he tried to get rid of the rage, it ensnared him.

Love your enemies.

How many times had he told his fellow slaves the same message? Now, it felt like a burden, a weight around his conscience. He felt defeated by the impossible task of forgiving Hob for the pain he'd inflicted and for the death of so many of his friends, for the death of his sister.

Do good to those who persecute you.

Paul spitefully shoved the head of the shovel back into the rubble and did his best to ignore his thoughts and disregard Hob's question. The man didn't deserve an answer. It was a challenge enough to keep digging into the remains of Hob's home, knowing he was helping the monster.

But Paul knew he needed to do it. Part of him wanted to run, to hide in the burned-out mountain, to wander off and find his way through the darkness. But he couldn't. There were still slaves to be freed. He had work to do.

Eventually, Hob understood Paul's silence and departed. Paul was relieved to be free of any harassment. Hob had been more oppressive than usual. Everyone, even his men, felt his anger and frustration. Many received the barbed end of Hob's whip whenever he disapproved of their response, their work, their idleness. Hob had immediately cracked down on any dissenting conversations which portrayed him as anything other than in power. But, it was hard to convey control when his home was in ruins.

Paul dumped another shovelful of debris into the wheelbarrow and decided it was time to throw it over the edge of the cliff. A pile of rocks and pieces was already collected at the bottom. Piece by piece, everything which belonged to Hob was thrown away. Paul couldn't help but smirk at the thought.

Paul came to a stop at the drop-off point and tilted the wheelbarrow upside down. Glass, rock, and metal tumbled down the hill with finality. He turned with a limp as pain radiated throughout his body. He could feel it with every breath. Ignoring the agony, Paul pushed the wheelbarrow forward. He was about to round the corner and head back to his position when he heard Hob speaking in harsh, hushed tones. He stopped and leaned forward to listen.

"Seriously!?" Hob hissed.

"Yes, sir. They plan on sending a delegation which will arrive in six cycles," spoke another man with earnest. Paul could hear Hob swear loudly.

"And who is sending the delegation? Rais?"

31

Paul assumed the second man nodded as Hob tore the air open with another wave of disparaging words.

"How did this get out!?"

"We don't know, sir. In the aftermath of the earthquake, we assume somebody let slip you had built the tanks. There's word that the Lord Protector has removed the nonviolent laws and now needs the tanks to maintain order."

"Order!? I built them so that there wouldn't be any order! They have no right demanding me to turn over what I created. They are mine, and mine alone," Hob said vehemently. Paul could feel the heat from Hob's words.

"Rais thinks they belong to the Lord Protector."

"Quit calling him that! His name is Lorenzo, and if my brother wants to send Rais like a lap dog down here to get my tanks, he can come himself. I'll show him where they belong."

"Yes, sir. But what do we do?"

There was a heavy silence as Hob worked through his own twisted and corrupted thoughts.

"We get ready. Prepare the men."

Dread filled Paul's heart. Hob was about to bring destruction down upon their heads.

"Anyone who can walk must fight," Hob declared.

Chapter 7: Hunters

Sebastian, Industry Protectorate, Tunnels

The walls squeezed around Sebastian. His chest was crushed by a pressure he couldn't see. His head felt rigid—locked in place by flashes of pain. A force was moving him, like an elevator, except the elevator was falling on top of him. The agony was building, and his legs felt like they were going to snap in half. Sebastian went to scream, but couldn't breathe, couldn't speak, as the words were pushed inside of himself.

Suddenly, the pain receded. Sebastian emptied into a tunnel. His whole body throbbed. He could still feel the hastily made chute enclosed around him.

Sebastian heard voices, and agonizingly rose to his feet. He was just on the edge of the emergency lights from the Station. Like a vapor, he crept to the edge of the buttery light.

"Where'd he go!?" A woman shouted—the same woman who had pointed Sebastian out in the first place. People looked around, certain one of them had to be the Diseased Figure. Sebastian dipped back into the shadows as gazes turned toward his direction.

"He must have used his manipulor to get into the room on the other side of this wall. That means he is probably in one of the Quarters. We'll have to search every single one of them," posited the Enforcer who'd manufactured Sebastian's escape.

Immediately the Station emptied as everyone left to search for the criminal. The Enforcer was the last to leave and turned his head in Sebastian's direction. With a curt nod, he too departed. Only the wounded and the Caretakers remained.

Sebastian melted away from the light. The tunnel swallowed him, and a terrifying safety enveloped him. Striking despair birthed inside his chest. He tried to fight it, to push it down, to employ every tactic he knew to prevent it from rising and consuming him, but it was bursting to life like flames feasting upon oxygen.

He was a fugitive—the hunted.

Beams of light filled the tunnel as searchers returned to look in the darkness. Sebastian had no option except to run. The choice burned in his feet as he fled into the shadows.

Myra, Location Unknown

Myra bit her lip until it bled. She was hesitant about following Adam. As he led the way through the barren land—his weapon illuminating a brilliant light which brought clarity and carved a path of luminance before them—her trepidation grew.

What if he was leading them into a trap?

What did he know about the bodies?

They floated before her eyes.

"Everybody stay together," Markus whispered shrilly.

The group was beginning to spread too wide. Like a shepherd, Markus drove them closer together. Myra felt her irrelevance and bit her lip harder. Her eyes scanned over the slaves. She knew all of them by name, including the ones who died along the way. How many more would she lose? This question haunted and paralyzed her.

Adam stopped and held up his hand. He extinguished his light with a flick of his wrist. The staff recoiled into his arm as if it were a part of him and Myra glimpsed something encased around his forearm. Adam crouched low.

Silence stalked them. Myra could see Adam's head tilt as if he were listening. In the darkness, the fear and uncertainty ate at her. Finally, she broke away from her position.

"Why'd we stop?" Myra whispered. Adam didn't respond as his eyes scanned the dusty gloom. Myra could see in the dark, but even she didn't recognize anything except rugged hills. She went to ask again, but he cut her off.

"It would benefit you to be quiet, miss," he said in terse politeness. "There are things out here that'll find us if we aren't careful," Adam stated ominously as he moved to his belly.

Just as the sentence rolled off his tongue, she heard a humming noise, which made the hair stand up on her neck. It conjured a memory of when she was a little girl as she stumbled across a beehive. Silvery assailants were upon her in seconds, injecting her with poison and pain. It was Paul, of course, who picked her up in a smothering embrace as the creatures stabbed him instead.

But, this sound was nightmarish.

The noise was above. It was amongst them. As Myra's eyes scanned the landscape, a black, disk-shaped machine descended out of the darkness and drifted near a ball of light embedded in the earth—like a black wasp hovering near a flame. On its underbelly were four metallic clamps shaped like pincers. It twitched back and forth as if sensing the air.

It was searching.

"What is it?" Her voice quivered.

"Hunters," he said in a hushed, still whisper.

"What do they do?"

Instead of explaining, Adam pointed as another disk-shaped object appeared. In its clutches was a pale, limp body that was still dripping with water. The Hunter paused next to the first and seemingly communicated information before it flew away in the darkness. The first machine moved in the opposite direction towards the water. The whole scene only took a few seconds to unfold, but it made Myra's skin crawl.

"They're gathering. We have to move. Let's go," Adam said without gusto as he rose. Myra stood up and motioned to Markus to get the others up as well. Adam was already a few paces ahead of them. He skirted the edge of the light and started to lead them around its illumination.

Uncertainty clouded Myra's thoughts. There was something Adam wasn't telling them. What were those things? Why were there bodies floating in the water? She was tired of not knowing the answers. Hastily, as the slaves continued their slow and agonizing attempt at getting ready to move, Myra caught up to Adam and grabbed him by the arm.

"Wait! Before we continue following you, I need to know what's happening!" Myra stated firmly. Adam swung back around, and though the light was behind him, she could see him weighing his options. The glare she gave him made up his mind.

"You really have no idea, do you?"

"None. Like I said, up until recently, we were all slaves. I've never known or seen anything except the slave compound."

"Fine, but I'll have to explain as we move. Keep up with me," Adam commanded as he turned. Myra blew out frustrated air but knew she had no other choice. She quickened her pace and fell in beside Adam.

"So, explain," she commanded with false bravado. Adam shirked her comment as he glanced around once again. It was a few seconds before he responded.

"Seven cycles ago, one of the Diseased destroyed the Dam at Hydra Station. The result was catastrophic. The water behind the Dam swept into the valley below and took out the Industry Protectorate, including one of the Industry Quarters." Myra pictured his words with sadness.

"Those bodies you saw out on the water? They belonged to Figures who worked and lived in Industry and are the result of a murderer—1C118—a Figure so warped and twisted by the Disease that he left carnage and chaos in his wake." Adam paused.

"To prevent the sickness from spreading, the Lord Protector, in mercy and wisdom, suspended the laws of nonviolence and took it upon himself to root out any who are likewise contaminated," Adam stated with little emotion.

Though Myra felt the prick of fear and concern in her chest, she was surprised to find Adam hadn't conveyed a single ounce of apprehension, or anxiety, or any emotion at all while he shared his story. The only time his voice rose in inflection was when he spoke of the Lord Protector.

"And the Hunters? Do they belong to the Lord Protector or these diseased individuals?" Myra was still trying to wrap her head around the situation. The strangeness of the society she had stepped into was overwhelming. The fear and apprehension were palpable upon the land.

Adam paused as he searched for an answer.

"I can only assume these machines belong to the Diseased. Their purposes seem..."

"Evil?"

"What?" Adam asked with a confused tilt of his head.

"You know, designed for the harm of others with a disregard for the sacredness of life. Actions which can only be carried out in the darkness and not in the exposure of the light," Myra explained as disbelief edged into her tone.

"Yeah... I guess they're evil?"

The question hung in the air, but Myra didn't know how to answer. She pushed forward through the awkwardness.

"So, where are we going now?"

"Back to where I live. Where I found you is the lower portion of the Agriculture Protectorate. We share a border with Industry. Before the Dam ruptured, we used the water to help grow our crops. I'm from the Greenhouse Sector in the upper part of Agriculture. That's where we're going and since the Train is down, we have to go on foot. Usually, we'd get there in three cycles. Your wounded will put us at five cycles."

Though it wasn't an accusation, his comment stung and made her feel inadequate. With a flick of her attention, she cast the thought aside. They continued to trudge along in silence, and Myra understood Adam was finished explaining. She fell back a few steps and thought through what he'd told her.

This was Axiom? The Axiom she had heard about from the guards. The Axiom with a glittering, golden Citadel at its head? A land full of pleasure and prosperity? But the Axiom she had hoped for was not the Axiom Adam described. His words birthed an unquenchable loneliness in Myra.

Despite what Adam had told her, one question kept nagging Myra.

Why was Adam so far away from his home?

It didn't make sense.

Myra pondered this as shadows clung to her skin.

Sebastian's breath came in stinging gasps. Sweat clotted in his eyes like beads of heavy vapor. His feet ran, his heartbeat painfully in his chest, and his mind raced through the onyx tunnels. He'd been running aimlessly for so long.

Where was he going?

What was his plan?

Sebastian felt the tunnel close in around him. He was making choices with options he didn't have. Sebastian was a wanted person—a criminal—the Diseased. He felt the sickness of fear and condemnation reign down upon his mind.

It was this fear that festered in his veins. He felt it curdle in his blood.

He's to blame.

That's what the woman had shouted.

It was true, and the truth was enslavement.

No matter how hard he fought it, the image of Hydra breaking apart filled his memories. Like pressure building up in his body, the reality of his situation pounded down upon him. He was running, running, running, but where was his freedom?

All those people. All those who followed him believed in him, and they were gone. They were dead. Just like Sam.

But, could Sam protect him from the water?

Could Sam protect Sebastian from his own foolishness?

From blame? From guilt?

No.

Sebastian stumbled. He fell in the dark and smacked his head into the ground as pain exploded across his scalp. He felt feverish and cold as he curled into a ball.

He was Diseased.

He was sick.

There was no healing for his mistakes. No atonement. No way of repairing the lives he'd broken. Hydra was ruptured. The wall was coming down. The water was pouring in.

Huddled in the dark, Sebastian was sinking.

Myra walked ten paces behind Adam with her head bowed. He had his light stick-weapon-armband out again. Adam had stopped looking around with caution and had even slowed his pace a little, which Myra assumed meant they were safe. The climb was beginning to get steeper as he led them all up a relentless slope.

Myra couldn't ignore the questions which swam around in her head. Adam was a mystery. He was closed off, but not purposefully. He was silent, but not to ignore her. He was as dark as the landscape. Myra couldn't figure him out and didn't understand his motivations.

"How's it going?" Markus asked as he shuffled up alongside Myra.

"Adam said we have five cycle's worth of walking ahead of us, but there's food close by. I think a cycle means a day?"

"Yeah. You told me already. I'm asking about you, though. How are you doing?"

Myra was caught off guard by the concern.

"I'm fine, Markus. How's everyone else?"

"They're making it. Some are going slower than others, but we have a system in place. The strong ones help the weaker and then trade off the responsibility when they get tired. Seems to be working. But, I think you're ignoring my question, My. You've been off. I can tell," he said genuinely.

Myra bit her lip. Markus was right.

"I miss Paul. I miss him badly."

Markus was silent.

"Me too, Myra. He'd be proud of you, though."

"Would he?" Myra asked abruptly. She didn't mean for it to tumble out, but it had been burning in her thoughts.

"Yes, My. Why wouldn't he?"

Myra hesitated but knew Markus was one of the few she could afford to be vulnerable.

"Because of Damien. Because I miss him even though he betrayed us. Because I didn't get everyone out and because I wasn't good enough and people died. Because you're better at this than I am. They listen to you, and you get them to follow you. What good have I done?"

"Stop doing that to yourself," Markus commanded.

"Doing what?"

"Doubting yourself. Listen, you got us out of those tunnels because you were brave enough to jump in the water. You convinced Adam to help us by appealing to his good nature despite the fact he's as thick as a rock. Our friends follow me because I follow you. Not the other way around."

Myra took his words like cool water on parched lips.

"Thank you, Markus."

"Anytime. We trust you, Myra, because you can hear Theo better than all of us. We're behind you. Now, could you convince blockhead up there to let us stop for a rest? This climb is wearing us down," he huffed.

Myra nodded and turned towards Adam. She suddenly pictured him with a rock for a head, and a goofy grin broke open upon her face.

It felt good to smile.

"Get up, Sebastian!"

The voice sounded distorted. Like coming from underwater. Everything in Sebastian's body felt distant and detached. He tried to sit upright as his head swam.

"Can you hear me!? You need ...of here...coming. They're coming...you!"

The voice was close. It echoed off the tunnel walls. But Sebastian couldn't see anyone. There was no one else in the darkness with him. Suddenly, the wall in front of him flickered with traces of blue light as a faded image of a girl appeared.

"Get away....coming...."

Sebastian tilted his head in confusion. Her words were broken and distorted as if she was trying to talk to him with bad reception. But that was impossible. The NOOM system allowed for nearly perfect and immediate communication. That was how the Lord Protector had managed to project his will across all of Axiom and destroy Hydra.

"I can't hear you! What are you trying to tell me?" Sebastian shouted mindlessly. He leaned forward as if getting closer to the girl with purple hair would help him understand. Her hands were working frantically at the bottom of the screen, and her lips moved inaudibly. Sebastian could see the fear and worry in her eyes.

Finally, her voice rang clear and strong.

"They're coming for you! Run!"

Her image became too distorted to recognize as lines of red invaded. Sebastian's brow furrowed as his eyes followed the red veins down the tunnel. His heart caught in his throat at what his mind failed to understand.

The tunnel was bleeding.

A chill ran down Sebastian's spine as a low hum filled the tunnel. He watched the red lines advance, but it was not this which brought terror to his heart. At the edge of the gory gloom, something was stirring.

The darkness married the murderous red, which made it hard to see until it was too late. A disc-shaped object, black and sleek with metallic appendages on its underbelly, grew out of the darkness like it lived there. The red from the walls reflected dully off of its sleek, black shell.

Before Sebastian could wrap his mind around the danger, the machine tipped forward and lunged towards him. A spike of fear plunged into him as he ducked. He felt the machine churn the air just above his head as it landed a couple of feet away from his crouched form. The metallic feet snapped shut in an attempt to capture Sebastian but only managed to shoot sparks and become embedded in the ground.

Sebastian saw his opportunity and ran.

The machine shook itself loose and darted upwards.

The sound of its angry hum brought terror to Sebastian's steps as he sprinted down the tunnel.

The red lines were all around him, filling the tunnel, his vision, and were even reaching out to him. He could feel their touch like tongues of fire.

A fork was approaching. Sebastian could smell the machine—like charred wires.

Sebastian heard the claws open and saw them in his peripheral vision. The wind from the drone buffeted him.

The claws swung close, cutting the air. Sebastian felt the metal bite into his back and slice his skin open. He heard a ripping noise as a scream tumbled from his lips. He stumbled and fell, his back exposed as the machine changed course.

The fork in the tunnel was close. All Sebastian had to do was beat it there.

A fire, more potent than the pain, brought him scrambling to his feet. He heard the clack, clack of the machine as it tore the shirt to pieces before resuming its hunt.

Sebastian couldn't breathe.

Tears and sweat and blood ran freely.

His back was a mosaic of agony.

The fork was just ahead. Sebastian aimed his body to go to the right, the darkness beyond inviting into safety. He hoped the machine was matching his change of direction. He heard a faint scraping noise as it nicked the edge of the tunnel when it leaned to the right.

The two tunnels loomed in front of him. He heard the claws open and saw them glint menacingly. Sebastian tensed every muscle.

The claws snapped shut around empty air as Sebastian rolled into the tunnel on the left. The machine continued onward, momentarily unaware of the change. Sebastian didn't hesitate as he came up from his roll and continued running. His legs felt like a limp hose. He knew he'd afforded himself an extra twenty seconds. The machine was almost as wide as the tunnel, which meant it couldn't turn around very well.

The light was ahead of him.

A station! Sebastian didn't know which one it could be, but he decided he didn't care. He needed to get out of the tunnel. He needed to hide.

A hum filled him.

The machine had made its way into his branch.

Sebastian pumped his arms.

The light was growing brighter.

Hope fueled his steps.

Sebastian burst out of the tunnel, ready to vault himself upward onto the platform.

"Stop!"

Sebastian froze in his tracks as a dozen Enforcers stepped out from behind columns with weapons aimed. The sweat on his body turned to ice.

An ambush.

The claws opened and snapped shut like a prison. A painful jolt embedded into his lower back as numbness swam over him. Sebastian went limp, as darkness swept him under.

Chapter 8: Theo

Damien, Technology Protectorate

Damien felt naked and vulnerable. Though it was a tremendous gamble to show his face and to go without protection, he'd abandoned the armor because it was a dead giveaway. He trusted his instincts.

But, where he was going now wasn't based on his instincts. He couldn't explain it, but Damien knew he was headed in the right direction as his feet took him through the coated alley. Like being drawn to the warmth of a campfire, he knew he was approaching his destination.

The alley ended. Glaring, exposing light infiltrated the darkness. Damien peered around a corner and assessed a street littered with people. He saw many individuals with ridiculous goggles covering their faces. He'd never put them on himself, but Abby had explained how they displayed a constant video feed and accessed parts of their brains needed to coordinate muscular movement. None of it made sense to him, but the tech seemed to be doing its job as Damien watched an army of people moving seamlessly, without having to see where they were going.

Despite the fact they were distracted by their goggles, Damien didn't want to expose himself. All it would take would be for one guard to see him navigating the crowd without the contraption over his face. They'd quickly piece together that he didn't belong. He had to find another way.

Damien turned, but just as he was about to head in the opposite direction, he felt a tingling sensation up and down his spine. Someone was watching him. Slowly, he revolved and searched the mob of people from the shadowy comfort.

Initially, nothing and no one stood out. But, as his eyes traveled the sea of faces, his skin crawled with the awareness of a presence he could not see. He searched, and searched, and saw a sliver of a face staring at him from across the street.

At first, Damien couldn't believe what he was seeing. Rather, he couldn't believe who he was seeing. The man extended his arm, with his hand stretched out to Damien. He was beckoning to Damien, asking him to come to him. The faint smile on the man's lips told Damien that he was safe.

Damien eyed the crowd. He saw the Enforcers down the street. He knew if he weren't careful, he'd be spotted and arrested—thrown back in the cell to rot.

The man still had his hand extended.

Damien took a deep breath and exited the alley. He winced when the lights struck his eyes, but Damien was soon weaving in and out of the crowd. The people didn't even know Damien was there, as their bodies responded to electrical pulses and mental tugs. He ducked under an arm and slid past another person. He was almost halfway to the other side.

To his right, Damien saw an onyx armored Enforcer enter the stream of people. He was heading right to Damien. Damien's heart quickened, and he picked up the pace. His eyes navigated as he strategized his route. All he could see were people, on all sides, closed in around him.

Damien looked for the other side of the street, for the man's outstretched hand, and could not see him. A wave of people was crashing all around him. He could see the top of the Enforcer's black helmet. He couldn't breathe. He couldn't get out. Damien tripped and fell. He couldn't get up. He was drowning in an ocean of individuals.

It was over.

"Damien?"

The young man looked up. The man was squatting a few feet away from where Damien had fallen.

"Why are you on the ground?" He asked. The question was full of curiosity and humor.

"I fell," Damien said weakly. The man's grinned wider.

"Everyone falls, Damien. Let's get up, now," he said as he extended his hand. Damien took it and allowed the man to pull him to his feet. Nimbly, the man led Damien through the crowd and onto the other side of the street as the people parted all around them like a stream moving around a boulder. Together, they made their way to a café, though everyone was vanished behind their goggles instead of talking to each other.

The man pulled out a chair for Damien before he too sat down across from him. A long, comfortable silence fell between them both. Damien didn't want to disturb the stillness, but the questions burned in his throat.

"It's good to see you again, Damien," the man said warmly. His eyes were the morning sky. What baffled Damien was how incredibly normal Theo looked. He was flesh and blood, not mysticism and glory. Damien had expected something else, something less human. Or more than human. He didn't know.

"Where did you go? One minute you were there, and then you weren't. I was alone."

The man received the indictments patiently.

"No, Damien. I promised you—I would never leave you. You may not have seen me, but I was there," he reassured. Damien hadn't meant for the accusations to spill from his lips, but he was full of questions.

"And what about everyone else? All these people? Do they see you?"

Damien had to know he wasn't insane. It was likely he had finally cracked and made all of this up. The man's smile fell until the corners were heavy with sorrow.

"They do not want to see me, Damien. I do not force them to open their eyes. But, I am not here for them right now."

The idea seemed preposterous to Damien. If this man presented himself to Axiom, to the world, so much would be changed. Lives would be changed, histories rewritten, and empires would bow. It didn't make sense for him to remain hidden, in the shadows, waiting on people to see him. Why was he not acting?

"I am patient," the man stated as he put his hands together on the table. Damien hadn't realized he was sitting in complete silence, caught up in his thinking.

"What did you do to me?"

Damien was afraid of the answer. Ever since he'd seen Theo for the first time, things were different. There was no longer a cloud of fear and anger raging within him like a desert storm. There was peace. It scared him.

"There is much I want to tell you, Damien, but we are running out of time. I will explain more as you go, but for now, I ask you to trust me."

Damien didn't like not having his questions answered but could tell it wasn't worth pushing. At the idea of a mission, a task, his curiosity grew.

"What would you have me do? I assume you wanted me to rescue Father James, correct? That was you, I assume—in my head," he said hesitantly. Once the words rolled off his tongue, he realized how stupid they sounded. Then again, he'd seen three-headed mutants and sand wraiths, so the idea of a voice in his head wasn't completely absurd.

"A shadow of me, yes. But now I must give you all of myself. Hold out your arm, Damien," the man said mystically. Damien was confused but obeyed. He held out his arm, and the man placed his hand on top of Damien's. Both of their faces lit up as tendrils of white light flowed from the man and into Damien. It felt like a whisper was filling his body.

The man retracted as the last bit of light slipped into Damien's forearm. There was once bare skin; now, there was a silvery-white cuff, similar in design to a manipulor. Despite the resemblance, though, it was different. It felt cool on his skin, lightweight, and he could feel its energy roll up his arm.

Damien searched himself, his mind, his heartbeat, to find what the man had given him. But, all he saw was silence. It wasn't an empty silence, though. It was full, deep, and wide.

"I need you to find the old man, Damien," the man stated thoughtfully. Damien's gaze was still on his arm as he watched the beads of light completely fade into his skin. He looked up at the man with confusion.

"Wait. You aren't going with me?"

The man's eyes flashed humorously.

"I promised you I wouldn't leave you."

Damien was starting to get a little annoyed about the man's mysticism and ambiguity. How was he supposed to be with him if he wasn't actually with him? Made no sense.

"What did you put inside of me? A weapon? A communicator? A food and drink dispenser? A portable toilet?"

The man laughed, and it caught Damien off-guard. He looked around, shocked and afraid the man's outburst would get them noticed. But, no one seemed to care. Eventually, the man calmed down as Damien fidgeted.

"There's your humor you've hidden for so long."

Damien didn't like how personal the conversation was becoming as he grew red and shrank in his seat. He was naked before Theo, and it made him uncomfortable.

"I missed it," the man said genuinely.

"Anyways. Back to the plan," Damien interrupted.

"Yes, yes. The plan. I need you to find him, but to do so, I need you to go to those you've betrayed," he said casually.

The heat returned in Damien's cheeks. He didn't like being called out.

"Why?"

"Because you are the result of the relationships around you, Damien. I need you to restore what you broke. You need to get them to trust you." Damien grew clammy.

"And what if they don't hear me out? What if they don't forgive me?"

"They will, Damien. Fear and uncertainty dwell in their lives, and forgiveness is a beacon they cannot ignore. Trust me."

Damien did. A fond silence fell between them.

"It is time for me to go, Damien," the man began as he leaned forward, "It was amazing to see you. Remember. I—"

"—Will be with you." Damien interrupted. Theo laughed again as he leaned back in his chair.

"You got it, Damien."

Damien stood. He turned away to scurry back into the darkness of the alley as he searched for the courage to speak. He turned back around to look at the man still sitting at the table whose eyes longingly roamed the surge of faces moving past him. As everyone hurried along to their tasks and destinations, he was a statue, a relic, a reminder of what it meant to be human.

"Theo?" The man looked upwards at Damien with a look Damien hadn't seen in years. "Thank you," Damien stated.

"Always, Damien."

Damien nodded and then turned to the task at hand. Already the feeling of deep, fathomless rest was fading as he walked away from the man casually sitting at the café.

Chapter 9: The Depository

Myra, Agriculture Protectorate, Ag Unit 007

Myra led the slaves down the hill. It was a painstaking process as many leaned upon one another for strength or to stay awake as death drowsed them. The process crawled onward as they made their way to the buildings at the bottom.

It hadn't taken long for Adam to give them the all-clear. Myra didn't know if he'd been thorough, but the hope of food, water, and rest guided her more than the fear of being caught.

Adam met them at the bottom of the hill and led Markus and the rest of the group to a tube-shaped building. Adam pulled open the double doors, and a light flickered to life, revealing rows of crates.

"The food is in the crates," he said firmly as he pointed into the building. "Let me open them, and ya'll can dig in."

Purposefully, Adam went to the nearest crate as a collective gurgle erupted from the mass of empty stomachs waiting in the doorway. Myra watched with curiosity as Adam's metal armband extended out in front of him and became a tool that easily peeled away the nearest crate's lid.

Adam did this for a whole row before turning back to the mouths hungrily hanging open. Before he could gesture, everyone was tearing into the food. Myra hung back but eventually gave in to the loud roar emitting from her stomach.

"There's plenty to go around," Adam conveyed as he went to the next row of crates. Myra pushed her way through the crowd, which was beginning to thin as everyone stepped back with armloads of food. She peered into the container in front of her at small, round pieces of food. She reached in and pulled out the brown item. It had coarse, rough skin and smelled of dirt.

"Potatoes," Adam said from behind her. Myra turned to face him, the food still clutched in her hand. "Grown not far from here. Try it. You'll like it." Myra obeyed and bit into the brown skin. Immediately, she tasted dirt and sugar and pleasure as new flavors broke over her tongue. She tore off another bite and wolfed it down. Adam smirked at her.

"Told you," he said casually. The tool he had used to open the crates was changed, again, and now bore a staff's resemblance, which he leaned on slightly.

"Got any water?" Markus broke into their conversation through a mouthful of potatoes.

"Sure. Follow me," Adam said as he turned to lead the way. Markus turned to Myra with a handful of potatoes clutched to his chest.

"Guy's alright, I guess." Myra rolled her eyes.

"Because he gave you food, right?" Markus gave her a goofy grin before following after Adam.

Soon, the entire group was stretched out with full stomachs and thirsts quenched. Some sat up against the building, talking in low tones with each other. Others slept in secluded corners. For the first time in a long time, they were able to rest.

Myra moved amongst the people, treating wounds the best she could. They'd managed to find fresh bandages and burlap in a nearby building. However, Myra hadn't seen any medicine, which meant receiving proper medical attention was still the highest priority.

Myra worked despite the weariness which ached up and down her back as she changed dressings and tended to wounds. Finally, Markus pulled her aside and convinced her to rest. Myra tried to argue, but loathsome tiredness overcame her. She stumbled towards Adam, who was sitting alone.

"Mind if I keep you company?" He didn't respond, but she saw him nod his head. Myra sat down on the crate next to him. Her body felt ragged and worn, and sitting eased some of the throbbing. The two of them sat in silence. Through the lights provided for the small compound, she could see his eyes scanning the darkened landscape.

"Your people get enough to eat?" Adam asked quietly.

"Yes. Thank you. For all your help. We wouldn't have survived without you."

51

Adam paused.

"You're welcome." He looked down and started prodding the dirt with his staff.

"What is that?" Myra asked curiously as she pointed. He stopped and brought it eye level. It glimmered in the light.

"It's called a manipulor. Everyone in Axiom receives one after Training. It's how we stay connected to the rest of Axiom."

"It changes shape?" Myra inquired.

"Some do. I work in Agriculture, so I use it for more than simply opening doors," he stated with an edge of superiority.

"I see," she replied despite still not fully understanding. "And what about this place? Do you work here, too?" She said with a sweep of her hands. Adam didn't follow her gaze.

"I work at the Lake in the Greenhouse Sector. This is a depository. It's where they store the food units before they are shipped to Citadel."

"Citadel?"

"Our capital city. It's a place every Figure dreams of being invited. A place of luxury and ease. The Prominent dwell within Citadel's boundaries. If a Figure performs their Role well or otherwise accomplishes acts of worth, he or she might become eligible to become a Prominent." His voice was a mixture of keenness and melancholy.

"But something has happened. This food is meant for Citadel but hasn't been received. The system has been disrupted. Things are not the way they are supposed to be." The sudden pleading and longing for normalcy in his voice made Myra uncomfortable.

"What happened?"

"A Figure brought a sickness into Axiom."

Myra was surprised at the fear in his voice.

"What sickness?"

Adam looked at her long and hard. The worry in his eyes was palpable.

"You don't have to tell me," she offered. What could be so terrible that speaking about it caused terror?

"Where I am from, it's forbidden to speak about it. To give it words is to give it life," he said cryptically.

"I understand. There are some things too evil to talk about," Myra said with a shrug of her shoulders, despite the fact she disagreed with her own words. For her, to speak of the darkness was to expose it. Adam tilted his head in response.

"That word. Evil. You told me about it earlier. What is it like?" He asked innocently.

The question caught her off-guard. She looked upward as she searched her mind for an adequate answer. Her toe dug into the dirt, and she had a quick idea. She stooped down and cupped soil in her hands.

"What happens if the soil you use to grow the potatoes is no longer healthy?"

The soil felt grainy in her hands and slipped between her fingers. She put a pile in Adam's palm.

"Nothing grows," Adam said simply. He gently worked the soil in between his fingers.

"Exactly! Evil is like soil that is unhealthy. Nothing good grows because of it."

"But, can you fix the evil?"

Adam sifted the dirt back and forth in his hands. There was a tenderness to the way he treated the soil. Myra watched his motion as she thought about her response.

"What do you do to the soil if it's gone bad?"

"Add good soil back into it. Soil rich in nutrients and minerals—the kind which helps the plants grow," Adam said knowledgeably. Myra nodded.

"When it comes to evil, it's pretty much the same. You replace the evil within a person with good—the highest and purest good."

"Can there be such a thing?" He asked with a hint of sorrow. Myra's brow creased together in confusion at the sudden depth of emotion. She opened her mouth to respond, but they were interrupted by a humming noise growing louder as it hovered across the darkness. Adam's eyes grew wide.

"Get inside," he whispered harshly as he stood.

Myra quickly got to her feet and followed Adam's gaze out onto the onyx landscape. The humming was now a buzz as it drew closer. Adam turned to her as his manipulor took on another shape.

"They've found us!" Adam hissed.

The Hunter entered the light cast by the Ag Unit with a rush of wind and a deep, jarring hum. In the glow, it looked almost alive as it searched back and forth. Myra crouched next to Adam. Cold fear coiled inside her chest. She could hear the dreadful machine moving across the Unit like a predator.

"What do we do!?" Myra whispered sharply to Adam. Adam brought his finger to his lips and beckoned for her to follow. They crept around the side of the crates. The Hunter was on the other side of the Unit, spraying the air with a black, inky liquid which became vapor and merged into the darkness beyond the light. The two of them stooped low and moved to a building that provided better coverage.

Myra heard voices and felt the stab of fear. The door to the food reservoirs was wide open, and light poured out from inside. None one knew they were in danger. None of them knew their voices were about to give them away. Myra started to turn away from Adam and felt his hand dig into her arm. She turned to face him, and he was shaking his head.

"No! It'll see you," Adam warned.

"I can't just let it get them!" Myra stated firmly as she jerked her arm out of his grip. His nails pulled away at her skin and left marks, but she ignored the flash of pain as she peered around the corner. The Hunter was about to enter one of the buildings they'd already raided. Thankfully, it was empty.

Myra waited with bated breath until it started to go inside to investigate. Once it turned away from her, she darted out from beside the building. Her feet carried her silently across the open space as she kept her eyes on the Hunter.

"Hey, My! You'll never guess what I found in here," Markus shouted as he emerged from the food unit.

Terror crashed into Myra and brought her to a sudden halt. Markus wore a confused look as he saw the evident fear on Myra's pale face. Both of their eyes flew to the Hunter, which hovered just inside the empty doorway. Its carapace gleamed with intelligent hunger. Markus looked at Myra with wretched fear as the Hunter lunged forward.

"Over here!" Myra shouted as she waved her hands frantically. The Hunter immediately changed course. "Get inside!" Myra yelled as she ran in the opposite direction. The sound of the Hunter was deafening as it shortened the space between predator and prey. Myra could hear its menacing whine as her body was buffeted by its fierce approach.

Myra dove behind a stack of crates and landed with a rush of air. She heard a jarring noise as the machine clipped the top box and looked up in terror as the container came crashing down. She felt her body shoved out of the way as Markus collided with her. The two of them rolled over each other in a tangle of limbs, but managed to get out of the way.

"Go!" Markus shouted as he brought her to her feet. She glanced backward and saw the Hunter righting itself. It attempted to take off, but it appeared to be damaged and struggled to get off the ground. Despite this, it crawled around like a monstrous insect and continued its chase. Myra turned around as she heard the machine's claws punching into the soil.

"Over there!" Markus yelled as he pointed to rows of crates stacked close together. The machine drew closer. She could smell its oily parts and feel it breathing on the back of her legs. The crates loomed in front of them. The machine made a horrible grinding noise as it lunged at them.

The walls of the boxes closed around them as the Hunter collided with the crates. They turned around and watched it flail its claw-like legs at them. It was too big to get in between the rows and soon gave up its failed attempts. The machine backed up and seemed to glare at them before it slunk back into the shadow.

A terrifying stillness settled.

Myra's breath came in ragged gasps.

"Where'd it go?" Her voice shook. Markus didn't respond but started to silently move forward. Myra followed despite the terror pounding in her chest. She grabbed his hand and tried to pull him back into safety. He slowly peered outward, moving his head to the left and to the right. He recoiled back inside and turned to face her.

"Probably going after the others. Do you see anything we could use as a weapon?" Myra glanced around, hoping to find something sharp or heavy.

The crates shifted around them. Markus's finger moved to his lips. His eyes widened as he looked over Myra's shoulder at the Hunter walking on the top of the crates. It made a series of clicking noises as its legs rapped against the containers.

Tears welled up in Myra's eyes. She couldn't see it but knew it was there.

"Look at me, My," Markus whispered sharply. Myra's legs trembled. It was above her. She felt its heat on her neck.

Myra couldn't fight it any longer. Her eyes traveled upward as she stared at the underbelly of the Hunter. She watched in petrified horror as a razor-sharp tube extended from the middle of the machine like a stinger. The Hunter arched upwards and brought its body rushing back down with the stinger aimed at her chest.

Markus pushed Myra out of the way. Myra's blood curdled as his scream echoed throughout the Depository. Markus was ripped off his feet and dragged backward out of the safety of the crates.

"Myra! Myra!" Markus screamed. Once the Hunter had him out in the open, it retracted its stinger out of his shoulder. His body lifted as the stinger withdrew with a spray of blood.

Myra watched in horror as the stinger slid back out. This time, it was aimed at his chest.

Markus was pinned by the machine's legs.

Myra was paralyzed.

He looked at Myra with desperate pleading.

The machine arched upwards and lunged back down.

A metal pipe struck the Hunter's broad side, and the machine lost its aim as the stinger stabbed into the soil next to Markus's head. Adam brought the pipe crashing back down as the Hunter's armor splintered into shards. The Hunter lifted off of Markus and turned its attention to Adam.

Adam swung again, but this time the Hunter anticipated the strike and grabbed his only weapon with a clawed leg. It threw the pipe down and started a wobbly advance toward Adam. Adam stumbled backward and fell. He scurried away but collided with a wall of crates.

There was nowhere to go. The Hunter chirped triumphantly and slid its stinger back out as its clawed legs held Adam down like a piece of meat about to be cut into pieces.

Myra swung the pipe as hard as she could. She heard the sound of cracking metal and smelled the charred smell of exposed wires. The Hunter turned its attention to her just as she swung a second time. This time, the pipe struck the machine and crunched right through the covering.

With a resounding whine and a shower of sparks, the machine heaved forward and crumbled in a heap of mangled metal. Myra could only stare down in heaving disbelief as the swirling dust settled on her skin and upon the pools of blood that were already being smothered.

Chapter 10: Plans Made in the Dark

Byron, Citadel, The Refuge

The Coms flickered to life in front of Byron's face as the leaders came into focus. He saw Horrus, the Head of Security for Citadel. He nodded slightly at Theres, who was the Head of the Industry Protectorate. She wore a grim countenance and didn't return the nod.

Byron acknowledged Soren, the Administrator of Agriculture, who he was sure would be an ally in the coming conversation. The fourth com did not materialize. It seemed one of his primary contacts in the Medical Protectorate declined the opportunity to connect with the rest of the Hajj leadership.

Byron's thoughts lingered on the blank screen before he switched gears.

"Ladies and gentlemen, as you are all aware, the situation is not what we had anticipated," Byron began in a low, even tone. Despite knowing the severity of their present circumstances, he didn't want to worry the others.

"That's an understatement, Byron," Horrus barked. His thick mustache brimmed with activity.

"Let's not be coy, Byron. Tell us the extent of the damage," Theres cut in. Her steel gray eyes spoke a severity.

"Of course. I know it's a sacrifice for all of you to meet like this, so I'll cut to the chase. As you all know, the Lord Protector brought down the Dam in Hydra Sector. The result was a fifty-five percent loss of industrial capacity. Electricity was hit immediately, but it seems Lorenzo had consolidated the electrical grid and moved it away from Industry before the event. Apparently, he has been consolidating and relocating most of Axiom's subsystems."

"He moved it prior? Why?" Soren asked gently. In the group, he was the youngest. He was still being reinstructed to not see Lorenzo as the reverent, all-powerful Lord Protector, but his Agriculture position was strategically advantageous.

"Because what happened in Industry was not an accident. It was not impulsive. It was not on a whim. It was not spontaneous. It was premeditated, calculated, and purposeful," Byron stated with a heaviness in his tone. He let the idea sink into their minds before he continued.

"You ask me why. Why did he do this? I do not know. All I know is Lorenzo murdered hundreds of people in a single moment and then blamed it on an ambiguous enemy to create chaos and disorder—a chaos and disorder that works in favor of his machinations and schemes according to a plan we can hardly understand at the moment. Ladies and gentlemen, we're not dealing with a madman. We are dealing with a genius. We have to understand that going forward. There is not a plan he has not conceived already, so we must be methodical and purposeful. We must be tactful and disciplined, or we risk walking right into his hands."

A protracted silence fell amongst them. Resistance looked feeble in light of this reality.

"And what prevents him from listening in to our conversation right now, eh? How can we know we are safe?" Horrus asked gruffly as he broke the silence. Byron went to respond but was cut off by Abby as she stepped forward.

"I can answer that question," Abby spoke confidently as her purple spiked hair bobbed up and down. Byron stepped aside slightly to give her some room.

"And who are you?" Theres inquired crisply.

Abby looked at Byron, who nodded his assent.

"My name is Abigail. Byron is my father," she stated frankly. Horrus choked back his astonishment, and Theres conveyed a look of shock and disbelief. Soren seemed unchanged by the information. Abigail looked to her father, who had a smile.

"Byron, dear, this information is astonishing," Theres began as she chose her words carefully. "Why the secrecy? Why have we not ever seen this daughter of yours?"

"Yes, it seems odd to have kept this nugget to yourself, Byron. Almost as if you didn't think we were trustworthy," Horrus accused with an edge in his voice.

"My reasons are my own. I'm sorry if this isn't sufficient enough of an answer for you, but I have to hold a couple pieces close to my chest. Me revealing Abby to you should be enough to show you how much I trust each of you. You each know the penalty for an unregistered child in Axiom, so I'm delivering my fate and hers into your hands. Regardless, she is part of all of this, and you can rest assured, Abby has made it impossible for this conversation to be breached."

"How can we be sure?" Horrus scrutinized.

"Do you recall the ten-minute blackout which struck Citadel one hundred cycles ago?"

"Yes, yes, I do. It was committed by the Hajj, a group of hijackers who broke into the NOOM," Soren stated knowledgeably.

"That was me," Abby quipped triumphantly. Collective admiration rolled through the three people on the Coms. Abby smiled meekly. "Within the last five minutes of this conversation, your Coms have downloaded and dispersed hand-tailored nanoparticles which I designed. I assume you all understand how the NOOM system works, correct?"

"Yes, of course," Horrus cut in, "What's the point?"

"I don't mean to sound naïve, but could you explain?" Soren interjected. Horrus scoffed.

"Certainly," Abby began, "the NOOM system was designed so that we could interface with Axiom directly. In essence, we could design and create Axiom based off of our wills alone. In the beginning, we were granted the ability to be the architects of a great civilization. However, once Lorenzo took control, he limited Axiom's capabilities. Basically, we cannot create impenetrable buildings, fortresses, etc., without his authorization. But, for him to maintain control over all the citizens of Axiom, he must be aware of everyone's presence at all times." She paused to take a breath. She could tell she had everyone's attention now.

"The NOOM system also prevented, up until recently, the ability to cause violence to one another. The NOOM system accomplishes this task through the nanoparticle security system found in Technology. The nanites are everywhere. We breathe them in. They're in our blood, our bones, our brains. They record and analyze every chemical, every synaptic connection, every movement—all to prevent danger to one another."

"All information we already knew," Horrus said sarcastically. Byron's frustration mounted at his disrespect.

"Continue, Abby," Byron said tersely.

"However, in the wrong hands, the nanites also provide a constant stream of information to the Directory—feeding them our every movement and emotion," she stated bluntly. Everyone listened, but it was Soren who was leaning forward in his chair as he digested this new information.

"You asked my father why he never mentioned that he had a child," she began as she glanced over at Byron. He wore a look of confusion but did not move to shut her down. "If I were to present myself to the nanites in the air, they'd pick up my DNA and recognize me as a foreign entity. Because I am not in the system, they don't see me. I'm invisible."

"But how do you accomplish this all the time? Surely there are nano...nanites in the room?" Soren asked curiously.

"Yes, Soren. There are. But I made them. The nanoparticles in this room, in my blood, are designed to mimic the behavior of ordinary nanites. The only difference is they relay false information to the Directory," she stated confidently.

"And what false information is that?" Soren asked.

Abby swallowed hard. She looked at her father. Despite the weary sorrow gathering in his chest, Byron nodded.

"That of my mother," Abby said softly. Byron watched the sadness tremble in her eyes.

"That can't be possible," Theres began, "If at any point the security system picked up a duplicate copy of your mother's DNA, alarms would sound immediately. Since this has obviously not happened, that would mean your mother is—,"

"—Dead," Abby responded flatly.

A stunned silence fell amongst them.

"Richard," Theres began softly, "I'm so sorry. We did not know. How long?"

"—A long time," Byron said quickly. "Which is why this information is the most dangerous information I have ever given you. As you all know, Director Florence has been a part of the Directory for years. If it were to be made known my daughter poses as my wife every cycle, then my daughter's life would be in immediate danger, as would my own. I am trusting all of you with this information," Byron said tersely. There was a hardness in his tone—a warning. Everyone was silent as they digested this information.

"Well, I guess this means we have nothing to worry about, eh? If your nanites have duped the system this long, then I'm confident they are doing their job on our end," Soren suggested. The others agreed. Byron nodded at his daughter and stepped back into the full view of the camera as she melted backward into the fabricated darkness.

"Now that we have that out of the way let's discuss the whole reason why I have you all gathered right now," Byron stated flatly as he went down to business. "How Lorenzo has accumulated and wielded his power is unprecedented. Needless to say, shock and awe were effective, and now his authority is spreading throughout all of Axiom. Abby estimates that the entire code for the NOOM system will be overridden within fifty cycles or less. That means, ladies and gentlemen, Lorenzo will have complete and utter control of Axiom," Byron stated grimly.

"How is this possible? The NOOM system was foolproof. It was designed to prevent violence and to protect us from one another. How did Lorenzo break the system? Did he use some sort of virus to corrupt the code?" Soren asked.

"Unfortunately, he is the virus. His will, refined and honed by centuries, broke the NOOM system and reversed the order of things. I believe he's preparing Axiom for something—something big. We've lost communications with our asset in the slave compound—Paul—but there've been massive shifts in the work the slaves were doing," Abby provided. "We believe he's preparing for war," she said with a shudder.

"This means we must strike. Our next course of action needs to be precise and effective. So far, Lorenzo doesn't suspect our presence. His attention has been on some unfortunate Figure who dared cross him," Byron conveyed.

"Yes," Horrus cut in, "on that young Figure—1C118."

"Sebastian," Abby added. Byron gave her a confused look. He was not aware she'd been researching the young man.

"Whatever his name is, he's been most effective in distracting Lorenzo," Theres conveyed. "He's even been blamed for the recent earthquake. We still aren't aware of what caused it?" She said with a raise of her eyebrow.

"No. But, I think the removal of the nonviolent laws had something to do with it. Regardless, 1C118 has become Lorenzo's poster boy for all things malicious and of ill-intent," Byron responded sagely.

"Personally, I thought he was working for you, Richard," Theres said as she nodded at Byron. Byron shook his head, but his mind started to work.

"No, but perhaps he could be useful to us none the less," he suggested faintly.

"What do you mean?" Soren asked. Byron paced.

"Maybe we could use him as a diversion. If we could plant misinformation, draw Lorenzo's forces away from Citadel, then maybe we could take crucial pieces off the board. We could even attack key departments which would further weaken his control—possibly slow him down."

Everyone was silent as they mulled over the thought.

"How do we even know he's still alive?" Soren inquired.

"He was spotted by one of our assets just after the earthquake. An Enforcer who works for us," Byron provided.

"Where is he now?" Theres inquired.

"Abby?" Byron asked with a tilt of his head. Abby moved to one of her own personal Coms, and her fingers worked feverishly. Byron watched as she hacked into the NOOM primary systems and did a search for 1C118's DNA sequence. Almost immediately, she got a hit as a map of Axiom appeared, showing the routes he'd taken.

"Oh no...," she said softly. Byron swore to himself.

"It appears he has been captured and is being detained in Armament," he stated as he turned back to the displays.

"Of course!" Horrus grunted. Everyone was crestfallen.

"But, that's a good thing," Soren provided.

"How so?" Byron asked as his brow furrowed.

"Comande Duval is dead, which means the leadership structure in Armament is in disarray. As far as I understand, no replacement has been selected, though Rais is taking control at an alarming rate. Until he steps in on an official capacity, we could infiltrate and remove Sebastian with relative ease."

Everyone paused as they digested the idea.

"Abby, any way you can see if the command structure has been restored? Or if any one of the Administrators has been reassigned to Armament?"

Abby went to work. She typed in the parameters and got a single result.

"Rais. He departed this cycle," she said bluntly. Byron swore to himself.

"Alright, ladies and gentlemen. We have a limited window of opportunity, but we are going to act before it is too late," he stated firmly as he placed his hands on his hips.

"What did you have in mind?" Theres inquired.

"We're going to have to wage war on multiple sides, unfortunately. On the one side, we need to retrieve 1C118. He can become the face of the problems occurring in Axiom. But, if he's locked up, he won't be very useful. Second, we assault the Technology Protectorate. With Rais away from his perch, we can take his Protectorate by surprise and hamper the nanoparticle security system's effectiveness in Axiom. That should buy us some time and allow us to move some of our people into key areas inside Citadel without being detected."

"Are you sure taking down the nanite system will be effective? What about the NOOM system? What's stopping the Lord Protector from barricading himself in Citadel behind massive walls or boxing us all in once we get our forces too close?" Soren asked seriously.

"We will lose the element of surprise, yes, but I am confident the lack of nanoparticles will allow us to get within arm's reach of the Directory and of Lorenzo. As long as he doesn't see us gathering at his feet, he won't know he's about to fall until it is too late."

"Agreed," Horrus started, "but how can we accomplish a war on two sides, Richard? Our resources are stretched thin already. Do you have an asset who can infiltrate Armament undetected, find 1C118 and free him, and do so without getting caught? It seems like a tall order if you ask me."

It did seem like an impossible task. One Byron had not yet figured out how to accomplish.

"No,...But give me until the end of the cycle, and I will figure this part out. In the meantime, Theres, I need you to get your network ready to move on to Technology. Once we have 1C118 in our grasp, we will start our assault. It may take a couple cycles, so make sure your people don't give anything away. I've heard Lorenzo created a new Role—the Paraclete— who has been given complete authority and power. I've heard of numerous Admins who've already been interrogated and prosecuted for suspected involvement. We wouldn't want to let slip what we are planning, so keep the details to a minimum and watch your confidences," Byron instructed.

"Of course," Theres quipped.

"Soren, I will need you to prepare a diversion for us. Once we have 1C118, you'll feed misinformation about his whereabouts in Agriculture. This will draw any more remaining forces from Citadel and Technology."

"Yes, sir," Soren said enthusiastically.

"Horrus," Byron started as he looked in the man's direction, "I need to know everything you can find about Citadel's infrastructure," he said curtly. Horrus simply grunted.

The group fell silent as the weight of rebellion settled.

"As soon as I can, I will contact you all. Good luck," Byron stated as he closed the meeting. Everyone responded the same as their Coms went blank. The last to leave was Soren, who smiled at Abby. Abby grinned back as his Com went dark.

Byron turned to his daughter. Concern and worry were already gathering on his brow.

"Now, where are we going to find somebody who will save 1C118?" He voiced aloud.

Abby looked over his shoulder at the Com looking into the alley. She could swear she saw a familiar face. The person moved, and sure enough, she knew who it was. A grin broke open on her face.

"I know exactly who we need to save Sebastian," she said as she pressed the button to open the secret passageway.

Chapter 11: Radiant

Mary, Medical Protectorate, Radiant Sector

Mary felt the uneasiness gather in her heart as her feet carried her off the Train and down an uncertain path. She recalled the cryptic orders she'd received on her manipulor:

P31, you are being reassigned to Radiant. You are to report to duty on your next cycle. Do not return to your previous Role. Do not inform anyone of the change in your Role. This is a binding and immediate change, Figure. Failure to be present in your Role will result in a severe penalty.

Now, as Mary approached the doors to a featureless building, her heart pounded, and her mind swirled.

Radiant.

Mary had heard rumors about the Sector, but she assumed they were just that—rumors. Radiant was shrouded in secrecy. What did they do in Radiant? Was it true Caretakers who worked in Radiant never returned?

Mary didn't know. But, she was about to find out. Her manipulor glowed a mustard yellow, the color of muddy bewilderment quickly evolving into apprehension. She'd never been to this part of the Medical Protectorate. She'd never been beyond her Role.

Except when she was in his arms. In his Quarters.

But that was so long ago.

A distant memory that flared up like a bruise.

It throbbed with its tenderness and warmth.

Her manipulor changed color, and she chased the memory away. Mary concentrated on the map glowing from her manipulor and let uneasiness return. The arrow hovering above her wrist pointed at the building looming over her. A single light peered into the darkness and illuminated a set of doors.

Cautiously, Mary approached the doors. She stopped a couple of feet away as her eyes scanned the emptiness around her. Suddenly, the doors burst open as a woman stepped out.

"Well, are you coming?" An exuberant voice clipped. Mary jumped as the woman stepped through the darkened doors, and a rush of aroma struck Mary's nostrils.

The woman looked unusual. She was wearing a flamboyantly pink set of clothes that curved around her body. Her hair was brought up above her head in a tight bun, and her hands were wrapped around a clipboard.

"Come on, sugar. I don't have all day. Step inside," the woman said as she ushered with her hand. Hesitantly, Mary walked through the doorway. "Right this way," the woman said as she led Mary to her right. Dutifully, Mary followed as they approached a door with a plaque that said, "Receptionist." Without a word, the woman held the door open.

Mary entered. Her eyes roamed around the room. The room itself was unlike anything she'd ever seen. It had green plants in pots in each corner. There were chairs arranged neatly, with small, flimsy books on tables next to the chairs. The room smelled sweet, and the walls were a light tan color.

"Name?"

Mary turned to the woman as she walked behind a counter. The woman sat down. A Com unit, an archaic keyboard, and loose papers filled the space in front of her. As she took it all in, Mary began to piece together the significance of the room. It was a replica of an office—a building designed for ancient Caretakers called doctors.

Before the wars, the bombs, and the worldwide plagues and famines, doctors used to receive patients daily for treatment and checkups. She felt a wave of curious nostalgia roll over her as the room hummed with fluorescent light.

"What's your name, sugar?" The receptionist asked. Mary snapped to attention.

"Sorry. It's P31. I'm from the Hospital."

"Sign in, here," the woman interrupted, pointing with long fingernails which gleamed in the sharp lighting.

Polished nails?

How in the world did she acquire nail polish? Such luxuries didn't exist. Mary stepped forward, her curiosity growing monstrous in her chest. What *was* Radiant?

She picked up the pen and scribbled her name the best she could. Her hand felt cramped and awkward. Writing was another rare commodity. Carefully, she placed the pen back down and dropped her hands to her side. After a couple of seconds, the receptionist looked at her with an amused stare.

"You people are all the same. You can go sit down," the receptionist said as she pointed to an empty chair. Mary felt the heat rise in her cheeks as she embarrassedly shuffled to the chair. The chair creaked when she sat, and the smell of leather puffed out from underneath her. She did her best to sit still and wait for whatever was next, but she couldn't stop her eyes from taking in the relics of Radiant.

Mary read the posters on the wall, which gave her instructions on washing her hands, covering her cough, and eating healthy. Her mind swam. At one point, she even reached out to touch the plant on the table next to her, only to find that it was plastic. She was caught up in the smooth texture, and Mary didn't hear the door open.

"P31?" Mary jumped as the deep voice echoed. "Mary?" Mary turned to the voice. The man was and wore a thin, white coat and loose pants. He read from a clipboard and called her name again as if he couldn't see her sitting right in front of him.

"That's me," Mary volunteered. The man looked up from his notes and smiled.

"Excellent. Right this way, please," he said with a gesture as he held the door open. The earnestness in his eyes made Mary uneasy. She stared into the hallway beyond, which turned a corner out of sight. "Don't you worry, Mary. We're going to take good care of you," he promised with a nod towards the open door and a flashy grin.

With trepidation building in her chest, Mary stepped through the doorway. The man closed the door behind Mary with a soft click.

"Follow me," he said as he touched her elbow and directed her to the left. A sickening feeling was collecting in the back of Mary's throat.

The walls were light blue—happy and cheerful.

"I'm Doctor Josef Clauberg," he began as he walked beside her.

"Why am I here? What is this place?" She asked weakly. The man gave her a wide grin.

"First, we'll take your temperature, height, and weight. Then, we can discuss the real reason why you've been sent to me. Step inside," Doctor Clauberg stated as he pointed into a small room. Reluctantly, Mary followed his orders and entered. The room had a small countertop, a sink, and a waist-high bed covered in white paper.

"If you will step on the scale." Sheepishly, Mary did so. Her confusion weighed down on her mind as she frantically went through the possible scenarios. Why was she being tested like this? Who had changed her Role and why?

Was she Diseased?

"Excellent, excellent. Now let me take your temperature. Just hold still." A cold, uncomfortable probe touched her temple. She resisted the strong desire to pull away but held herself in place. Seconds later, the probe chirped.

"Good, good. Well, you are certainly in great health. Congratulations!" Mary's head swam. His grin filled up his face as he leaned up against the counter. "Now, as my patient, do you have any questions or concerns?"

Plenty.

"Forgive me, but I must ask. What is this place? Why am I here? Who are you?" Doctor Clauberg straightened. His face grew somber and grave.

"Follow me, please," he said as he beckoned. Still bewildered, Mary followed. The two of them left the room and journeyed down the hallway. They stopped at a door with a plaque on it which read, "Radiant Clinic." The Doctor typed a code into a keypad.

The keypad chirped, and then he pushed the door open. The smell of antiseptic wafted out and met Mary, causing her nostrils to burn. As she peered into the unlit room, her eyes began to pick up the glint of metal, and she could hear the sound of machinery humming.

Doctor Clauberg stepped into a room scarcely illuminated. As Mary entered the room, her heart fell. Rows of gurneys lined the room, but the gurneys weren't empty. Every single one she could see contained a Figure strapped in as various tubes ran from their bodies into machines which hummed and chirped. Their closed eyes and lifeless bodies made Mary feel the prick of anxiety.

"Welcome to Radiant, Mary," Doctor Clauberg stated with pride as he extended his arms. How he spoke her name made chills run down her spine. Her eyes lingered on the gurneys. They all looked helpless and small.

"Are they...?" She hesitated. Dare she say the word?

"Oh, no. The patients aren't dead. They're very much alive. Just unconscious. See," Doctor Clauberg began as he approached one of the gurneys. He waved in the Figure's face, snapped his fingers, and even lightly tapped the person's cheek like an insolent child. "Out cold. For their benefit, of course."

For their benefit?

A lump gathered in MMary'sthroat.

"Are they Diseased?" She croaked hoarsely.

"Quite the contrary. They're pure—the purest in Axiom. And we at Radiant would like to keep it that way. Which brings me to your new Role, Mary," he said in an approachable tone as he took a few steps forward. She could smell pungent cologne, and the sweat gathered in his armpits.

"Your job is to make sure these patients have everything they need. You will monitor them, give them nutrients, and clean them if necessary. You will do whatever it takes to keep them in tip-top health. Understood?" His friendliness and charm molded into a stern, sharp tone.

"Yes, Doctor. But why are they here?" She asked with razor-thin curiosity. His plastered smile fell.

71

"There are certain things I will not tolerate at Radiant, Mary, and questions are one of them. I am the Doctor, and what the Doctor says needs to be carried out. Understood?" His eyebrows arched as he stared into Mary. The heat rose in her cheeks, and she felt the urge to run. She held her ground but lowered her gaze.

"Of course, Doctor."

"Thank you. Head Mother Cynthia here will guide you to your work station and show you around." As soon as he'd spoken, a woman appeared as if she'd been waiting for her cue. She wore an old-fashioned Nurse's outfit—the kind Mary had seen in the training manuals.

The design was meant to evoke a feeling of care and warmth, but the woman was everything but warm. Her face was pointed and hollowed, and she wore another rarity in Axiom— makeup. It made her eyes look dark and moody and her lips full.

"I have some demanding needs I must attend. You two have fun. Tah tah," he said as he walked away, heading back to the doorway they'd entered.

"This way," The Head Mother stated crisply. Still caught in the unusual circumstances, Mary could only follow in a confused daze. The Head Mother's heels clicked on the polished floor and became a rhythm of steps connected to the beeping and chirping of the machines all around them.

"You will be here at approximately 0900 each cycle. Tardiness will not be tolerated. Failure to show will have...*consequences*," the Head Mother said hollowly.

Mary didn't want to find out what those consequences might be. The Mother led them through double doors, which opened at the touch of a button. They entered a hallway that branched off into multiple rooms. They passed numerous doors, each one closed and windowless.

"You will sign in at the waiting room and wait to be retrieved. It will either be myself or an orderly. Any questions? Ask now or don't ask at all," she said pointedly. So many swirled through Mary's mind.

"Will I see Doctor Clauberg often?" Mary asked.

"On the rare occasion. The Doctor is very busy. We receive patients almost every day, and he has to examine them before they hit the floor. If they do not meet his standards, they're sent...elsewhere. But, if they do, you must monitor them and keep them comfortable, administering to their every need."

There was a sinister knowledge in her voice that made Mary shudder. The Head Mother led her through another set of doors and into a rectangular room. In the middle were long tables with small seats attached to the tables. At the tables were a handful of women leaning forward in a still silence as they brought food to their mouths.

"The Cafeteria. You will be eating here every day. You will dress in your standard Caretaker clothing, but when you arrive, you will take off those contaminated clothes," she said as her eyes roamed up and down Mary's body. Mary was suddenly self-conscious of her clothes. "And get a sterile set of scrubs from your locker through that door," she said as she pointed.

"Work stations are through those doors. You get your supplies, your orders, and your readouts from your work station. It's mobile, so take it with you."

Mary felt overwhelmed, but it seemed the Head Mother finished explaining. A stiff silence fell between them. The Mother gave her a solid, resonating glare, and Mary was the first to look away.

"We expect professionalism at Radiant. The Doctor may show you respect by referring to your first name, but I don't have to show any. You're here because somebody pulled the right strings, but that doesn't make you valuable. Understand?" Mary was used to not being valuable. She nodded.

"Good. Now, I suggest you meet the rest of your team," the Head Mother said with another long point. Mary followed her gaze to the group of women still sitting at the table, each of them at least six feet away from each other, eating in silence.

Not knowing what else to do, Mary found her feet carrying her to the table. She sat away from the other women and stared at the space in front of her. The door to the cafeteria closed with a clap as the Head Mother left the room.

There was a sudden rush of air and motion as the women left their spots and closed around Mary.

"Hey!"

"How ya doing?"

"What's your name?"

"How'd you get assigned to Radiant?"

The questions were overwhelming, and the unexpected presence of four women around her made her feel the heat rising. Each stared at her with interest as they waited on her answers. Mary's eyes flew to the door the Mother had just departed through as nervousness crawled in her chest.

"Well, come out with it. Who are you?" Asked the tallest of the four women. She had red hair, and her lips were a deep pink. Such colors didn't exist in Axiom.

"I'm P31: Caretaker." The women laughed together. Mary wasn't insulted but felt herself blush. "Or Mary."

"You're a newbie, so I guess you have to get used to us, but we don't care too much for the formalities," spoke the redheaded woman. "From here on out, you'll be Mother Mary. I'm Veronica, that's Tess and Mags, and Gigi, and right over there sulking because she's no longer the new blood is Mother Kapplin." Mary listened fully.

Mary found the group of women to be disarming and comforting despite their smothering nature. Her eyes went to each face as Mother Veronica pointed them out. Each woman gave a curt nod and a welcoming smile. Even Mother Kapplin gave a small wave.

"I'm sure you have a bunch of questions after the whole show the Doc and Mother Tightwad put on when you arrived," Mags suggested. Despite knowing questions were forbidden, Mary found herself nodding.

"Well, then. Out with it! What do you want to know first?" The women hugged in tighter towards Mary as they crowded their heads together. Mary felt the fear prickle in her chest, and her manipulor started to change color to reflect her worry. The women glanced down at Mary's arm as she tried to cover the color emitting from her wrist.

"Don't worry about it," Mother Gigi instructed. Her hair was short and closely cropped. Mary had never seen a woman have short hair. "They turn them off once you arrive, so the light doesn't disturb the patients cuz they don't want them coming out of la-la land. Like that one time with Cynthia." A collective shudder rolled through the women.

Mary's interest grew.

"What is this place?" Mary asked.

"What place? Radiant doesn't exist. Not officially, that is." All the girls nodded in tune with Tess's comments. "Unofficially, this is a suckhole that drains every single person who steps through the door. Most of the time, the new patients come from The Directory, but occasionally Armament snags a couple and sends them our way."

"Doctor Clauberg said something about them being pure? What does that mean?"

"Ahh, good ol' Doctor Claw. He's a funny man," Mother Veronica began, "And I don't mean he makes me have the giggles. He has a flair for the nostalgic. He likes the old way of doing things around here. Why do you think you walked into a waiting room when you got to Radiant? And why we're wearing makeup and outdated Mother uniforms? The guy's a coocoo. But, he's in charge of Radiant and in charge of setting up the procedures with the patients."

"What procedures? Is he trying to get them better like in the Hospital?" Mary was growing more and more confused the longer they spoke. They snickered to themselves.

"You don't get it, do you, doll?" Mother Kapplin interjected after having let all the others have their go. "People don't come here to get better," she said ominously. An unsettling silence fell on their shoulders.

"Then, why do they come?" Mary said with a waver in her voice. She was afraid of the answer but she had to know.

"They come to get drained. Every single person out there gets drained of their soul or lifeforce. We've heard a couple of names for it, but it's a byproduct of intense devotion

75

and concentration which activates chemicals in the brain and body. They get sucked dry until there's nothing left."

A tight knot was forming in Mary's stomach.

"Why?" She whispered.

The women paused and looked at each other.

"Oh, dearie," Tess began, "so that the Lord Protector can live forever."

Chapter 12: Restored

Damien, Citadel, The Refuge

Damien peered up the stairway as it materialized in front of him. At the top was a door framed in silver. The color gave him hope, for it meant the murderous red color hadn't yet infected Abby's refuge. He took a deep breath and began his ascent. His footsteps felt heavy as he climbed as he thought, for the thousandth time, about what he was going to say.

The door opened ahead of him. He swallowed the knot in his throat and entered.

For a moment, the room blinded him with its vibrant light. It was like he was back to the moment he'd first stepped foot into this room—seconds after a woman had rushed him inside to prevent his capture. The memory seemed ancient.

"Damien?" Abby spoke softly.

Damien looked at the girl who had, on countless occasions, saved his life. The one who he'd betrayed by ignoring her advice and selfishly doing what he wanted.

"Abby," Damien returned.

"How are you here?"

"Yes," a voice resounded as Byron stepped forward. Another wave of guilt crashed over Damien at the sight of yet another person whose trust he'd broken. "The last I heard, you were imprisoned. How do we know you aren't a spy—an infiltrator," Byron accused as he towered in front of Damien.

Damien looked at Byron and then at Abby, his tongue still tied in his mouth. The words bubbled on his skin. Byron's stare bore into him.

"Forgive me," he whispered. Byron's brow folded.

"What?"

"Forgive me. Please. I'm sorry for what I did. I'm sorry I broke your trust." Damien glanced around Byron at Abby. "Both of you. I'm sorry."

A stunned silence consumed their conversation. Abby stepped forward until she was beside her father.

"I forgive you, Damien."

Damien felt the heat rise in his cheeks.

"How'd you get here, D?" Abby asked. Damien could hear the friendliness in her voice. His heartbeat calmed.

"Theo," he said confidently.

"Who?" Byron asked. Now, Damien to be confused.

"Theo. You know, the Master?"

Their faces were filled with empty understanding.

"Who is Theo?" Byron asked, now an edge to his voice. "And how did *he* help you escape?"

"It's hard to explain. He kinda gave me himself, I guess."

They still weren't getting it.

"Watch. I'll show you," Damien suggested as he went to the wall. His fingers touched the cold surface, and the white lines caressed the wall. They moved, like liquid, in all directions, connecting and merging. Every nanoparticle in the room glowed with ambient brilliance so bright the lights in the room looked dim in comparison.

The lines converged in the center of the room, forming a structure that resembled a tree with branches made of light reaching out in an embrace. Damien looked to them with a wild grin on his face, but they still wore shock and confusion.

"Damien...what exactly are we supposed to be seeing?"

The truth sunk into the pit of his stomach.

They couldn't see it. None of it. The image flickered and faded, and the room returned to normal. Damien's hand receded from the wall. An unsettled emotion stirred inside of him, and he felt loneliness creep into his chest.

"I don't know how to explain it, but Theo sent me. He said you'd need me."

"This Theo seems to know too much information," Byron growled. Damien felt the hair stand up on the back of his neck as he watched Byron's fists clench.

"When did he send you?" Abby asked as she stepped in front of her father.

"Two cycles ago. I think." Abby turned back to Byron.

"He's not lying, dad. Whoever this Theo is, he seems to have foreseen our predicament and our need ahead of time."

"I don't trust a source I have never met," Byron said tersely with a shake of his head.

"I trust Damien, dad," Abby said softly. Damien felt his heart flutter with hope. "Besides, we have no other choice. Who else has his skills?"

Byron stared at his daughter as he chewed on her statement. Finally, he looked at Damien with resigned distrust.

"Whoever Theo is," he began, "I'm going to need to talk to him. In the meantime, we need your help, Damien."

"I'm here to find the old man. Joshua O'Reilly. He was in the cell next to me. If I find him first, I'll help you," Damien said staunchly. Byron's eyebrow rose, but he didn't argue.

"Abby? Whereabouts?"

Abby went to the keyboard. Damien maintained a static gaze with Byron. In Byron's cheek, a muscle kept clenching.

"No way! Look at this," Abby said to Byron. Byron broke his gaze and went to his daughter. He looked over her shoulder.

"Huh." He turned back to Damien. "Well, it's your lucky day, Damien. Your old man is in the Military Protectorate. It seems he is being taken to Retirement soon. But he doesn't move out again for another couple of cycles. It looks like you'll have an opportunity to grab our guy and yours," Byron stated flatly. Damien could tell his mind was still swirling.

"Is it going to be dangerous?" Damien asked them both.

"Most likely," Abby responded.

Damien grinned. It was just like old times.

Chapter 13: The Confined

Sebastian, Armament

Hungry flames wrapped around Sam as he spoke.

Sebastian, what does it mean to be human?

Sebastian woke with a start as he jerked into existence. He groggily scanned the room, which was barren and lifeless, as numbness ebbed out of his bones. His arms, which were encased in a pair of manipulors up to his elbows, felt heavy.

Sebastian was confused. Why would they give him a manipulor? He tapped at each of them, but no display appeared, and nothing occurred. He shook his head in wonder and tried his best to stand. As he stood, the manipulors glowed and prevented him from advancing as bolts of red light shot outward in arcs and dragged him to the wall.

Now he understood.

The manipulors were his prison.

An agonizing weight settled upon Sebastian as his throat tightened and his stomach churned. What were they going to do to him? He was Diseased—a terrorist. In the past—when violence wasn't an option—such people were Extracted, exiled from Axiom, and assigned to a certain death outside of Axiom's walls. But, violence and death were part of the fabric of Axiom, now. The great black cloud of savagery had found its way inside.

It was he who had opened the door.

Sam's question still haunted him. How long had it been since his death on the Train?

So long.

Yet, his question was what had provoked Sebastian to search for answers. It was in this pursuit that Sebastian opened up his mind to what was forbidden—his emotions. At first, these emotions were an idea he had to ignore, but once they took root inside his imagination, they gave birth to action. He let anger, passion, vindication, rage, and desire consume him until he was a pillar of fire that others came to watch burn.

And people came.

Stephen, and dozens of others.

But, now they were dead. Because Sebastian had tried to bring them into his light, to get them to agree with his pain. He tried to convince them to bring down Axiom.

Sebastian could still see the projection of the Lord Protector standing in front of him as Hydra crumbled.

Sebastian was a fool. That was what the Lord Protector had called him. He remembered the words, the voice cutting through him just seconds before Hydra was destroyed. Destroyed because of Sebastian's irrationality and arrogance.

What did it mean to be human?

The question was foul in his mouth.

Inside of him was more pain than he could redeem.

Perhaps this was what it meant to be human.

To hurt and be broken.

Sebastian was brought out of his thoughts by a chirp as the door slid open. A stiff, broad-shouldered man entered, and Sebastian immediately recognized the military insignia across his chest. He was confined in Armament.

Sebastian remembered the last time he was in Armament. It was the day he encountered the old man who gave him a book. It was the day he rejected the laws of Axiom.

"Figure, stand up."

Sometimes he remembered the words. They were etched in his brain, lingering like a whisper. He remembered pouring over their intimacy and feasting upon each syllable. In moments of terrible clarity, he could recall the phrases and statements like they were in front of his eyes.

"Stand. I won't ask again," the Enforcer threatened.

Now, one sentence glared from its veil of mystery.

Though I walk in darkness, I will not fear, for you are with me.

It didn't make any sense to him. Like the rest of the book, the phrase was an enigma—one he no longer had the energy to solve. Besides, the rest of the book was on his manipulor, which his father had taken moments before he stabbed him. Whatever truth it contained was lost to him.

Numbed by his new reality, Sebastian stood though his heart did not stand with him. It was still chained to the floor. Somehow, he managed the courage to speak.

"Where am I going?"

The Enforcer did not answer immediately. Instead, he pressed a button as the pressure pulling Sebastian's arms released. Before he could react, though, the Enforcer pressed another button. In response, both arms were jerked forward in front of him until the two manipulors combined into a single cuff. The Enforcer's lip curled into a sneer.

"You're going for...questioning."

Sebastian had the distinct impression he would not like how they got the answers out of him. He was jerked forward by an invisible cord and forced to follow the Enforcer.

Paul, Slave Compound

When Paul arrived at the depot, he immediately recognized the throng of people, slaves and guards alike, working feverishly to create barricades out of debris and loose materials. The depot itself was a squat building at the end of a railway that emerged between two mountains.

Paul was familiar with the design, for it was similar to the carriage house in the Mountain. It, too, had a depot from which Paul corresponded with the Hajj, a group trying to overthrow their oppressive regime.

But something had gone terribly wrong. The *Lord Protector*—the moniker felt awkward and uncomfortable—was sending his men to obtain the machines Hob built, which indicated the resistance and uprising had failed. All his hopes for a future for himself and his people were ashes, now. For the first time in a long time, Paul did not know what to do. He didn't know the next step. He didn't know where to go.

"Move it!" A guard shouted and prodded him in the back. Paul's feet responded even as his mind sunk lower into his thoughts. He approached a group of men and women who were hard at work, creating a wall. His hands went to work as his eyes roamed the expansive depot. He followed the train tracks to the point where they were swallowed in the darkness between the mountains. The light didn't penetrate the gulley between the giants, and Paul felt a foreboding feeling creep up his spine.

Darkness approached.

How long did they have before the delegation arrived? He remembered the conversation he'd overheard—the man said a few cycles. Paul assumed whoever was coming was coming in force. Out here, beyond the protection of Axiom, violence, and suffering were the law of the land. Hob wasn't going to give away his creations willingly.

Paul's hands were bleeding, cut on a piece of metal he'd been transferring. He stopped and looked around himself as he tore cloth to wrap around his hand. He felt immensely weary, more tired than he'd ever felt in his whole life. Even when he labored in the factories, flames licking his skin, he always possessed a vigor beyond himself. Now, he was worn out.

Something caught his eye. Paul's eyes moved over the terrain, across the depot, and up a squat hill to his right. He surveyed the emplacements they were building and immediately saw the foolishness in their position. Where Hob had them constructing barricades would be too close to the valley. They'd be overrun instantly.

"Quit you're dawdling," an aggravated voice shouted.

Paul turned to the man, a guard whose clothes were torn and unkempt. The man looked just as worn out as Paul.

"I need to speak to Hob," Paul stated firmly. The guard looked at him, blankly. "It's urgent," Paul attempted again.

"What you need is a good beating," the guard threatened as his hand went to his waist.

"Do you want to die?" Paul asked. His face darkened.

"Are you threatening me!?" The guard shouted as he pulled out his club. Paul didn't flinch.

"If I don't talk to Hob, then everyone here is going to be slaughtered, including yourself," Paul assured bluntly. The guard's face fell, and Paul drew closer. "What's your name?" Paul inquired in a hushed voice.

"Preva Jennings. But most call me Logan," he said lowly.

"Logan, it's good to meet you. How'd you get assigned to us slaves?"

Logan looked at him curiously.

"I was transferred from Armament."

"Transferred? You're being punished?"

Logan's gaze crumbled.

"I failed to apprehend a fugitive, and he fell into the wrong hands—a man whom my Comande didn't trust. I was supposed to be transferred back ten cycles ago, but my Comande is dead," he said flatly.

"I see. And do you have any children? A family?"

"Armament is my family," Logan said honestly.

"And do you want to be back in Armament?"

"Of course," Logan responded earnestly.

"Then let me speak to Hob. Please. Our lives depend upon it." Logan hesitated for a moment but then nodded.

"Follow me."

Sebastian didn't know where he was being led, but he followed dutifully. He felt hollow and empty on the inside—preferring death instead of the shame of each breath. Sebastian's hands were bound together in front of him, and a thin light streamed from his cuffs into the Enforcer's manipulor. Each time the Enforcer walked too many paces in front of Sebastian, the rope became taught and yanked Sebastian forward in a humiliating jolt.

After the fourth consecutive yank, Sebastian stumbled into the Enforcer.

"Watch it, filth! I don't want your disease!" The Enforcer shouted as he pushed Sebastian away. Sebastian, despite himself, felt embarrassed.

Sebastian felt dirty.

"I'm sorry," he mumbled, hiding the red deepening across his face.

"Not yet, you aren't," the Enforcer stated forebodingly as he tugged on the light rope. "After Rais gets through with you, I'm sure you'll understand the weight of your crimes," he said with a snort.

Rais.

Sebastian had heard of the man. Aside from the Lord Protector, no one else held as much power in Axiom as Rais. The man was the Director of Technology, but his influence stretched much farther. Evidently, now it reached into Armament.

Fear washed over Sebastian. He wanted to fight it, but he knew it was futile. What was in store for him was going to be worse than death. Sebastian continued to sink. The water was eye level. He was drowning despite being able to see.

"We're here," the Enforcer barked as he pulled Sebastian to a stop. Sebastian clutched the wall as the Enforcer typed a code into the panel. The door slid open to reveal a room twice as large as his previous cell. In the center of the room was an unremarkable table and chair. On the table, however, were metal tools that glinted menacingly.

Sebastian was shoved into the room. All warmth eased out of his skin like he'd been drenched in a bucket of cold water. The Enforcer forced Sebastian to the chair and cuffed his hands to the back. Immediately, an ache spread through his shoulder blades as his muscles stretched to their limits. Now, he was forced to stare at the tools on the metal table—a small, razor-sharp saw, a hammer, and an assortment of ancient devices.

"As for you," the Enforcer spoke as he straightened. "It's time for you to go to Retirement."

"Is it really that time?" A voice behind Sebastian started with a chuckle. Sebastian's attention had been on the table when he entered, and he missed the other occupant in the room. "I feel like my work is just beginning. A bit too early to retire, if you ask me," the voice said again with another short laugh. Sebastian recognized the voice.

"Whatever, old man. Hold out your hands," the Enforcer demanded. Sebastian heard the clicking noise of cuffs locking. The Enforcer brought the man around and paused at the door as he typed in the code. The man turned.

Sebastian's breath caught in his throat.

"Hello, Sebastian. It is good to see you again," the old man said with a grin and glittering eyes.

"You...," Sebastian managed to croak as disbelief clogged his throat. The old man was just as Sebastian had seen him last—ancient and wizened with age and understanding.

The panel flashed red as the passcode was denied. The Enforcer cursed under his breath and feverishly typed the number back into the keypad. The memory of their encounter was a burning thought in Sebastian's mind. The flames wrapped around Sebastian's emotions as his hands trembled.

"I take it you read the book?"

"You!? You did this to me! You gave me that book and now look where I am!" Sebastian accused.

"Shut it!" The Enforcer snapped. He was now beating upon the panel, trying to force it to open.

"I see you," the old man said warmly. Sebastian was shaking with indignation.

"Yes! Imprisoned. A criminal."

"I see someone who has fewer shackles than before," the old man said cryptically.

"I said, shut it!"

The anger was subsiding. In a way, the old man was right. Despite being in chains, he was freer than before. He had more understanding, but with it came the weight of knowledge--of knowing but being unable to do anything about what he understood. The feeling was heavy and made him weary.

"Why did you do this to me?"

The old man gave Sebastian a tender look.

"Because you are important, Sebastian."

The door finally slid open, and the Enforcer yanked on the old man's tether.

"Diamonds are made in the dark," he said sagely as he was being pulled out of view. "Don't give up hope." With a final tug, the old man was taken away. The mystery of his words carved away at Sebastian. He put his head down on the cool, metal table as his mind swam.

Chapter 14: Bleeding Out

Myra, Agriculture Protectorate, Ag Unit 7

Myra couldn't stop the bleeding. Her hands were covered in the sticky fluid as it flowed through her fingertips. Markus screamed in pain as she applied more pressure to the gaping wound in his shoulder. Adam ran to her side.

"What can I do?" He asked breathlessly. A million thoughts surged through Myra's mind. The blood overwhelmed her. The destroyed Hunter just feet away still sizzled and spat out sparks. She couldn't think straight. Nothing made sense.

"Myra, what do you need me to do?" She shook the fog out of her mind.

"Find something I can use to stop the bleeding."

Adam raced into the darkness.

"And a needle and thread!" Myra shouted without raising her head. Markus groaned, his breathing coming in ragged gasps. He clenched his eyes shut as he fought the agony. "Talk to me, Markus," she demanded.

Myra needed Markus to speak to her. To distract her from the four-inch gash which cut through his shoulder and came out his chest.

"It hurts," he said with a wince.

"Why'd you come after me, silly boy? You should have gone back inside with the others," Myra said sorrowfully. Markus forced a genuine grin to replace the mask of pain.

"I'm always coming after you, My." It was the truth. Despite herself, she returned the smile.

"Well, it's my turn. Is there anything else I can do?" She asked earnestly. It wasn't a question he would have an answer for, but she needed him to stay alert.

"I've never had a hamburger before. I hear it's delicious. Maybe one of those?"

"You're crazy." She admired him for it.

"A real nutcase. But, a man can hope."

But, he was hardly yet a man. As she stared at him, though, she could see through the layers of suffering etched in scars. But, in those scars, she also saw Damien. Myra shook him out her head and concentrated on Markus. His breathing, now, was growing irregular. Adam came bounding back over.

"I found this," Adam offered as he held out his hand and revealed strips of cloth. They weren't bandages, but it worked.

"Keep looking. Water, needle and thread, anything," she directed as she started to wrap his wound. Without a word, Adam departed. Markus let out a low moan, and pain ran across his face. "Hang in there, Markus. Stay with me," she said softly as thick silence settled in around her.

The air tasted like dirt and circuitry. His skin felt clammy and cold. Myra pressed firmly into his wound, applying as much pressure as she could without making him spasm in pain. She shushed him softly, hoping the soft noise would soothe him. Adam came running back with an assortment of items clutched loosely in his arms. He deposited the materials unceremoniously at her side and bent down.

"Want me to grab anything else?" Adam asked anxiously. Myra glanced over at the items he'd brought. She saw a canteen, more cloth, some thin cord, and a sharp object she could use as a makeshift needle. She lifted the material off his wound to inspect the bleeding. As soon as she lifted, blood flowed like water. She put the cloth back down and applied pressure as the blood started to seep through.

"That's good. Please find everyone. Make sure they're safe. Can you do that?" She asked through thin lips. Adam nodded. "Good. Don't tell them about Markus. That's something I'll need to do," Myra said with calm urgency.

Without a word, Adam left again. His absence settled in upon Myra. Gingerly, she lifted the cloth again, peering under the makeshift bandage to see if it was working.

"You should've gone with him," Markus said weakly.

"I'm where I need to be," she said gently. Markus's face, even in the dim light coming from the buildings, was ashen. She unscrewed the cap on the flask and sniffed the contents. No aroma met her nostrils, so she assumed it was water.

Myra tilted the liquid back and let it cascade over her tongue. It was sweet and cold on her lips. She held the water in her mouth, hesitating as she thought through her next decision. If the water was poisoned, then she would know immediately. But, she couldn't give it to Markus without ruling this out. Myra swallowed. The water rolled down a throat aching for more. Myra waited a few seconds, but nothing happened.

"Drink," she said softly as she brought the canteen to his cracked lips.

"Yes, ma'me," Markus responded with a hint of sarcasm. He did his best to tilt his head as liquid lapped against his mouth. He took a couple of big gulps before another wave of pain forced him to lay back down again. Myra checked under the bandage again. The bleeding had faded to a trickle.

"It looks like the bleeding has stopped for now."

"Doubt I have much left," he said with a faint chuckle.

"But, I have to close up the wound, or you will tear it open again and continue bleeding out."

"Doesn't sound so bad."

"It isn't funny, Markus. You could die." Her voice was a mixture of weakness and authority. The very idea of losing him was unthinkable.

"Okay, My. Tell me what I need to do."

"*You* don't have to do anything. I have to seal the wound. It looks like I have the right materials, but I have to go and sterilize the needle."

"So, you're leaving me. I thought we were just getting cozy," Markus said with a snort. Myra rolled her eyes.

"I need you to hold pressure, okay?" She said sternly as she lifted her hand and put his in place. The movement brought a fresh wave of agony, but he didn't complain. "I'll be right back. I promise." Myra rose to her feet, uncertain if she wanted to leave him. Another Hunter could be out there. Markus would be completely vulnerable.

"Alright, My. I'll just be here. Might even take a nap."

Myra looked down at the sharp object in her hand and then out into the darkness beyond the light. Nothing moved. She glanced down at Markus, took a deep breath, and ran.

Myra didn't even know where to start looking. Her best guess was to find a flame of some sort. She sprinted away from Markus and towards the building with all of the food. Although it wasn't too far, she found the exhaustion and fatigue eat away at her as she ran. She hadn't slept in almost two days. Her body felt hollow and numb. Myra ignored these feelings and pushed herself towards the food depot. She grabbed the door handle and jerked it open.

Inside, the rest of the slaves were all gathered in various groups. They were talking together, even laughing, as they held open containers of food. Gaunt faces were beginning to fill in with color as the nourishment settled into their stomachs.

"Hey, have you seen Adam?" Myra asked. Numerous heads shook back and forth. Frustration bit into Myra.

"I think I saw him slip outside a couple of minutes ago," a black-haired woman—Maggie—provided. Myra nodded appreciatively and slipped back out the door. Her eyes scanned the space in front of her. Where could he be?

Myra heard voices. She froze and tilted her head as she attempted to listen.

"Figure...considered to be dangerous...use...caution... report...sightings."

The voice was close. It sounded female but was empty of emotion. Myra cautiously followed the sound of the voice as it repeated the same words. It emanated from the side of the building. As she got closer, she picked out more dialogue.

"—has been spotted in the Agriculture Protectorate, Sector 7. This Figure is considered dangerous and should not be approached except by Enforcers. Use caution around this Figure, and do not let him contaminate you by physical contact. Report any sightings to an Enforcer using callsign Onlooker."

"What is that?" Myra asked Adam, who had his back bowed to her. He stiffened at the sound of her voice and turned around with a sheepish look on his face.

"It's a Word—a broadcast from Citadel. See," he said as he showed her his wrist. Extended from his manipulor was a three-dimensional display of a red-colored head. It looked human, except the eyes were closed, and the scalp didn't have any hair. The female voice started to repeat the message.

"What does it mean?" Myra asked with an edge to her voice. Adam pressed the side of his manipulor, and the image disappeared into his wrist.

"A dangerous criminal has been spotted in Agriculture. The announcement was probably extended across all of Agriculture to warn everybody." Myra's eyes narrowed. It made sense, but he still seemed a little suspicious.

"It said he was seen in Sector 7. What Sector are we in?" Myra inquired.

"Sector 12. We're not even close to where they're looking," he said confidently. Myra let a sigh of relief escape.

"Great. Well, let's hope it stays that way. For now, I am going to use this as a needle," she began as she brought the sharp object up into the light, "but I need to sterilize it. Do you know where I can find an open flame?"

"I do. Follow me," Adam beckoned as he quickly walked away from Myra.

When Myra finally got back to Markus, he had his eyes closed and a hand behind his head. The color had left his face entirely, and his blood stained the ground around him.

"Markus?" Myra asked hesitantly.

"Bout time you came back. I was about to get old," Markus said weakly.

Myra bent low and felt his skin. It was cold and clammy.

"How do you feel? Honestly."

"Tired. I'm getting a little spacy," he said slowly.

"Let me see," she said softly. She moved his hand away from where he was applying pressure. He winced but didn't speak. Myra lifted the bandage. The wound was lifeless, and the ragged flesh was beginning to turn gray around the edges. She pressed her lips firmly together. She had to act quickly.

"How's it look, Doc?" Myra didn't respond. Her eyes roamed around the instruments and materials she had at her disposal. This wasn't going to be easy. "That bad, huh?"

"I'm going to stitch you up, but I have to warn you. It's going to hurt."

"I'm pretty tough," he said bravely. He wasn't lying. Still, Myra was hesitant. It was not in her nature to inflict pain willingly, but she knew the pain was the only thing that would get him better. She lowered herself to her knees beside him. He gave her a meager smile, which she appreciated.

Myra went to work, creating the stitching out of the fabric and string. It wasn't going to be very strong, so she had to close the wound as tight as possible to prevent the thread from giving away and tearing the wound open anew. Once she had everything prepared, she took a steadying breath.

"Ready?"

Markus nodded as Myra slid the sharpened tip into his skin. Markus grimaced but held back any comments. Myra worked hastily, moving the thread back and forth across his wound, drawing the edges closer and closer together. As she worked, she bit into her cheek, trying hard not to think of anything other than the task at hand.

"You're quite good at that. Where'd you learn how to stitch someone up?"

"Paul used to come back to the hovel with gashes and wounds where he'd saved someone's neck in the factories. I had to learn the hard way, but I mostly practiced on him."

"Well, I sure am glad you've had your practice," Markus retorted. At the sound of Paul's name coming from her lips, Myra grew melancholy. She missed her brother desperately. She missed the mountain, its dark tunnels where she could hide, the ancient cavern where they used to worship. She felt safe there—like being in an embrace.

The mountain was where she met with Theo. She missed the mountain. Her community, her people, were shattered. They were on the run, hiding, wounded. All of the choices she'd made so far only got them in greater danger, in greater pain, which was why she knew they all needed to get back to Paul as soon as possible.

"Almost done," Myra said softly. Beads of sweat were forming on her forehead. Her hair was matted to her neck and lay in tangled knots.

"Good. I was wondering what was taking so long," Markus chided.

"Haha," she said sarcastically. She dabbed at a trickle of blood that had appeared.

"So, where's good ol' Adam?"

"He's with the others."

Markus was silent for a moment. Myra started on her last few stitches. Her fingers ached, but she did not relent.

"I don't trust him, My. Be careful with him."

Myra's thoughts flew to the sight of him listening to the broadcast from Citadel. The look of guilt on his face was still fresh in her mind.

"Hold still. I'm almost done."

"Yes, boss lady." Markus fell silent as Myra completed her work. She analyzed her efforts. It wasn't her best, but it would hold until she got him to a real doctor.

"Alright. I'm going to make a sling for you and find you something to lay on. Your arm will be immobilized for a while, but you'll thank me later."

"I'll thank you now if you don't mind. Can I sit up?"

"Yes. Slowly. Take my hand." Myra extended her hand, and Markus took it, allowing her to do most of the work as she pulled him to a sitting position. She kept a close eye on the suture, looking for any ripping, but it managed to hold. His arm hung limp in his lap, and he hid behind a mask of pain.

Myra's hand was growing warm and sweaty. She looked down and realized she was still holding onto Markus's. Hastily, she let go and started creating a sling out of the fabric.

"It's crazy, isn't it?"

"What is?" She asked as she tore the fabric into strips.

"Who we become. A couple of days ago, we were just slaves. Now, look at us."

Myra didn't want to look. She didn't want to meet his gaze, but she did anyway. His eyes were swimming with pain and longing. She could see herself in them. Myra was close enough to breathe Markus in.

The distance between them was getting smaller as if gravity were pulling them towards one another. They were just inches apart. Markus stared into her with an unblinking, unrelenting desire. She hadn't been this close to someone since the moment Damien told her he loved her.

"I found more supplies," Adam spoke as he drew near. Myra flinched and immediately withdrew from Markus. Her eyes flew to Adam as he emerged from the darkness with an armful of random materials. He wore a bemused look when he saw how close the two of them were to each other.

"Thank you, Adam. I think what he needs now is to get to a real hospital," Myra interjected before he could ask awkward questions. He gave them both a long look.

"Well, there is a hospital in the Medical Protectorate. That would be your only option."

"Can you get us there?"

Adam paused and put both hands in his pockets. He bit into his cheek as he thought about her question.

"I wouldn't say it's impossible, but it would be a challenge," he reflected. A challenge? What exactly had they already endured, if not a challenge?

"We leave soon," she stated bluntly.

"Alright. I'll get everyone ready," Adam offered.

"Thank you, Adam. That's helpful."

"No problem. I'll meet you guys on the other side of the Unit." Myra nodded. With a nod, Adam departed and merged back into the darkness. She looked back at Markus, whose eyebrows were arched. The both of them knew how close they'd been to each other. Their intentions electrified the air.

"Let me put this on you," she whispered. Markus nodded. Gingerly, she slipped his arm in the sling. His skin felt warm again. Or maybe it was just her.

"Can we talk about—."

94

"—No. You need to rest. You've lost a lot of blood, and your body is tired. If we are going to leave soon, you need to be rested enough to do so."

"Glad you're looking out for me," Markus responded with veiled sarcasm. Myra ignored the comment and stood.

"I'm going to go and get something for you to lean on." An awkward silence pushed them apart. "I'll be right back." Without looking back, she merged with the darkness.

Chapter 15: From the Shadows

Paul, Slave Compound

Paul was determined. He was determined to convince Hob that his forces' position was a tactical disadvantage, and he was going to be overwhelmed almost immediately if he didn't reposition. This was just the first of many issues he could see were wrong, and he didn't understand why it was not apparent to Hob himself. Regardless, as Jennings led him towards Hob, Paul's mind worked over the conversation in his head. Hob was going to have to listen to him.

"What do you want?" Hob clapped once Jennings came to a halt in the doorway to a makeshift headquarters. The building itself leaned precariously and threatened to capsize.

"My apologies, sir, but I have someone here who wants to speak to you. He says it is urgent."

Paul could practically hear Hob's scowl.

"Did he now? Of course it's urgent. Send him in, and then get back to work!" Preva Jennings reappeared and gave Paul a look of dismay.

"He's not in a good mood. Good luck."

"Thank you, Preva," Paul said softly as he entered through the door. Hob's eyes lifted from a crude map and briefly landed on Paul. Hob's glower became a crater in his face.

"Why are you here?" Hob's voice was heavy with tension, weariness, and worry.

"You need to move your forces. They're going to be overwhelmed," Paul said bluntly. There was no point in beating around the bush with Hob.

"You think so, eh? And what, while you've been working away on undermining my authority by holding secret meetings in caves and infesting my slaves with rebellious ideas, you somehow became a brilliant military tactician?"

"You need to move your forces, Hob. It's going to be a slaughter." Hob scoffed.

"If it weren't for you, boy, I'd have plenty of fodder to throw at the enemy. But, you convinced your dear sister she needed to take over a quarter of slaves with her to her death."

At the mention of his sister, Paul could see the mountain ignite with fire. He fought against the loss as it bubbled to the surface.

"Hob," Paul said gently despite the anger and rage boiling in his chest, "many people—your people—are about to die if you do not act. I plead with you to listen to me and move your troops to these positions," Paul said as he pointed to the map. Hob didn't even give him the courtesy of looking down at where he was pointing.

"They aren't my people, boy. You act under the presumption that I care about their lives. Besides, why are you so concerned? A zealot like yourself should be begging and pleading the enemy for mercy, not preparing to fight. Revealing your true nature, eh?" Hob stated with a wicked smile. It was as if the man relished in the idea that Paul was no better than him.

"I care about the people, slave or free. If defending their lives means defending this Compound, then that is what I must do. It's not my desire to harm, but the light must often harm the darkness."

"Such pretty words and empty philosophy," Hob said with a snort. "It's hollow, vain ideas like light and dark that got us all in this mess to begin with." Hob was speaking almost to himself with a great degree of derision and scorn. Paul received his words patiently.

"So, you'll do nothing? Nothing to protect these people? In the least, you should arm the slaves and let them defend themselves," he said sharply.

Hob laughed like distant thunder.

"Arm the slaves? You're joking, right. Why would I give the people I oppress the very weapons of the oppressor? That is an insult, boy." Hob's face darkened as a shadow closed in around his eyes. "You continue to test my patience with nonsense and continue questioning my authority, and I promise you that the beating you received will pale in comparison to the pain I will pour on you. Understood?"

Paul felt an angry retort build up in his throat. His jaw clenched as he held it at bay.

"Now, run along, boy. Go to the front lines and prepare for war. Die for your fellow man if you so desire, but do not underestimate my resolve nor my aggression again."

Paul remained, motionless in place, his mind passive and calm. Hob did not scare him. His threats seemed idle and empty. Paul also knew Hob was capricious and stubborn, which meant there was little hope in convincing the man to see reason. After a few long seconds, Paul turned and retreated through the gaping doorway.

Preva Jennings was standing not far from the dilapidated building. Paul was surprised he had waited on him. If Hob wouldn't listen to him, then Paul would have to undermine Hob's authority and do things his way. If Hob found out, he'd condemn Paul for treason, or betrayal, or whatever arbitrary crime Hob wanted to pin on him. But Paul knew he had to act. He had to save lives. This thought was clear as he approached Jennings.

"Did you get the response you needed?" Preva Jennings asked casually.

Paul nodded.

"Yes, and we have work to do."

Byron, Citadel, The Refuge

There were dark circles under Byron's eyes. He stared at the blank Coms in front of him as he worked through his plan, choosing his words carefully, seeing to the very end all possible routes—foreseen and unforeseen. Finally satisfied, he keyed a command into the Coms—*Ariel*—his wife's name.

Minutes passed in silence and weighty solitude as he waited. He wasn't alone. The room was warmed with Abby's presence, and yet he felt loneliness none the less. Eventually, the faces of those whom he trusted and relied upon filled the screens. Their faces were a mixture of confusion and concern, which reflected luminously off of Byron's eyes.

"Hello, everyone. I'm sorry to call upon you so abruptly, but an opportunity has presented itself that we must act upon," Byron said mysteriously.

"It better be a significant opportunity. I was in the middle of an Administrative meeting when my manipulor started flashing," Horrus conveyed with fear-laden disdain.

"Yes, unscheduled interruptions like this put us in jeopardy, Byron. We must tread carefully," Theres warned. Horrus grunted in approval.

"We knew the danger when we agreed to follow his leadership," Soren provided curtly. Horrus rolled his eyes. "So, what is this great opportunity, Byron?"

"1C118 has been found and is being removed from the equation. He will be a nonfactor soon, so we can commence with our two-fold plan. Soren, you need to continue spreading false information stating Sebastian has been located in Agriculture. The last message worked, but we need to draw more forces away. We want as much of Armament and Rais's forces relocated from Technology as possible."

"Is it true a large faction of Rais's forces are on their way to Infrastructure?" Horrus inquired.

"Yes. He seems to be allocating a substantial amount of his resources to the slave compound," Byron provided.

"Why?" Abby spoke up from the shadows. Byron jerked his head around at the sound of his daughter's voice. She wore a look of genuine concern. In all the times they'd related to the slave compound, it was always Abby who corresponded.

"Does it *matter*?" Horrus asked. "This is unheard of, Byron. How can our meetings stay secret if so many people are privy to the information we share?" Horrus barked. Byron turned back around and fixed Horrus with a glare.

"My daughter is not just anyone, Reginald. I trust her with my life, and I assure you she is invested in this just as much as all of you. Regardless, her question is valid. Why is Rais sending units to the slave compound?"

"I did some more digging and have heard they are seeking to acquire a piece of machinery which will help solidify Lorenzo's control. Some kind of mobile weapon system," Theres offered. "But, knowing the Lord Protector, I assume it's more than just resource seizure."

Byron cursed under his breath. If this was true, then they had to act faster than he'd anticipated. If Lorenzo obtained this weapon system, the Hajj would be over before it began.

"All the more reason why we need to commence with our original plan of action," Byron began with severity. "While Rais's units are stretched thin, we need to attack his Protectorate. We need to cut off his communication capabilities. If we sever his security system, we can tighten the noose around Lorenzo's neck. I know I told you last time we had more time, but time is of the essence now. How soon can we get forces prepared for an assault, Theres?"

"Within two cycles," she offered.

"Good. That's all the time we need."

"Lethal force?" Horrus inquired. The question hung over all of them. The darkness under Byron's eyes deepened.

"Yes. As necessary. Soren, move forward with the misdirection. Horrus, I need you to keep an eye on Lorenzo. Assure him he doesn't need to shut down Citadel and that he is in no present danger." Horrus grunted out his response.

A heavy silence settled between them all. They knew that there was no returning from this point. If they were caught, they'd be murdered for treason.

"Thank you. All of you. Good luck," Byron said fully. Each of them nodded in return before the Coms became a muted darkness.

Chapter 16: Bastille

Damien, Armament, Bastille Sector

"You're going to want to go south," Abby directed gently. It was good to have her in his head, again, and her earnestness made him smile.

"Armament is a maze of barracks, training grounds, and warehouses. Still, most of the attention is towards the Protectorate center, where I planted false information about a potential threat. It should draw most of the Enforcers away, but be careful," she cautioned.

"I won't do anything foolish or dangerous or illegal," he chided, knowing full well he was accomplishing all three. But, he also knew he was doing the right thing. He knew, somehow, that if he rescued Sebastian, he'd find the old man—Father O'Reilly. Damien didn't know how or why Sebastian was connected to the old man, but he accepted that there were some things he didn't have to understand.

Damien worked himself deeper into Armament, which was a Protectorate not like all the others he'd encountered. There was an obscure danger he couldn't place—like being surrounded by fog as he walked alongside the edge of a cliff.

"So, what exactly am I looking for?" He asked to distract himself from the foreboding feeling.

"It's a vast prison structure. Expect high walls, barbed wire, and guards. Bastille Prison is used for those who are meant to be Extracted. You know, disease carriers, crazed lunatics, rebellious infidels, the usual crowd," she said humorously.

"Sounds like my kind of people," Damien chided. "How am I getting in?"

"Working on that," Abby responded. "That red stuff is spreading further and further outward away from Citadel, and it's getting harder to make changes to the NOOM system. Pretty soon, I'll be completely locked out of the system." Her voice carried urgent desperation.

"Then I guess I should hurry. And this Sebastian character. What should I expect from him?"

"Medium build, brown hair, greenish-gray eyes. He worked in Hydra, so he'll have some definition to him. A strong jawline and broad hands..."

"How long have you stared at him?" Damien prodded.

"Not long," Abby said with a hint of embarrassment. "I just wanted you to have all the details. You know, to make it easier to find him."

"Uh-huh. How about a cell number? Would that be too hard?" He said sarcastically.

"Oh. Yeah. Good idea. Let me check." Damien shook his head in amusement as the sound of typing filled his ears.

"Got it. He'll be in C-Block, Cell 316."

Damien grunted out his gratitude.

"Uh-oh. It looks like they've already moved him to the Interrogation Section."

"Has Rais arrived?"

There was a moment of silence which aggravated Damien. He had so many mixed emotions towards Rais—hatred rebuffed with mercy. The incongruity made his head spin.

"He just arrived in Armament and will be at the prison in half a cycle."

Damien's heart skipped.

"Alright. I'll pick up the pace. Keep working on getting me inside, and I'll let you know when I am outside the prison. "

"Okay. And Damien?"

"Yeah?"

"I'm sorry I gave you the sedative and agreed to have you sent away."

The pain in her voice moved him.

"It's okay, Abby. You did the right thing. I'll contact you soon." The line went silent, and Damien stared into the gloom.

He had half a cycle before Rais got to Sebastian. Half a cycle before the man tortured Sebastian to the point of death.

That was all the time he needed.

Bastille Prison emerged out of the shadows like a sleeping giant. The pale concrete walls and glinting razor topped surfaces stood as still as a mountain threatening to come crashing down. Its gates were open, like a gaping mouth.

The top of the prison reached upwards into the swirling darkness, and Damien wondered if it touched the very domed ceiling itself. Faint lights glowed like eyes that peered in the eternal night. A searchlight swept over the barren land in front of him. His eyes scanned the prison, searching for weaknesses, penetrable possible points of entry, seeing blind spots.

Two guards at the front entrance.

Three guards on the perimeter.

Two searchlights followed a predictable arc, overlapping in the middle but creating pockets of shadows and solitude he could hide within.

The situation reminded him of the time he infiltrated the Outrider's operations base to steal the keys to the Red Creek mineshaft. The scenario was eerily similar.

Damien heard a whining noise as a grouping of sleek, black monstrosities traveled across the landscape in front of him. They hovered almost twenty feet off the ground and communicated with each other in chirps and beeps.

Those were definitely not like the Outrider's base.

A chill ran down his back. If he didn't know any better, he'd assume these machines were alive. Their mechanical design was alien enough to make him uncomfortable. Wherever the guards were not marching, and the light did not expose, the machines hovered. The prison was guarded beyond measure. Getting in would be impossible.

Almost impossible.

Damien's eyes scanned the prison walls as a plan formed in his mind. All he needed was for Abby to carry out her end, and then he'd be inside. His hand flew to his ear as he switched on his communicator.

"Abby? I'm in position. Ready when you are," he said in a low voice. He waited a few seconds for a response, but none came. He pressed firmly on his ear. "Abby? Can you hear me? I said I am ready to go!"

His voice came out in a sharp whisper. He was just loud enough to catch the attention of one of the machines. It fitfully jerked away from the others and headed in his direction.

Reflexively, Damien ducked behind the rocky outcropping he'd been using for reconnaissance. The whining hum from the machine grew louder as it approached. Damien tensed every muscle and willed himself to become smaller. He knew if he were to make a run for it, he'd be seen immediately.

There was nowhere for him to go.

The machine was above him. Heat bombarded the top of his head as dry gusts of wind battered him. The cacophony of his dread and the machine combined into a flurry of noise and trepidation. The monster tilted forward, then scanned to the left and right.

Seemingly satisfied, it slowly withdrew and rejoined the rest of the flock. Damien allowed his muscles to uncoil, but he did not dare move. Predators could wait forever for prey to make the first move.

"Damien... can't...losing control...Copy?"

Abby's voice was faint and garbled, and the static overrode her words. Damien's hand went to his ear as he responded in a still whisper.

"I can't hear you, Abby. Say again."

The static increased. Damien's brow furrowed as frantic thoughts darted through his mind. Was Abby in danger? Why couldn't she reach him? His eyes scanned the darkness in front of him, searching for an answer that wasn't readily available.

But then he saw it.

The ground was moving, squirming like it was infested with fiery worms. The red color was advancing towards him, reaching out like agony. It was only ten feet away, a wounded snake sliding closer and closer to the trapped mouse.

Damien's eyes darted over the rock. The machines were gone, but the guards weren't clear. He would be directly in their line of sight. He glanced back at the advancing red mass as apprehension caught in his throat.

The red mass was only a couple feet away. Damien reacted reflexively and jumped up on the rock to escape. His hands gripped the rough surface, and light gleamed at his touch.

The white light sprang from his fingertips, shooting outwards towards Bastille. A faint shimmer appeared on the outer wall of the prison. Damien lifted his hand off the rock, and the shimmering stopped.

Immediately, he understood. But, there was no time. The red lines were crawling up the rock surface, reaching for his leg. The searchlights exposed the landscape. The guards weren't far enough apart to justify his plan.

Damien felt a stinging sensation in his calf. He looked down, and a tendril of the rust-color was digging into his leg.

Damien leaped off the rock and came crashing down onto the barren ground. There was no cover, no hesitation permitted. His heels dug into the soil as he sprinted towards where the two searchlights overlapped.

Just as he neared the edge of exposure, the beams pulled apart, and he continued onward in cool, shadowy darkness. The guards were walking with their backs turned away from each other, but Damien knew that the one on the right was going to turn around in ten steps.

Damien was still too far from the wall. There was no way he'd make it in time. His breath came in thin gasps as he pulled at his body for more speed. Static erupted in his ear as Abby attempted another round of communication, but her voice was still distorted and distant.

The guard reached the end of his route.

His shoulders started to turn.

Damien was still too far away. He prepared himself for the fight. He could take on three guards, but he'd lose the element of surprise.

A brilliant sapphire glow illuminated the prison as a structure took form to his right. The guard stopped turning and watched as a monolith appeared. It dazzled in the gloom and spread a warm blue haze across Bastille's surface.

It was Abby's distraction.

It was all Damien needed.

The walls of Bastille loomed above him, and despite his instincts, Damien jumped upwards as if onto a platform. To his hope and amazement, his feet fell onto a stable, unseen surface. Where his feet made contact, puddles of light rippled. He didn't hesitate as he continued upward. Each step was gut-wrenching and made his stomach clench into a knot, but each step was rewarded with light.

He was soon level with the wall, and the next step carried him over, though his unease did not dissipate until he was on the ground on the other side. Fighting the shock and awe bubbling in his chest, Damien melted into the shadows.

He was in Bastille. Now, where was Sebastian?

Abby had stated he was in C-Block, in Interrogation. He didn't have any idea where he was, nor did he have access to schematics or Bastille's layout.

Things were getting easier by the second.

Chapter 17: The First Wave

Paul, Slave Compound

Paul worked feverishly as he raised the large stone and stacked it onto the pile of rubble. The makeshift barrier shifted under the weight, but still held firm. All around him, slaves and guards worked in unison, carrying debris far enough to hand it off to the next person as uneasiness hung in the air.

No one spoke. Except for grunts of effort and the sound of construction, no sound permeated the general anxiety gathered amongst them.

Hob hadn't been seen in hours. But Paul was not bothered. If Hob didn't want to protect anyone, then he didn't deserve to be amongst them. Despite his courage, though, Paul felt anxious about what lay ahead. He knew Hob wasn't about to relinquish his tanks, which meant whoever was coming would wrest it out of Hob's hands through violence.

A low, jarring noise interrupted their silence. Everyone's head turned to the tunnel between the mountains. The noise hissed through their work and brought a fog of worry. Everyone watched as a sleek, black train emerged from out of the gloom. The machine, elegant and deadly in design, was a whisper across the land as it approached. The train hovered above the ground like smoke.

"Alright, everyone," Paul began, "you know what to do." There was a flurry of responsive movement as everyone went to their designated locations. Some moved into dilapidated buildings and behind barriers.

The train slowed as it approached. Its windows remained darkened and empty. At long last, it came to a halt with a rush of wind which stirred Paul's tattered clothes. The train loomed over him even from nearly twenty feet away.

Paul held his breath and waited for what was next. His hand wrapped around a pipe, which he had braced against his leg. Paul didn't know if he was prepared to use the weapon. Paul knew he couldn't take a man's life, but he needed to defend those he cared about.

His hand was sweaty against the metal.

A door opened on the side of the train. Steps descended to the ground automatically. Paul tightened his grip on the pipe and watched for any sign of misdirection, but none came. Instead, a lone man descended the stairs. Once the man got to the bottom step, he finally turned his head.

The man gave Paul a mildly shocked look as if he wasn't expecting anyone, let alone a group of individuals with dirt coated skin and rags clinging to hunger honed bodies. The man shuffled over to Paul with a broad grin etched onto his face. As he approached, his feet kicked up dust and brought him to a coughing fit.

"Hello! My name is Eberry." The man coughed into his elbow. "I was sent to speak to the person in charge."

No one stepped forward. They were a silent, hesitant wave, afraid to crash upon the shore. Paul felt the draw of his feet. He set the pipe against the wall and left his position.

"I'm in charge," Paul stated.

"Ah, good! Good! Like I said, my name is Eberry. I am the Lord Protector's Ambassador," the man said in a fast-paced tone. The top of his head fell just under Paul's nose, and he looked upward from a face shining with perspiration. Wrapped around his wrist was a gauntlet, which glowed.

"I'm Paul. I have no title," he said bluntly. The Ambassador raised an eyebrow.

"No title, eh? But, you're in charge."

"Someone has to be. What exactly do you need from us, Ambassador?" Paul asked pointedly.

"To the point, I see. I like it. Well, we have arrived under peaceful terms with the intent of obtaining the armored assault units created in this sector—one of the finest sectors, I assume. Word has traveled throughout Axiom and has graced the attention of the Lord Protector."

The man paused as if expecting Paul to comment. Sensing Paul's disregard, he continued.

"The Lord Protector has heard your hard work and efforts in this part of our great society and wanted to see for himself the fruits of your labors. So, if you will lead me to these creations, he will be more than pleased."

"They are not mine to hand over, Ambassador. I am merely a slave. In this *fine* section, we are all slaves," Paul stated firmly as he spread his arms around. "With that being said, I am confident you have come all this way for nothing, Ambassador."

The Ambassador forced a chuckle.

"Surely, you misunderstand! What did you say your name was?"

"It's Paul," Eberry's eyes narrowed.

"Do you happen to have a sister, Paul?"

Paul's heart rushed to his cheeks.

"You know about Myra? Do you know where she is? Is she alive?" Paul's questions were passionate, despite his best efforts to wrestle them down. A mischievous light shone in Eberry's eyes.

"How about we talk inside?" The Ambassador suggested as he inclined his head toward the train. Paul felt apprehension crawl up his arms.

"What can be said in there can be said out here," he said coolly. Paul didn't trust the man.

"Alright. Suit yourself. We have your sister in custody. She requires great medical attention and will not live much longer if she does not get help," Eberry said bluntly. His words rang in Paul's ears. Myra was alive? But, he saw the mountain on fire—the same mountain he'd told Myra to use as an escape.

"Can I see her?" Paul asked in a hoarse whisper.

"Not right now. Give in to our demands, and we will consider giving her medical attention and some time with her brother." Paul felt tears brimming in his eyes. His heart fluttered in his chest.

"What do I do?" Paul asked. Eberry smiled.

"Our demands are simple. Hand over the mobile weapons platforms, let us take you into custody, and we will unite you with your sister and leave. Plain and simple," he said matter-of-factly.

"And you'll leave all of us alone. Just take what you want and go?" Paul asked.

"Of course. Trust me, Paul. I am not here to cause any harm. What belongs to Hob belongs to the rest of Axiom. The Lord Protector is just here to collect what is already his."

Including me.

But, what would he give to see his sister?

What do I do, Theo? Please, help me.

Silence was Theo's response. Paul felt alone and rejected. Why wasn't he being heard—especially when the stakes were so high, and the cost of a single mistake would mean devastation? He needed something—a sign that pointed him in the right direction.

"Well, what do you think?" Eberry prodded.

"I need to see her. To confirm what you are saying is true," Paul said softly.

"Not going to happen. Not until we have what we came for." Paul felt exasperation crawl in his chest. He longed for Myra but didn't know if Eberry was telling the truth. He could be essentially longing for someone dead.

But, Paul's heart yearned for his little sister, and he wanted her to be alive. He wanted to hold her close and let her know everything was going to be okay. He wanted to see her radiant smile and her golden locks that never lost the light.

An idea settled into Paul's mouth.

"What color is her hair?" Paul asked. Eberry paused, his plastered smile faltering.

"What do you mean?"

"If you have her, then you'll know her hair color."

"This isn't some game. Hand it over, now, or you will never see your sister again."

"My sister is not with you, Eberry." Paul felt power coursing through his words. "Is she?" Eberry's face contorted from indignation to a twisted, cruel grin.

"I knew you were smart," he said.

"And I know you're a liar. You haven't come to make peace, have you?" Eberry didn't answer. "You came for a fight,"

Paul declared. Paul didn't turn, but he could hear the others catching on as the movement carried on behind him. Eberry's eyes darted to the people over Paul's shoulder. "You weren't going to spare us, were you?" Paul asked, knowing the answer. Eberry's gaze finally returned to his face as his lip curled.

"I only pitied wasting the firepower," he cackled.

"I don't want to fight you, Ambassador. But, these people are not the same as me, and they would not hesitate. Please, leave. Before this gets any worse," Paul said with a heavy dose of compassion. He honestly didn't want bloodshed. Eberry was just a man following orders—a human being caught up in loyalty. Maybe, though, he would listen to reason.

"Fine. Have it your way," Eberry said nastily as he stared into Paul with a hatred so deep Paul was afraid he might get lost within it. The Ambassador broke his gaze, however, as he strode defiantly in the opposite direction. Paul watched his steps, confident he was going to turn around at any moment.

The little man eventually made it to the steps and climbed them with crimson etched into his cheeks. The Ambassador disappeared inside without another glance.

As soon as the steps retracted into the train and the door snapped shut, the people around Paul started to cheer. Paul didn't join in. It couldn't be this easy. Yet, the train began backing out of the Depot, emitting its low hum as it slipped away from the broken Compound.

Paul held his breath, waiting, anticipating, anxiety bubbling in his chest. The train crept back into the darkness between the mountains until it was completely swallowed up. Everyone continued to jeer and throw insults. After a few seconds, Paul finally let go of the tension winding in his back. He let a small grin appear on his lips.

But then he heard it. It was like an itch in his ear. Like an insect pestering at his thoughts. Like angry hornets. His eyes went to the darkness. The cheering died down as others began to hear the same noise breaking through the jubilation. The sound grew louder and louder as an unexplainable dread settled into Paul's heart. He turned to his people with fear in his eyes.

"Run!"

From the darkness, dozens of flying shapes emerged. They descended upon the slave compound like a swarm of hungry locusts. As soon as they were in range, the machines spewed red.

"Hide!" Paul shouted. Panic struck him in the chest. He pushed others forward as they ducked into a collapsed building. He felt the rush of heat as the projectiles dug into the walls around him.

Once inside, Paul turned around and looked outward. He watched in horror as the machines slaughtered mercilessly. Screams tore the air as the gunfire cut people down in the middle of their escape. The drones invaded the Depot, hunting for individuals who had managed to dive behind cover before the assault began.

The machines ripped them out of their hiding spots, suspended them just high enough in the air to offer a target for another drone, and then filled the victims with red streaks of violence. Angry, violent desperation burned inside of Paul. His people were dying, and there was nothing he could do.

Paul heard the whine just as he ducked into the shadows. Across the room, the two people he'd pushed inside the building—a man and a woman—were cowering together behind a tattered couch. Paul put his finger to his lips and signaled them to remain quiet.

The machine entered. Paul clung to the dark corner he inhabited. The machine made the air warm with fear and exhaust as the stench clung to his nostrils. It filled the doorway like sleek, black death.

Dust showered from the dilapidated second floor. The machine tilted its sensor-laden dome upward as it proceeded forward. Above their heads, the second floor creaked and groaned. Paul's eyes darted to the stairs just as the machine tilted in the same direction. If they were lucky, it would wander upstairs and allow them to escape.

Paul watched with bated breath as the machine hung motionless in the air. If it turned even the slightest, it would see him. His hand tightened around the metal pipe as he prepared for an inevitable assault.

The machine drifted towards the stairs. Dust cascaded through the air as it ascended the derelict steps. Soon, it was out of sight as dust fell from above. Paul waited until the machine moved away from the landing and into one of the rooms. He looked down at the terror-stricken individuals huddled on the other side of the room.

"Come on!" Paul commanded in a sharp whisper as he frantically waved his hand. The man hesitated and glanced upstairs, his eyes welled with dark lines. "Hurry!" Paul urged.

The man swallowed heavily and started towards Paul. His hand was wrapped around the woman's as she followed. Paul kept his eyes on the stairway, hoping the machine didn't descend while the couple was out in the open.

A sudden ripping noise abbreviated the silence. Paul's heart rocketed in his chest as his eyes flew to the woman. Her dress, merely rags sewn together, had gotten caught on the arm of the couch. It didn't take much to pull it apart as the rip ascended throughout the house. Paul held up a hand, and the two of them immediately stopped. The guilt and anguish on the woman's face brought sorrow to Paul's heart as his eyes went to the stairs expecting to see death descending upon them.

The stairs were vacant.

Paul waited with bated breath, but the drone didn't come down. He paused another half-second before waving the couple towards him. The woman readjusted her dress, now with a gash rising to her waist, and followed the man.

A creak penetrated the silence. Paul cocked his head but kept waving the two people towards him. Just as he reached out his hand for the man, the air was torn into pieces as the drone burst through the second story floor. The woman shouted as she was plucked off the ground. Debris showered down upon Paul, and for a moment, dust blinded him.

As soon as he could gather his bearings, Paul slashed outwards with his pipe. He felt the jarring sensation of metal on metal, and though his vision was still blurry, he didn't relent. He brought the weapon and brought it crashing down.

The machine whirred and whined as the woman dropped from its grasp. Paul saw the gun on the undercarriage swing towards him and reacted without thinking as he dove.

Gunfire erupted.

The air smelled of crackling energy and burning wood. Red streaks spat in all directions, and Paul watched helplessly as the woman crumpled to the floor with curtains of blood descending down her abdomen. The man sprinted towards the stairs, and the machine turned its attention to its next victim. Paul watched the blood seep out of the woman's open lips as the light faded from her eyes.

A helpless rage ignited in his chest. Paul bellowed as he rose to his feet, climbed onto the couch, and leaped onto the attacker. The machine dipped, and the spray of gunfire missed the man running for the stairs. The machine bucked and surged in an attempt to throw Paul off, but he didn't let go.

Paul felt his legs impact walls and furniture as pain radiated throughout his body. Paul gritted his teeth and fought to stay on. His grip was slipping, though, and he knew once he was kicked off, the drone would simply turn on him and kill him before he could rise to his feet.

The machine swerved, and man and machine collided with the wall. The drone punched through the wall with him in tow. He felt pain and blood spread throughout his abdomen as pieces of wood dug into his flesh.

Paul felt his fingers slip as he started to plummet. In desperation, he grabbed onto the last section of the machine before it spun out of reach. The metal from the drone's weapon was still hot from use as a burning sensation pulsed in his hand.

Paul looked down. The ground spun below him, and he knew out in the open he was an easy target. If Paul didn't jump now, his demise would be sooner rather than later. Before he could make this decision, however, he was suddenly weightless. The ground rushed up to meet him and then spread through his legs and knees as he slammed into the dirt. His teeth clacked together, and his shoulder crunched grossly, but he managed to roll into a sitting position.

The world was foggy. Paul could hear shouting and screams. He tried to shake the ringing out of his ears, but his movements seemed slow and exaggerated. His vision settled, and eventually, he was able to make sense of the devastation unfolding around him.

Paul rose unsteadily to his feet. Why was he not dead? He searched for the drone that had carried him out of the house. Just a few feet away were the disintegrated remains. A large piece of wood penetrated the front of the drone and exited the back. The weapon Paul had held onto as a last resort hung by a single sinewy piece of metal.

"Is it safe!?" The man shouted from inside the house. Paul's eyes darted across the desolate landscape. Bodies were strewn across the broken Depot. Smoke and dust swirled in the air, but no machines inhabited the bloody gloom.

"You're clear!" Paul shouted hoarsely. His body throbbed with pain. Distant screams carried across the still air. The battle—if it could be called that—had pushed deeper into the Compound. A heavy, throttling feeling weighed upon Paul.

"Linda... she's dead," the man reflected gravely. Paul looked behind him and followed the man's gaze. Linda lay face down just inside the doorway wrapped in a puddle of deepening crimson. Paul felt the sorrow of her loss wash over him.

"Yes, and she won't be the last," Paul stated firmly.

"What are we supposed to do?"

Paul's mind worked through the Compound and immediately knew where to go and what to do.

"What's your name?" Paul inquired.

"Gregory," the man responded.

"Alright, Gregory. What we have to do is not going to be easy. But it has to be done." Gregory looked up.

"Just tell me what to do."

Paul nodded slowly as a plan forced itself violently into his mind.

Chapter 18: Strangers

Sebastian, Armament, Bastille Sector

Sebastian stared numbly at the table in front of him, which gleamed dully. The room was a dreadful silence. He'd been alone for a long time, and though he was hungry, his unease overrode this desire and replaced it with a mottled fear which rolled up and down his spine.

He knew he was going to die. The knowledge haunted him, but in a manner which satisfied.

Sebastian had failed. It was better this way. It was better if he were not around to be the reason why so much death and violence were occurring. A part of him wished his father had succeeded in murdering him. He still felt the jagged memory of the metal penetrating his stomach.

Sebastian knew what was ahead of him. Torture. Suffering. Questions for which he had no answers. He deserved it, though. This was the fate he had created, and it was inescapable. So, he'd wait. Wait for the inevitable end which submerged him as he sat under the dull light, staring at the instruments of agony displayed in front of him.

He heard a noise. Footsteps were approaching. A shudder rolled through his body. He was trying to be brave, but it wasn't enough. No emotion could defend or protect him now. His head sunk down. His shoulders broke. His eyes wanted tears, but even the fear drank those dry.

The footsteps stopped right outside his door. Sebastian drew in a deep, steadying breath.

The door slid open with a chirp. Sebastian's heart was too weak to carry up his gaze, and deep, paralyzing despair weighed his bones down. Consequence had ensnared him.

"Sebastian?"

It was a young man's voice. The words lacked menace or aggression and were steeped in a curious eagerness. Sebastian looked up and his breath departed his body. Immediate fear and revulsion collected in the back of his throat. What he was seeing was impossible.

"Sam?!"

Sebastian's thoughts were filled with flames as the inferno wrapped around Sam's body and smothered him in death. And yet, Sam was standing right in front of him. How? Tears of joy welled up in his eyes, but then they turned into bricks and sank back down.

It was a trick!

"Get away from me!" Sebastian shouted as he struggled against his cuffs. "You're not really him. Guards!"

"Shut up!" A rough voice spoke heatedly. It was definitely not Sam's sagacity woven into his words. "I don't think you know who I am, Sebastian," the fake Sam said as he raised his palms.

"I do! You're an imposter! A liar and a thief! How dare you wear his face!"

"Ooh," the imposter said. Sebastian watched as his hand went to his neck. The imposter put two fingers behind his ear, and suddenly Sam's face dissolved and disappeared.

Sebastian's brow furrowed into rivulets as he stared into the face of someone who was his own age.

His eyes radiated with energy and controlled power. Yet, there was an infinite amount of weariness upon his body. His shoulders were broad and arched. Scars ran up and down his arms. Sebastian had never seen scars before. They seemed almost perverse on the young man's skin.

"Are you Sebastian?" He inquired in a hurried tone. Sebastian nodded as he worked through his confusion. Why would they send someone so young to get rid of him? "Good. I've been sent to rescue you. You need to follow me."

Confusion broke out on Sebastian's forehead. Was this still a trick? A snare to implicate him in an escape? The young man glanced out the door and down the hallway.

"Listen, I've already surrendered. There's no need for this," Sebastian provided.

The young man brought his head back in and approached Sebastian with a stern gaze.

117

"No. You need to listen to me, Sebastian. We're running out of time. We need to leave now!" The earnestness in the young man's voice made Sebastian feel uncomfortable. He straightened in his chair and glared.

"I have accepted my fate. I am done running!"

The young man looked both worried and frustrated. His eyes darted to the gaping door and then back at Sebastian. His lips formed a firm line, and he pressed his palms into the table. He leaned towards Sebastian and spoke in a terse, calm voice.

"You really don't matter to me, and if it weren't for the fact they sent me to get you, I'd leave you here to wallow in your own self-pity. But, they want you, and you were part of the package, so I have to deliver you to them."

More heaps of confusion collected in Sebastian's mind.

"Who sent you? Who are you?"

The young man's jaw worked furiously.

"I can answer those questions later. Right now, we need to leave. We still have to find the old man."

"You know the old man?" Sebastian inquired.

"You mean Father O'Reilly? Do you know him too?" He asked as he loomed over Sebastian. Sebastian tried to read his face and could only see curiosity and disbelief. Clearly, this person was not here to do him harm.

"I guess. I don't know his name. I just know he's old. And a man." He gave Sebastian an annoyed look. "There's not many of them around here, so he's probably the person you're looking for. But, you're not going to find him here," Sebastian said plainly.

"Why not?"

"He's being sent to Retirement. He left a half-cycle ago," Sebastian offered. The young man hung his head for a second but then quickly brought it back up.

"I assume you know how to get there?"

Sebastian bit his lip. Could he trust this person? Did he want to trust him?

"I do. It's on the other side of Axiom. About four cycles away. I can draw a map for you or show you on a manipulor."

118

"That's not going to work. You're coming with me, Sebastian. You're not going to argue with me about it, either. You have no choice."

When did he ever have a choice? He looked at the young man and saw determined hardness.

"Fine. But, if we get caught, you'll be considered one of the Diseased. You'll be tortured and executed," Sebastian conveyed in vain. A sly grin spread on the young man's face.

"I've seen worse."

Sebastian believed him.

"Got a key?" Sebastian asked as he indicated to his locked hands, still clasped firmly behind him. Sebastian watched him bite his cheek before he moved behind Sebastian with a determined expression. Sebastian was surprised a few seconds later when the cuffs fell off and hit the floor with a clack. Sebastian brought his arms around and rubbed his wrists from where his skin was raw.

"How'd you do that?"

"You ask too many questions. We need to go!"

The young man made his way to the door and peered out. Sebastian felt heat rising in his neck. He didn't like his brashness. His words were curt and rude. His stance was hostile and aggressive. His eyes were sharp and prodding.

"Fine. But I need to know your name. And I need to know why I should help you."

The young man turned back in and, despite his annoyance, answered the question.

"My name is Damien. I don't need your help. You need mine. So, let's go."

Damien ducked out of the room and left Sebastian in aggravated silence. Despite his frustration, Sebastian followed.

Damien poked his head around the corner as his eyes darted down the vacant hallway. Good. No one heard them, despite Sebastian's stupid shouting.

But, Damien knew they were quickly running out of time. If what Abby said was true, the further Damien wandered from her hideout, the weaker her nanoparticles strength, which

119

meant whatever security system was in place would eventually recognize him. And the walls were starting to take on a gory hue as the red invaded Bastille.

Damien heard loud shuffling as Sebastian exited his cell. Damien almost regretted having to drag him along, but Sebastian knew more about Axiom than Damien. Without Abby's assistance in his ear, he needed a guide. Judging from what Damien saw, though, he felt like it would be the lame leading the blind.

"What are we waiting on?" Sebastian whispered loudly.

"Do you possess any survival skills?" Damien asked over his shoulder. There was a brief silence.

"No?"

"Then be quiet and let me figure this out," Damien snapped. A retreated silence formed. The problem was Damien had known how to get to Sebastian, but without Abby, he didn't know how to get out. The only choice he had was to stay out of sight and retrace his steps. Damien's hand flew to his ear as his mask—a face which belonged to someone Sebastian knew—materialized.

"Follow me," Damien beckoned as he moved forward. He hugged the wall and touched the smooth stone with his open hand so he could create a doorway at a moment's notice. They approached the point where the white stone merged with the tide of red moving towards them as they walked. Damien hesitated over the conquering color.

"Be careful," Sebastian said softly. Damien could hear the fear in his voice and felt the awkward concern. His open hand reached out to the red stone. It felt moist to the touch and oddly spongy—as if the color had changed the structure of the stone. Damien withdrew his hand and saw a deep maroon fluid.

Sharp, piercing alarms slaughtered the silence as a cacophony reverberated throughout the prison. Damien winced, and Sebastian's hands flew to his ears. A drop of fear accumulated in Damien's chest as footsteps echoed.

"In here!" Damien shouted as he placed his palm on the wall. The light flew out from his fingertips and weaved into the tendrils of red. The two clashed and struggled against each other, but the light prevailed as a doorway took shape. Damien ducked inside and went to close the door, but Sebastian wasn't right behind him. A flare of panic and anger sparked inside of him as he looked at Sebastian's cowering form in the middle of the hallway. He still had his hands clamped firmly over his ears.

"I don't have time for this!" Damien shouted vainly. The footsteps were getting louder. Damien gripped Sebastian's shirt and jerked him into the room. Without looking to see where he landed, Damien turned his attention to the gaping wound in the wall. He could hear the jingling of the guards' armor as they approached. There was no time to close the wall completely!

Damien concentrated. He imagined.

The alarm faded.

The Enforcers stopped directly in front of him with weapons drawn. Damien held his breath and stood unmoving. One of the guards turned and looked straight at him.

He couldn't see Damien. The trick had worked.

Damien hadn't had time to create a complete wall, so he made one which hid him, but not the guards. The guard turned his head and took a step further down the hall. Damien let out a rush of air as he relaxed his tensed muscles.

"They can see us!" Sebastian shouted in a whisper. Damien started to grow hot.

"Did you hear something?" Spoke a muffled voice. The guard turned back around to face him. He leaned forward.

"What are we supposed to do!" Sebastian asked as he grabbed the back of Damien's shoulder. Heat crawled up Damien's neck. The guard brought up his hand and tried to reverse the portal Damien was maintaining.

"We have to surrender!"

Damien brought his hand around and slammed it into Sebastian's jaw. There was an audible crack as Sebastian went tumbling, but it was good enough to shut him up. Damien turned back around and did his best to keep his wall in place.

The guard cocked his head. The man pulled his gloved hand away and looked at his palm. When he saw the oily, red fluid, he rubbed it off on his black armor and continued scrutinizing the wall in front of him.

"Hey! Down here," the second Enforcer shouted. The man in front of Damien took a step away from the wall and wandered after his partner. The tension eased out of his body, and his shoulders slumped. Behind him, Damien heard sniffling. A pang of regret ate at him as he turned towards Sebastian.

"Listen, I'm sorry I had to do that..."

The sentence was interrupted as Sebastian slammed into Damien—his shoulder thrusting deep into his gut. The air rushed out of Damien's lungs as the two of them fell to the floor and tumbled in the darkness.

Damien's head snapped backward and smacked against the ground, but he quickly rolled away and got into a defensive stance. Sebastian barely got to one knee before he was swinging wildly. Damien ducked under a blow and swiftly wrapped Sebastian in a chokehold.

"Are you done!?" He shouted into Sebastian's ear. Sebastian struggled harder, kicking frantically at the ground. He didn't even attempt to pull Damien's arm away as Damien tightened the hold. Damien could smell the fear and aggression exuding off of Sebastian. He could hear Sebastian's ragged breathing in his ear.

"Just stop, and I'll let go." If he didn't ease up, Sebastian would be an unconscious burden whom Damien would have to leave behind. In a last, feeble attempt, Sebastian reached up and grabbed Damien's arm.

Light blinded Damien. As soon as Sebastian's hand grazed Damien's arm, streams of light blossomed outward in shards of luminescence. Damien dazedly relaxed his grip on Sebastian's neck as he tried to shake the spots dancing in front of his eyes. When he finally saw clearly, he was amazed to find letters emanating from where they touched.

The letters filled the room. They formed words that Damien found hard to read and comprehend. Some of the words joined together in phrases and sentences which floated ethereally in front of them.

Damien jerked away from Sebastian and stood up abruptly. Immediately, the words disappeared. For a moment, all that remained was the darkness. But, this too was replaced by the tendrils of red which found its way into the room. Soon, the room was a pulsing blood vessel.

"What did you do?" Damien asked with shaky accusation. Sebastian was staring up at the ceiling. His eyes roamed, searched, yearned as his chest rose with shallow breaths. "I asked you a question," Damien said tersely. Finally, Sebastian looked at him. There was an awe in his face, which made Damien uncomfortable.

"Where'd you get that?" Sebastian asked as he pointed to the white cuff wrapped around Damien's wrist and forearm.

"Does it matter?"

"It does. I've seen those words before."

"Where?"

Sebastian hesitated, but Damien glared at him.

"They were given to me."

"And where are they now?"

"They were taken from me." Sebastian's words had an echo of melancholy to them, but Damien pushed forward without hesitation.

"Unless they're a map to get us out of here, I don't see how they matter."

"They matter. All we are are words, Damien."

Damien fought the urge to hit him again.

"We need to get out of here. Do you know the layout of the prison?" The question caught Damien off guard. He expected more brooding and ambiguity.

"*No.*" Damien didn't attempt to hide his disdain.

"Then perhaps you should let me figure this out," Sebastian suggested. "I was an Administrative Apprentice, so I've had a cursory understanding of most of the Protectorates, including this one."

Damien didn't have any clue what most of what he said meant and resigned to a shrug of his shoulders. Sebastian started to pace, with his hand under his chin, as if holding his head up would help him think better. Damien's patience held out for the entirety of two minutes.

"So, what's the plan, *Apprentice*?" Sebastian didn't react to the jab, much to Damien's dismay. But, eventually, he halted.

"Can I use that?" Sebastian asked as he pointed at Damien's cuff.

"No," he said abruptly. The very idea of giving away what Theo gave to him felt like abandonment, like a betrayal.

"Didn't think you would. Though it certainly would have made this an easier process. Then again, you did manage to create a see-through wall, so maybe this won't be too impossible for you," Sebastian rambled.

"Stop that. Stop being so vague. It's annoying. Just tell me what I'm supposed to do," Damien retorted.

"Fine. Do you understand how a manipulor works?"

"Sure. It allows you to do what you're thinking about."

"Not really, but close," Sebastian began. Damien bit back a retort. "It works off of a person's will, which is a combination of what a person desires, their intelligence, the level of their discipline, their imagination, and their insight into the world around them. These help shape a person's choices, and when you apply them to the manipulor, it allows us to shape the very world around us. Understood?" Damien genuinely didn't like Sebastian, nor his condescension.

"Sure. It's what makes us human. But what's it got to do with our plan?"

"If you can concentrate hard enough, extend your will out beyond yourself, beyond these walls, into the very fabric of Bastille itself, then you can create a map of the entire prison. Which would be helpful if you can do it."

If?

"I can do it," Damien declared.

"Do you want me to walk you through it?"

Damien snorted.

"No. I got this." Damien rubbed his hands together and approached the wall. The red oozed over its surface, and he was almost hesitant to touch it. He didn't want Sebastian's input or encouragement, though, so he immediately put his hand on it.

"Just concentrate," Sebastian started, but Damien waved him off. The young man fell silent and let Damien think. His thoughts roamed throughout his head as he searched for an idea, an insight into the prison's layout.

White light glowed at his fingertips and moved outwards in spirals. But, these spirals met only the darkness of what Damien didn't know. He bit into his cheek as his frustration mounted. The lines of light receded backward as if stemmed by the tide of red. Damien removed his hand.

"Fine! You can explain the process. But, I swear. If you touch me again, you'll be on the floor," Damien threatened.

Sebastian was unmoved by his comment, though, and continued to stare into Damien as if he was a parent waiting on a child to stop talking despite the fact they were almost the same age.

"Squat down and touch the floor," Sebastian instructed. Damien did so, and Sebastian soon joined him at his level. "Now, close your eyes."

"I'm not closing my eyes," Damien said in defiance.

"Damien, I need you to be able to see beyond what is in front of you. So, please. Close your eyes." Before he did so, Damien rolled them again. His hand found the floor, and he planted it firmly in place. "Now, I want you to think about how the floor feels. I want you to think about the walls in this room. But I don't want you to stop there. I want you to extend your concentration beyond these walls as if you understood every surface, every pore, every crack, and crevice."

Damien followed his instructions. He thought about the surfaces. He thought about what he was feeling. All of the information seemed like an overload, and he didn't know how to organize it into a pattern he could use.

"This is impossible!" He said through gritted teeth.

"Where you are unsure, use your imagination. Use the intelligence you have available from when we were in the hallway. I'm sure you know the prison's general dimensions from when you were outside of it, so use this as a template. It doesn't have to be perfect. Your manipulor will fill in the blank spaces." Sebastian's tone was slow and patient as he explained the process. Damien listened carefully as he doubled his efforts.

An image started to take shape in his thoughts. He thought about the room he was in, imagined its surfaces when he was uncertain. But, he didn't stop there. His awareness spilled into the hallway, through the twists and turns, real or imagined. His concentration traveled through the route he'd taken to find Sebastian until he was standing outside the prison—no, in the air above the prison when he'd ascended the outer wall. From this vantage point, he could see the entire layout of Bastille.

"Alright, I think I have a clear picture. What's next?"

"Now, think about what you desire. What do you want to do with all of this information?"

Damien knew exactly what he needed to do. He made the entire prison smaller and smaller in his mind until it could fit in a space just in front of him. He could see into every corner of Bastille as if he was a giant standing over a village.

"Well done, Damien. You can open your eyes."

Damien's eyes fluttered open. A luminous glow emitted from in front of him. A spark of excitement burst in his chest when he saw Bastille laid out before them. It radiated with light, which shimmered and swam on the walls. Damien pushed himself up and approached the replica. It wasn't exactly how he had imagined the layout, but he knew it was the corrected form of what he had assumed.

"Woah," he reflected.

"Good job. Now, we can figure out how to get out of here." Sebastian walked around the model of Bastille with his hand again under his chin. It was his thinking face. Damien marveled at his creation and felt an immense sense of pride and accomplishment as Sebastian paced.

"I think I know how to get us out of here," Sebastian said at long last. "But, it's going to involve some creativity."

"Creativity?"

"Yes. You see this room right there?" Damien followed Sebastian's finger to a long, open room with multiple doors lined with bars.

"I see it. So?"

"That's the primary path to getting out. Now that the alarms have gone off, there will be Enforcers at every exit."

"Including that one. How are we supposed to get out?"

"I understand how the Enforcers operate. A little. And they will tighten up their most vulnerable locations."

"And this, I assume, is not a vulnerable location?"

"It will be heavily guarded."

"Then why are we even considering it? I thought you said you knew what you were doing!?"

"It's a matter of execution," Sebastian said sagely.

"Just tell me the plan and skip the speech," Damien retorted. A wounded wave rolled across Sebastian's face but quickly receded back into the depths of his stoicism.

"We're going to go above them," Sebastian said simply.

"Right. Above them. Got it," Damien said sarcastically.

"It'll make more sense when we get there."

"It better. But, let's not waste any more time."

"Agreed."

The two of them moved to the wall. Damien looked back and saw Sebastian admiring Damien's creation.

"Sorry about hitting you. Really," Damien said softly. "And thanks for walking me through making that," Damien said as he tilted his head at the model.

"Don't thank me yet, Damien. Is the coast clear?"

Damien turned and made the wall transparent.

"Yeah."

"Alright. Then let's go."

Chapter 19: The Paraclete

Abby, Citadel, The Directory

The air was thick with tension, and a veil of anxiety cloaked the Atrium. Abby's shoulders ached with the apprehension that weighed upon each Director. Even the Head Director, usually regal and stoic, showed signs of the trepidation on his gaunt face.

Each Director sat with their backs straight as their gaze directed towards the chair in the center of a pool of exposing light. A man stepped forward. He wore specialized armor that was black accentuated by red, angular lines.

The Paraclete.

The sight of the shadowy figure made the hairs on Abby's neck stand up. A mask obscured his face, yet managed to convey malice in the sharp, black lines. The man was a silent haunt and bore more authority than all of the Directors.

The Paraclete was the tip of the Lord Protector's spear and led the attack against the Disease. The Paraclete had access to everyone—every word—every emotion.

Nothing was hidden from the Paraclete.

"We do not appreciate being summoned out of session, Paraclete. This better be important. Do you have another accused?" The Head Director spat irritably.

"I do," the Paraclete stated plainly. His voice was stale as it filtered through the helmet.

"Let's hear it, then. I want to get on with this. Bring the guilty party into the room."

Abby couldn't take her eyes off the mask. She wondered what kind of person hid behind its hostile veneer. The Paraclete was an enigma, a mystery.

Shortly after the death of Comande Duval, many sweeping changes went into immediate effect, including the creation of the wholly ambiguous position of the Paraclete. No one truly understood the Paraclete's role except that the Paraclete was a position created for the specific occasion whose job was to expose dissent at all costs.

And so, the accused arrived.

At first, the suspects were brought in front of the Directory on meaningless charges that had little bearing to any laws that could be broken. But one after another, the innocent were sentenced and sent to the Bastille.

But, the Directors' hands were tied. They served the will of the Lord Protector, and it was his will to use the Paraclete. The truth bent toward him. Evidence found favor in his direction. And there was nothing they could do to stop it.

But, Abby couldn't take it much longer. She felt the crushing grip of the lies. They choked out her voice and made it impossible to breathe. With each passing cycle, more and more individuals were brought into the Atrium. Each victim pleaded and begged, but their sentence was already determined. The Directors were merely a formality, now, and most of them recognized this sobering fact.

"Of course, Head Director. But, I don't have to bring them into the room. The person in question is already here."

Gasps and murmuring buzzed amongst the Directors. There was a cacophony of shuffling as Directors sought to distance themselves from one another. Abby felt fear take flight.

"You dare accuse one of the Directors? On what evidence?" Director Malisa interjected. Abby could see that even Director Malisa was visibly shaken.

"Oh, I have plenty, Director. This person has long been connected with supporting and working for the Hajj and has demonstrated the Disease's symptoms in multiple variations, including a willingness to pursue establishing a political system unanchored from the Lord Protector. This individual consistently seeks to undermine the Lord Protector."

Abby's ears were growing hot. The Paraclete's visor flinched in her direction. Her feet burned with the desire to run, but her legs were heavy with indecision. If she ran, they'd catch her before she got out the door. She could fight, but to what end? There was no way out of this except to defend herself against a broken, corrupt system.

"Further, this individual has been known to be in contact with 1C118. This alone is a treason of the highest kind." The Directors were silent as each of them fought the dread building up in their seats.

"A name, Paraclete. We need a name," the Head Director persisted. How would he react when it was Director Florence who he accused? Abby prepared herself for what was coming next. She'd always recognized the risks of what she did to undermine the Lord Protector.

But, of course, she had fail-safes in place.

Abby tapped a button on her manipulor. There was no way she was going to go down without a fight. The Paraclete nodded at the Head Director and continued.

"The guilty know already," the Paraclete began as his head swiveled in Abby's direction. Dozens of eyes followed his gaze as the Paraclete approached. Abby could feel the weight of his accusations. The relieved condemnation that each Director conveyed was a death sentence. She tensed her muscles and prepared to leap over the railing in front of her.

The Paraclete stopped in front of her. Abby could see herself reflected in his black mask.

"Isn't that right, Director Justains?"

The room sucked in its breath. Abby's brow broke open into confusion. The Communication and Social Interaction Director next to her, Lisa Justains, rose shakily to her feet.

"It's not me! I swear!" The woman intreated as she looked from face to face looking for absolution. But, the Directors leaned back and hid in the shadows. Lisa turned to Abby, begging in her jeweled eyes.

"Bring the accused forward," the Head Director commanded firmly. There was a hollowness to his voice— disbelief. But, he had a job to do—a Role to perform.

"Please," Director Justains pleaded to Abby. A weight settled into Abby's gut that prevented her from rising. The Enforcers shuffled into the seats and made their way past tangles of legs and purple robes. Aside from trying to let them through, no one dared move. No one dared speak, lest they became an object of scrutiny as well. "I didn't do this."

Real tears swelled in her eyes.

The Enforcers grabbed her around the shoulders as defeat etched into her countenance. In the face of violent options, there was no use resisting. The Enforcers marched her down the row of Directors. Nobody looked up into the face of their fellow Director. No one dared touch her soiled robes.

Abby watched her depart, as the empty seat next to her bellowed. The Enforcers brought Director Justains to the chair, forced her to sit, and wrapped the chains around her wrists. The clink of metal on metal slapped the silence with sound.

The Enforcers stepped back and merged with the darkness. The Paraclete, with hands clasped behind his back, paced behind the chair. Revulsion and hatred boiled in Abby's veins. How could he do this!?

How could Abby let it happen?

"How does the accused respond to these declarations?" The Paraclete inquired as he paced.

"My response is the same! I am not guilty of these crimes. I am loyal. I have served the Lord Protector all my life. Ask any of them," Director Justains said as she nodded in the direction of the Directors. The Paraclete stopped pacing and turned his attention to the audience.

"Is there any credible evidence for this claim, Directors?" The Head Director asked. The Paraclete looked at each of them, imploring them to speak up on her behalf. To see one of their Directors standing accused meant any one of them could be accused. This haunted reality glistened in the Head Director's hooded eyes. "Director Malisa? Director Frederik?"

"I'm sorry, Head Director," Director Frederik began. His beady eyes blinked aggressively as the strain in his voice carried across the Atrium. "But, we haven't had adequate time to study this situation. We have no evidence to the contrary," he said hollowly. Abby knew it was hopeless. Nobody in this room knew the other personally—they were intimate strangers.

"Director Florence," the Head Director began as he looked in Abby's direction, "as Administrator of Training, surely you worked the closest with Director Justains. Perhaps you can shed some light on the matter."

Abby swallowed heavily as her tongue grew thick. Director Justains was Administrator of Communication and Social Interactions, which was remarkably different from Abby's position. Abby had gotten so used to wearing her mother's face and pretending to be a Director that she never stopped to get to know and understand the woman who sat beside her.

"This is preposterous!" Director Justains shouted as she leaned forward in her chair. "Head Director, you have to see common sense. This is a lie. It cannot be the truth!"

"What is truth, Director?" The Head Director asked evenly. Director Justains' face fell as she settled back into the chair. Her fate was sealed, and she knew it.

"Evidently, it's whatever you decide it to be," Director Justains said sorrowfully. "You will regret this—all of you. Don't think for a second that any of you are safe from this," she said darkly. Abby knew she was right. Already, the regret was building in her chest and crushing her down into her seat.

"Take her away, Paraclete," the Head Director commanded. His voice had lost its strength. Abby watched in horror as the Enforcers approached the chair, unclasped the restraints, and brought the broken woman to her feet. Lisa stumbled. The Paraclete turned to follow.

"You can't do this!" Abby was on her feet without knowing she had stood. A high-pitched ringing sound resounded in her head as all eyes turned in her direction. The Paraclete paused but did not turn around. Everyone listened with bated breath as fear ingrained them into the stone seats.

"This is wrong, and you know it is. This woman is innocent. They've *all* been innocent."

The silence in the Atrium was heavy. Abby felt pins and needles radiating up and down her arms. She was lightheaded but emboldened at the same time as indignant rage churned in her chest. "Take your mask off and face us, coward," she said through gritted teeth.

"Director?" Abby tore her eyes away from the Paraclete and towards the Head Director. The look on his face was one of confusion and shock. Her eyes scanned the audience, looking for support. But, she was alone. She was terribly alone.

For the first time, Abigail had merged her rebellious personality into her role as Director Florence. But, now she was exposed—vulnerable. Her heart fluttered as she scanned empty, pitiless faces. There was no hiding, now.

"As you wish, Director," the Paraclete spoke evenly. Abby's eyes flashed back to the shadow-armored man. His hands rose to the bottom of his helmet as he fumbled with the clasp. The man lifted the helmet off his head as brown, matted hair appeared. Abby held her breath as the man turned.

E64 bore no anger or surprise on his face. Abby's heart dropped. The recording of him stabbing Sebastian replayed in her mind. She could see over and over the needle penetrating Sebastian's abdomen.

Was he the Paraclete? It made sense. Such a terrible Role belonged to the father who tried to murder his son.

"You have no right," Abby conveyed once she found her voice. She was trembling.

"On the contrary, Director. I have the only right. What is your name?" A thick stillness penetrated the room as everyone watched the drama unfolding. Abby could feel their scrutiny, their jubilation, their relief that it wasn't one of them who finally stood up to the Paraclete.

"Director Florence."

"The Head of Training?"

"Yes." Abby felt distinctly uncomfortable as a spark of understanding flashed through E64's haunted eyes.

"Interesting," he said casually. Abby bit the inside of her cheek. She was undoubtedly failing anonymity, but she was tired of the fear and trepidation, the intimidation and abuse.

"I find it interesting that the Lord Protector has allowed an Administrator with no extensive background in the laws to perpetuate these investigations. From where I am standing, I see the suggestion of someone whose modus operandi is full of fallacy and self-serving mechanisms," Abby accused.

E64 smirked.

"If you would like to insinuate something, Director, then do so. There's no point in ambiguity."

"Fine. I accuse you of having a hidden agenda that suits your goals and not the goals and desires of the Lord Protector."

"That is a high accusation. One that you would have to prove. Do you have any evidence?"

No. Abby didn't. All she had was common sense and her intuition. Something about E64 was off, and she knew it.

"I take it from your silence that you do not. If that's the case, then I must depart. I have more pressing matters to attend to." The Paraclete turned.

Abby wanted to speak, to level her authority against the Paraclete, to stop him from choking out the laws and reason. Nothing he was doing made sense. In the least, the Directors had a system, a method that could be applied to all situations, all Figures—even if it served a false ideal. But, the Paraclete seemed above the law, and beyond reason.

Abby opened her mouth to respond, but before she could put together a syllable, an Enforcer came sprinting into the Atrium. The man was without his helmet, and a trickle of blood oozed out of a cut above his eyebrow. It mingled with his sweat and fell down his face like tears.

"I apologize, Directors, but this is urgent," he said breathlessly. Abby's brow creased together.

"Speak, Preva. What is the manner of this interruption?" The Head Director asked.

"Sir, there is a situation unfolding just outside the Directory," he gasped out.

"A situation?" The Paraclete inquired. The Enforcer turned to the night-clad man.

"Yes," he began anxiously. An explosion boomed throughout the Directory as the ground shook.

"We're under attack!"

Chapter 20: Prison Break

Damien, Armament, Bastille Prison

Damien stared down at the Enforcer. The fact that he was directly above the black-armored guard was dizzying, but Damien maintained his balance. Carefully, stealthily, he moved down the bridge he'd created.

The bridge hadn't been an easy concept to create, but Sebastian had coached him through the process of building a set of steps that led upward to a bridge suspended off the ground.

Transparent on one side, Damien could see down, but if any of the Enforcers looked up, they'd see a mirror reflection of themselves. It wasn't foolproof, but Damien hoped the ensuing confusion would provide enough time to get them out of Bastille Prison.

Damien heard shuffling. He peered over his shoulder at Sebastian and gave him a cross look. Could he be any louder? Sebastian granted Damien a sheepish look as Damien glowered. Damien glanced down at the Enforcer, but the soldier hadn't looked upward.

Damien crept forward. They were already almost halfway across the room. He could see the end in sight, though two Enforcers still blocked it. How were they going to get them both to vacate their positions? Damien pondered as his feet pattered across the bridge. He'd need to think of something fast. The end was approaching. Damien halted to think.

Sebastian didn't notice Damien stopped and collided with him. Damien whipped around just as Sebastian's foot slipped off of the bridge. Reflexively, Damien reached out and grabbed a handful of his shirt. The older boy was no means light as Damien felt his balance begin to shift forward.

They were going to fall.

Damien dug his heels into the bridge and leaned backward. Sebastian's eyes gaped open in shock as Damien struggled to pull him towards him. Damien gripped the other side of the bridge with white knuckles. Finally, he was able to pull Sebastian back onto the bridge as the two of them collapsed next to one another.

Damien's breath came in angry bursts.

"Pay attention, idiot!" Damien whispered sharply.

Sebastian looked at him, remorsefully.

"Hey, did you hear something?" An Enforcer asked. Damien glanced down at a barrel pointed directly up at them. Damien held his breath. If his plan worked, then what the Enforcer was seeing was a mirror image of himself, and not two boys huddle in the dark.

A second Enforcer approached, and he too looked up.

"What is that?" The first Enforcer inquired. Damien could feel his muscles tense as he prepared to bolt.

"It looks like your ugly reflection," the second Enforcer responded with a chuckle.

"I get that, but why is it there? Have you ever noticed a full-length mirror running across the ceiling?" Damien was growing uneasy. So far, the mirror only served to baffle them. From his belly, Damien's eyes shot towards the remaining Enforcer still guarding their exit.

"Come on, move," he mumbled. Damien glanced back down at the two Enforcers. The first one had his head tilted. He stepped to his left one step, and then took another. Damien got as flat as he could and hoped Sebastian was doing the same.

The Enforcer stopped, with his weapon lowered.

"What do you see?" The second Enforcer asked. There was a long, agonizing silence. The Enforcer at the entrance took a few steps forward. Beads of sweat trickled down Damien's face, and his heart pounded against the bridge.

The Enforcer raised his weapon and aimed it at Damien.

"Wait!" Sebastian shouted as his hands extended over the edge of the bridge. Damien swore under his breath.

"What are you doing!?" Damien hissed.

"Trust me. Get ready to grab my arm and run," Sebastian said out of the corner of his mouth.

"We got someone up here!" The Enforcer shouted. Damien watched as the Enforcer by the entrance left his post.

Damien understood.

"State your number, Figure!"

"How'd he even get up there?" The second Enforcer murmured. The third Enforcer came up alongside the other two.

"My name is 1C118," Sebastian provided. "And I want to surrender." Damien got the hint. His hand extended and clamped down on Sebastian's arm. Immediately, bolts of bright light shot in all directions as all three Enforcers ducked, clutching their visors and shouting in agonized confusion.

Damien heaved Sebastian to his feet as they ran.

Chapter 21: Cloak and Dagger

Byron, Citadel, The Refuge

Byron stared into the Coms as he waited for the assault on the Technology Protectorate to commence. Enduring energy rolled through his body as his solemn gaze cycled through the multitude of screens projecting images from throughout Technology. Before she left, Abby programmed the Coms only to display critical areas within the Protectorate. Although it limited the amount of information Byron had access to, he wanted his full attention on the assault.

Byron paced. So much rested on this first strike. It would be the first time in history that a dissenting force within Axiom moved against the Lord Protector. It would be the first open challenge to Lorenzo's power. If the forces in motion didn't take down the security measures in Technology, then all of this would be for nothing. Was Byron scared?

Absolutely.

But, it had to be done.

After Rais appointed himself as de facto Comande, he'd taken control of all the forces and powers within Axiom. Byron knew it was only a matter of time before Rais turned his gaze upon Byron and started his quest for vengeance, but until that moment, Byron would use every second of Rais's hunger for power against him. Rais spread himself too thin, dipping in too many areas, attacking too many fronts. But, this worked to Byron's advantage. By the time Rais figured out what was happening, it would be too late.

Regardless, the next choice was important.

"Sir. This is Team Leader. We are in position," a gruff voice crackled through his manipulor. Byron keyed a command, and the Com in front of him flicked to an image of a squat building. The building didn't stand out, which was the point. Rais understood the necessity of subtlety, even if he possessed a flair for the sensational.

Inside the nondescript structure was a machine that coordinated the nanoparticles in Axiom's atmosphere. Cutting off this feedback was entirely necessary, and victory here paved the way for future success.

Failure would set them back into a corner where defeat took up residence. Whatever Byron said next could mean the beginning of the end of Lorenzo's tyranny or the end of everything he'd worked to accomplish.

Byron did not hesitate.

"Execute."

"Yes, Sir."

The room went silent as Byron held his breath. At first, he saw nothing on the Com, but eventually, armor-clad figures emptied the alleys on both sides of the building. He watched as the silent warriors—handpicked for their loyalty and skill—approached the door.

The building and street were soundless. There was an emptiness that unnerved Byron. Was Axiom prepared for what was coming next? No, but after Lorenzo brought death into Axiom, this was inevitable. Byron watched as one of the soldiers reached in a pouch and pulled out a miniature drone.

The machine lifted from his hand just as a second soldier cracked open the door entering the building. The drone nimbly slipped inside. A few seconds later, the screen erupted in a brilliant flash as the drone detonated.

"Breaching," the team leader conveyed. Byron was gripping the table with white knuckles. He watched as the blackened Enforcers slipped one by one into the building. A half-second after the last man entered, the algorithm Abby designed switched the point of view to a camera mounted on the team leader's helmet. Faint smoke from the flash drone lingered, but otherwise, the foyer was empty.

Byron's brow creased together. Something wasn't right. There was no way the building wasn't guarded, especially in light of recent events. Rais wouldn't be that stupid, surely. He watched with tense interest as the team of men checked in rooms to make sure they were clear.

The goal had never been to kill, thus the stunning drone, but to not encounter any resistance at all was unsettling. Byron tapped his fingers on the table as his mind worked through the scenario. He wasn't well-versed in tactics or combat, so the number of possible outcomes his mind navigated through was only a handful.

"Commence, sir?" The Team Leader inquired. He too was nervous. Byron could hear it in his voice.

"Keep moving forward. Be ready for anything," Byron said tersely.

"Yes, sir." The Team Leader gave a quick hand gesture, and the men moved deeper into the building. Byron continued to watch, mulling over the situation's irregularity, but was distracted by one of the Coms on his right. The screen was flashing red.

At first, he thought he imagined it, but the flashing continued. Byron tore his eyes off the screen in front of him and walked over to the Com. The flashing was growing more urgent, now, so Byron reached out and touched the glass. The Com responded to his touch and switched to a different image, which made Byron take a step backward.

The Directory was on fire. Byron watched in terrified awe as gunfire erupted from the colonnades on either side of the Directory. Whoever was locked in combat was pouring on a heavy attack. Byron watched in horror as men and women in purple clothes—the traditional garb for the Directory—got caught in the crossfire. Their bodies jerked before crumbling to the ground in grotesque heaps.

A battle was taking place at the Directory. Trepidation brew in his chest. How could this be happening!? He didn't authorize a strike on the Directory, and there was no way the numb residents of Citadel suddenly woke up out of their stupor and assaulted the Directory.

Byron panicked. He walked back to his Enforcers in Technology. They were still moving deeper into the building. He wasn't even sure if they'd encountered any resistance yet, but he didn't care. The situation was spiraling out of his control before it was even in his grasp.

There was only one person who could have put this together. Byron keyed a command into his manipulor and waited. The muscle in his jaw fluctuated as his anger accumulated. The Com in front of him grew into definition as Horrus filled the screen.

"Took you long enough," Horrus said dryly. Byron bit back the avalanche of anger brewing.

"What are you doing, Horrus?" The man's beady eyes narrowed. Byron could feel the blood rushing to his head.

"I'm doing what needs to be done, Byron."

"What needs to be done!? My daughter is in that building, Horrus!" Byron's wrath spewed from his mouth. His chest heaved as the implications settled into him like gravity.

"A fact that is unfortunate, really, but she knew the dangers of her position when she took on the face of your wife. I had this planned before you revealed her identity, so the fact that she is your daughter was unknown. If you had shared this information with us sooner, perhaps this wouldn't —."

"—You're blaming me for this!? You're a fool, Horrus. You've tipped our hand. Not only have you made our objectives blatantly obvious, but you also went behind my back." Byron was seething. Horrus's mustache twitched aggressively.

"I went ahead of you, Byron, not behind you. This was never about you, and quite frankly, I didn't need your authorization. The Directory will fall, and Citadel will be primed for takeover because I acted decisively. If you strike hard enough, you knock the enemy down. Act swift enough, and they won't get back up."

"People are dying!" Byron's voice shook as his fist came crashing down onto the table. Horrus clasped his hands under his chin, and his face darkened.

"A most unfortunate reality, but the reality I'm replacing is far worse. Victory comes at a cost, Byron."

A stiff silence settled between the two men. Byron knew he couldn't reason with Horrus, which meant he had to do damage control instead. There was no way to reverse what was already in motion.

"Whose forces are currently repelling the assault on the Directory?" Byron asked as evenly as he could.

"My own. As Administrator of Citadel Security—."

"—Spare me the introduction, Horrus. I understand what you accomplished. By using your forces to both assault and repel, your hands are clean." Horrus beamed.

"Precisely."

Byron bit into his cheek. In all, it was a well-crafted plan, even if it was out of his control. Byron glanced back at the Com projecting the Directory. More of the ancient building was on fire. Columns lay in ruins next to heaps of bodies. A despairing, powerless sadness seeped into Byron.

This was not how it was supposed to be—at least not this early in the fight. Bloodshed was going to occur, but Byron wanted to limit the number of casualties, not encourage them. He turned his attention back to Horrus, who wore an amused look on his face.

"Can you do me a favor, Horrus, if anything?" Horrus didn't respond, but Byron continued. "Find my daughter. Get her out," Byron pleaded. He felt fatigued and weary as the rush of anger ebbed out of him, and resignation took its place.

"I'll tell them to keep an eye out for Director Florence."

"Thank you."

An impregnable silence stood between them. Byron couldn't look the man in the eye.

"Did you take down the security site?" Horrus asked. Byron's head came back up as his eyes flew to the Coms. In the turn of events, he'd forgotten about his team. He pressed a button on his manipulor, an aggressive maroon color, and spoke into the device.

"Team Leader. What's your situation?" Byron watched the screens as the armored men continued opening doors and entering rooms. Their flashlights revealed emptiness.

"Disabled, sir. We're just searching for any backup devices. We met some resistance, but nothing we couldn't handle," the team leader conveyed evenly.

"Any casualties?"

"A few incapacitated but merely unconscious." Relief flooded Byron. He glanced at Horrus, who wore a smug look.

"Excellent work, Team Leader. Gather your team and get out of there. Despite your success, I have a feeling the Lord Protector is aware of what is happening," Byron stated evenly as he flashed Horrus a sour look.

"Yes, sir. We'll be out in ten."

"Thank you. Don't communicate until I give you the all-clear. Great work." Byron said genially. Byron watched the Com a few more seconds as the men started their retreat.

"You should thank me. Without my distraction, your plan may have never succeeded."

"I am not going to thank you, Horrus. You put a lot of our goals in jeopardy with this stunt," he said tersely.

"Perhaps. But, we succeeded today. I got what I wanted, and you got what you wanted," Horrus suggested with a shrug of his shoulders. Byron knew it wasn't that easy, though. Something about his raid on the security site didn't feel right. Frankly, it felt too easy.

"I want you to find my daughter and get her out, Horrus. That's the least you can do."

Without letting him comment further, Byron silenced his Com and hung his head. Worry creased his brow as he thought about Abby. It took everything in him to not run to her side, but doing so would expose her and him simultaneously. No, he'd have to wait and trust Horrus to get her out.

Byron tried not to think about losing her. He lifted his head and stared into the Com showing the unfolding battle at the Directory. The fire was raging, but most of the gunfire had abated. He watched, hoping to see his wife's figure emerge from the building.

Byron felt helpless. How could he help Abby if he was stuck in this room? Aggravation curled on his tongue, and the desire to put his fist through the Com rose in his arms. He felt like a prisoner.

A prisoner.

That was it. Byron knew exactly how he could help. He went to the command desk on his left and started to tap the keys rapidly. He certainly didn't know much about hacking and hijacking the system like his daughter, but she'd shown him a thing or two. He created the strand of code, made sure it made sense, and then sent the information into the steady stream of data making its way to the Observers.

Byron waited. The response would be sent to every Enforcer in Axiom, including the Com in front of him.

ICII8 spotted in Citadel. All personnel available proceed to the Directory. Neutralize target on sight. Advance with caution.

Byron smiled to himself. This would draw forces to the Directory and give Abby the best chance to escape. He knew that Horrus's forces would be destroyed in the process, but it was necessary. Byron was so engrossed in this thought that he didn't see the Com on the edge of the display rapidly flashing.

Chapter 22: The Broken Seat

Abby, Citadel, The Directory

Abby couldn't believe what she was hearing. The Directory was under attack? That was impossible, improbable. No one would implement a strike so dangerous and so brazen—especially not her father. He wouldn't expose Hajj so openly. Besides, she knew he was assaulting the security site in Technology. It wasn't possible that he coordinated the assault and planned the attack on the Directory without her knowing.

And yet, the ground shook.

Dust reigned down upon them, and a distant booming noise echoed down the hall and into the room. A couple of Directors stared in disbelief at the Enforcer standing just in the doorway, blood cascading down an open head wound. Others were already on their feet, glancing desperately around for the exit. Abby leaned forward, trying to listen.

"What do you mean we are under attack? By who?" The Paraclete asked hoarsely to the Enforcer.

"Unknown, sir. The assailants struck from the southern end of the colonnade and pushed us inside. We barricaded ourselves and have prevented them from advancing, but it appears they have set fire to the Directory and destroyed several infrastructures," the Enforcer explained fearfully.

His face was growing whiter with each word, and Abby was afraid the man was going to pass out. The Paraclete—E64—didn't respond.

"They're trying to break through the barricade, and I'm not sure how long we have before it doesn't hold them back. What do we do, sir?"

The Paraclete paced. A hunger of conversation buzzed around the room. Abby watched him, knowing that E64 had no military training of any kind. He was a man of the hour, after all, and the hour had passed. Axiom was in a different phase, now. Axiom was at war. Abby was shocked that it had escalated to this point, and she struggled with this new reality.

More dust showered from above. Abby knew the building wasn't going to stand much longer. The Directory was an old building erected long before Axiom, and flames were feasting on its ancient bones.

"We need to get out of here," Abby inserted. The Paraclete and the Enforcer both looked in her direction.

"But how? The front entrance is barred," E64 inquired.

"I know a way out," Abby offered. "If we go through the Library, there are a couple of exterior access points. The closest one is on the northwest corner of the Library—."

"—Near the music room," E64 injected.

"Yeah...Right next to it," Abby drew out.

"If that's the case, then we need to leave now," the Enforcer reflected. "There's no way of knowing if the Directory's been breached already," he said ominously. The Paraclete nodded and moved to the stand in front of the chair.

"Directors!" He began as the men and women quieted. "As you are all aware, the Directory is under attack. The attackers may already be in the building, but we have a plan to get everyone out. This means we have to leave right now."

"Leave? Why would we do that? Could we not just close the door and wait for help to arrive?" Director Malisa asked almost to herself. Abby could see the vulnerable fear—a childlike terror—in her eyes.

"The Directory is on fire," the Paraclete conveyed. Abby heard several Directors suck in their breath. "And if help doesn't arrive in time, the Directory will fall."

"Nonsense," the Head Director interrupted. "The Directory is the seat of the government. It has stood since the beginning of Axiom, and it will not fall." There was a cHorrus of agreements. Abby's heart sank as their voices rose in unison.

"The Directory *has* stood since the beginning, but these fires will bring it down," Abby provided. "It's not built to withstand these pressures. Besides, the Directory is not a building. It's all of us," Abby said as she extended her hands. The room was silent as her words soaked in.

"Preposterous! It's better to stay here and wait for help," the Head Director stated firmly. The Directors around him nodded. Abby couldn't believe their ignorance.

"That's your decision, but for anyone who wants to get out, follow me," the Paraclete said as he slipped his helmet back over his face. With a click, it locked into place. Abby was the first to leave her place and walk to where he was standing. She turned around and was shocked to see only two Directors also leaving their seats. What could she say to convince them that hadn't already been spoken? E64 turned to the Enforcer.

"Preva, I need you to stay here and guard the entrance to this room. These Directors may be obstinate, but we cannot leave them undefended."

The Preva nodded, though Abby could tell the man wouldn't be able to travel very far regardless of whether or not Directors were staying. The wound on his head had still not clotted as crimson seeped out of the cut. Abby's head swam, but she kept her nerve.

"Yes, sir!" The Preva said with dignity. The Paraclete turned to the three Directors behind him.

"Regardless of what we encounter, we need to stick together. Let me handle anything that comes at us, understood?"

"Why?" Abby started in. "Have you ever fired a gun?"

"Have you?" E64 quipped. Abby fell silent. She was dubious but had no other option than to trust the man who, without hesitation, stabbed his child. "Follow me," the Paraclete said firmly as he led them out of the Atrium.

Once they withdrew from the Atrium, a choking silence settled amongst them. Every sound resounded off the inky walls. The air smelled of smoke and was noticeably warmer. Panic pounded in her veins. She could see the red outline of the Paraclete's armor, but otherwise, choking darkness smothered the hallways.

Who attacked? Abby knew this wasn't her father's plan. He wouldn't put her life at risk. Was this the Lord Protector? Was he taking a preemptive strike against his people to prevent

147

rebellion? Although the idea seemed farfetched and deranged, it fit Lorenzo's penchant for dominance.

"Not much further," the Paraclete said over his shoulder. Abby could hear the uneasiness in his voice. Her confidence was quickly abating. Surely whoever was behind this wouldn't try to kill her. She was, after all, Byron's daughter.

But how many people knew that?

In the dark, she was Director Florence.

A pounding noise shattered the silence. The four looked back as the gunfire echoed eerily down the hallway. They'd already been traveling for five minutes, but there was no mistaking it came from the Atrium. Loose, mangled screams followed. The cries gave birth to a throttled silence.

How many shots were fired? Abby couldn't remember. Despite herself, despite her duplicity and the years she'd lied to her fellow Directors, Abby felt a stab of loss overwhelm her. She knew those people, even if they didn't know her.

"We have to keep moving," E64 stated evenly. He was doing a good job hiding his fear. Abby could feel it hugging her closer than the darkness and smoke. She walked closer to E64, longing for safety. She could hear the ragged, fear-ridden breath of the other two Directors behind her. Sweat clung to her body like soiled clothing.

"Through here." Abby followed, knowing they had to take a long way around. Some of the routes were so choked with smoke and the threat of fire, to proceed would be foolish.

A thunderous crash echoed through the Directory as parts of the ancient building came tumbling down. The ground shook, and Abby's teeth clattered. Dust cascaded down on top of their heads, and one of the Directors screamed. Abby felt herself being pushed from behind as her feet quickened their pace. Behind them, more booming claps reverberated as the Directory started to break.

"Get in!" The Paraclete shouted from ahead of her. Abby's heart pounded wildly in her throat as a gale of debris infested wind buffeted her from behind. Shards of stone pelted against her back, and she knew the walls were tumbling behind her. She could see the light through the smoke, faint and distant, and it spurred her onward.

"Hurry!"The Paraclete shouted.

The air cracked—like the sound of dry bones. She heard a scream get cut in half as the hallway slammed into place.

The Directory was going to be her tomb.

Chapter 23: Retribution

Paul, Slave Compound, Factory District

Sweat stung Paul's eyes like angry sparks of fire. His chest burned as his lungs sought out desperately for oxygen. He ignored the pain in his side and continued his sprint. He could hear the machines closing in behind him as the air churned with hostile vibration. Paul reflexively changed his course a few degrees. The shot singed his hair as it passed. The volley struck the ground in front of him, kicking up dirt and debris that showered him and turned his sweat into sticky mud.

The horde of discs hunted him. Panic gathered in his throat. His world was starting to tunnel and narrow as his stamina ran dry. His heart pounded painfully in his chest. Another shot barely missed him, this time splashing at his heels and lashing his legs with fire. A pained, agonizing shout erupted from his lips. They were zeroing in on him. Paul couldn't tell how close they were, but the next shot would be lethal if he didn't get out of their sight.

Paul could see the smokestacks of Factory Number 1. They leaned and loomed over him, threatening to fall upon the squat buildings just beneath. The air curdled as multiple machines prepared to fire. Paul knew there was no way he could dodge more than one strike. His legs felt like liquid metal. His body was about to give out. Death was about to descend.

But, a corner was approaching.

Paul gave a final burst of power and aimed for the turn. The assault tore the air. He could hear walls splinter and crumble. The maimed earth shook with violence. Paul veered to his left, strafing the corner with his shoulder. The Factory filled his vision—offering safety and salvation.

At last.

The discs banked poorly, having to swing wide to follow in Paul's direction. The frenzy of movement caused many of them to collide with each other. Paul felt searing pain pelt him like needles as pieces rained down on his head. Stray shots splashed against the ground ahead of him as the Factory loomed. All he had to do was get into the vast open doors, and then he'd be safe.

The air hummed. Paul knew that there was no way he was going to escape what was coming next. But, life burned inside of him because survival meant more than himself. He was almost inside the gaping mouth of the Factory. The first wave of gunfire burned the air with bubbling ferocity.

Paul stumbled.

The ground came up to meet him as his demise dragged him down. Paul did his best to tuck his shoulder as he dropped into a roll. Dust kicked up as the machines closed in upon his helpless form. When Paul finally came to a stop on his back, he attempted to rise and managed to get onto his elbows. He scurried backward as a black wave of discs came to a halt. The ranks of machinery thinned as the wretched machines lined up to destroy their prey.

Paul swallowed heavily.

This was his end.

Paul squeezed his eyes shut and waited for the pain to blind his senses. A second passed that ate into his terror. A new sound seized the violence as a metallic, jarring noise filled the air. Paul opened his eyes and saw machines wavering and swerving in sporadic jerks. From above, metal rods hurtled down on top of the drones like missiles.

A flash of hope birthed in his chest.

Paul scrambled to his feet as a disc came crashing down. He felt the pieces punch him in the back, but he didn't slow. He dove behind a low wall and landed next to Gregory.

"It's working!" Gregory shouted over the racket. Paul glanced back over the wall at the unfolding battle. Guards and slaves pelted the machines from above.

The rods, typically used for smelting, weren't delivering death blows, but each strike did more and more damage to the unprotected disc—something Paul had deduced when he'd brought one down at the Depot.

"We're not out yet," Paul reflected. "Look!" Paul pointed at the swarm of machines. What was once random dipping and ducking was now a pattern. A cloud of discs broke into smaller sections as each machine tilted in the second floor's direction. The hum of their weapons charged the furnace with a high-pitched whine as the drones retaliated. As their first volley struck the second floor, most of the assault force ducked. Some, however, weren't as fortunate. Paul watched in horror as bodies tumbled from the second floor.

The firing stopped. Dust and debris swirled. Paul waited with bated breath for the discs to make their move. He didn't have to wait long as the entire column of machines started to ascend to the second floor. Paul's heart plummeted. Those on the second floor were too exposed and would be slaughtered. Paul grabbed a metal rod at his feet, swiftly stood, and hurled it into the heart of the drones.

"Over here!" Paul shouted raucously as his throw glanced off of a couple of discs. Almost half of the drone swarm turned in his direction. That wasn't good enough. Paul sprinted towards the machines as a feverish fire burst in his chest.

"Paul! What are you doing!?" Gregory shouted.

"Improvising! Get to Furnace C!" Paul shouted over his shoulder. Paul didn't check to see if Gregory understood. The mass of nightmarish machines turned in his direction. The air hummed with energy as the discs chased after their prey.

Paul's heart pounded in his chest, and cold sweat cascaded down his back. The sound of the drones was all he could hear as they pursued him through the corridors. Even in the tighter space, they were still close. Paul knew the Factory like the back of his hand, though. He knew every sharp corner, every detour, and every scarred surface.

A ball of energy dug into the wall beside him as flakes of burning concrete splashed across his arms. He ignored the pain and slipped around a corner. The machine crashed into the wall as a sharp crack slapped off the concrete surfaces. The reprieve didn't last long as two more took its place.

Paul slipped into a vast room. The walls were curved and funneled and formed a thin tube at the very top. Paul's eyes moved over the walls. There was no door in front of him.

An aggravated hum filled the room. Paul turned to face a massive cloud of discs that was thickening with each breath. The swarm bristled as each machine charged with energy. Like a face deepening with embarrassment, a rose color shimmered across each carapace. The final drone entered the room.

Paul was cornered.

"Now!" Paul shouted as he lay flat on the ground and started to roll. The door to the furnace closed resolutely as the drones fired. The projectiles struck where he'd been previously, but he was already rolling under the wall. As soon as his body was under, flames erupted throughout the massive furnace.

Paul's heart pounded in his chest as the fires followed under the wall. He shimmied as quick as he could as the temperature rose intensely. He could hear the inferno raging and chasing after him. He could feel the flames licking his skin, but he didn't stop.

Paul could feel cool, clear air. Smoke and heat filled his lungs as the flames encircled him. Paul slammed his eyes shut, hoping desperately that he was still rolling in the right direction. Suddenly, Paul felt hands grip his arms as he was forcibly pulled out of the fire. Fresh, sweet air brought relief to his skin. His eyes fluttered open.

"I gotcha," Gregory said. Paul looked down at his body. Steam rolled off his singed clothes. His skin tingled painfully, and his beard smelled of charred hair.

"Did we get them?" Paul said with a cough.

"They're roasted."

"Good," Paul said weakly. He ignored his pain and allowed Gregory to pull him to his feet. "We need to make sure the whole building is clear of them. Let's go," Paul stated firmly as he led the way. Pain erupted with each step, and he was sure he had severe burns on his legs, but he ignored the pain.

The halls were mostly empty. Still, Paul was hesitant, taking his time to check behind corners. Eventually, the corridors opened up to the main entryway. Relief flooded him when he saw numerous people—slaves and guards alike—sifting through the drone remains. Biting back his pain, he jogged over to where they were gathered.

"Anybody hurt?"

"Not seriously," a slave, Frederik, said. A cut above his eye was crusted over. "Thank you for leading them away. You saved us," he said solemnly. Paul shrugged.

"You'd have done the same, Frederick."

The two were silent a moment, and a thick weariness collected on Paul's chest. Paul knew they'd lost over twenty in the first wave. Preventing more deaths was his highest priority.

"What do we do now?" Frederik inquired. Paul's eyes scanned the area. He looked at the ragtag group of slaves and free men but couldn't tell who was a master or slave. No one had weapons, though. Aside from the rods, they had little in the way of defense.

"We need to gather supplies. Figure out if we can use anything from the machines."

"Think we can somehow use their weapon system?"

"I don't know. I assume there are fail-safes in place to prevent a downed machine from being useful," Paul stated hollowly. It was just now registering to him that to the drones, he was the enemy. He shook the idea out of his head. "It's worth a shot, though. We need to be quick. There's no way of knowing when the second wave will attack."

Frederik opened his mouth to respond, but a jarring sound drowned his voice. Everyone's eyes flew to the main entrance as a loud, grinding noise intensified.

Paul's heart pounded as reinforcements rounded the corner. At first, he didn't quite understand what he was seeing. In front of a column of armed soldiers were metal devices that looked like spiders—spiders ridden by a single mounted soldier. His eyes traveled over the barrel of a turret that each mounted soldier grasped in their hands.

The pieces fell into horrifying clarity.

"Hide!" Paul shouted just as the first row of soldiers opened fire. Paul tackled Frederik to the ground as red slashes of death created mayhem and carnage all around them. The two of them crawled on their bellies as men and women all around them screamed. Finally, the two of them were able to reach a pile of debris high enough to hide behind.

"We're being slaughtered!" Frederik yelled over the firefight. Paul glanced over the makeshift barrier at the massacre unfolding. The spiders were already inside the vast archway—some were even scaling the walls as their clawed legs dug into the stone. As Paul watched people he knew and loved die, a hot rage bubbled up inside of him.

They were cornered. Outmatched. Beaten.

Theo, help us.

The gunfire abated just as quickly as it had begun. An ill silence settled as dust swam in the air. Paul's eyes darted over the barrier at the army standing at the ready. He watched as a man stepped forward, the same man Paul spoke to when the train arrived—Eberry. The cowed man who had stepped out of the train was replaced with a stiffened commander who wore malice like it was his skin.

"Paul!" Paul and Frederik exchanged glances. "There is no need for any more bloodshed, Paul. Just surrender to us, and we will leave immediately." Eberry's said wistfully.

"It's a trap!" Frederik whispered sharply.

"Most likely," Paul responded as he continued to stare at Eberry. An uncomfortable dread accumulated in his chest. What did Eberry want with him? Why was he doing this?

"Come on out, Paul. Let's talk like adults. No one else will get hurt. I promise."

"Don't do it, Paul."

Paul didn't know what to do. Whatever decision he made, someone was going to die.

"I'm going to count to three, Paul!"

Paul was afraid. With every fiber, he was terrified.

"One!"

"He'll kill you, Paul!" Frederik said.

"Two!"

Paul knew death was probable.

"Three!"

Paul stood.

"Stop!" Paul shouted as he put his hands in the air. Each soldier turned their weapon in his direction, and Paul immediately felt the intensity of their aim as he approached.

"Ahhh," Eberry began. "You are a smart man, Paul."

"Give me your word that no one else will be hurt," Paul demanded. Eberry gave a curt smile.

"Of course. As soon as you are in our custody and we have the tanks, we will pack up and leave."

Paul knew he was lying. Yet, his feet took him to the man. Paul stopped in front of him as deep anxiety birthed in his chest. Why did they want him of all people? He was a nobody. Paul held out his hands as he subjugated himself to Eberry. Eberry gave a sly smile and nodded to one of the soldiers who placed a pair of cuffs on his wrists.

"And the others, sir?" The soldier asked as he turned to Eberry. Malice kindled in Eberry's eyes.

"Wipe them out," he said simply.

"No!" Paul shouted as he lunged at Eberry. The soldier brought the butt of his weapon crashing down into his gut and pain exploded in a fury of feeling. The soldier dragged Paul forward as he choked on the need to breathe. "Run...," he croaked as the soldiers advanced into the Factory.

A deafening explosion shook the ground, and a roaring wave of energy almost knocked Paul off his feet. He turned his head in time to see another ball of fire erupt just outside the factory entrance. Soldiers and machinery flew in all directions. The remaining soldiers darted, not knowing how to respond to this sudden retaliation.

A familiar roar charged the air as smoke curled around a colossal mechanism that emerged out of the fire. The flames licked at the blackened metal, but the machine did not slow down. Another discordant explosion ruptured the battlefield as debris and bodies flew through the air.

The shock wave knocked Paul off his feet. He came up on one elbow and tried to piece together the puzzle of confusion and chaos. Eberry was waving his arms and yelling, but Paul couldn't hear him through the ringing in his head.

The tanks continued to roll towards the Factory. They did not slow down, no matter who was in their way. The ground felt like liquid underneath Paul as he watched Eberry and his men stumble away from the battle they could not win. Just as quickly as they'd arrived, the soldiers and their meager machines disappeared into the swirling debris.

The advancing tanks stopped just outside the Factory. Paul rose to his feet as pain curled up his leg from the top of his right knee. He ignored it but didn't move. He didn't know if the tanks represented friend or foe. The last time he'd seen them, they were death.

A hatch opened from the top of the nearest tank. A pair of hands appeared as a man pulled himself up.

Hob jumped from the tank and landed in a cloud of fire and smoke.

Chapter 24: Convictions

Damien, Armament

Damien's breath came in flagged gasps. He hadn't run for this long since being chased by a basilound near Briton. His vision swam in front of his eyes, and though he was only a few paces behind Sebastian, he was struggling to keep up. He cursed his weakness and pushed forward. If Sebastian wasn't slowing down, then neither was he.

"Can we take a break?" Sebastian asked over his shoulder. Relief flooded Damien.

"Yes. There's an outcropping up ahead. We can use it to hide while we rest," Damien said in between breaths. On their right was a massive blank wall, the outside of Armament. The surface stretched onward into the consuming gloom. So far, it served as a reference point as they fled through the darkness.

"An outcropping? Where? I don't see anything."

"It's there. Trust me. Just ahead."

Sebastian fell into silent confirmation. As one who'd grown up in a hostile environment, adapting to the demands of survival created in Damien certain advantages. Sebastian was a child of Axiom. He was unaccustomed to darkness.

Then again, he knew very little about Sebastian. All he knew was Damien just broke him out of prison. Prisoners weren't always guilty of wrongdoing, and Axiom's laws were infuriatingly confining, so his imprisonment could be wrong. Or, Sebastian could be a cruel, evil individual who'd committed heinous crimes who'd end up stabbing Damien in the back.

"I feel like I'm going to vomit. How much further?" Sebastian whined.

Probably not *too* heinous.

"Forthty more feet," Damien said exasperatedly.

"Do you mean forty more feet?" Sebastian corrected. Damien fumed.

"Sure."

Sebastian merely nodded. Damien's jog lessened as they approached. Hopefully, they were safe by now. They'd been running for hours. Sebastian finally saw the outcropping as he slowed to a walk and put his hands on his waist. His shoulders rose in deep, desperate gulps.

Damien, feigning resilience, picked his feet up, and rushed past him. Not until he was in front of Sebastian did he finally slow down. A huffing, mottled silence fell between them.

Damien knew they couldn't remain immobile for very long. Presently, they possessed the advantage of confusion and speed, but these assets would quickly run thin if they weren't careful. Damien considered contacting Abby, but he'd received no response the last time he'd checked in.

Either she was unable to reach him due to interference as the Lord Protector's grip tightened around their throats, or she was caught and captured. Or maybe she was just busy. Damien forced himself to trust the latter, optimistic version.

"What do we do now?" Sebastian asked. Damien was quiet. He knew where he was leading Sebastian, though he'd not informed him, and the less Sebastian knew, the better. Not satisfied with his silence, Sebastian pressed tersely. "Damien, what are we doing?"

Damien hadn't been entirely transparent. Sebastian had probably assumed they were on a desperate flee in a random direction. In reality, Damien had chosen the route purposefully. Regardless of Sebastian's importance to the resistance, Damien had to find Father James. He'd completed his assignment by breaking Sebastian out, but now it was his turn.

Damien took a few steps backward. Sebastian couldn't see very far in the dark, which meant all Damien had to do was run. Yes, it might mean Sebastian would get caught again, but the two were on different agendas, different mindsets. He'd only end up slowing Damien down. Damien knew he'd be remorseful, but his priority was finding the old man.

As if sensing Damien's departure, Sebastian stared into Damien. Damien was on the edge of Sebastian's vision, now. If he slipped behind the rock outcropping, he could get away without Sebastian knowing which direction he'd fled.

"Damien?" Sebastian's voice was hollow, scared. Damien put his hand on the rough stone and prepared to propel himself into the dark. "Please..."

Damien felt the pang of guilt—a new emotion that he was still trying to get used to—but knew this decision needed to be made. His legs tensed as he readied his body.

The landscape around them burst into life. Luminous strands of light bathed the world as a colossal image projected across the sky. The sudden disruption from dark to light made spots swim in front of Damien's eyes, but as his vision cleared, he saw the radiant source. Sebastian's headshot floated high above the land. Beneath the image was a message:

Warning! Warning! Sighting of Fugitive IC118. Citadel, Directory Sector
Wanted in connection to assault on the Directory
Wanted in connection with destruction of Hydra
Warning! Warning! Sighting of Fugitive IC118 . Citadel, Directory Sector...

Damien watched the message scroll back and forth. Sebastian's image darkened as anger creased across his face. He bared his teeth aggressively and a fiery look birthed in his eyes. The young man that Axiom displayed was a monster.

Damien looked at Sebastian. The light swam in the wells of his eyes, and fear accumulated on the furrows of his brow. Pity curled up inside Damien's chest.

"Is it true?" Damien asked. The image above them receded, and sooty darkness settled. Sebastian nodded slowly.

"Most of it," he said solemnly.

"What do you mean, most of it? Obviously, you didn't just assault the Directory, and you're not in Citadel, so what is fact and what is fiction?"

"Fiction is fact, Damien," Sebastian said mystically. Sebastian was silent for a moment. Even in the dark, Damien could see him struggling to put to words what he'd experienced. Damien started to grow impatient.

160

"Why don't you just start from the beginning?" He coaxed. "When did all of this begin?" Again, Sebastian was quiet. Damien bit his cheek and held back his irritation.

"I lost someone," he said soberly. "A friend. Though I didn't know he was my friend at the time."

Damien hesitated. "He died?" The question felt sacred. Death had always been his reality, yet this was the first time Damien had ever cared enough to ask such a question.

"Yes. His name is Sam. You were wearing his face."

It sounded like an accusation.

"That's not my fault. I didn't choose to put it on."

"I didn't say it was, Damien. Just an observation," he said coolly. A brief, stiff silence bristled between them before Sebastian continued.

"This all began when he died. His death introduced the idea that Axiom was fallible, that life in Axiom was not promised. I stood in front of the Directors, trying so desperately to believe in a system that no longer satisfied—a code of law that said I couldn't, shouldn't, be human. But, no matter how hard I tried—no matter how much I submitted to Axiom—I was left empty."

Damien understood the feeling. The echoes of recent barrenness, like a faint memory, in his mind.

"So, what did you do?" Sebastian paused and put his hands on his hips. He peered into the darkness as if seeing past the inky night.

"I gave in. I gave in to the emotional demands that weighed upon me. I tasted what was forbidden, and I was devoured." His voice trembled with passion. Damien could only guess what memories replayed in his fractured mind. "I experienced what it meant to be alive—not simply to be a conduit of nature, but to exist."

"But, this existence was brittle, fragile, and it needed to be protected, so I hid it. I tried to bring it to the Directors to help it grow, but they didn't listen. I convinced myself they were feeding me lies and corrupting what I knew to be real. They tried to tell me I was only an animal and that emotions were indecent, illogical, forbidden. I tried to set them free, to help them see there was nothing to fear, but they rejected me."

The bitterness in his voice was potent. Damien could feel the heat of his anger like it was a fire blazing into life. But, Damien could also relate. He remembered how he was tossed from Abby to Myra, rejected for trying to do what he had thought at the time was the best thing to do. Sebastian, despite his melancholy, was not much different from Damien.

"I assume you didn't just pack up your stuff and move on, right?" Sebastian shook his head.

"No. I was on fire. There was something in me that had to get out. I couldn't sit idly by while Axiom slumbered. It just didn't seem right. I knew I had to do something, anything, to wake the world." Again, Sebastian's voice radiated with intensity. Damien could feel the strength of his words. "So, I created a room—a place where people like me—people longing for freedom—could meet. What began as a place where we could think and feel as free beings became a staging ground."

"A staging ground?" Damien asked. "For what?" In the dark, a wry smile appeared on Sebastian's lips.

"Revolution." Damien did his best not to roll his eyes. Everyone wanted a revolution. It was tiresome sometimes.

"Just a guess, but I'm sure it sounded like the removal of the present rule of law, the overthrow of the tyrannous regime, and the assimilation of freedoms and rights held back from the common people?" Sebastian's eyes narrowed in the dark.

"Yes…?"

"Thought so. Was it successful?"

Sebastian looked away into the bleak nothingness.

"In the beginning, yes. Word began to spread, and soon we were almost one hundred strong—"

"—Wait a minute. You said all of this happened recently. Do you mean to tell me you amassed a following of over one hundred people who wanted to join you in this crusade in that short of a time? How did *you* manage that?"

"Almost one hundred, but yes. Many struggled with the same desires I struggled with. The whole time, they'd just been waiting for the opportunity to feel. For someone to come forward and call them out of hiding."

"That's impressive," Damien reflected.

"Hardly. It didn't amount to anything. The whole time, the Lord Protector knew. He knew what we were trying to do. He knew, and he watched," Sebastian said with hollow despair.

Damien wondered why. Why did the Lord Protector sit back and watch Sebastian unfold his plans? Was it to see what Sebastian would do? Was he analyzing Sebastian like a specimen in a lab? Or was he a predator watching his prey?

"And then, he acted on what he saw," Sebastian said sorrowfully. Damien could see, from the way horror dripped from Sebastian's face, the Lord Protector's terrifying response.

"What did he do?"

Sebastian looked up.

"He destroyed Hydra. I tried to stop him, but I was no match for his power. The whole time I believed I could defeat him and save everyone." Sebastian was conquered. Damien could hear it in his voice. "I was a fool. And because of me, hundreds of people are dead. So yes, I am to blame. I committed the crime. Because I gave into what was forbidden and poisoned the minds of others, I infected Axiom. Now, it is a lawless land of destruction and violence."

Damien rolled his eyes this time.

"So, you're to blame for the power outages, the violence tearing Axiom apart, the slave compound within Axiom, as well as all the deaths caused by the destruction of Hydra?" Sebastian didn't respond. "And I assume you're also to blame because I was imprisoned and tortured by a lunatic?"

"I don't know," he said lowly.

"Exactly! I don't know you, Sebastian, and I'm not sure I'm one to give sage advice, but I am not from Axiom. I'm from the outside—from the Scar—and one thing I have learned throughout my life is that the world is full of evil people who are willing to do evil things so good people will feel like it was their fault. Now, I don't know if you're innocent from all of it, but Axiom was sick long before you caused the fever."

Damien couldn't believe the words were coming from his mouth. In the past, he'd have told people like Sebastian to suck it up and move on.

"It's because of me that hundreds are dead. I have their blood on my hands."

"Everyone has blood on their hands, Sebastian. You just have to wash it off," he said bluntly.

"How? I tried to fix things. I set aside my rigid logic and took up the fluidity and freedom of emotions. But, to what end? What did it gain? I am more lost than I was before. Instead of wading through what I was feeling and trying to figure it out, I brought others down into the mess with me. What am I supposed to do now? I can't fix this."

Damien knew the answer. There was nothing Sebastian could do to reverse what the Lord Protector had put in motion. There was nothing he could do to bring the dead back to life. But, Damien knew that Sebastian was aware of this. He was asking what he was supposed to do to come out from under the blame, the guilt.

Damien could point to a distinct moment when his guilt and remorse, his shame, was not only lifted but repurposed in such a way that it became his strength. He could even convey to Sebastian how he, too, could find purpose in pain. But, his tongue didn't want to speak the words. The conversation was already awkward, with its intensity and vulnerability. There was no sense in making it worse.

"I don't know, Sebastian. But, I do know you'll just have to find peace within yourself. Maybe find a balance between logic and emotion. Like a compromise." The suggestions sounded trite and pathetic. They were a bandage on a gushing wound. "This has been a...lovely conversation, but we need to keep moving. We don't want to stay in one spot for very long," he suggested. It took a second for the words to penetrate Sebastian's wall of self-pity, but eventually, he nodded in return.

With Sebastian's acceptance, Damien turned and started walking. Sebastian followed suit close at Damien's heels. To help him out, Damien activated light on his manipulor. He dimmed it so that it didn't give away their position but made sure it was strong enough for Sebastian to follow. The two young men walked in steady, rhythmic silence.

"Where are we going?" The question caught Damien off guard after long minutes of cloaked silence. Damien bit his tongue. Should he disclose to Sebastian the nature of his plan, or should he remain ambiguous and vague?

"I'm part of the Hajj—the rebellion—Sebastian. And you aren't the only part of my mission." The words sounded more ridiculous than he intended. "Like I said when I busted you out, my goal is to find the old man," he responded.

"Do you know the way?"

"Generally," Damien flaunted.

"Then I'm generally sure you are aware that we are not going the right way?" Damien cursed under his breath.

"I'm taking a long way," he responded.

"I see," Sebastian said. Damien's irritation festered.

"Fine. What's the best route?" He asked irritably.

"I could show you on your manipulor. Just let me see it," Sebastian suggested as he pointed. Damien didn't like the idea of handing over his manipulor.

"Why don't you just show me on yours?" Sebastian looked crestfallen.

"My father took it from me. Right before he tried to kill me," Sebastian said sadly.

"Well, I killed my mother, so that makes my life worse. Can we move on and get to the part where you're showing me how to get to the old man?" Damien said through gritted teeth. Damien was tired of Sebastian's downcast, depressed attitude. It was exhausting. Sebastian gave him a wide-eyed, shocked look, but Damien didn't care.

"Sure... Let me see your arm." Damien extended it. Sebastian moved closer but then hesitated as he frowned down at Damien's manipulor. Suddenly self-conscious, Damien withdrew his hand.

"What's wrong?"

"Nothing. I was just thinking about what happened last time I touched your arm." Damien could still see the shards of light dancing before his eyes.

Damien felt a resounding loss.

A memory took form in his mind, dug up by the light. Myra was standing in a circle of warm radiance, inviting him to come inside. He remembered her forehead on his chest, her arms around him. Such a sweet embrace felt like a distant remembrance, now. Damien felt the absence of her presence like a weight around his heart.

In the room, what did it say?" Damien asked steadily. Sebastian was silent. "Is it something bad?" Damien asked with a little more eagerness.

"No."

"Then what is it?"

"It doesn't matter. Let's keep moving," he said as he turned back around.

"No. You need to tell me what you saw, Sebastian," Damien said sternly.

"Do not be afraid, for I am with you," Sebastian relented. The words plummeted down Damien's spine as goosebumps erupted all over his body. Elation and fear mingled together into an intimate euphoria. Damien had heard those words before. Words that were like food to him. Judging from Sebastian's reaction, he, too, had seen them in the past. But his response was not the same as Damien's.

"You've seen them before?" Damien inquired.

Sebastian nodded.

"Yes." Damien didn't fully comprehend. Sebastian seemed upset, not the intoxicating joy that Damien was feeling.

"What do they mean?"

"They're nonsense. Given to me by the old man many cycles ago." Sebastian turned his gaze to the massive wall that represented Armament. "I met him here, in Armament. He pretended to know me, and then he gave me a book." Damien listened raptly.

"What was in the book?"

"My demise. The words led me to...to this," he said with arms outstretched. "It all started with those words—an empty promise telling me that I wasn't alone anymore. But, it was a lie. All I've ever been is alone."

"Do you honestly think this is all about you? There is a fight going on much bigger than yourself," Damien began in a low whisper. They were approaching the edge of the Armament. The vast building that seemed to stretch on forever was nearing a corner. Damien didn't know what was beyond and feared their voices might alert a patrol. "I get it. You feel lost."

"I doubt you do, Damien. Everything I have ever believed in has amounted to nothing. Axiom is my home, but I don't know if I can live within in its walls anymore," Sebastian said melodramatically.

"That's dumb. I used to trust luck and chance, but now I think it's no coincidence that the old man—the same old man I need to find—gave you that book. There're too many things that don't make sense. Do you have any idea how the book was projected? You don't have a manipulor, and yet the words were still conjured—as if they were a part of you. As if you are the display. Does that not make you wonder? Do you not want to know the answers?"

Sebastian sighed and shook his head.

"I don't know if I want answers anymore," he resigned. Damien didn't respond as they neared the corner. The vast building ended in a fine point. Damien held up his hand and approached the edge. He peered around, hoping to see another stretch of an empty landscape, but was dismayed to see a whole platoon of Enforcers lined up in rows.

The Enforcers stood motionless as one unit boarded a train humming above the tracks. Judging from how slow the process was developing, it would take a long time for the area to clear. Damien felt Sebastian's presence as he, too, joined him at the corner.

"Doesn't look like we'll be going that way. Any ideas?"

"Yeah. Some. I'm not too well versed with the area, but I know of another route. It would actually be quicker."

Damien turned sharply and glared at Sebastian.

"Then why haven't we taken it?" He asked irritably. Sebastian looked away.

"It cuts through Industry." Damien still didn't understand. Why wouldn't they go the shortest route? It made the most sense.

"There's no other option. Now, show me the way." Damien didn't leave any room for arguing as he extended his wrist. Sebastian glared at him but otherwise complied. Careful not to touch his arm, Sebastian typed in a set of commands into his manipulor. Once he was finished, an arrow appeared above his wrist that pointed away from the Enforcers.

"Excellent. Let's go," Damien stated abruptly as he led the way into the darkness.

Chapter 25: E64

Abby, Citadel, The Directory

"We're safe. For now," E64 said unenthusiastically as he held out his hand. Abby took it and allowed him to pull her up. She stared into his visor, wondering what look was in his eyes.

"But we can't stay long. We need to keep moving," he suggested. As soon as the words left his mouth, Abby felt dizzying pain travel up her arm. She looked down at her hand and saw drops of blood pooling at her feet.

"Ow," she said weakly. The Paraclete looked down, too.

"Let me see," he said. Abby hesitated. Here was a man who was more monster than human. Yet, his hands were gentle. "Looks deep, but probably not very damaging. Let me clean it and bandage it up."

Abby nodded as her gaze wandered. The room they'd made it to was not like the rest of the Directory. It wasn't made of stone, nor did it look old. The walls glistened with a newness only Axiom provided, which meant they were in a created room, a room designed by will.

Her attention kept moving as she saw the makeshift bed in the corner. Beside the cot was a stack of thin books, one of which was open. She approached it as E64 moved about the room, gathering supplies for the cut on her hand. The book was old and faded, and part of the page was torn.

At first, she thought the words were simply gibberish. She'd read many books as Director, but what she was seeing was more symbolic than literature. But, the more she looked, the more she understood what the lines and marks meant.

Music.

Abby looked up and into the face of E64. He'd taken off his helmet and was staring at her with a melancholy, tortured look of uncertainty. There were cascading melodies of meaning in his eyes.

"Is he alive?" E64 asked softly. Abby's heart dropped.

"Is who alive?" She didn't have to ask, though. She knew what he wanted to know. Abby watched the man struggle to breathe, to break.

"Is Sebastian alive?"

Abby's gut tightened. This could be a trap. The only way she would know whether or not he was alive was if she worked for Hajj. By confirming her knowledge, Abby would be implicating herself. Was the man in front of her asking as a father or asking as the Paraclete? Abby didn't know, and she wouldn't know if it was a mistake until too late.

"I don't know what you're talking about," she deflected. The heat was rising in her throat.

"I know who you are, Director," he began irritably, "and I have known for a while." Abby's head swam, and she felt faint, but she maintained her presence. If he wanted to arrest her, the Paraclete would have done so already. E64's complexion softened. "Please, I need to know. Is my son okay?"

Abby softened.

"Sebastian is alive. The last I knew, he was near Bastille." E64's eyes lowered.

"He was caught? What about everything I've seen about possible sightings?"

Abby chewed on the inside of her cheek. One wrong word and she could blow the cover of everyone involved. The earnestness of E64 moved her, though. She saw the dark circles under his eyes, the unshaven patches on his jaw, and the furrow of his brow. He was not the Paraclete.

"We got him out." Abby saw relief in E64's eyes. The man stepped backward and steadied himself against a table. "That's all I can say," Abby provided.

"I understand." A steady silence fell between them. So many questions swirled in her head. Why was he helping out the Lord Protector? What was the purpose of accusing all those people and bringing them to trial?

Abby wanted answers, but E64 transfixed his gaze upon the ground in front of him. She resolved to giving him his space. Abby's eyes wandered, again, as she continued investigating the room. Distant booms sounded, but they sounded like they were from another world entirely. Indeed, the room was not part of the Directory, so she assumed they were safe. She glanced back down at the music, and with clarity, the pieces all fell into place.

"You live here, don't you?" E64 looked up.

"Yes. Let me have your hand," E64 said bluntly. He started to dab at it with a clean cloth. Abby felt the sting roll up and down her arm. The pain gave way to comfort as he wound the bandage around the wound, applying the right pressure and gentleness when needed.

"Why?"

E64 shrugged. "I am alone," he said somberly. He looked at Abby with a watery stare. "Finished. I'm not a Medic, but I know you'll need to rest it for a few days. I have an assumption that the Hospital will be too busy for a small wound like that," he said with shadowy humor.

"Thank you, E64."

"It's Richard. No sense hiding, now. There are no more laws after this, so it won't matter if you know, Director."

"Ab—Ariel. Ariel Florence," Abby said as her face went red. She'd almost slipped out her real name, and that would have been a deadly mistake no matter how trustworthy Richard was. "So, this room connects to the Library, I assume?" Richard nodded as Abby changed the subject. "And I'm sure it comes out in the Music Room, right?" Again, Richard dipped his head.

"Yes. I'm waiting on the thunder to stop. From my assumptions, the fires would have taken down the east and south sides of the Directory, but probably not the north and west end. The Library, though, is almost directly in the middle, so there's no way of knowing if the collapse went that far," he remarked evenly.

"Well, it's been a couple of minutes since the last noise. What if we looked?"

"Alright," Richard said as he pushed himself off the table and grabbed his helmet. Together, they approached the far wall. Richard placed his palm on the surface as a small slit appeared. He waited, watching to see if flames fed on the new source of oxygen. No orange tongues leaped at them, so he enlarged the gap until it was a doorway.

"Let me go first," Richard suggested as he pulled his weapon from his hip. It hummed in his hand as he went through the open space. Abby watched him enter into the smoky darkness of the Music Room until his red outline disappeared around a corner.

Abby was alone and felt the loneliness soak into her. She wanted desperately to be with her father and knew he was probably frantic. However, she feared most what Lorenzo was going to do in response to this attack. The man was everything but forgiving.

Death was everywhere. It wasn't just out in the Scar or secreted away in the Slave Compound. It was in the walls that came crashing down. It was at the end of a gun pointed at people she knew. It wasn't a whisper anymore. It was a reality.

Since she was born, Abby had been groomed to be her mother. Her father trained and raised to infiltrate the system, erode Axiom from within, and remove Lorenzo for good. Along the way, Abby had her moments of rejection—of wanting to be free of the responsibility and the burden of resisting a world she'd never freely walked as herself.

But, she'd remained steadfast and compliant. Abby did her best to live up to the sacrifices her parents made, to live up to the life her mother surrendered. So, Abby adorned her mask and paraded around as Director Florence. She built a network of defense measures. She infiltrated Axiom.

For what result?

Axiom was coming undone. Something had irreparably shattered. She could still feel the gusts of violence buffet her body as the Directory crumbled behind her. Abby had never been close to death, but in those moments, death was close to her. Her whole body shook as the adrenaline wore off. Fatigue and heavy sorrow settled into her bones.

Could she honestly live up to what her parents expected of her? What was once solid resolve was now splintered doubt. It may have been the resistance that struck and brought the

Directory tumbling down, but it was the Lord Protector who made such violence possible. No matter what happened, he would win. That fact was heavier than all the stones in the Directory combined.

"We're clear. Follow me and watch your step," Richard stated as he came back into view. His red suit bathed the walls in the color of blood. Abby nodded and trailed in his wake.

The air smelled of ash, and dust swam in clouds. Shafts of red light poured through cracks in the ceiling, but the stones didn't shift as they walked through the gloom. Abby's foot collided with an object on the ground, and she looked down.

Abby saw the faint light gleam dully off metal. It was bent and warped where the fire tried to devour it, but otherwise, the musical instrument was intact. Still, though, the sight of it lying on the ground in ashes made Abby somber.

Eventually, the two of them made their way to the Library. Abby's heart sank once they stepped into the vast room. Most of the shelves had capsized. Books lay in heaps, broken and burned. She was standing in a graveyard, and it was the imagination that had become the corpse. Abby's heart tugged at her. She wanted to stay here, to sift through the ashes, to find the words that remained.

The Paraclete held up his fist.

"Hold up." Abby stopped and watched the arcs of light sweep back and forth.

"Enforcers?" Abby whispered.

"No idea. It could be the other guys. Best if you hide," Richard suggested. Abby slipped behind a teetering bookshelf. She watched Richard take a couple of steps forward to distance himself from her hiding spot.

"Halt," he demanded, "state your name and classification," Richard commanded in a gruff tone. The two beams of light bathed Richard in a white glow. Richard remained motionless. She could see his hand gripping his weapon firmly.

"Preva 287B and Preva 314C," one of the men shouted. A flicker of relief sparked in Abby.

"Good to see you. I'm the Paraclete. Are you Enforcers alone?" The Paraclete probed.

"Yes, sir. We were sent in to notify any Enforcers that we're pulling out."

"Pulling out? Why? What about the attackers? Are they still in the building?" The edge of fear in Richard's voice made Abby uncomfortable. Abby could see the mottled, sweaty face of one of the Prevas.

"The fugitive—1C118—has been spotted, and we're being reassigned to this priority. As for the attackers, most of them were either killed by the building collapsing or chased away during the firefight," the Preva said triumphantly.

"I see. Did anyone else get out? Any of the Directors?" Abby held her breath.

"Some got out. An attacker assaulted the Atrium and killed a couple of them, but a Preva subdued the assailant."

Abby's breath eased out of her with relief. The sorrow of loss was still there, though, knowing some of her fellow Directors were dead.

"Okay. I hate to say it, but the way behind me is completely blocked off. There are no more survivors on this side of the Directory," Richard said calmly. Abby's heart skipped a beat. "But, I haven't looked into the north end of the Directory. Perhaps there are more survivors there," he offered.

"Yes, sir. We'll give it a brief check, but our orders are to get out sooner rather than later."

"Understood. I hope those who are still here understand how much we tried looking for them. I hope they know how much we wanted to find them," Richard said ambiguously.

Abby knew this message was for her. The Prevas responded with silence. "Well, let's be off, gentlemen. It's time we caught 1C118," he said woefully. Abby watched them leave. Once the lights disappeared into the sooty dark, a silent weariness settled into her bones. She waited a few more minutes before she crept out from behind her hiding place.

Abby's head was spinning as fatigue languished her body. She took steadying breaths and headed for the exit. As she walked, tears slipped silently down her cheeks, though she didn't know for what she mourned. Perhaps all of it. Perhaps none of it. Her manipulor glowed a confusing mosaic of colors as it interpreted her pain.

When Abby pushed through the door, cool air welcomed her. Her face felt haggard and dry as the air caressed her skin. She walked numbly, allowing her feet to take her where her mind was too weighed down to follow. Eventually, she was far enough away from the Directory to turn around and see the demise of the once distinguished building.

More tears sprang to Abby's eyes. The Directory was in ruins, a broken reminder of what Axiom had become. Fortitude loomed above the desecrated building. Abby took a steadying breath. Axiom was broken, but she could fix it—they could fix it. This was what she was born to do—to reverse the grip of tyranny and to bring wholeness to Axiom.

But, Abby knew she could no longer do this as Director Florence. Her next decisions would have to be as Abigail Florence, and no matter what she did, Abby knew it would cost her everything.

Chapter 26: The Farm

Myra, Agriculture Protectorate, The Lake Sector

Myra watched the erratic rise and fall of Markus's chest. He was unconscious, his face flashing between moments of pain and stillness. Honestly, it was the moments when he was tranquil that she worried the most.

It had been over two days since he was hurt, and now his breathing was ragged. Myra knew if they didn't get medical help soon, his blood was going to become toxic. She'd seen it plenty of times amongst the slaves as incurable wounds turned foul and deadly. In the end, it was a slow, agonizing death.

Theo, help him. Please!

The muted response tore at her. Myra wanted confirmation—tangible hope. She wanted Markus to be healed. She knew she needed to trust Theo—in his timing and his ways.

But, could she trust Theo if Markus died?

Myra didn't know the answer anymore.

"My?" Markus said as he stirred with a groan. His makeshift stretcher bounced and swayed as the two men—Jacob and Tyler—carried him forward. Myra was at his side as she leaned in to hear his whispered, strained words.

"Yes, Markus?" Her voice shimmered with emotion.

"Are we there yet?" He asked with a hint of a smile that birthed another volley of pain.

"I'm not sure, Markus. Do you need anything?"

Markus bobbed up and down as the two men holding him walked. The caravan of slaves had been walking for what felt like ages. To Myra, though, it was a blur. She hadn't left Markus's side since he slipped into a fitful rest. The whole time, Myra clasped his hand. Like an anchor that held her by his side, it was a comfort to Myra.

"A back rub. And tell them that their driving is terrible." Both Tyler and Jacob displayed small grins. A stiff silence fell between them. Markus had yet to open his eyes.

"Seriously, Markus. What can I do?" His brow furrowed in concentration. Markus chanced the opportunity to open his eyes. Pain swirled within their glassy depths. Myra's heart sank. There was no child behind those eyes.

"How much longer, My? Where is *he* leading us?"

Myra knew Markus was referring to Adam. She glanced past Markus and to the young man who stood almost ten paces away from the rest of the group. He clutched his staff in his hand, and he walked with a sense of purpose. He neither looked behind him to observe the slaves, nor did he look side to side for danger. Markus didn't trust Adam, and despite herself, his pessimism towards Adam was starting to shape Myra's views.

"To the tunnels, Markus. I told you that already. Don't you listen?" She teased emptily.

"Sometimes. I don't know about him, My. We could be going in circles, and we'd never know until it was too late," he said cynically. Myra shook her head.

"I'll go pick his brain. Since you want me to."

"That's assuming he has a brain, Myra. He's a farmer. His mind is made of fluff."

"You're made of fluff, Markus. Stop fretting like an old woman and let me go ask."

"Yes, mother. I'll go back to my crocheting and sleepless nights," he said sardonically.

"Cry-baby. I'll be right back."

Myra let go of his hand and departed. She felt the warmth of his grip leave her as she walked away. She also felt the exhaustion settle into her bones. Their jesting did little to abate the ebb and flow of her anxiety and concern. Myra did her best to stuff it down, to cast it aside, as she quickened her pace. When she drew up next to him, Adam did not immediately acknowledge her presence. The two walked in nimble silence.

"You're probably wondering where we are?" Adam said in a low voice.

"Yes, Adam. We've been walking for a long time. Are we close to our destination?" Adam answered with another long pause. His staff dug into the ground with each step and made a grating sound with each strike. Myra bit her cheek. "It's just my people are exhausted, and Markus isn't doing very well. We need to get him to a doctor sooner rather than later."

"We'll be there soon," he said cryptically.

"How soon?" Myra asked with a testiness in her voice.

"We've been following the shoreline for almost a cycle. The tunnels are not far from here. We are approaching the Greenhouse Sector, and we'll rest then. I'm sorry it's taken so long, but we've had to go around some critical points where I assumed sentries and drones would be patrolling."

Myra felt a pang of guilt.

"Thank you, Adam. I know we present a great danger to you. You have no idea how grateful I am," she said softly.

"Of course." Resolute silence gathered like dust. She didn't depart from his side, though. The two of them walked without speaking for minutes, and Myra's mind began to wander. She occasionally glanced over at Adam, but the young man was inscrutable, even in the light. Finally, discontent with the silence, she spoke.

"Do you have a family, Adam?" His face coiled slightly.

"We aren't permitted the right to have a family," he said hollowly. Myra was dumbfounded.

"Aren't permitted?"

"No. It's not allowed—illegal."

"Why?" Adam merely shrugged.

"I don't ask questions, Myra."

Myra was sad for him. The idea of such an existence was empty. Even her relationship with Theo would be without dimension, lifeless without those around her to share it.

"So, you're alone?"

"Not having a family doesn't mean I'm alone," Adam responded disdainfully.

"I'm sorry. I didn't mean to insinuate." Adam sighed.

"Don't worry about it. How would you know about how my world works?"

"How does it work, Adam?"

178

"Very simply. I work in a Unit. We cultivate the soil and harvest the crops. We are the caretakers of the earth," he said fondly. "Without us, Axiom would starve. Something that goes ignored," Adam pointed out as he switched to bitterness. Myra felt the frustration but let him continue in his seething. "And ever since Hydra ruptured, nothing has been the same," he said ambiguously. Myra could hear the fear in his tone.

"What do you mean?"

"Nothing," he said curtly. Myra didn't push. She could tell he wasn't in the mood to elaborate. "We're here," he said as they eclipsed a hill.

Adam turned off his staff as the two of them looked down onto the shallow valley below. Numerous structures dotted the landscape. They were shaped like long tubes rounded on the top. Darkness shrouded many of the buildings, but some flickered with a pale, white light shown through opaque walls. An eerie stillness rested on the area like a fog.

"What is this place?" Myra whispered. She was afraid she'd break the unsettling silence.

"We call it The Farm," Adam stated with a strained tone. "Let's go. Food and water in those greenhouses." Adam pushed forward down the hill towards The Farm. Myra followed as a penetrating dread began to accumulate in her chest.

As Adam and Myra approached the first derelict greenhouse, a chill ran down Myra's spine.

"What happened here?" She asked in a whisper.

"Enforcers. It looks like they took what they wanted."

"Food?"

"People," he said bluntly. A hollow, sinking feeling settled in Myra's gut.

"That's evil."

"That's Axiom." Adam's voice carried a nuance Myra didn't quite understand, but that made her uneasy none the less. "There should be food in those greenhouses over there," he said as he pointed, "and over there should be clean water. Inform your people that they need to remain quiet. The tunnels are just over there," Adam said as he pointed into the darkness. Myra couldn't see anything but trusted him at his word.

"Thank you, Adam. I'll let the others know." Adam silently nodded as Myra pulled away. As soon as she reconnected with the rest of the column of slaves, she handed out the instructions. Everyone was elated about reaching a spot to rest and replenish their stomachs.

Myra was still on edge, though. Something about the empty greenhouses, with their flickering lights and milky walls, creeped her out. She was brought out of her anxiety by a low moan. In a moment, she was at Markus's side.

"We're here, Markus. The tunnels are just over there," she said with forced enthusiasm as she pointed. His eyes did not open, and his face was a pallid mask of agony. She lifted his bandages and glanced at the wound. The edges of the wound were turning gray, and she knew that irreversible decay was already settling into his body. With deep, resounding sadness, Myra put the dressing back on the wound and brought a flask of water to his lips. "Drink a little, Markus."

Markus did his best to lift his head. Water spilled from his cracked lips and dribbled down his chin. Myra watched his lips eventually open and receive some of the water. She tilted the flask back as a small hope birthed in her heart. A sudden choking noise broke her hope as Markus started to sputter and spit out the water.

"Sorry!" Myra brought the flask back down. She quickly dabbed at Markus's lips, trying to help him not get soaked. Deep, penetrating despair started to creep in, but Myra fought it. She focused instead on cleaning Markus. It was strange to be this close to him, again, as comfort spread through her.

Silent grief interrupted and bore down upon her shoulders. Myra didn't want to think about him, but no matter how hard she tried to forget about Damien, he was in her thoughts. She didn't want to think about him because she knew she'd made a mistake. Myra could still feel the lever's cold metal under her hand as she sealed his fate—as she sent him hurtling into the darkness. Myra had been angry when she did it, and now she just felt the emptiness of his presence.

"You like what you see?" Markus said with a chuckle. Myra snapped to attention as Markus's face came into focus. She hadn't realized she was aimlessly staring at him.

"How are you feeling?" Myra said softly.

"Other than having to prevent myself from drowning, I'm wonderful," he said mockingly. Myra smirked at him.

"Honestly?" His eyes narrowed.

"Don't ask. I'll be fine. I promise. Did you say that we're near the tunnels?" Myra nodded.

"I'm going to go and tell the others. Okay?"

"Oh, don't worry about me. I'll be here. Miserably wasting away." Myra rolled her eyes, but as she walked away, she couldn't help but fear that Markus was speaking the truth.

Chapter 27: The Good Physician

Mary, Medical Protectorate, Radiant

Mary carried the tray with both hands. She kept her eyes forward as she passed each patient—each victim--trying her best not to see the lifeless, pallid bodies. Mary tried to ignore the smell of humans wasting away. She tried to ignore the steady drip of sedatives and medicines that poured into their bodies—allowing chemicals to stall death.

Mary wanted to ignore the low moans of some who were on the edge of consciousness. She tried to forget that their muscles were eroding, atrophying. She did her best not to see the sunken faces eaten alive by hunger.

But, there was no way to ignore it all.

There was no way not to care.

No matter how hard she tried to "just do her job," Mary felt the task cut into her like needles. Each face she passed haunted her. Each life she walked by was a life she felt like she was taking. But what was she supposed to do?

The only thing that she had the power over was their comfort, and towards this, she worked tirelessly. There were so many whose food supply wasn't keeping up with their metabolic rate. She saw gaunt faces that were slipping into rapid malnourishment. She saw hollowed-out cheeks of adults. Young men and women. Children.

Then, there was sanitation. Thus far, the routine was the bare minimum. Each bed was a stench of unwashed clothes, soiled undergarments, clogged catheters.

The catharsis from the other Mothers was so significant that she doubted they cared about the patients. There was no need, no prerogative amongst the other Mothers, to go above and beyond. Aside from when Doctor Clauberg or the Head Mother was present, the other women scraped by on the minimum requirement. Mary enjoyed their company—their friendship—but the way they casually handled the human beings in Radiant disturbed her.

"How are our patients today?" A young man asked as he approached. Mary's eyes traveled to the crisp, toothy smile and hungry stare of Doctor Clauberg. He wore a stethoscope around his neck, and his clothes were stiff as they sculpted his upper body. "Are they comfortable and taken care of, Mother Mary?" He asked with a heavy dose of concern behind a mask of compassion. Mary felt his deceptiveness.

"The patients need better care, Doctor Clauberg," Mary responded bitterly.

"And that is exactly why you are here, Mother Mary. You provide such a pivotal role in the process of providing top of the line comfort and care for our patients here at Radiant," he said whimsically. Mary wanted to roll her eyes, but the anger was brewing beneath her skin. Her manipulor pulsed an aggressive amber tone.

"You mean we provide comfort while they are killed, correct?" The question came out of her mouth before she could stop it. Before she could push it down and bury it next to her pain, next to her fears, alongside the deadened emotions and the corrosive anxieties festering like open wounds—the words tumbled from her lips. Doctor Clauberg's face darkened.

"Now, Mother Mary, let's be reasonable. These patients," he indicated with a wave of his hand, "are vital to the success and advancement of the human race. Everyone here is a participant in a grand gesture of sacrifice and devotion for their fellow man. They *volunteered* for these positions," he said earnestly. Mary was finding it very difficult to believe him.

"So, no one is here, coercively?"

"Absolutely not, Mother Mary. Radiant is a respectable establishment," he said as if he was offended. "These people understand their role. After all, everyone has a role, Mother Mary. And yours is to take care of my patients," Doctor Clauberg said with open hands.

Despite the feigned attempt at genuineness, Mary got the point. Her job was to ensure these people were drained of their life energy and not ask questions about it. "Now, I have significant work to do, Mother. Some new patients need to be received and incorporated into the program. I will check in on you over the next few cycles to make sure you are adjusting appropriately to this position."

The threat hung just above his glistening lips. "And remember, Mother—let's put a Radiant smile on our face." Mary's lips pursed and broke into a forced smile. With a curt nod, Dr. Clauberg departed. The indignation in Mary's blood boiled as she watched him go.

"Have a nice chat with the good Doctor?" Mother Veronica probed as she suddenly appeared at Mary's elbow. Her abrupt arrival caught Mary off guard.

"What did you guys talk about, eh? Anything juicy?" Mother Tess asked with a sly grin.

Mary looked at the young faces of the girls around her. In their presence, amidst their youthful enthusiasm, she was much older than all of them. Her age was sifted and filtered through the girls. Indeed, she could still see in their eyes the hope and expectations that were drained from her like an open wound. Their faces were glowing, beaming, hungry.

In many ways, the girls looked up to Mary, though Mary did little to warrant such attention. As they hung on her arm, looking for answers, Mary felt the weight of their curiosity.

"I was simply voicing my opinion on matters," she responded vaguely. Mary knew she had to be careful. She did not understand why she'd been placed in Radiant, but she was hesitant about including others in on her frustrations.

If the Head Mother, discovered she was causing unrest, then she'd report Mary. She was already second guessing her outburst. Even as she recalled her bitter words, she felt the weariness settle into her bones as the fires dissipated.

"And what are those opinions, Mother Mary?" Mother Tess asked in a tone Mary couldn't place.

"Just the usual. Needing more supplies and such. Requiring better care for the patients." The word—*patients*—felt unpleasant on her tongue. They were lambs, and Dr. Clauberg was a predator.

"Oh come, now, Mama Mary," Mother Tess flapped, "We all know there is much more to complain about in Radiant. If we just started off with the food itself, we'd be here all day," she said with a short laugh.

"Yes, tell us," Mother Veronica chipped in. "We haven't had anything to talk about lately!" Mary knew they weren't going to relent.

Mary opened her mouth to speak but then saw something out of the corner of her eye that caught her attention. Mary's brow creased together as she watched a man exit Patient Intake and walk across the Main Floor. Even though he was at a distance and obscured by a shadowy helmet, his gait was recognizable.

"Excuse me. I have to go," Mary said abruptly. She shrugged the girls off her shoulders and hurried towards the man clad in red-rimmed armor heading towards the exit. She felt her legs pick up their pace as he reached for the handle.

"Stop!" She commanded sharply. The man froze with his hand on the door handle as his back went rigid. Mary felt a flurry of competing emotions brew in her chest.

"Turn around," she whispered. The man didn't move. But, she needed to see his face. "Turn around, Richard." With great hesitation in his movements, E64 turned.

As if knowing she'd ask him anyway, he reached for his mask and tapped a button on the side. His visor revealed deep, shadowed eyes and cheeks hollowed and gaunt. A cut, crusted and inflamed, hung just above his brow.

"P31," E64 said flatly.

"You will call me by my name," Mary said briskly. A rebuke flashed in his eyes, but then that spark became a trail of smoke. Her gaze traveled over his armor, over the dents and the scratches, over the wounds. She saw a symbol etched into the shoulder piece—a winged staff jeweled with an all-seeing eye and two serpents wrapped around the staff handle.

The Paraclete.

Mary's disappointment deepened. She barely recognized the man in front of her. She wondered if he even recognized himself. She recalled their last conversation—the one where she reached out in vulnerability, in hope. Richard's response had been cold and cruel, but it taught her a lesson. She couldn't trust her emotions—even if they were powerful. No, she had to mask them behind her bitterness and cynicism. It was the only way.

"Why did you assign me to Radiant?" She asked with grave accusation. It had taken her a couple of cycles of wondering and pondering, but as soon as she'd seen him, Mary knew. She wasn't in Radiant by accident.

Somebody had put her here, boxed her in, hemmed her in like a prisoner. The only person who had the power to do so was the man staring into her with deep, haunted eyes.

"I did what I needed to do," he said softly.

"What you needed to do? You mean, what was convenient for you? Get me out of the way, and you can do whatever you want, right?" His lips formed a hard line.

"You have no idea what I want," Richard said lowly. Mary smirked as her blood boiled. She wanted to smack him, to incite him to passion and fury, anything other than his exhausted words. "And you have no idea what I've had to do."

"I know what you've done. I know every single face you have condemned to death. I know all your victims, Paraclete," she bit at him. She could see the remaining color fall from his face. A heavy, choked silence grew between them. Mary felt the sour words gather on her lips. "You are not the man I love anymore. You're a monster, Richard."

Mary's words weighed the Paraclete's shoulders down.

"I know," Richard responded solemnly.

Despite herself, Mary felt sickened tears rising to her eyes. She just wanted him to respond, be angry, and send a volley of words and accusations, but his barrels were empty.

"Where is our son, Richard?" His face flushed with color. "Is he okay?" Richard took a deep, calming breath.

"He's safe," he provided. Despite herself, despite her anger, her cynicism, Mary believed him.

"Where is he?"

Richard's face fell.

"I don't know." An uneasy silence fell as Richard chewed on the inside of his cheek. Mary felt a desperate anxiety bubble in her throat. "But, you can't go looking for him. I need you to keep your head down." Mary felt a flash of anger.

"Or what? You'll punish me? You'll get them to strap me to one of these chairs?" The resentment felt good. Richard's face was crestfallen.

"Please, Mary. For Sebastian's sake, stay out of trouble. You don't know what's happening."

"Because you had me locked away." Now, it was Richard's face that bore irritation.

"I didn't lock you away. You wouldn't even understand what choices I've made," Richard said bitterly.

"I don't care, Richard. There's nothing you could say that would convince me that your hands are clean. Just look around at all this," she said as she spread out her arms. "This is you're doing. How can you live with yourself?"

Richard paused.

"I can't."

Mary almost felt sorry for him. Almost.

"Goodbye, Paraclete," Mary hissed as she turned on her heel. She walked away and didn't turn back.

As Mary walked, she felt the distance between them grow and grow. She wanted to turn back around and see if he was watching her leave but retained her straight-backed composure. There was no way she was going to listen to him. She wasn't his pet. Eventually, she heard the door behind her open and close with finality.

Would that be the last time she saw him?

Did she want it to be the last time?

Mary didn't know.

A flurry of motion brought Mary out of her musing. Her attention flew to a patient strapped to a bed only three gurneys away. For a second, she couldn't quite comprehend what was happening as the man's body twitched and spasmed erratically.

But, as soon as frothy foam appeared on his pale lips, her mind and body moved into action.

"Help!" She shouted as she ran towards her patient. Sticky anxiety clouded her thoughts as she stood over him, desperately searching for what she was supposed to do.

There was no training for this.

The foam poured from his mouth, and she could hear him choking. Her instincts took over as she pushed the Com away from the man's face and tilted his head.

The man's body jerked violently. Mary heard a snapping noise as the restraints holding the young man in place broke. The two of them spilled onto the floor as Mary took the brunt of his weight. The wind rushed from her lungs, and pain ruptured throughout her body.

"Help!" She screamed. Her eyes darted around frantically, searching for aid, but no one was coming. She maintained her grip on the young man's neck as her fingernails dug into his skin. His breathing sounded less ragged, but his eyes roved madly.

"Shhh. It's okay. I'm here. Shhh," Mary soothed as she gently patted his forehead. The young man's skin was cold and clammy. His lips were a dark shade of blue. She continued to soothe him, pulling from deep within herself the maternal nature she'd locked away.

The young man's breathing slowed, and his body relaxed in her arms.

"That's it. Shhh. Let's calm down now."

The young man's eyes stopped dancing long enough for the two of them to lock gazes. There was a childlike desperation in his stare.

"Help me," he begged.

The light disappeared from the young man's eyes. His chest heaved one last time and then fell still.

Anguish welled up in Mary as tears slid down her face.

The young man was dead.

Chapter 28: An Open Wound

Damien, Industry Protectorate, Hydra Sector

Damien had lost track of time. He followed the route on his manipulor, but even this had to be scrapped and changed throughout as they encountered patrols of Enforcers and vast stretches of red-laced surfaces—like fields oozing lava. Damien also contended with Sebastian's reluctance and hesitation. Mostly, they walked in silence as Sebastian got lost in brooding.

"What did you mean?"

"What do you mean, what did I mean?"

Sebastian glanced at Damien.

"You said that you used to trust luck and chance. What did you mean by that? What changed?" Sebastian asked.

Damien frowned. He didn't want to get into this conversation. Not because he didn't believe that Theo had changed him—he knew this without a doubt—but he still didn't understand it fully. How was he supposed to describe a transformation that he was still undergoing? He'd only end up sounding like an idiot.

But, Sebastian was still looking at him with expectation.

"I don't know. I just stopped trusting the way I used to see the world," Damien replied with a quick shrug of his shoulders. Sebastian continued walking in silence, and Damien hoped he was willing to let the answer suffice.

"What do you trust now?" Damien groaned inwardly. There was no avoiding it.

"I trust in Theo," he said with a rush of words.

"What is a Theo?"

"Theo is a person...I think." Sebastian threw him a furrowed brow.

"I'm confused."

You and me both.

"All I know is after meeting Theo, things started to change in me. I no longer needed to rely on my old way of thinking," he said reflectively. It was the first time he put into words this new reality.

A deep, uncomfortable silence settled between them.

"That doesn't make any sense, Damien," Sebastian began lowly as he walked. "How can a single person make that much of a difference?"

Damien didn't immediately respond as he chewed on the question. He grasped for an answer and tried to remember all the things he'd overheard Paul say all those days he spent with him in the mountain. If only he'd paid more attention! The heat rose in his cheeks as Sebastian continued to stare with anticipation.

"Have you ever had someone speak so powerfully into your life that what they said made it impossible for you to be the same person?" It was the best he could do. Sebastian was silent a moment. Damien watched his shoulders rise with a deep, steady breath.

"His name was Sam. He told me we had a purpose—that I had a purpose. I didn't get it at the time, but those words have never left me. I hear them sometimes—like wisps of steam. They're a reminder," he said solemnly.

"Exactly. Theo is that voice that reminds me that I have a purpose—that I'm not alone."

"I see." Sebastian was silent again. "So where is this Theo? I have never heard about him before." Damien chewed on his lip. He was growing tired of this conversation and just wanted to go back to mobile silence.

"He's everywhere. Axiom. The Scar. Everywhere." Sebastian stopped walking and turned to face Damien. His hands went to his waist, and a wry smile flicked across Sebastian's face as if he knew something Damien didn't.

"Ahhh. So, Theo is everywhere? All-seeing, I assume? All good and willing to do anything for us mere mortal and pathetic figures?" There was something in Sebastian's voice that made Damien's skin crawl.

"I mean, sure. You could say that," Damien relented.

"Thought so." Sebastian turned back around and resumed his silence. Damien struggled to find words, but the finality of the conversation was evident. Sebastian's downcast attitude and stooped shoulders were replaced with straight-backed annoyance. Damien followed him and busied himself with reading the map of their route, though this was pointless. He knew it like the back of his hand.

Eventually, Damien brought himself out of his empty distraction as he noticed a shift in the smell and taste of the air around him. The moist, muddy air was chalky on his tongue, and there was a pungent aroma of a recent fire, though the smoke had long dissipated. The ground was littered with debris and felt spongy—as if it had freshly rained and saturated the soil. It reminded Damien of the tsunamis that occurred in the Scar.

And a noise. At first, it was low and constant—so much so that Damien didn't pick it out from the background. But, eventually, it emerged from the silence. As they climbed a hill and approached the crest, it grew in volume.

"What is that?" Damien asked as Sebastian paused. At first, Sebastian didn't answer. But, as Damien drew up alongside him, Sebastian tilted his head. Damien followed his gaze to the edge of a great, frothing river that bubbled and boiled with activity. Lights lined the landscape, but even some of these were submerged. The roar was almost deafening as the river carved itself through the valley, through human structures somehow still standing as water gushed through windows. Other buildings lay in ruins as the water teemed with debris.

"What happened here?" Damien wondered. It was like a flood had swept civilization away.

"That, Damien, is what happens when you try to defy a man who is everywhere," Sebastian stated as he looked out over the valley.

Chapter 29: Disparity

Abby, Citadel, The Refuge

Abby glanced around, making sure no one followed. Angry beads of sweat dotted her forehead and gathered her hair in dirty clumps. She felt exhausted and emotionally drained but was glad to be home. She put her hand on the wall in front of her, ignoring the sensation of the red tendrils stinging her skin as she touched the surface.

For a second, nothing happened. No hidden door appeared. No pocket receded backward to allow Abby the climb into her Refuge. Her brow knitted together in fear as her eyes darted behind her, expecting dark figures to emerge from the shadows. Panic pricked at her heart. Had she been discovered?

Abby attempted to pull her hand away but could only lift it a few inches off the wall. She felt a sickening, desperate sensation scream in her chest as she yanked at her hand. Alarms sounded in her head, and fear sent hot tears down her cheeks.

A hole appeared where her hand was, and as it widened, she fell into the recess. Abby crumbled to her knees and scrambled into the safety of the small room. Hastily, she bound up the steps two at a time. Abby stumbled into her room as a vibrant, warm light enclosed her.

"Abigail?" Byron asked as he pulled his attention off of the monitors. Abby didn't respond as she ran to him. She buried her head into his chest as deep anxiety finally caught up to her. Byron stroked her head in silence. "It's okay. You're safe."

Abby remained silent. Once she was centered, she pulled away and tapped at her manipulor. Her mother's face disappeared to reveal a grief-stricken teenager.

"We were attacked, dad."

"I know. It was Horrus. The coward," he said through gritted teeth. Abby saw a fiery anger flash in his eyes. "How dare he put your life in danger. If it wasn't for me sending in reinforcements, I'm sure his forces would have overrun all of Citadel," he said spitefully.

There was something in his voice—a vindication—that Abby hadn't heard before. She remembered the dozens of Enforcers swarming the Directory—their pervasive nature as they searched and interrogated. Abby felt their accusations and the way they followed her before she'd slipped out of their grasp. It was strange to know that it was her father who'd sent them. She couldn't help but feel a confusing betrayal.

But, Abby knew the anger she heard in his voice was not just because his daughter's life had been in danger. It was something else, something more carnal rising to the surface. Her eyes scanned his face as the fire subsided.

"Are you hurt?" Abby shook her head.

"No. I was helped. By the Paraclete." Her dad gave her a darkened, confused look. "He knew. He knew who I was, dad," she said lowly. Her father's face clouded again. He leaned back against the wall and crossed his arms.

"He didn't arrest you," Byron said slowly.

"No. I don't know why not," Abby said.

"Me neither. And not knowing is troubling. What kind of leverage is he trying to build up against us?" Byron wondered.

"He only wanted to know if Sebastian was okay."

"Why?"

"Sebastian is his son."

A knowing look flashed across Byron's face.

"I see. This means he intends on using what he knows about us as leverage to obtain Sebastian," Byron suggested forebodingly. Abby shook her head.

"No. I saw a man who just wanted to know if his son was still alive. Nothing more. I didn't get the feeling that he was trying to use me."

"Perhaps, but one shouldn't rely on their feelings alone. You are prone to trust people no matter what evidence to the contrary." Abby felt the subtle sting of his words.

"I've been in this game for longer than you give me credit, Dad," she retorted. She could feel her face getting flushed with heat and exhaustion.

"Then you understand the danger. The Paraclete works directly for Lorenzo. If the Paraclete knows who we are, then it is best to assume Lorenzo knows or will know."

"Or maybe he could become an ally?" Byron was already shaking his head. "Somebody who can work for us on the inside, within Lorenzo's inner circle?"

"No. Too risky." Byron started to pace. "We may have to do something a little more drastic," he said gravely. "A little more permanent." A weight settled in Abby's stomach.

"You want to kill him? Are you serious?" The idea seemed appalling to her.

"What other option do we have?" Abby felt anger rise in her throat.

"I don't know, but murder shouldn't be one of them!" Byron's face grew ashen. Abby held his gaze, not flinching in her resolve. Her eyes searched her father, but his anger and fear were clouding his countenance. She barely recognized him. As she searched, a flashing screen behind Byron caught her eye.

"What is that?" Abby voiced as she walked past her father. Her fingers found their home and rushed over the keys. She brought the image up in front of her. Abby's mind frantically worked as she pieced together what she was seeing.

Abby designed her system so that it would pick up anyone who entered into Axiom. She knew if she didn't find them first, then the Observers would. It was how she picked up Damien the first time. Usually, the new genetic information was from a single or two people. Yet, on the screen, she recognized numerous foreign DNA sequences—a massive amount of new information clustered in the Agriculture Protectorate.

"How long has this been flashing?" Panic pulsed in her temple as Myra stared at the screen.

"Since the assault," Byron said steadily. Abby's heart plummeted. She typed frantically, watching any outgoing transmissions from the surrounding area. There were a couple of messages that got out, but she couldn't trace them to their source. She gritted her teeth. Why was there this mass of new genetic material? It didn't make sense.

Unless...

"Have we heard from Paul and his people lately?"

"No. We lost communication."

"Probably because this," she said as she pointed at the screen, "is the group of slaves." Byron drew closer and peered into the image.

"That's impossible."

"Maybe not. Please tell me you sent reinforcements to investigate this." Byron gave her a blank stare as he shook his head. "Well, who's in the area? Who can we send to pick them up before the Observers catch their scent?" Byron continued to shake his head as his lips pursed.

"I don't think you understand the gravity of our situation, Abby. Lorenzo's grip is tightening. His power, instead of being curbed and pushed back, is growing. Our people are spread thin."

"Dad, these *are* our people. How long have they helped us? We owe it to them."

"I'm sorry, Abby. It's just not possible." Byron said with a small, heavy shrug.

"We have to make it possible! We can't abandon them."

Byron drew a deep sigh.

"We have to make choices, Abby. Choices that are not easy. Choices that won't be clean. I know you may not understand this, but I have to do what is best."

And defending the defenseless is not best.

"They will be killed," she said pleadingly.

"There is nothing I can do." Abby stared into him, hoping the intensity of her sorrow would move him. It did not. "I know it's not what you want to hear, but it's the unfortunate situation we are in. Horrus acted rashly, and now I have to do cleanup before everything spirals out of control. I'm sorry, but it's the best I can do right now."

Abby could see on his face that he was genuinely sorry.

"Okay, dad."

A melancholy silence enveloped them both. Abby felt like something intangible had been lost.

"You must be hungry?" Byron suggested. Even as he spoke, a wave of fatigue and hunger washed over Abby. She felt weak and steadied herself on the computer display.

"Yeah. I am. Could you go downstairs and get me something to eat? I'm going to check some more of the feeds to make sure I wasn't followed."

"Good thinking. Anything in particular?"

Abby shook her head. Byron gave a smile and approached. He kissed her on the forehead and departed. Abby remained in place as she watched him leave.

As soon as his footsteps receded down the stairs, she started typing her message.

Chapter 30: The Nature of Evil

Myra, Agriculture Protectorate, Greenhouse Sector

Myra stirred with a low moan. She blinked back tired, bewildered tears as her body informed her of the myriad of bruises, aches, and pains that she'd accumulated. At first, she hadn't wanted to go to sleep, but as her fellow slaves sat down to eat and relax, their heads began to bob, and their eyes drooped. Even for Myra, exhaustion was victorious.

Myra felt her pillow stir.

Myra jerked into a sitting position and looked at Markus, who was her pillow. Myra remembered going from person to person, making sure they had what they needed. She remembered redressing Markus's wounds as a great heaviness consumed her strength. Myra didn't know how long she slept, but she woke with her head on his shoulder. A mixture of emotions rose in her heart as she stared down at him.

Myra missed Paul. When she first felt her head buried in Markus's arms, she thought she was still back in the hovel stirring from one of her dreams—rubbing her eyes, as Paul gave one of his reassuring grins. Somehow, the hovel was like a distant memory—like looking back at a younger version of herself that she didn't recognize.

"We need to start moving," Adam whispered as he approached. Myra took her eyes and feelings off of Markus and went to Adam. His countenance was grave.

"What's wrong?"

"We've been here long enough," Adam said tersely.

"Understood. I'll get everyone on their feet." Adam gave a curt nod and wandered away. Myra stared back down at Markus. She watched his chest rise again before she rose to her feet. The rest had done him some good—the color in his face had returned. She'd let him sleep a little longer.

Myra wove through the slaves, touching gently, stirring softly. She received bleary-eyed stares and grunts of disapproval, but soon she had everyone awake and ready.

"What's taking you so long? You should be ready to go, grandma." Markus teased as she approached. Myra saw the shimmer of pain, but he didn't complain.

"You still need to be in your stretcher."

"It sounds like I don't have much of an option."

"Doctor's orders," she said with a tilt of her head as she looked back down at the stretcher.

"Yes, Mother," Markus surrendered as he laid back down. She nodded at two guys who picked him up.

"I need you to hang in there until we can get to the *real* doctor. Okay?"

"Are we there yet?" He whined.

"Soon. I promise," Myra responded.

I hope.

Myra held back her pessimism as she pulled away from Markus. She wished she had all the answers but found more and more she didn't have any. Myra looked around at everyone, and despite the rest, there were still layers of weariness upon each of them—exhaustion rooted within their hearts that had grown from the seeds of suffering.

They were slaves in transition—orphans longing for physical freedom but seemingly never arriving. Even Myra, who felt freer than she'd ever been—even more so than before she'd become enslaved—even she felt the curtain of doubt hanging over her. Would they ever be truly free? Or would they always be pilgrims in a foreign land?

"Cast your worries upon Theo, Myra," Paul began in her head. She could feel his gentle, calloused hands weaving in and out of her hair. "They're going to come out anyway, so give them to Theo. He cares for you," Paul reassured. His words eased her mind as she worked through her anxieties and gave them away.

Myra spied Adam standing alone ahead of the rising train of people. She broke away.

"We're ready," she said simply. Adam nodded and started to pull away. Myra looked backward at the mass of people who clutched their meager belongings. Compassion stirred deep in her heart. She tore her eyes away from them and looked at Adam. He held his staff and was walking with quiet determination.

"You said this was your home?" Myra asked softly. Adam merely nodded. "What did you do here?" She continued despite his silence.

"Hydroponics. Though I maintained irrigation efforts and crop utilization," Adam responded crisply. "I make sure efforts in feeding Axiom are maximized and efficient."

"I see. Was it difficult work?"

"Depends on how you define difficult. Judging from the way you carry your shoulders when you're tired, the cuts on your arms, and how you keep going despite exhaustion—I'd assume you were not a stranger to hard labor," he said bluntly. Myra felt her face flush with sudden emotion.

"You're right. Was it that obvious?"

"People who work for what they earn are easy to spot," he offered, though Myra couldn't tell if it was a compliment.

"Did you work alone?"

"No. I worked in a Unit with my Figurehead and a couple of other Figures."

"Figures?"

"Yeah. People."

"I see." Truly, she didn't. It was a strange way to describe a person. "Were you all close?"

"Our work required us to be in proximity, yes."

"No," she started with a short laugh, "did you have any friends or family?" Adam shot her a furrowed brow.

"What are those?" Myra wanted to laugh again until she understood he was serious.

"Ummm. People who you know and trust, who you can go to when you need help, who you care for and love. Surely you have some of those?"

Adam slowly shook his head as his manipulor turned to a glowing yellow.

"Such things are not allowed," he said passively. "Relationships are forbidden for they lead to compromise." Again, Myra felt sad for him.

"But...," Adam began hesitantly, "over the cycles, I have developed associations with other Figures. Up until now, the Agriculture Protectorate was largely left to itself—to work and cultivate. We did not seek out the other Protectorates. We had no dealings with anyone other than each other. We were in isolation—a chosen solitude between us and the earth, land, and creature." There was a deep melancholy in his voice. "But everything's changed, now."

Myra understood his pain. She understood the great, deep disconnect. As they walked, the ground was getting soggier. They'd left the greenhouses and were traversing an open stretch of land. The faint, flickering light from the greenhouses cast long shadows. Myra could hear the lapping of water as it caressed the edge of the shore to their right.

"What do you do now?"

"What I must," he said bluntly. The two of them approached the edge of the shoreline. Myra could hear the squelch of her shoes in the mud. The ground began to slant downward, and she could tell that the land they were walking was at one time underwater.

"Tunnel's right over here," Adam said as he pointed. Myra followed his finger to the mouth of a tunnel draped in darkness and obscurity. Long tendrils of vegetation hung over the entrance like serpents. "After the Lake drained, this appeared. It seems it was under the water the whole time."

Myra had a sudden image of a dark, fathomless hole.

"And you're confident it will get us to the hospital? That it doesn't just end somewhere?"

"Yes. Just gather your people in the entrance, and we will all go in together," he said.

Myra nodded and then turned to the rest of the slaves. Eventually, she had instructed them all to link together to avoid getting lost. When at last she had everyone together, she turned to Adam.

"We're ready."

"Good. Let's move," Adam said as he led the way. Myra followed, looking upward at the branches of vegetation still dripping. The air smelled musty and damp, and her clothes clung to her body like sweat. She turned her attention to Adam as she pondered his situation.

"Things will work out, Adam," Myra reflected openly.

"How can you be so sure?" Adam inquired.

"I believe good always overcomes evil. Remember when I talked about the highest and purest good?" Adam nodded. "Well, this purest good is a person, and I am confident he will rescue us."

Adam was silent for a couple of paces.

"Do you really believe that?"

"Yes. I do. And I believe he wants the highest good for all of us," Myra stated confidently.

Another wave of noiselessness ensued, which was only broken by the wet spatter of mud and dripping water. The cave's mouth loomed above them like a hungry mouth as a chill ran down Myra's spine.

"I'm sorry, Myra," Adam said as he broke the silence.

"Don't be sorry, Adam. The point is not trying to measure up, rather surrender."

"No. Not about that," Adam said ambiguously.

"Then what are you sorry about?"

Adam stopped walking and turned to face her. His manipulor churned with a dark, somber color. Goosebumps erupted on Myra's skin.

"I'm sorry for being evil," he replied in a whisper.

Lights ignited as darkened men spilled from the tunnels.

Chapter 31: The Edge

Damien, Hydra Sector, Industry Protectorate

Damien followed Sebastian in strained silence as the two of them descended lower into the valley. Sebastian hadn't gone into great detail about what had happened—about why a whole town was wiped away.

But, when Damien's eyes glanced at Sebastian, he saw his stooped shoulders, his steps that dragged behind him, and the shallow, pained breath that escaped firm lips. Damien saw someone who was broken.

Damien was compelled to mend the wounds Sebastian bled so freely. But, what could he say that would fix any of this? Damien was still in the process of mending, healing from scars that he'd worn for a long time. What had he to offer Sebastian whose injuries were so fresh?

Their descent slowed as the ground leveled. Damien glanced around and followed the cliff face behind him. It bent around a corner and blocked the view of the dam.

"They didn't even see it coming," Sebastian reflected heavily. Goosebumps broke out on Damien's skin as everything came into focus.

The landscape around them was heavy with agony and destruction. Broken, shattered pieces of buildings lay in heaps and clogged jams—jutting upward where they'd tried to resist the onslaught. The ground was moist and congested, like milk that was beginning to curdle. The air was thick and throttled like a noose around the neck. Aside from their footsteps squelching in the mud, silence left them to sink into misery.

Damien's eyes wandered over the shattered terrain. He could see the foundations of massive buildings. The lights on the cliff face behind them flicked ominously and offered intermittent details to translate the annihilation around him.

Everything was gone. Not a single building had been able to resist. Damien imagined in his mind just how massive the wave had been that ripped structures from their foundations. A shudder ran up and down his spine, and the thought was too heavy to ponder.

Damien turned his attention back to Sebastian, but Damien was alone. His eyes searched the darkness in frantic fervor. Where had he gone? Damien quickened his pace as he scanned the ground for footprints. He finally found Sebastian's trail and pushed after him.

Eventually, Damien found Sebastian. Sebastian stood on the very edge of a cliff as watery mist curled around him from below. Sebastian didn't hear Damien as he approached, or at least didn't make any indication as he continued to stare downward at the water beneath his feet. As he neared the edge of the churning, writhing river, Damien knew what Sebastian wanted to do—the only choice he felt he had left.

"Sebastian?"

The young man didn't move, though Damien felt like he wasn't standing still. Damien stepped towards him, hesitant and slow in his approach. He knew what a cornered, caged animal looked like. Eventually, Damien drew up alongside him. The two of them stood on the edge of the embankment. Six feet below their feet was a channel of water bubbling and wrestling over the surface. The cacophony clashed in his ears, though Damien was certain Sebastian couldn't hear it at all.

"Sebastian, you don't have to do this," Damien said as he peered at Sebastian.

"What is there left to do, Damien?" A knot formed in Damien's throat. Words rapidly formed on his lips as his tongue worked faster than his mind.

"I know what it is like to carry shame," Damien began. Myra's face filled his mind, and his heart dropped. "I know what it is like to lose someone because of my mistakes."

"I lost everyone!" Sebastian shouted over the mighty waters. "Sam! Stephen! Everyone! Their faces are here, in this water, staring up at me. I was their leader, Damien. Worse, I was their friend. I promised them something better than this," he indicated as he held his hands out over the gray water.

Sebastian was silent as his words sunk deeper into his soul. "I failed, and now they're dead. Because of me. It's fitting that you led me here, Damien," Sebastian said ironically. "I deserve to see this. I deserve to feel this pain. And I deserve to die because of it."

"You cannot mean that, Sebastian." Damien struggled for words, for anything coherent, for anything compelling. "Your life is much more meaningful than your mistakes. It has to be bigger than that. You're listening to your pain, and I get it, but you are much more than what you are feeling."

"I am not Axiom's savior," Sebastian voiced hollowly. The two of them fell into a strangled silence. "I was the herald of its destruction. I listened to what I felt, and now I must listen to what makes sense. If I die, maybe all of this will be over. Maybe Axiom will return to what it once was," Sebastian suggested with a shrug of his shoulders.

"But why would you want that? Why would anyone want the way things used to be?"

Sebastian looked up at him with an uncertain sorrow.

"Because I wasn't in control before. And now that I am, I am lost." Damien looked into him, into a young man who could see no other option, and he knew that there was nothing he could say that would save Sebastian from himself.

"This must be done. For the good of Axiom."

Damien's fists curled. A single strike to Sebastian's jaw would leave him sprawling. A follow up to his temple might knock him out. What Damien would do after that was unknown. He just had to get Sebastian away from the ledge.

"Don't try to stop me," Sebastian said with a simple grin. "Though I appreciate the effort. Goodbye, Damien."

Damien lunged as Sebastian fell.

Chapter 32: Fortitude

The Lord Protector, Citadel, Fortitude

The Lord Protector stared out over Citadel with a fixed, durable gaze. His hands were clasped firmly behind his back as his mind roamed over the great city. He carefully considered what he was about to do as he numbered his steps. It was like playing chess in four dimensions—up and down, forward and backward, and throughout time. He wandered through every foreseeable consequence, pondering thousands of scenarios, browsing through motives and actions like they were pages in a cheap magazine.

A magazine.

An ironic smile played across his lips. He hadn't held a magazine in centuries. It was strange how the memory reminded him of the old way of things. Like small pebbles stuck in his shoes, occasionally, he stepped the wrong way and was reminded of what was beneath him.

Time had its way of crawling backward in his mind. Like lost love, it whispered and enticed, promising pleasure but only guaranteeing emptiness. The past was an empty tomb.

The Star bathed his body in a maroon glow. Red veins radiated throughout the room, wrapping him in bleeding dusk. The red color had been an unexpected consequence of introducing violence into Axiom. It was incredibly Draconian and reminded him of some of the ancient rhetoric prescribed by politicians and pundits. Like light and dark, white and black, red versus blue. Petty notions for ineffectual individuals.

Yet, he knew the color provided a wrinkle, a veiled suggestion, a hole in the armor of his planning. People hated what they could see—whether it was a color, a man. But, he could leverage their fear and disconnect to the benefit of Axiom. In this pursuit, he did not rest. He did not find respite. There was no end, for Lorenzo was the Protector of humanity.

Humankind had erred. Like a rebellious teenager, they'd grown entitled and demanding until the immaturity became humanity's undoing. It was his job to mature Man. It was his prerogative to lead them into adulthood.

Still, it had taken longer than expected. He was tired. Worn. Yet, there was still a tremendous amount of work to be done. There were threats to Axiom, to mankind, which he had been analyzing and scrutinizing for centuries. Now, the pieces were in place for the perfect defense against these threats.

But the cost was great.

As he stared outward, watching, seeing, consuming, this cost coursed through his thoughts.

"You're conflicted," a soft voice spoke from behind him.

The sound of someone else in the room caught the Lord Protector off guard. He turned slightly to face the person. He was sitting almost a dozen feet away, one leg folded over the other, his hands clasped in his lap. Upon seeing him, the Lord Protector's lip curled a little in the corner. He was genuinely surprised but turned back around to face the window.

"Am I?" A rich, intimate silence fell. "I did what I needed to do. Axiom—mankind—must be protected at all costs, and sacrifice was essential."

"I agree. Sacrifice is entirely necessary. And yet, you regret the decision."

"Of course!" The Lord Protector said sharply as passion inflected in his tone. "The loss of a single human being is a weight," he said as his voice bore tremendous sadness. "If I had it my way, I'd provide immortality to all of them. But, they are so uncivilized, so ill-prepared for freedom. You give them everything they need, and they will still go and break plates."

"The cost of what it means to be human."

"The cost of arrogance and stupidity. Such behavior can be changed, though. Unlearned. Rewritten. All humanity needs is someone to teach them and to hold them on one path. Someone who can remove distractions—even the greatest distractions—to give humanity time to step away from its baggage and become something more, something stronger, something purer," the Lord Protector stated vehemently. His heart felt fresh. He hadn't felt this passionate in decades.

"And yet, you are still conflicted."

The Lord Protector's lips formed a thin line. His eyes roamed Citadel. Great darkness lay ahead. Great pain and suffering were on the horizon. But diamonds are made under pressure, in the dark of the Earth, and it was time to apply the greatest pressure he could without breaking the bond he had with his people.

"It is not conflict, I feel. I hesitate because there is much suffering ahead."

"There typically is when a child is being born," the voice said sagely. The Lord Protector had to agree. It was precisely how he saw Axiom—a child needing to be coaxed from the darkness and brought into the light. "But, as soon as you bring a child into the world, it will forever have the chance to rebel, to break your trust."

This, too, was true. It was why it had taken the Lord Protector so long to conform all of reality to his plan. Too much time was necessary for this moment. So much rested on the young man.

"You know he is not going to become who you want him to be, Lorenzo." The Lord Protector sneered. He hated being called by his name. It felt antiquated—like it belonged to someone else—a man he stepped away from millennia ago.

"That is where you are wrong, Theo. Sebastian is playing right into my hands. He is doing exactly what I want him to do. There is no stopping what has begun," the Lord Protector stated with firm confidence. "The only person who would try to stop me is you, but you're not actually here. You're just part of my subconscious. A part of me I stamped out a long time ago," the Lord Protector chided.

"And here yet, I am."

The Lord Protector snorted.

"Wordplay. You failed, and I will succeed. As we speak, my devices are in motion, unfolding from hundreds of years of planning. I will not be deterred. Not even by you."

His pronouncement was met with silence. The Lord Protector turned to find he was again, alone.

"Of course," he said scornfully. He turned back around and stared out onto Citadel. His eyes swam with rubies as he became more solidified in his position.

It was time.

The Lord Protector extended his will. He filled Citadel with his mind, coursing through walls, corridors, streets. He embraced every fiber of Axiom with his mind, letting himself weave into the world like smoke filling a room. Once the Lord Protector reached the edge of Citadel, he initiated a set of commands and recoiled his conscious as the changes began.

A low rumble filled Citadel. It shook the streets and stirred dust from the buildings. Even the Star, unmoved for generations, swayed slightly. At the edge of Citadel, walls rose out of the ground like spires. They rose upwards until they towered over the city. The rumbling faded as the walls slid into position, connecting into an impenetrable barrier.

Citadel was a fortress.

Part II

Chapter 33: Ramifications

Paul, Slave Compound

"No."

Unrelieved flames flashed through Paul. He leaned over the table as it groaned beneath the weight of his frustration.

"*Yes*. You saw what Eberry and his forces can do. If you don't provide your guards and at least a quarter of the rest with weapons, then Eberry will overrun us within the hour," Paul stated bluntly.

"I said no," Hob reiterated with force as he sat deep into his cheap armchair. Paul had been working on him for almost an hour but to no avail. The man was impenitent, stubborn, and extremely short-sighted. Paul could only see a man who was intent on clinging to what little power he still contained. If Hob did not budge, then what Paul had stated ominously would most certainly come into fruition.

"Hob, there is no other way!" Paul said firmly.

"You fought them off. Surely, you can think of something," Hob patronized.

More anger congregated in Paul's chest, but he swallowed it and stared meaningfully into a man who was willing to condemn hundreds. What Paul didn't understand was why. Why wasn't Hob mounting a better defense? Why was he letting Eberry come to him instead of staging a counterattack?

"Yes, I did fight them off. But, we lost many good people in the process," Paul stated heavily. The weight of their deaths was beginning to seep into his heart. They were a crown of shame upon his brow.

"Expendable resources to get the job done," Hob suggested. Paul fought the urge to throttle the man with his whip. Why did Hob even need it anymore? It was just a symbol—a broken epigraph of the power Hob once possessed.

"And when all of them are dead, they'll come for you," Paul said evenly. He let that reality settle into the man. A flash of turmoil rolled across Hob's face, and Paul watched as he bit into his cheek. An uneasy, festering silence brew between them, and Paul's eyebrows rose aggressively.

Paul felt alive with tension and knew he wouldn't give into Hob's ridiculous demands. Men like Hob knew only fear. For all the threats and punishments, all the bodies and shallow graves, he'd amassed over the years, his position yielded him no leverage if those he'd abused struck out at their persecutor.

"I will arm the guards. That's it," Hob stated.

"That's enough. For now. Eberry will be back with reinforcements soon."

"You act like you understand his tactics?"

Paul paused as he reflected on his knowledge. It was true: he was confident every step of the way that he understood his enemy. He did not know where he'd gained this insight but was wise enough to use it to protect others.

"It's simple. You showed up with your...tanks and forced him to retreat to the depot. From there, he's gathering his next wave—presumably with some show of strength that will rival your own."

Hob smirked, but Paul didn't find anything about their conversation to be amusing.

"And where exactly where will his next assault take place?" Hob asked as he glanced down at a map spread out on the table. Paul looked down and immediately recognized the layout of the compound.

There were symbols and scribbled notes that he didn't understand, but the buildings and design were the same as the alleys, streets, and structures that had filled his life for years. His eyes lingered on the silhouette of the mountain. Just the image alone called to him—to a sanctuary that time itself had failed to forget.

For now, though, it was Paul who had to forget.

"Here," Paul pointed with certainty. Hob stood and peered down at where Paul indicated.

"In the Manufacturing Sector? What makes you think he'll go there?" Hob asked with a creased brow. Paul held back his impatience. How could the man *not* see it?

"Eberry caught us by surprise at the Depot—hitting us with a force of those flying things—"

"—Drones. They're called drones," Hob corrected.

"With those drones," Paul said slowly as he continued. "And he had one of two choices. He could push inward towards the Slave Quarters and from there overwhelm your mansion, or he could turn his attention to the Factory Sector. Now, I provided a little bit of incentive by drawing his forces towards the factories, but it was too easy, which means that he intended to go there to begin with—his original plan," Paul said.

"So? Why does that matter? He could've just chosen it at random," Hob said incredulously.

"Maybe. Or maybe he knows that we make the bombs in the factories," Paul suggested. A flash of disdain rolled across Hob's face.

"How would you know what you were making? You're just a slave!"

"But, I am not a fool. And neither is Eberry. He's obviously been gathering information about what you were doing here, Hob. He knew exactly where to strike." An uneasy silence settled between them, and Hob bit his lip violently.

"A spy? In my ranks? They wouldn't dare turn on me," he threatened openly to no one in particular.

"You know of no one who would hate you so much that they'd be willing to give Eberry information to bring about your downfall? I'm sure there are plenty of people you've betrayed, hurt, and otherwise treated unfairly and without justice," Paul said with more sarcasm than he'd planned.

"You mean someone like you?"

A stony, warm silence fell between them. Paul could see blackened violence curdle in Hob's eyes as his thoughts towards Paul started to melt into aggression and paranoia. Hob's hand was already on his beltline, resting against his gun.

"David, I have nothing to gain in killing you. My goal is to prevent bloodshed. Not create it." Hob didn't respond, though the violence subsided in the wells of his eyes.

"Eberry will focus his attention on the next layer of your tanks by hitting your fuel source."

"Which is in Manufacturing," Hob said in resignation.

"Precisely. Eberry is not going to hit you head-on. Especially after seeing how much firepower you have. No, he's going to continue to dismantle your defense strategy until you have nothing left. Then, and only then, will he come for you."

Hob was silent again as he stared down at the map. Paul could see the information wrestling within his eyes as they darted across the paper. Finally, he sat down in resignation. Paul felt the seconds tick agonizingly in his head. In the silence, though, his thoughts returned to what he did not understand.

"Tell me something. Why is Eberry really here?" Hob flashed a look of indignation.

"What do you mean?"

"You know what I mean, David." At the sound of his name, so personal and intentional from Paul's lips, Hob gave Paul a staunch glare. "Eberry isn't here only to dethrone you. He's here for something else. What is it?"

"That doesn't concern you," Hob said reflexively. Paul could feel the heat travel up his neck.

"It most certainly does. You owe it to me—."

"—I owe you nothing. You forget that you are a slave," Hob said with a hollow laugh. The retaliation bit into Paul, but he took no heed to his words.

"And look where I am standing."

Hob glowered as defeated hatred burned in his eyes. He was silent, again, which brought Paul enough time to get his anger back into place.

"You don't know what to do, Hob. And I do. Don't ask me how or why I know, but you need me. Frankly, I don't need to help you," Hob granted him a look that understood, "But, I will. It would help me if I knew why Eberry was attacking us with so much ferocity."

"Because of my brother," Hob said softly. Paul almost didn't catch the words.

"Your brother?"

"Yes. My brother is Lorenzo—the Lord Protector."

Something in the back of Paul's mind recognized the name. He searched through his memories until he found the name—a name that he'd picked up from his correspondence with the resistance on the other side of the mine shaft. It was a name that was reviled, hated even.

In the midst of Paul's enslavement, he'd never believed it was this Lord Protector who had him bound. It was easier to blame Hob than someone he'd never seen. But, how David's face grew paler and paler made Paul understand the gravity of the situation.

"And what does your brother want?"

Hob looked up at him with a look that Paul had never seen him wear—a glimpse of pity.

"You. The Lord Protector wants you."

Chapter 34: Intervention

Mary, Medical Protectorate, Radiant

Mary couldn't remove the young man's face out of her mind. His eyes stared up at her with a lifelessness that bore into her. His skin, fading from pink to gray as it lost its warmth, felt clammy on her palms. His death brought a sickening clarity to her world.

Mary's feet were moving her towards the table stretched out before her. A single Mother sat alone with her back turned to Mary. Mary didn't know what else to do—who else to go to, but she trusted her gut. She'd ignored it for so long, sacrificing little bits and pieces of herself every time she pushed her conscience down, down, deep. Mary was tired of ignoring her intuition. She was tired of retreating from what she knew in her heart was the right thing to do.

Mary was tired of being weak.

For so long, she'd avoided an inevitable conflict. First, she failed to fight for the man she loved—a man who was forced to make impossible choices. Then, she could not fight for her son—offering him up to a system that promised to keep him safe. She failed to protect herself—to protect her heart. And it was all these failures that weighed so heavily upon her that her knees could no longer take the weight.

But, Mary was no longer on her knees.

Mary steadied herself and sat next to Mother Veronica.

"Hey, Veronica."

"Hey, yourself. I heard all about that kerfuffle earlier. Are you alright?"

"No. I held a young man in my arms as he died."

"Oh," Mother V said evenly as her face fell a little. "That's too bad. Sometimes, though, there's nothing you can do," she said indifferently.

"But, there is something we can do," Mary said through gritted teeth.

"What do you mean, dearie? We do our job, take care of the patient, ease their suffering, and when the time comes, send them on their merry way."

The way she spoke about the whole process unnerved Mary. Almost to the point where she was reconsidering what she was about to say. But, she recognized that Mother Veronica had the most influence amongst the rest of the Mothers. She laughed, and they laughed. She gossiped, and they gossiped.

"What if...," Mary began as her eyes darted around. She wanted to make sure the Head Mother was nowhere close. If she found out about this conversation, then Mary was likely to be thrown out of Radiant, or worse. "What if we did something about the system?"

Mother Veronica flashed her a dumbfounded look.

"Whatever do you mean?"

"I mean, we bring down Radiant," Mary stated firmly as defiance bubbled in her heart. Mother Veronica continued to stare at her with mouth agape. "Surely you have questioned all of this, right? How can we sit idly by while people suffer—suffering that only brings longevity and health for a select few?"

"But, that's just the way it is, dearie." Mary's heart began to curl inward upon itself as it flinched beneath Mother Veronica's calm disregard.

"But, it's not the way it's supposed to be. Surely, you understand this? Understand that these are human beings we're draining of what is most precious to them—their life. How do you not see the wrong in what we do?"

"What we do is keep them comfortable. These people are patriots—living emblems of what it means to be a citizen of Axiom. They have chosen to sacrifice themselves. Who are we to deprive them of their right?"

"I don't believe that for one second, and I know deep down, neither do you. Why else would all of them be restrained? Why else would we give them drugs that keep them numb and immobile? Something is not right, and I can't swallow any of it much longer," Mary hissed. Her ears were hot, and beads of vindicated sweat dotted her brow. The two of them were silent as her heartbeat ruptured in her ears.

"I'll admit, Mother Mary, I have had my suspicions along the way. But, to throw the baby out with the bath water seems a bit...outlandish. Don't you agree?"

"I do not. For once in my life, I disagree and aim to do something about it."

"And what do you plan on doing?"

The question hung between them like an omen.

"I don't know. I only know I need to do something. All I am asking is that you think about it. If I were to act on this, I would need your help and the help of the other Mothers."

"I see. So, you didn't come to me to confide. You came to convince," Mother Veronica said with an air of insult. Mary couldn't believe how petty she was being.

"I came to you because I had no one else. But, if you don't want to help, that's fine."

"Now, don't get hasty. I didn't say I wouldn't. You did ask me to think about it, after all."

A glimmer of hope surged in her chest.

"Yes. That's all I need for right now."

"Alright."

Another unscheduled silence ensued as Mary fought to offer simple words amidst a complex conversation.

"I think it's best you run along, now. Wouldn't want to arouse suspicion," Mother Veronica suggested. At this, Mary's eyes wandered around the room.

"You're right. Thank you, Veronica. I wouldn't trust all of this with anyone. Only you."

"Delighted. I will see you later, Mother Mary. And in the meantime, I will give your suggestion a great deal of thought."

"That's all I ask. I will talk to you later," Mary promised as she rose from her seat. She felt weighted, heavy, even though she'd just let go of so much emotional baggage and turmoil that had been accumulating. Despite this feeling, Mary felt accomplished, even free. Now, she just hoped that something good would come out of her boldness.

Chapter 35: Sinking

Sebastian, Industry Protectorate, Hydra Sector

The water enclosed around Sebastian's head in a tender embrace. It pulled him under, collected every piece of him that had floated away and gone adrift. Sebastian descended like a stone—like a block of concrete weighed down with grief inside the churning, raging depths.

Sebastian could still see the light shimmering off the water above him. He held his breath, even though soon he was going to take a gasping, gulping breath of watery death. Something inside of him, something consistent, wanted to enjoy the last of his life he still held between clamped lips.

The current took him with a sudden jerk. He flipped end over end as his world spun wildly out of control. The peaceful departure that he desired flew from his fingertips as his hands extended outward to grab hold of any surface that offered strength. Finally, his body came to a stop, though he couldn't tell where he was and which direction was toward the surface.

The light was gone.

All around him was a deep, black tomb. Sebastian knew his lungs couldn't resist much longer. He knew that as soon as he gave in to the hunger for life and his mouth opened, he'd swallow his demise. Panic coupled with his heart until they were on the same beat. Petrifying fear curdled in his veins and compelled his body to act, to kick, to swim, to push upward.

But, in Sebastian's mind, he had already given up. He could no longer feel the water on his skin. It was like he was in a nightmarish dream, drifting through the dark.

Sebastian opened up his lungs and breathed. Immediately, terror swamped his body as water rushed into his throat. He clawed at the emptiness around him, kicked and squirmed against his own decision. Pain clamped down upon his chest, and his heart was a gong across the deep. His thoughts, once so strong and so reliant, were faded and worn.

He was dying.

Sebastian had finally come to the end of himself.

As the end closed in, Sebastian could feel his body growing more and more fatigued. It was not triumph he felt, instead surrender to an inglorious end. His mind was sober as his vision began to blur into meaninglessness.

Sebastian felt the overwhelming desire to rest, to give in to the drought that thirsted upon his awareness. Yes, if he shut it all down, closed off every part of him that made sense out of the world, then he'd find peace.

You give your people peace.

Colors danced in front of his eyes—varying shades of iridescent blue. He'd never seen such beautiful sadness.

Sebastian could see Sam. He was swimming towards Sebastian. A thick, sick sorrow gurgled inside Sebastian's heart. Sam had given up his life to protect Sebastian, but it was a waste. All of Sebastian's striving and trying had resulted in such a tremendous loss of life that it was surely a mistake that it was Sebastian who hadn't died on the train the day it exploded. It should have been him, not Sam.

Yet, Sam was still swimming towards him.

I'm sorry, Sam.

Sebastian could see blue veins of light close in around his body and embrace him. But, he couldn't stay awake as darkness settled into his bones.

Chapter 36: Broken Surfaces

Myra, Lake Sector, Agriculture Protectorate

Myra heard a high-pitched whining as fear gathered in her throat. She watched in horror as a dozen men encircled their group. Adam stood in front of her, with arms crossed and an apologetic look on his face.

"I'm sorry. They took—" Adam was interrupted by a strong, strangled bellow that erupted from behind Myra. She turned just in time to catch Markus, who was advancing with pure hatred in his eyes.

"You coward! You sold us out. You filthy piece—"

"—Markus! Stop!" Myra yelled into his ear. His face was a mask of pain and anger, and his color was fading fast. She could see drops of crimson beginning to ooze through the fresh bandage. In his fit of wrath, he'd torn open the wound.

But, this wasn't her only concern. Her eyes darted to all of the men who were tightening their circle. She looked to all the frightened faces of people she'd unknowingly led to their demise. Panic and pain exchanged places in her heart— alternating with each beat in her chest. Myra didn't have time to be angry. She only had time to protect everyone.

The circle of soot cloaked adversaries tightened.

"Please. I did what you asked. Let me see them," Adam pleaded as he faced one of the men who was indistinguishable from the rest except for a red insignia across his chest. "I won't tell anyone about what I saw. I promise," he said in a voice that was finally cracking with emotion. His staff was in his hand, digging into the ground. It glowed a mottled purple and green.

The response from the soldier was swift. Myra watched in shock as Adam received a punch that doubled him over in rolling agony. His face turned red as questions hung in his eyes.

"Put him with the rest," the man barked. Two of the men grabbed Adam by the shoulders and shoved him forcefully. He staggered into the mass of scared slaves who gave off short cries of alarm but managed to catch him. "Search them. Find out if any of the targets are here," the man snapped once more.

"Alright! Line up back to back so we can get a good look at you," one of the men barked. Nobody moved. Although they were used to tyranny and terror, it had always had a face. These men, obscured by their helmets, were their imagination's worst ideas. The man in charge shook his head as if annoyed at their lack of haste.

"Shoot one of them," he commanded. Panic jolted throughout Myra as she watched one of the men comply with this order. She couldn't feel her feet moving, but her body was in motion as she jumped forward.

"No! You will not," she barked as she held out her body in front of the group.

"A martyr, eh?" The man spoke slowly as he came to a stop in front of Myra.

"You will not harm them," Myra said courageously. Her body was shaking uncontrollably, and her arms, held out as a shield, were growing heavy.

"And I suppose you plan on stopping me? Did you hear that, boys? She's going to stop us!" Laughter, low and hollow, bubbled around her. Without recognizing the movement, he pulled a weapon out from a holster. Myra stared down at the gun. "You'll just have to be the first to go, then," he promised.

Myra closed her eyes and reached out to Theo, hoping he could hear her frantic pleas. The response was a short chirp that echoed sharply across the lake. Myra opened her eyes and stared down the barrel of the man's weapon. His wrist was pulsating with a green glow that bathed the stricken faces of the slaves in an emerald hue.

"Odd," he said mostly to himself. He turned his head to the rest of the soldiers. "She's one of the targets."

He turned back to Myra, and though he wore a helmet that covered his face, she could feel his stare scrutinizing her. "It seems you're more important than you let on, missy. Take her and scan the others," he ordered.

Myra immediately felt hands grip her shoulders as she was shoved forward. Bewilderment and confusion tumbled headlong with her as she tried to piece together the sudden change of events. Behind her, she could hear the frightened sound of the slaves as they were shoved and scanned.

"Sir, what do we do with those who are negative?" Asked a voice behind her. The leader of the group inclined his head and again looked in Myra's direction with intention.

"Kill them," he said crisply.

Myra struggled against her captors as screams of terror tore the air behind her.

Damien, Industry Protectorate, Hydra Sector

Sebastian was heavy. His body dragged Damien down like an anchor. Damien's legs burned as he kicked and fluttered his feet, trying desperately to bring them both to the surface. His lungs cramped in his chest and begged him to let go of the foolish, stupid person he was trying to save. But, the surface was just above his head. It called to him—a siren song that mocked more than invited.

Was Sebastian even alive? When Damien had found him, he was at the bottom of the river. He'd expected to see a body, floating with the current, eyes open and glossed over. Yet, what he'd found was a blue membrane surrounding Sebastian—like a shield. As soon as Damien touched it, it dissolved, and Sebastian fell into his grip.

Damien continued his climb as his heart felt sick in his chest. He couldn't know if Sebastian was still alive, but he had to try and get him to the surface. His free hand gripped invisible handholds as he churned the water. His vision started to slip, descending quickly into oblivion as the edges of his understanding crept into the darkness.

Let him go.

The voice was haunting, enticing. It was familiar, like Damien was staring into a mirror and hearing his own voice.

He's already dead, and so you will you. Let him go.

223

Damien pushed upward, bubbles escaping his clamped lips and ascending upward. He didn't know if he was advancing. The surface seemed like a distant memory.

Look out for yourself, Damien. It's what you've always done. It's what has saved you time and time again.

Damien was the voice. He wanted to listen, too. To let go and watch Sebastian drift downward into the grave he chose.

Your life is the only life that matters, Damien.

The darkness was consuming his sight. He could hear his heart beating in his mind as it slowed and slowed in its approach towards death. His body felt laden down with a burden that wasn't his own. Damien felt his fingers open, and his grip loosen.

Don't let go, Damien.

The voice didn't belong to him, but it was enough to give Damien a last burst of energy as he frantically sought oxygen. Damien broke the surface with a tremendous gasp and brought Sebastian up out of the water. After a few desperate breaths, he turned his attention to the limp body in his arms. Damien tried his best to keep Sebastian's head up, but it rolled lifelessly side to side.

Damien searched around frantically for the edge of the river. In the darkness, nothing made sense as the raging waters carried them. His head dipped below the water, and he choked on a mouthful of water. Damien came up but couldn't make out much more than Sebastian's face in front of his own.

Damien felt a stabbing pain in his back as they collided against a jagged surface. The two of them bounced off, and Damien barely managed to keep his grip on Sebastian's body. Panic spiked in his chest. If he didn't find the shore soon, he'd drown just as much as Sebastian had already.

Light pierced the gloom and blinded Damien. He held up his free hand and tried to make sense of what he was perceiving. The light moved on, sweeping to the right. Damien wasn't sure if it was a rescue or somebody trying to find them but knew he needed to decide.

"Help! Please!"

Another mouthful of water cascaded into his throat. He choked and spat out the contents. "Help!" The light spun back around, and despite his instincts, Damien waved frantically as the current continued to carry them onward. He heard a low, guttural roar and distant voices.

Pain stabbed his ribcage as they bounced off another unseen obstacle. Damien felt Sebastian fall out of his grip. Frantically, he searched for his body and managed to snag it in his outstretched fingertips. The two of them spun in the water as Damien lost complete control.

Damien struck another surface. Stars and pain burst into life as his head clapped against the stone. Before he could comprehend his demise, the world lost all understanding.

Myra broke free from her captors and sprinted towards the slaves as feverish protection accumulated in her feet. They were her people, and she would not let them die. She watched as the first soldier raised his weapon at Mama Beth. The woman did not flinch and did not look fearful—rather almost relieved. Myra gritted her teeth as she positioned herself in between the old woman and the soldier.

"No!" She shouted defiantly. "You will not hurt them!"

Everyone was staring at her.

There was a fire in their eyes, and Myra had lit the fuse.

Myra got caught in a torrent of motion and combat. Her fellow slaves grabbed at weapons, ripped off armor, tore helmets from shoulders. The soldiers were momentarily caught off guard as a wave of angry and oppressed humans bombarded them with blows. Myra couldn't make sense of everything as men and women rolled around in the mud. Grunts and sharp cries of pain broke open like an ongoing conversation.

The sound of a weapon charging up—a high-pitched whine that made Myra recoil—added its voice to the melee.

"No! No! No! Stop fighting! They'll kill us!"

Myra shouted in vain. A luminous plume of red ignited the darkness as it poured from a soldier's weapon. Myra watched in horror as it struck a man—Cedric—squarely in the chest. Pain and confusion singed his face as the projectile burned through his life and left him in a crumpled, empty heap.

The color of blood bathed the darkness as more soldiers joined retaliated. Instinctively, Myra ducked as the air grew heavy with the smell of suffering.

"Cease fire! Cease fire! You're going to hit the girl!" The leader of the group bellowed. Immediately, the firing subsided as an unsettling silence ensued. Myra scrambled towards a young woman, Dalilah, who wore a mask of pain.

"Shhh. Let me see," Myra said in a whisper. Somehow, she'd managed to end up in the middle, and none of the soldiers could see her. Through elbows and knees, Myra could see out but did her best to remain hidden. She looked at Delilah's wound, a burn that started at her wrist and carved its way up to her elbow.

The wound was a glancing blow, but the skin was charred and pouring blood. Delilah whimpered in evident pain, and Myra looked around for anything that would bring relief. She reached down underneath her feet and grabbed a handful of soft mud.

"This is going to hurt," she guaranteed as she slathered the cool, dense mud onto the wound. Delilah winced and bit back her agony, but otherwise held the pain inside her throat.

"Come out, now, Myra, and no one else will get hurt." Icy, cold dread cascaded down her back. How did they know her name? Myra felt the slaves around her shift ever so slightly as they tightened her concealment. She looked through legs until she found the man in charge.

His helmet was off, and a trickle of blood ran down his chin, but otherwise he looked composed and in control. Myra watched him move to the right and saw in horror that he was pointing his weapon at Markus, whom he held firmly in his grip.

Without hesitation, Myra rose and pushed her way forward. Once she was free, she could feel all the soldiers turn their weapons in her direction. She walked a couple of steps forward from her people and stood in between them and the soldier in front of her.

"Let him go," Myra said coolly. The man grinned with teeth stained with blood.

"Come with us, and no one else will get hurt."

"I don't believe you."

"Then you'll just have to trust me," he said as he licked his ruby lips.

"Trust you? You'll kill everyone as soon as you have me," Myra spat.

"You have no choice. I saw how this one," he indicated as he pressed the tip of his weapon into Markus's neck. Markus struggled, but his pallid face revealed he hadn't much strength even to stand. "Tried to defend you. I bet he's important. If you don't comply, no one will die. No one except him." Markus stopped trying to break free and looked at Myra. "So, tell me. How important is he?"

Myra looked at Markus. Myra knew how important Markus was to her. But, she knew if she walked away from her people, she sealed their fate, too. Frustrated pain catapulted in her chest. What was she supposed to do?

"I'll count to three. One..."

"Don't, Myra. He's a liar!" Markus shouted.

"Two..."

Myra's heart swam. She couldn't make this kind of decision, but the words were already coming from her mouth.

"Stop! We have you surrounded!" A booming voice echoed as a host of people poured from the tunnel, descended the hill, and sprinted across the marshy shore. There was a moment of confusion and bewilderment as the soldiers frantically searched around, looking for a way out.

"Drop your weapons!"

There was no escape.

The soldiers surrendered. The man in front of Myra held his ground as his eyes frantically bounced around.

"I said drop it," an icy female voice clipped as she pressed a weapon against the man's head. His eyes finally settled on Myra as a smirk played across his lips. He let go of his gun as it fell from his grip. Markus stumbled towards Myra, and the two of them caught one another.

Markus held her in an embrace, more for support than comfort, though it quickly took on shades of affection. He pulled himself apart as his gaze went to the men and women stripping the soldiers of their weapons.

"Did you call them in?" Markus asked with a chuckle.

"Yeah. In between babysitting you and getting us captured," Myra volleyed back.

"Who are they?"

Myra shook her head. She had no idea. As if sensing their muddled questions, a soldier approached them with their weapon pointed at the ground.

"Myra?" Myra nodded through her confusion as her brow folded together. "My name is Preva Adair. Abby sent us. We're from the Hajj."

Damien blinked back a wave of nausea and blurring pain. He felt the ground beneath his body heave and roll as waves of ear-splitting headaches pounced upon his head. It took him a moment to understand that he was sitting upright. Judging from the way the water sprayed his face and the wind whipped his hair, he assumed he was on a boat.

Damien wanted to move into a crouching, defensive position, but his body was heavy. Pain stabbed his skull, and he knew he was suffering from a concussion—a familiar agony.

Damien's movements were sluggish as he fumbled for a handhold. Slowly, clumsily, he rose to his feet and prepared to attack whoever dragged him aboard. His body swayed with the waves, but his senses were beginning to sharpen.

There were three assailants in front of him—all of them oblivious to the dangerous young man they'd made the mistake of trying to capture. Damien gathered his strength, clenched his jaw, balled his fists, and readied himself to attack.

The boat turned sharply, and Damien stumbled. The men reacted to his presence, and one of them caught Damien.

"Woah, now. Easy."

228

Damien wanted to resist—to fight back, but his vision was swaying haphazardly. He mumbled a threat through thick, fuzzy teeth.

"You won't force me by take," he guaranteed.

"Let's sit down, friend. You've done enough." With an odd amount of gentleness, the man guided Damien back to a sitting position. Damien didn't like it, but he permitted the man none the less. "You took a nasty hit on the rocks, I'm afraid. It'll be a while before you can stand."

Damien could still feel the nasty hit. It was sharp and jagged on the edge of his skull.

"Where am I?" He managed to choke out.

"You're safe. At least we are for now."

"For now?" Damien said as he peered up at a bearded man with beady eyes. Even in the gloom, his face was gaunt, and shadows rimmed his eyes.

"We might have picked up their scent when we were dragging you two out of the water. We had to get the two of you out of there fast, so there's no telling if they're following."

The two of you.

"The other guy? Is he okay?" Damien was reluctant to disclose Sebastian's name. He didn't know this man, nor did he know his intentions.

"He's alive." Damien felt the tension ease out of his body just a little. "I appreciate you saving my friend," the man continued. "Sebastian and I go back quite a bit."

Chapter 37: Countermoves

Paul, Slave Compound

The air was growing heavy with tension as the sound of Eberry's troops courted with silence. For long hours, they'd heard swarms of drones fading in and out of earshot. The ground shook with movement, but they did not witness its source. Yet, they waited. From his vantage point above the street, Paul could see dozens of men and women hidden amongst the rubble, poised for the counterattack.

They had only one shot at this. The discomfort clenched in Paul's gut. He knew people were going to die, and he hated having to make this choice. But, Paul also knew that Eberry wasn't here to spare anyone. Men like him didn't show mercy. For all of his grandiose sadism, Hob in the least valued human beings for their function. To him, people were useful. Though such an idea hung like smoke in the bottom of Paul's lungs, Eberry was a different type of evil.

Eberry saw people as vermin needing extermination.

"Any word on the size of their unit?" Paul asked into a black device that fit in the palm of his hand. It garbled before falling silent. Hob had explained to him that despite being given scant resources to operate hundreds of individuals, he'd at least procured communication devices from his brother. Though rarely used, now they were essential to the minutes being drawn out like a strip of thin metal. Minutes that still allowed his plan to be mandible, but soon would become too brittle to withstand any change.

"Not yet," came the broken response.

Paul bit his lip. There was so much information he didn't know. So many missing pieces.

"Your plan better work," Hob threatened from his position on the edge of a window. Paul's gaze went to Hob. Hob was looking down at the street below, which was darkened and ruined from the earthquakes. They were positioned in the old city—what was left of a time and humanity long forgotten. Even in the gloom, though, Paul could see the fear in his eyes.

But, Hob was right. Paul's plan had better work. He was confident, though he didn't understand why. Paul was not prone to ambition. Yet, every time Hob tried to create a plan, Paul spoke over him and firmly stated what needed to be done. He was confident of himself and had a surety that he could not explain but trusted.

"Three columns of soldiers on foot—my guess is over two dozen," the voice spoke through the box. Paul's pulse quickened. Two dozen? That was less than he anticipated.

"Do you see anything else? Any drones?" Paul asked into the device as he pressed the transmission button. A moment of silence followed.

"No. Just the soldiers. They're almost passed me. You should see them coming around the corner in a few minutes," the voice said with a hint of relief. Paul didn't buy it. There was no way Eberry was running low on resources.

"Keep your eyes open and let me know if you see anything else," Paul stated.

"Okay."

The device fell silent, and Paul's mind started to work. Hob gave him a furtive glance as a soft, warm wind wove its way through the broken windows. Paul could feel his heart growing sick with dread.

"Just two dozen, eh? Are you sure you picked the right spot?" Hob asked with no reserve in cynicism.

Paul ignored him and continued to think, going over the map of the Compound in his head. He went down narrow alleys—too narrow for drones and machinery. He moved throughout the Manufacturing Sector, through the abandoned city, to the edge of the Factory sector, before going down to the Depot. It didn't make sense. Why would Eberry send such a small force to capture Manufacturing?

"Looks like he fooled you," Hob chimed.

"Quiet. I'm thinking," Paul snapped with more heat than he anticipated. He didn't understand where he'd gotten it wrong. They'd abandoned the Factory sector and reinforced Manufacturing. With the firepower Hob had granted them, they could effectively stage a concerted counterattack from a defendable position.

It clicked.

Paul's face grew heavy with trepidation as his eyes traveled to the large smokestack protruding upward from the Factory sector. He was in a perfect position to see the monolith that extended to the very ceiling of the dome.

The chimney was designed to take all the smoke from the Factory sector and empty it outside of Axiom, but ages ago, it disconnected, and now all of its contents seasoned the area with soot. Now it was a silent epitaph. Its shadow bathed Manufacturing and the city in a smoky gloom.

"We have to move everyone back," Paul said as his voice shook. Hob's brow creased together.

"Retreat? Already? I figured you for a coward."

"We don't have time for this!" Paul retorted. "Any second now, Eberry is going to detonate charges that will bring that chimney down on our heads," Paul grimly stated as he pointed. Hob's eyes flashed out the window.

"Preposterous. All that would do is obscure his route to the Manufacturing sector. It'll hit our location, maybe, but it would be a superficial blow. No worse than a couple of bricks coming down on our heads," Hob said sarcastically.

"And then Eberry will have us cornered by a couple of bricks blocking our route," Paul said bluntly. Hob grew solemn, and the scar on his face flushed a deep purple.

"You're certain of this?"

"It doesn't matter if I am. He may be taking all this time to go around Factory and come up through the Guard's Quarters. No one would be there right now. The whole sector is empty," Paul said knowledgeably. Hob's agitation grew, and his denial festered, though Paul knew he was beginning to see the point Paul was making. "If I am wrong, then I am wrong. But, if I am right, then he has the upper hand, and we have our backs up against the wall."

"What do we do?" Hob sounded deflated and looked at Paul for guidance. Paul felt a tremendous discomfort twist in his gut. He wasn't made for this. He saved people—but maybe he still had that chance—the chance to protect people differently. Paul's thoughts lit up as a new plan formed in his mind. It would be daring, and the timing would have to be perfect, but it might turn the tide in the other direction.

"Where are your tanks right now?"

"Near the Slave sector."

A vivid image of the hovels, the homes of so many of his friends and companions, doused in gorging flames flushed through his thoughts. He could still hear the tremendous booming of the tanks as they poured destruction down on the innocent. He could feel each blast as it rolled through every scar and wound he bore on his back.

"Move them." Paul squatted down and drew in the dust. His fingers, calloused and burned from years of base labor, outlined the Slave Compound so that it resembled the map they'd poured over for hours. "Here. To your mansion." Paul hid a smirk. Hob's mansion was a pile of rubble and ruin. He was equal to those whose homes and lives he destroyed.

"What purpose would that serve? That would put them out of action. If we keep them in the Slave sector, we can come in behind him just like he is doing. Then we'll have the upper hand, and we will destroy him from two fronts," Hob said with a hint of glee.

"No. He's going to see that coming. We have to bring the chimney down before he does," Paul said plainly.

"Bring it down? Are you stupid? That would put us in the exact same predicament!"

"Not exactly. You see, Eberry is going to blow the chimney on the farthest side, which would bring it down behind us—cornering us. Where your tanks will be positioned, you could strike it on the near side. Judging from the angle, it would fall along this line, here," Paul indicated as he drew the projected path. "Which would put it in front of us." Paul looked up at Hob, but could tell he still did not understand the full implications of what he was suggesting.

"And then we'll be attacked on two sides! On one side, it'll be his soldiers on foot. The other will be the forces he's bringing up from behind. Add on top of that his drones, and we'll be slaughtered," Hob said bitingly. "If we bring down the chimney, we are sealing our fate."

"That chimney is coming down already."

"Says you."

"Says common sense! If we beat him to the punch, then you can use your tanks to reign down fire just like you reigned down fire on my people," Paul said breathlessly. Hob smirked.

"So that's what this is all about, eh? You blame me for killing off a bunch of slaves."

"We don't have time for this, David."

"You think by invoking my name, you somehow have leverage over me? That somehow, I'm like you," he mocked.

"Can we please just get back to the plan," Paul said through a clenched jaw. A persistent ringing was growing in his ears as heat flushed up his neck.

"That somehow I'm human—redeemable even? That maybe if you treat me with enough goodness, I'll suddenly become good like you? Do you even believe that all of this is part of some grand plan? That you're here to set me straight? That all those lives that were lost will suddenly be worth it if you can turn me? That I'm just going to one day love your pathetic *Theo*—"

"—I blame you!" Paul yelled with a rush of vitriol. "I blame you for killing my friends. I blame you for making me suffer. I blame you for murdering my sister! I blame you for enslaving us, and ruining every chance we had at having our childhood. I BLAME YOU FOR ALL OF IT!"

Spit flew from Paul's rage as his fist balled into cudgels. The desire to punch Hob in the face thickened in his wrists as his pulse pounded throughout his body.

"No," Hob began with a smirk, "you don't blame me. You blame Theo. As you should. Do you even know what he wants you to do anymore, or are you just guessing?"

Tears rushed to Paul's eyes as he slowly shook his head.

"Then you're free," he stated evenly. "Now, as for your plan," Hob chirped as he dramatically switched his tone. "It's quite smart. We're going to be pinned down either way, and it's better if we pull the trigger before Eberry does. You're right about my tanks. With the range they have, they could obliterate Eberry's primary force. Without any way to retreat. Maybe if we're lucky, we'll make it out of this alive," Hob chirped.

Paul didn't feel alive. He felt hollow—burnt out. His head hung down as the tears lingered on the bottom of his pain. Hob's voice softened, surprisingly.

"Not everyone wants to be good, Paul. Remember that. Now suck it up and get ready to lead the ground forces. As far as I can assume, we can funnel the drones into this street and strike from above and below, but I'll need someone on the ground who knows what he is doing," Hob said as he turned and pulled out the communication device. Paul's attitude remained pensive as he glanced out the window at the street below.

Chapter 38: Shallow

Sebastian, Location Unknown

Sebastian languished between bitter disappointment and ragged despair. His body was bleary, throttled, weighed down. He felt emotionally scourged—burned from the inside out until all that was left was a hollow shaft.

His weariness was deep, sharp, as it stirred within Sebastian a fathomless melancholy. It was his body rising from death as his mind coped with the fact that he'd just attempted to take his own life.

Even his death had been a failure. He'd been so close to drowning. He could still feel the water clogging his lungs. He could still feel his body sinking down and finally coming to a rest on the river floor.

That was when Sam—and the blue—appeared. At first, he'd assumed it was his brain losing function as his mind lost its grip on the world around him. But, just before he blacked out, he remembered watching the blue coursing tendrils wrap around his face like a mask.

And here he was. Alive.

Why?

Sebastian heard voices as the fog lifted. They sounded distant but were coming into sharper distinction. He felt the ground beneath his body shift and lurch as his stomach flipped with each sudden change in direction.

At first, he thought he was back on the Train—a terrible notion that quickly died away as even greater lurches overtook him. No, whatever he was lying down upon was cold, damp, and smelled of mildew. As his body reenergized itself, Sebastian decided it was finally time to open up his eyes and face the world he'd sought to leave behind.

Sebastian sat up, and a sharp, constant throbbing sensation rose in his body and rested in the back of his skull. He winced and tried to peer through squinted eyes. At first, he did not understand what he saw as he rested his torso against a low wall. Directly across from him was another wall which rose up and down steadily, like liquid.

The floor beneath his body was wood haphazardly pieced together in an assortment of lengths and shapes. Sebastian looked to his left and saw two men standing at a machine as they conversed in low voices. One of the two had their hand on the waist-high device and pushed it back and forth in the direction the second man was pointing.

Sebastian tried his voice, but it came out in a crooked croak. Each breath was like inhaling fire, and he suddenly felt sticky and faint. Without being able to stop it, Sebastian vomited on the floor next to him.

"That's probably my fault," a familiar voice spoke over Sebastian's misery. Sluggishly, Sebastian turned his head as he wiped tears and vomit off of his face. "I did my best to stabilize the boat when I built her, but I had very little knowledge, so she's a bit rough," a man said as he squatted down to Sebastian's level. His face came into focus, and familiarity stirred in Sebastian.

"Stephen?"

"It's good to see you, Sebastian," Stephen said with a warm smile from the other side of his beard. "Drink this," he instructed as he handed a flask to Sebastian. Without hesitation, he took a deep gulp of water. It didn't put out the fire raging in his throat, but it beat back some of the flames.

Sebastian wiped the water from his chin and handed the flask back to Stephen. Sebastian was still in shock as he analyzed his friend. A part of him assumed it was his brain playing tricks on him again.

"I thought you were dead," Sebastian said shamefully.

"We got out. At least some of us did," Stephen reflected mournfully.

"How?"

"Your warning. It gave us enough time right before Hydra broke into pieces. They said it was your fault, but I know it wasn't. Just some accident they had to pin on someone," he

237

said with a shrug of his shoulders. Sebastian didn't care to try and correct him. It didn't matter.

"After we got out and watched half of Industry get wiped away, we thought about turning ourselves in—try to figure out what to do and where to go. Most of us lost our Quarters. Some of us lost everything. And everyone," he said with a somber tone. "But, we knew it was best that we remained in hiding, so that's what we've been doing," he said mildly. Sebastian's head was spinning.

"Where are we?" He croaked.

"We're on the river. On a boat, to be precise."

"A boat?"

"Yeah. Something from before Axiom—a relic. It's designed to float on water and move against even the strongest current," he said triumphantly.

"Where did it come from?"

"I built it," Stephen said proudly.

"You built this?" Sebastian said in awe.

"Yeah. It wasn't that hard once you understood buoyancy and aerodynamics. Combine all of that with the pieces of Hydra and the other sectors that got swept away, and you have enough materials to build a dozen of these," he said as he patted the wood paneling.

"I see. And this boat has allowed you to go undetected this whole time?"

"More or less. The nanites don't go near the water—you taught me that. The drones sometimes chase after us, but we can lose them with speed. We've had a few close calls with patrols of Enforcers, but they haven't caught us yet," Stephen said with a confident grin.

Sebastian didn't immediately respond as he digested this information. The pieces started to fall into place. Sebastian attempted to rise to his feet as he gripped the side of the boat.

"Here, let me help," Stephen offered. Sebastian felt his hands slip under his armpits as he rose. The world swayed, but Sebastian forced himself to remain focused. His eyes scanned his surroundings, analyzing and dissecting every detail.

The two men to his left had broken off their conversation and were looking out over the foamy water. Sebastian's gaze carried around to his right, past a bundle of cloths and straps, and eventually to the front of the boat.

In all, the boat couldn't have been more than twenty feet wide and three times as long. At the front, Sebastian saw a raised platform. Another man stood on top of it, with his eyes fixed ahead of him. Even as Sebastian sluggishly watched, the man shouted over his shoulder.

"Rock ahead. Thirty feet off our right side," he warned. Sebastian heard the two men shuffling as they adjusted the mechanism. The boat drifted to the left ever so slightly, but it was evidently enough to satisfy the man on the platform.

"It's not as advanced as the dampener I created, but it'll do the job," Stephen said sheepishly. Sebastian merely nodded his head. His attention wandered past the man on the platform to a young man sitting at the front of the boat. His back was turned, and his head angled down towards the water.

Damien.

"He saved your life. Must have swam forty feet down to get you from the river bottom," Stephen said.

"I wish he hadn't," Sebastian mumbled.

"You don't mean that," Stephen suggested.

"I do, Stephen. But I'm not going to try and explain. I just want you to keep him," Sebastian pointed at Damien, "away from me." Stephen didn't immediately respond as he gave Sebastian a deep, furrowed disbelief.

"Okay, Sebastian. It's a small boat, though, and I can't guarantee you won't see each other. We'll be here for a while."

"Why? Where are we going?" Sebastian asked sharply. The pounding was sharp behind his eyes.

"To Retirement," Stephen said evenly. Despite his discomfort, Sebastian's eyebrows rose.

"Retirement? Why?"

Stephen hesitated. "Maybe it's best if I show you," he offered. Sebastian's brow creased together like waves, but he let Stephen lead the way. His legs felt weak and uncertain as the boat swayed back and forth. Sebastian half followed, half stumbled after Stephen.

Eventually, he led Sebastian to the raised platform. On the other side was a tarp laid across the deck. Sebastian couldn't make out what was underneath as Stephen bent down and gripped the edge of the tarp.

"I must warn you, Sebastian," Stephen said softly as he looked up at him, "This isn't going to be pleasant." With a flourish, Stephen pulled the tarp away as a pungent odor slammed into Sebastian, nearly knocking him over.

Bodies.

Sebastian was staring down at bodies.

Their eyes were milky and empty, their skin blue and bloated, and their arms and legs hung at odd angles. Sebastian felt his stomach heave as he rushed to the edge of the boat and vomited. He heaved again, but only bile came out. There was nothing else left in him.

"We've been collecting them from the water for a while, now. Figured it was the right thing to do. The lucky ones stay close to the surface so we can see them," Stephen said calmly.

"Lucky!?" Sebastian spun despite the agony that swam throughout his body. "Are you serious!? They're dead, Stephen! Gone! Just a mass of wasted flesh, now. They're not lucky. They don't exist anymore," he said with venom.

"I don't understand, Sebastian. What about everything you taught us? What about the plans we created? I thought we were trying to set people free and find value." Sebastian felt rage rush in his chest. His body heaved up and down with anger.

"Do you see this, Stephen?" Sebastian said as he pointed at the bodies. "Do you see what I caused?" Stephen looked taken back. "Because of me, people—thousands of people—are dead. I caused that, Stephen. Because I was dissatisfied with the way things were. Because I was unhappy with myself and wanted others to be as miserable as I was. Because I was an ignorant fool who thought he could take on the Lord Protector!"

Stephen gave him a long, penetrating stare. The lapping of the water on the side of the boat and the engine's low hum were the only sounds shared between them.

"We can't let him win, Sebastian."

"He already has, Stephen. We just didn't want to accept it," Sebastian said lowly.

"I refuse to believe that, Sebastian. Axiom saved you for a reason. Just now, your friend found you at the bottom wrapped in blue—wrapped in Axiom. There is always a limit to how far the LP's influence can reach, and it is up to us to find that limit." Sebastian didn't respond. His head was pounding, and his throat burned from dehydration and anger.

"It doesn't matter, Stephen. Just leave me alone," Sebastian said as he sat back down. He closed his eyes and laid his head against the side of the boat. The rocking of the boat made his stomach feel unpleasant.

Stephen stood in silence for a moment.

"Do you need anything?" He asked softly. Despite his long list of demands, Sebastian shook his head. He wanted to be alone. "Okay. If you change your mind, I'll be at the front of the boat." Sebastian didn't respond as he worked through the throbbing at the center of his head. "Sebastian...you will get through this. We all will," Stephen promised as he walked away.

Sebastian kept his eyes shut. Stephen's words rang in his ears. He was probably right. They probably would get through this. But Sebastian didn't know if he wanted to.

Chapter 39: Seizure

Mary, Medical Protectorate, Radiant Sector

Mary's eyes scanned the room. Though the lights were dimmed, her gaze searched the dark corners for shadowy outlines. An adjustable lamp hung just above each bed, but otherwise the room was dark.

Mary timed it perfectly. She knew it was time for a shift change. The other Mothers would be going to their lockers to undress and gather their belongings. She wasn't supposed to be on the floor until another ten minutes. The gap in time was enough for her to do what she'd come to accomplish.

Mary heard a door open and close in the distance. Goosebumps erupted on her skin as her heart leapt to her throat. Her eyes darted around looking for the source, but no one was with her. Just the patients—the victims—whose chests rose and fell rhythmically. She felt a sharp stab of pity and anger in her chest and this was enough to encourage her to continue. She had to do this. She had to set these people free. It wasn't right what Doctor Clauberg and the others were doing to them.

Mary walked with purpose. Her feet were soft on the floor as she strode briskly to the service station. There were a dozen service stations just like the one she was approaching. Each location contained linens, toiletries, and medicines, though Mary knew the medicines were just poisons meant to keep the patients unconscious and subdued.

She didn't know exactly what type of drug they were using on the patients—something strong enough to elicit a fully cognitive and emotional response and yet keep the person physically paralyzed. All she had to know was what to replace. Her pockets clinked and clacked as vials of clear liquids rubbed together in the close confinement.

A door on the other side of the room burst open. Mary dove behind the service station as voices drifted towards her. Immediately, Mary picked out the voices of Mother Veronica and Mother Tess.

"Did you see the Struggler that Mother Mary had the other day? Poor girl was all shook up about it. Must have been her first time experiencing the death of one of the patients," Mother Tess said gaily.

"She came to me about it. You're right—she was quite out of her mind about it. I don't think she's cut out for this type of work if you ask me," Mother Veronica said darkly. Mary felt the slight stab of irritation. She'd gone to Mother Veronica in confidence, not to be gossiped about.

"Think she'll wash out like the other ones? End up on the table?" Mother Tess wondered.

"Maybe. She's too radical. I'd keep my distance if I were you. You don't want to get caught up in her mess when she gets caught up in fancy ideas," Mother Veronica said.

Mary's anger was surging in her veins. She fought the urge to stand up and give Mother Veronica the full measure of her mind, but knew that it would ultimately be pointless. Mother Veronica was part of Radiant. She was part of the problem, and no amount of convincing would change her mind. Mary was glad, though, that she'd overheard the conversation. She at least knew not to trust Mother Veronica.

Mary waited for the voices to fade as she crouched behind the service station. Her knees burned, but she ignored the discomfort. When she heard the door open and close, she eased herself into a more comfortable position. Cautiously, she peered over the edge of the station.

The room was filled with shadows, again. Other than the sound of the machines keeping the patients alive, Mary was met with silence. Hastily, she ducked down and felt around for the medicine drawer. She found the handle and pulled.

The drawer was a small refrigerated compartment built into the service station. Inside were dozens of clear bottles filled with transparent liquid. Her task was simple—she'd replace the ones in the drawer with the identical ones in her pocket. The job of the Mothers was to administer the drugs, and not to check them for authenticity. By the time the others had figured out something had been changed, it would be too late.

Mary eyed the bottles which were beginning to condensate. Cold vapor curled around her face as it left the refrigerator. Mary knew once she reached inside and grabbed them, she'd become a criminal. She had to be sure this was what she wanted to do.

Mary reached inside.

"And what exactly do you think you are doing?" A cold voice asked as the words cut through the silence. Mary was paralyzed as she felt cold terror drench her body. She recognized the voice that belonged to the Head Mother. It was the voice of the last person Mary wanted to hear. Once she rose to her feet, Mary was going to be facing the person who was going to get her sent to the Directory.

"I asked you what you were doing, Mother Mary. Stand up where I can see you," the woman barked.

Mary took a deep breath and stood. Her legs quivered underneath her and threatened to collapse. She stared into the face of the Head Mother, who wore a look of disappointment. Behind her, the patients slept in their cones of light, completely unaware of the drama unfolding mere feet away. Mary prepared her words as they rose to her tongue.

"I was refilling some of the medicines, Head Mother. I saw that they were running low yestercycle, and took the initiative to refill them," she lied.

Mother Cynthia's eyes narrowed.

"Nice try. I refilled them an hour ago, Mother Mary." Mary felt her chest tighten as her heart pounded in her throat. "So, tell me the truth. What were you doing?"

Mary knew it was over. She'd been caught. All the Head Mother had to do was test each solution to discover what Mary had concocted. She had nowhere to hide. She had no lie to defend herself with.

"I was changing out the formulas," she said bluntly. Her hands tightened into balls. The Head Mother was a tall, skinny woman. Mary had never gotten into a fight before, but she'd do her best.

"And why were you doing that?"

Where would she go from here? To Rick? No. He was a dead end and would probably turn her in as soon as he could. She'd have to go into hiding. Her life was over.

"I asked you a question," the Head Mother challenged.

"I did it so that everyone here would wake up. They'd wake up from whatever drug induced stupor they were in, and they'd fight back. They'd destroy Radiant and prevent any more harm from being done to the helpless," she said through her teeth. Mary prepared to defend herself. Her eyes poured into the Head Mother, waiting for her to make the first move.

The woman smirked.

"You need to follow me."

Mary followed the Head Mother with steps riddled with confusion. Why hadn't she been apprehended? Was she being led into a smaller room so that there was less of a chance she could escape? Was she going to be interrogated? Mary didn't know, yet she still followed. There was no use running, now.

But, it was only the Head Mother who knew what Mary was up to. A dark thought crept into her mind. What if she just got rid of the woman?

As soon as the question rose in her thoughts, Mary chased it back down with disgust. She wasn't a murderer. Not like them. No, there was little left for her to do than to continue after the Head Mother. If anything, she'd cooperate and hopefully get a lighter sentence.

"In here," the thin woman said as she held open a door. Inside, Mary could see Com screens. She assumed it was a room reserved for surveillance. Was this how the Head Mother had discovered her? Probably. But, why did she want Mary to go inside? To confirm the obvious? To show her that she was caught red-handed? "Quickly," the Head Mother urged. Mary complied as she entered the room.

Mary stood in front of the screens as her eyes bounced to each Com. She could see the two Mothers—Mother Veronica and Mother Tess—as they walked through the reception area. She saw Doctor Clauberg sitting behind a desk, tapping a pencil against the dark stained wood. She even saw a screen pointed down at the locker rooms where they changed into their uniforms. A shudder of disgust rolled down her spine, but this shudder was replaced with dread when she heard a lock slide in place behind her.

Mary didn't turn to meet her foe.

The Head Mother brushed past her and went to the Coms. Her fingers flew over a set of symbols and Mary watched as one of the Coms—the one looking down into the very service station Mary had attempted to sabotage—started to flicker and move. The Com was going backward.

The Head Mother let it stop on the moment Mary stood on the other side of the service station. Even from the grainy screen, Mary could see the indecision on her own face. Was the Head Mother merely going to confirm what came next? Still the woman had not spoken.

Mary watched as the woman's fingers moved back over the symbols. Eventually, she stood up straight and hit a final key on the board. The video resumed, except this time instead of showing Mary diving behind the station, it showed the two of them walking away from the service station. Mary's brow folded together as the Head Mother turned to face her.

"I'll hand it to you—it's smart. The best way to overthrow Radiant would be in reanimating the victims instead of attacking the guards. I wish I had thought of it myself."

Mary couldn't believe it. It was a trap. It had to be. But, the more Mary stared at the Head Mother and listened, the less threatened she felt.

"When Mother Veronica came to me about what you said to her, I at first didn't believe it. Why would a mild-mannered, quiet woman like yourself want to be involved in anything as dangerous and damaging as rebellion?" A flash of anger roared in Mary's ears. She'd trusted Mother Veronica, and in the end the woman turned on her.

"But, then I dug a little deeper. I read your file—the one that only Doctor Clauberg has privilege to read. You're his mother. You're Sebastian's mother."

At the sound of his name, her knees almost buckled. But, Mary held herself upright. She had to be strong, to wear her mask and pretend she didn't understand.

"I don't know what you're talking about," Mary feigned. The Head Mother shook her head.

"Mary. It's okay. You can trust me. You just saw me erase the recording. What else do you want me to do to show you I am on the same side?" Mary was struggling. She found it hard to see beyond the hard exterior the Head Mother portrayed for so long.

"And whose side is that?" The Head Mother smiled.

"I was hoping you'd ask. Let me show you," she said as she turned towards the Coms. The Head Mother started tapping away again, and Mary watched with strong curiosity. Who was this woman? A blank Com in front of the Head Mother flared to life. "Alpha-Tango-One-One-Three," the Head Mother said to no one in particular. The screen transitioned until the face of a male, young and full of energy, filled the Com.

"An unscheduled meeting, Cynthia. Tell me you have something good." His voice was smooth, rich. The Head Mother glanced at Mary with a sly grin.

"I do, Soren. We have the mother."

Chapter 40: Preva Adair

Myra, Agriculture Protectorate, Lake Sector

Myra was dumbstruck. Over a dozen soldiers with blue-lined armor surrounded the men who held Myra and the rest of the slaves at gunpoint. She felt a shudder crawl down her spine as she thought about how close they'd come to being killed.

Myra thanked Theo under her breath as an immense weariness settled over her.

"Are you hurt?"

The question caught her off-guard as a helmeted soldier approached her. Myra wearily eyed his weapon holstered against his hip.

"Excuse me?"

"We have some resources available to tend to small wounds. Are you hurt?" The question snapped her out of her pondering as her eyes darted around.

"Where's Markus?"

"I'm sorry. I don't know names. I'm Preva Smauth—"

"—He had a wound on his shoulder. Just here," Myra said as she pointed.

"Ah. There's not much we could do for him. We have him with a couple of the more seriously wounded over there," Preva Smauth responded as he pointed.

Myra followed his finger to a pocket of deep shadows. Jutting outward into the light was a leg coated in mud. Myra knew what she'd find when she went over there.

She'd find bodies. She'd find critically injured friends. She'd see the dying and the suffering. She'd find people who'd longed for freedom for so long that it had become a dream—a fairy tale that couldn't come true.

"And what will be done to help them?" Myra asked tersely. Preva Smauth paused. She couldn't see into his blue-tinged visor but assumed he was looking at her with calculation.

"We'll have to leave them here until we can get more medical supplies."

Myra felt her world start to spin as icy fear and rage rose in her heart.

"Let me speak to who's in charge," she demanded.

"I can't do that, ma 'me. Preva Adair is extremely—"

"—Let me speak to her." The rage and anguish continued to compete in her chest. The Preva paused before finally nodding.

"Fine. She's over there," Preva Smouth indicated with a flick of his head. Myra saw a woman standing with her hands on her hips and her helmet tucked under her arm. She barked out orders to the soldiers around her. Myra clenched her jaw and headed towards the woman.

Myra felt her feet get sucked into the mud, but she ripped them up and continued towards the woman. Her thoughts started to take shape in her mind like shards of stone. There was no way anyone was going to be left behind—alive or dead. But, what was she going to say to the woman in charge?

She didn't have the words, yet, and was grateful that the mud was slowing her down. She wracked her brain and tried to remember the conversations Paul held with her in the past. He always knew what to say. How would he do this?

Preva Adair loomed in front of Myra.

"Excuse me," Myra tried softly. The woman either didn't hear her or didn't care to acknowledge Myra.

"Establish a perimeter. We don't know what resources the LP has out here. And make sure those prisoners are carefully observed," the woman barked.

"Preva Adair? I need to speak to you."

Again, Preva Adair ignored Myra, and this time the woman glanced in her direction before moving onward with her authority. Hot anger rose in Myra's stomach.

"Start getting everyone on their feet. We'll need to leave soon," Preva Adair stated to a soldier who quickly went to his task. Myra felt foolish. Myra clenched her jaw as the anger continued to build.

"I'm talking to you!" Myra finally shouted. Preva Adair's head snapped in her direction.

"Yes. I see that. What do you need?" The woman was curt but held no ill-will in her tone.

"The seriously injured will be staying here? Is that true?" Preva Adair gave Myra a measured stare.

"That information is correct. We cannot take on extra weight. We're taking whoever can walk on their own, and we'll come back for the rest later," she stated matter-of-factly. Preva Adair started to turn as she closed the conversation.

"No." The woman stopped her turn and faced Myra.

"Excuse me?"

"I said no. We're not leaving anyone behind, or we're not going," Myra said defiantly. Preva Adair's eyes narrowed.

"Do you have any idea what's out there, Myra?" The question caught Myra off-guard, and she didn't respond. "This batch of goons were nothing compared to the arsenal of lethal forces that the LP has at his disposal. Even with our help, you are outmatched and outgunned. We have no direct access to Medical, which means we have no access to the care some of your people require."

Myra ingested the information but found most of it hard to swallow.

"So, there's no way of helping us?" Myra asked. Preva Adair's gaze was firm, but there was sympathy in her eyes.

"I know you don't want to hear this, but your unit—"

"—We're slaves—a family. We're not a unit," Myra said with a fond coldness.

"You're able-bodied individuals who can point a gun," Preva Adair responded bluntly. Myra felt pain creep into her chest. They weren't being rescued. They were being asked back into slavery of a different kind. Tears rose to her cheeks.

"I can't leave them," she said as they fell. Preva Adair put her hand on her shoulder.

"I understand. These people," she said as she pointed. "They follow you. Will you prevent them from helping us?"

Myra looked up at Adair and knew the challenge the woman was facing.

"I'll give them a choice. You promise them a bed and something to eat, and they'll follow you," Myra said.

"Duly noted. I'll leave two men to guard you. If you stay in the tunnel, you shouldn't be spotted," Adair promised.

Myra nodded.

"Thank you." Preva Adair gave her a nod and a soft squeeze before pulling away. Myra turned and headed back to the darkness where the dead rested.

Myra sat down next to Markus. The smell of decay and death gathered in the gloom, but she didn't mind. It was a familiar scent—like sweat and singed clothes.

A sudden, bellowing longing filled Myra. She wanted Paul so very much. Without his guidance, everything was falling apart. But, what happened next to her fellow slaves was out of her hands. Many of them opted to follow the comfort and safety of Preva Adair and her men.

Some stayed behind, but Myra knew they'd follow eventually. For Myra, though, she was going to stay. She wasn't going to leave the fallen and wounded to die alone.

Myra stared down at Markus. His face was pale, and his skin was cold. She moved his shaggy hair out of his eyes and pushed it off his face. He stirred with a groan as his eyes attempted to open. After a few seconds of struggling, they finally slid halfway open.

"My?"

"I'm here, Markus," she said as she grabbed his hand.

"How do I look?" His wound was black around the edges. She knew he didn't have much longer before he'd slip into the night and wake in the dawn. A desperate prayer rose.

Theo. Please. Save him.

"You're looking good. Help is on the way," she lied. Tears rose to her eyes, and she was grateful for the darkness.

"I was hoping you'd say I look handsome, but I'll take good looking." His laugh turned into a grating cough, and pain traveled across his face. "Can you tell me something?" He said in a tone that was more serious than he'd ever been.

"I'll tell you anything, Markus."

"Do you love me?"

The question hung between the living and the dying like a fine thread of light.

"I do, Markus. Now get some rest. Okay?"

"Okay," he said with a poorly concealed grin. His eyes fell back into their sockets as fatigue overtook him again. Myra's tears dripped from her chin. What was she supposed to do? How was she supposed to save him?

Myra couldn't. She was defeated by her inability to save him. She felt helpless and scared. More so than when she was a slave, bent to the will of another. More so than when she was in Hob's clutches, and the threat of death hung over her. Now, she felt alone, and that made everything worse. Myra hung her head and rested it on Markus's chest as she cried. His breathing was shallow, now. There wasn't much time left.

Myra heard footsteps. At first, she ignored them. But soon, the sound of squelching mud filled her thoughts as boots came to rest next to her. Myra raised her head.

"It seems you are in luck, Myra," Preva Adair said. Myra stared up at her visor.

"Luck?"

"Yes. A medical outpost not far from here needs to be seized. We can take your wounded with us." Preva Adair's soldiers formed up behind her as they waited for orders. A burst of joy erupted in Myra's chest. "These men will help you. We leave immediately." Preva Adair turned and walked off before Myra could thank her as her soldiers raised Myra.

"What do you mean?" Myra asked breathlessly. The Preva turned stared at Myra through a visor concealed silence. "What are we going to be doing?"

The Preva's tone was crisp and clear. "It means Radiant must fall, and we must be the ones who will bring it down."

Chapter 41: Reign

Paul, Slave Compound, Old City

The street was clogged with tension and debris as men and women cowered behind meager barriers and clutched weapons. The few distributed weapons glinted menacingly in the semidarkness. Sweaty hands fingered triggers nervously, and even the slightest cough or whisper was met with aggressive glances. Everyone was on edge as the sound of drones pulsated through the air, like a wave of wasps drawing nearer.

"Steady," Paul whispered to those around him. Paul clenched a gun in his hands. It felt distant in his grip—like it didn't belong to him. The metal oozed between his fingers. He was utterly against using violence as a means of asserting one's will against other human beings.

Drones, however, were not humans.

"We're almost in position," Hob gurgled over the communicator. Paul eyed it wearily as sweat dripped down his cheek. He knew he was trusting Hob with his life.

If Hob missed or if his aim was too short, then instead of bringing down the massive chimney and cutting off the enemy's retreat, he could very well hit the chimney at the wrong angle and bring it crashing down upon the paltry army huddled behind rubble and broken walls. But, there was no other option but to trust. If they tried to pull back towards Hob, then they'd get caught out in the open.

"Don't be a coward and run. Stand your ground," Hob instructed. Paul ignored him as he turned a dial. Hob's voice faded until he could barely hear it as Paul's heart continued exploding in his chest.

Though thousands surround me on all sides
I will not be afraid, for you are with me

Paul let the words repeat in his head. Though he couldn't feel any emotional connection to them, he hoped and trusted that they were true. Otherwise, he, and everyone around him, were truly and utterly alone. Paul pushed the thought out of his head as the first drone appeared at the end of the street. Reflexively, he crouched down.

"Hold your fire," Paul whispered.

They needed to wait until the drones were directly above them to strike in unison and hit them before they could redirect their flight patterns. This would also mean the soldiers would be entering the street. If timed correctly, then bringing down the tower would cut off the soldiers from the rest of their forces and make it easy to pick them off.

Everything had to go right, though. As he thought about the plan, Paul's legs cramped. His whole body could feel the tension coiling up inside.

The drone surveyed the street. Its front end tilted in either direction as a red light emitted from its underbelly. The light bathed the street in a maroon glow as it scanned the area. Paul felt pain roll up his legs, but he dared not move. The drone hovered in place, looking directly at them.

Two more drones appeared behind it as the red beam faded. A few seconds later, that number was doubled. Soon, the entire street was swarming with drones. The black-toned army advanced towards their hiding spots as the street swam with wind and dust.

Paul's eyes darted towards a man hiding behind a low wall. Both hands were gripping his gun with white-knuckled fear. Even in the darkness, Paul could see the uncertainty etched across his face.

The first drone flew a dozen feet above the man. The sound of the machine pounded off the walls. The man glanced at Paul as his features melted into terror. Paul mouthed the word "no," but the man broke eye contact as he stared at the underbelly of the drone. His weapon started to rise as he pointed at the machine's exposed apertures.

The first soldier rounded the corner. If the man fired, he'd be swarmed immediately and torn to pieces by the hungry drones that hung above the street like spiders dangling from invisible thread. Dust kicked up and struck the man across the face. The man's finger closed around the trigger.

The drone, as if sensing his presence, dipped its nose. The gun shook uncontrollably in his grip, and he steadied it with a pale grasp. The man squeezed his eyes shut.

Paul fired.

The weapon jolted in his hand, and he nearly dropped it as the sound of the gun cracked like Hob's whip through the narrow street. The shot missed as it easily deflected off the rounded head of the drone. The monstrous machine—a thing of Paul's living nightmares—turned its attention away from the man below it and focused on Paul.

Paul didn't hesitate.

"Fire!" He bellowed as men and women launched their attack. Gunfire, rocks, metal shards all reigned down upon the drones from below and above. Each volley was a personal vendetta—a release of rage and fear that spat out of barrels, descended from well-aimed throws, and penetrated carapaces with the crackle of electricity and screech of shattered metal. The street was soon littered with numerous drones' remains as they warbled and wobbled, only to get crushed by another drone crashing to the ground.

Paul fired multiple times, not really aiming and not knowing how, but emptying himself. With its red light that looked like a massive eye, the drone leader showered sparks on the street below as bullets pinged off its armored shell. Another shot caught it on one of its joints, which ruptured the clawed metal appendage. The piece hung limply underneath it as the machine started to move backward in retreat.

A new sound filled the street. Soldiers had joined the battle, now, as red jets of energy splashed across surfaces on either side of Paul. A man to his left careened off his feet as blood and spittle flew from his mouth. A massive crater smoked in the center of his chest. Paul ducked behind his pile of rocks as more projectiles launched towards him.

Screams ruptured the sodden dust gloom. Paul glanced over his shield at the approaching army. At least thirty or forty men were approaching like shadows silhouetted in the powdery air. The street was long, but he had to hold out as long as possible. If the attackers from above continued their barrage, it might give them all enough time.

But, they didn't have time.

Now reunited, the drone army surged forward and ducked away from the assault. The drone with the glowing, red light shot upwards and rotated. As it turned, it released its counterattack as balls of red energy spat from its underbelly.

The windows above the battle erupted in a shower of dust and carnage, which cascaded down upon the street below. Bits of metal and bone struck Paul as his hands flew to his head. Revulsion and terror rolled through Paul. His resolve and courage melted like metal dissolving in a lake of fire.

The soldiers were almost upon them.

Paul's eyes danced around madly as he searched for the communicator. Somehow, he'd lost it in the initial counterattack. A powerful blast struck his barrier, which threw him off his feet. Paul choked on dirt and blood as he crawled away from the detonation. His eyes found the small black object just a few feet away. Desperately, he crept faster.

The air hummed with the sound of a drone. The ground around him turned red like running blood. Paul did not turn around. He knew what was coming for him.

Paul's hand closed around the communicator as he forced it to his lips.

"Fire! Fire! Fire!" He shouted as he rolled to his left. The drone's outstretched claws dug into the ground, inches from where he'd been. Paul shimmied away as his mind clotted with terror. The drone ripped itself out of the ground as dirt and rock showered down in clumps.

It was trying to capture him.

Still, Hob hadn't responded to Paul's orders. Had he fled? The drone turned to face him. Paul looked in either direction, but there was nowhere for him to go. The drone's broken arm hung at an awkward angle as a black liquid oozed out of the wound.

A new sound, more terrible than anything he'd heard, bashed the air above the battle. The aerial attack sent sickening shivers up his spine as dozens of slave hovels burst into flame within his memories. This time, though, the tanks weren't aimed at his people.

The shots continued until they detonated a couple of streets over. Even with the buildings blocking the view, Paul could see flames leap into the air and smell the odor of destruction. The explosions repeated until at least a dozen roared past with silence in their wake. Even the drones stopped as all attention moved in the direction of the chimney.

Jagged, whispering cracks swept upward. The massive column shifted and swayed as it fought the inevitable, but still, the base held firm.

"Come on. Come on," Paul mumbled.

The chimney was still standing. Painful despair settled into Paul's gut.

The drone turned and bathed Paul in its amber haze. Paul brought the communicator to his lips. Before he could speak, a heavy groan splintered the apprehension. Paul watched as the rest of the chimney's base crumbled.

The chimney fell with a looming grace. The air before it was thrust aside like a veil. The soldiers in its shadow fled in terror, but there was nowhere to go. The chimney struck with a force that threw the world off its feet.

Paul was suddenly careening out of control. Buildings around him crumpled and toppled in ruin. Drones rolled end over end as the shock wave bounced off of the walls of the narrow street. Glass and rocks pelted Paul like sparks from an angry fire as screams of alarm borrowed the air.

A deathly, agonizing silence commenced as a cloud of dust settled on Paul's skin. He struggled to his feet, but the world felt funny and off-balance. The street looked like it was leaning. Every noise around him sounded muffled and strained as men and women clambered to their feet.

At the far end of the street, a massive wall of rock and time barred the way. The soldiers who'd been proudly marching towards Paul and the people around him were struggling to rise. The drone which had cornered Paul was skewered by a jagged pole that now stuck out of its dull, red eye. The counterattack was successful. More so than Paul had anticipated. His stomach churned as he heard his enemy beg for help from beneath mounds of rock and wreckage.

What had he done?

The second wave rolled over his head as the street exploded in violent plumes of fire and debris. Hob rained fire down upon them as bursts of light illuminated the dirty air. Paul stared numbly as his plan commenced. Blood curling silence muted lives caught in each blast. Paul couldn't look away as human beings were ripped off their feet and thrown through the air like weeds torn from the soil.

Wasn't this what he had wanted?

"Stop firing!" Paul shouted into his communicator. "Stop firing! They've been defeated, Hob. Stop firing!" His head grew sticky with sweat as he stared at the soldiers. Hob seemed to ignore him as more explosions ripped through the narrow street. Paul's clothes and hair rippled with each concussive blow. Dust stung his eyes as tears ran down his cheeks.

Please, Hob, stop.

The air grew still. Paul waited with bated breath. Ahead of him, the street was on fire with suffering and flames. Even the dust glittered with embers as they settled on his skin. Paul wanted to tend to their wounded, but he knew better than to surge forward without first checking on Hob.

"Am I free to move forward and assess the wounded?" Paul asked pointedly. He was met with a heavy silence. "I say again, am I free to move forward?"

A dark thought entered his mind. What if Hob was realigning and waiting on Paul to go forward so that he could take him and the rest of the slaves out with a couple of well-aimed attacks? Paul knew that Hob saw him as his enemy, and what better way to get rid of him than in the thick of battle?

A distant explosion turned Paul's attention. This was followed up by another muted explosion. Both sounded like they originated from Hob's mansion.

"Hob?" Paul asked slowly. Suddenly, the communicator gargled to life as the sound of gunfire and shouting pushed through the other end.

"We're under attack!" Hob shouted as his voice carried in and out. "We're being overrun!" A hot stone sank in Paul's gut as he stared numbly at the black object in his hands.

It was a trap.

Chapter 42: Wake

Damien, Location Unknown

Damien leaned over the edge of the boat as it skimmed over the water. Jets of cool, crisp wash sprayed his face like beads of silky dew. The light air of the valley swam around his body as the memory of early mornings talking to his mother over a cup of strong, bitter brothee emerged from years of neglect and abandonment. Yet, this time, he did not fight it. He did not denigrate it as foolish, immature ruminating. He didn't push it away out of an arbitrary survival instinct.

No, Damien let the ache spread through him as the memory turned from muddy dark, to pale and transparent, to vivid and radiant. With years behind her smile, he could see his mother. Damien stared into the youth in her eyes as she explained a dark world in a sunny way.

He could still feel the hot metal cup as his fingers clasped around it, not wanting to let go out of a boyish need to be tough. He could still smell the aroma of cooked beans strained, filtered, and poured out into a murky, aromatic soup.

With the thought came the flood of remorse—a sickly nostalgia that was potent. The thought of his mother brought tears like a caress to his eyes. For years, he'd barricaded himself from thinking about her—thinking about the woman whose love matched her smile—all warm and reassuring. As the boat pushed through the water, Damien's thoughts felt weightless and untethered as he waded through himself.

A wave of pain struck him. He could see his mother's body strewn out across the floor. He could see the trickle of blood on the corner of her pale lips. He could feel the gun in his hand. The sound of it still echoed in his head.

Damien didn't fight the uninvited memories. He recognized the effects of Rais's poison. It was still in his blood. It was a part of him. When he closed his eyes, his dreams were a reminder of his mistakes. He relived his deepest darkness. But, he wasn't afraid.

He'd made many mistakes in the past couple of years. He'd become a monster. But, all of that was being brought into the light so that it could be dealt with once and for all.

The light always finds a way in.

At the sound of her voice, Damien's heart grew heavy with a pungent longing. He wished he could talk to Myra. He wanted to show her the person he'd become.

But it was too late.

"Why'd you save me?" A heavy voice cut through Damien's reverie. Damien didn't have to turn to recognize Sebastian's somber tone.

"You were drowning," Damien said sarcastically. He didn't want to get into it with Sebastian. He needed to work things out, and Damien didn't want to be his sounding board. Sebastian, though, was stillness and silence behind Damien.

"I didn't want to be saved," Sebastian finally said.

"Well, you were saved. I guess that means now you have the chance to complain about it," Damien said heatedly. He could feel his anger rising as the water clotted together on his forehead in sticky clumps. Sebastian was ungrateful and annoying. He couldn't have been more than a couple of years older than Damien, yet there remained an immaturity about Sebastian that aggravated Damien.

"You don't understand," Sebastian said bluntly.

"There's nothing to understand, Sebastian. You got all sensitive and sad and then jumped into the water. You couldn't cut it, couldn't take it anymore, whatever, and you decided you wanted out," Damien said coldly. Sebastian recoiled and glared.

"I'm not weak. You have no idea what I've been through," he growled. "Just forget it," Sebastian finally said as he started to turn away. Damien bit his cheek. His words, his condemnation, were spoken in an all too familiar voice. The tough-guy approach wasn't going to work.

"Why'd you do it?" Damien asked with a barbed tongue. Sebastian stopped. Even though he wanted to be left alone, Damien pushed forward. "You say I don't get it, so explain."

261

"I had nowhere else to go," Sebastian said evenly. Damien leaned on his elbow and looked at Sebastian. His features were smoky and sullen, and his head was cowed.

"What does that even mean? You could run away. You could go hide with the slaves in their mountain. You could work for the Hajj. You could do any number of things."

"There is nowhere I can go that I won't be," Sebastian responded lowly.

Damien sighed. Now things were getting into deep, emotional territory. Damien didn't respond, not knowing how to do so. Sebastian, though, looked at him expectantly.

"And I assume that's a problem because...?"

"Because up until one hundred cycles ago, I didn't know I was. I was never aware of my existence. The first time I ever felt something, I felt fear. I've only ever known fear. I was born into it. I breathed it every day. It became a part of who I was. But, then something happened to me, and my fear became anger and rage. Rage created a plan, a drive, a goal to bring change and reform. I even rallied others around my desire to see the system broken," Sebastian said defensibly.

Damien could see the passion kindling in his eyes like distant fires dotting the Scar.

"But, in the end, the Lord Protector destroyed everything, and instead of crushing me, he let me watch. He said it was all for me. Every life washed away. Every building ripped from the foundation. Every bit of destruction was for me because I wanted to feel. Because I wanted to change."

A desolate silence settled on Sebastian's shoulders like heavy rain. Damien wanted to turn away. Wanted to stop listening. But, he knew this was what he was supposed to do. Knew it like thinking.

"I was born in anger and rage, Damien. And now, all I feel is an impenetrable loss."

Damien understood those emotions. He understood a life informed by one's fiercest natures. It was all barbed wire and jagged rocks.

"He beat me, Damien. I never even stood a chance," Sebastian said resignedly. Damien's temper flared, and he did his best to measure his words.

"You have to get over it, Sebastian." Sebastian flashed him a dark look. "Look, I'm not good at knowing what the right thing to do is, but it sounds like you were doing the right thing. But just because you're doing it don't mean it's going to be easy. You're going to get beat up," Damien said knowledgeably.

"You're gonna walk around with a target on your back. Trust me. I used to be the one hitting that target," Damien said, half-joking but fully serious. "Being good isn't easy. It's actually much harder because you have to care." Damien paused. Sebastian's gaze had fallen. "And it sounds like you still care, and that means you haven't been beaten." Sebastian looked up. "At least not all the way," Damien ended.

Sebastian's gaze lingered.

"But what do I do with all of it?" Sebastian asked as his voice cracked.

"With all of what?"

"The pain." His eyes softened like wax. "With everyone I lost. All I feel is sadness, Damien." Damien felt discomfort creep up his neck as he looked back out over the water. "How do I get rid of it?"

Damien's mother filled the space between memories.

"You don't. You have to let it become a part of you. Otherwise, you lose something."

"Lose what?"

"Them. You lose them. You stuff them away for so long that they get lost in between surviving and living."

The words had been his reality for so long that Damien still found it strange that they belonged to someone else—a different version of himself that he was shedding like removing layers of clothes that had been silently suffocating him.

"Somehow, you have to find a balance between what you feel and what you know."

Sebastian lived in one of his exhausting silences. The boat lapped against the water, and the motor hummed behind

263

them. Amid agonizing seconds that ticked off in Damien's head, the two of them heard footsteps approaching. Damien turned back around to face Sebastian and the new arrival. Stephen approached with a steady gaze.

"We've almost arrived," Stephen said.

Damien tilted his head. "Where are we?"

Stephen's face darkened like a brewing storm.

"A terrible place," he said ominously. No sooner had the words left his lips than a sour, putrid scent assaulted his senses. The pungent odor wafted above the water like a haze of sickly dew. A sharp stab of fear fermented in his chest.

Damien knew that stench.

It was the smell of the dead.

Chapter 43: Retaliation

Paul, Slave Compound, Old City

Paul stared in the direction of Hob's forces as the darkness bounced and squirmed with bursts of light. Thunder carried across the Compound. Paul glanced backward at the destroyed army and the chimney's ruins, which lay gray and lonely as it clogged the street.

Other than those who fought on his side, no one else left to fight behind him. The plan worked. The way to the Depot was clear, now. All Paul had to do was push his forces towards Eberry and cut him off.

But, Hob was in trouble.

Another tremendous detonation jingled amongst the glass windows.

Paul ran.

As his legs worked feverishly beneath his body, Paul could feel his lungs burning in his chest like coals feasting on dry wood. Yet, he did not stop even as the fire climbed up his legs and spat venomously at his heart.

Paul could hear the violence unfolding just beyond the buildings and felt the ground shake with booming explosions. As he ran, many guards and slaves—if they could even be called that anymore—were staring in the same direction.

"He needs our help!" Paul shouted as he swept past statues transfixed by conflict. "Hob needs our help! He's under attack!" He screamed desperately with half of a breath. The other half was caught in between heartbeats that ricocheted throughout his body as he pounded down the street.

The gray embrace of the shattered buildings opened as he stepped onto broad, rough terrain. Here time had eroded the relics of the past until only somber ruins left newly birthed mountains in their wake. Hob's mansion was just beyond a massive building that blocked his view and provided his unstable ascent. Paul labored up the building's bones, praying that what he found on the other side wasn't desolation.

A pounding explosion rolled through the ground and heaved the fragile hill on its side. Paul stumbled but caught himself before he fell. The air was heavy with the smell of being ripped open. His hands dug into shards of human history that cut into him like hot knives. He ignored the searing pain and pushed onward, knowing that with each passing second, it was more and more likely that Hob was dead. Finally, Paul eclipsed the hill and looked towards Hob's mansion.

The hill leading up to his mansion was ablaze with chaos and gunfire. In the low gloom, he could see drones and soldiers darting around at the bottom of the hill as red projectiles lobbed up towards Hob's remaining forces. Half of Hob's tanks were in smoldering ruins. He still had two on top of the hill, but they could not fire down at the amassing army of drones and soldiers at the bottom. Soon, there'd be enough to overwhelm Hob.

Desperate anguish crawled up Paul's spine and bit into his soul. If Hob fell, then Eberry would move onto the rest of the Slave Compound.

Paul didn't know what to do. He felt powerless and helpless in a way that he'd never felt before as the carnage grated against his desire to remain pure. He couldn't kill. He couldn't take another man's life. The very idea was agony to his soul. Yet, as he watched the battle unfolding and heard the screams rip through his heart, Paul knew his time of remaining neutral and unstained was ending.

But, what difference could he make?

Drones flitted across the darkness as they dove into Hob's forces. Each time these monstrous machines struck, he heard screams of suffering carry across the stale wind. Soldiers fired from entrenched positions and provided cover for the drones. Even if he fired his gun at the black cloud of drones, it would do nothing to stop the onslaught. His eyes shot frantically around as he searched for anyone who could help.

Paul saw his answer.

At the bottom of the hill, right behind the enemy's entrenched line, was one of Hob's tanks. The feverish machine was shrouded in smoke and shadows. Paul clung to the darkness as he made his way down the hill.

There was no way of knowing whether or not the gluttonous machine was operational, but as his body lunged towards the tank, it affirmed his need, his desire to do something—anything that would save lives. As he neared, the tank loomed over him like the shell of a massive, empty beast. He could still hear the screams. He could even see the hovels bursting in flames like sparks dancing across the darkness.

Paul's hand was on the ladder.

He heaved himself upward. With each rung, Paul left behind who he was until, with ragged breath, he was on top of the murderous structure.

Paul stared into a midnight hole. He couldn't see what was inside as the gloom peered up at him. It could be a sarcophagus filled with the dead. It could be so destroyed that he'd be jumping into jagged agony. He did not know. The drones turned the air into a whine. The soldiers shouted out orders as they prepared their weapons.

Paul dropped inside. Steely darkness swallowed him as his feet clapped like thunder. Once he had his bearings, he took a hesitant step forward. A bolt of electric pain stabbed into his forehead as he collided with the low ceiling. Paul readjusted his height, knowing by painful experience he didn't have enough room to stand up.

As the bursts of light dissipated, he peered into the shrouded darkness. If he could find a console of some sort, he could figure out the rest. Behind him, an explosion lit up the hill around the tank. Light escaped into the hole. For a moment, he could see what was in front of him as his eyes spotted lights. He hunched his back and made his way to the emerald glow.

Paul's finger caressed the console. He pressed random controls, hoping they were the right ones in the correct sequence. After the third attempt, the surface in front of him came to radiant life. A mossy shadow bathed the tank. Right next to his head was a pair of goggles. Reflexively, he stood so that they were in front of his eyes.

The landscape before the tank stood out in whispery contrast. Milky white fires lit the whole hillside. Paul pulled his head back and glanced down at the display. There was a single, blinking fiery button.

The button. The one which would render the air with destruction. The one that rained death upon his people. The one that could take life without pity.

That button was within reach.

Paul looked through the visor again. At the bottom of his view was the long, protruding barrel. However, the weapon was pointed at the ground, so Paul ripped his head away so he could search for a means of adjusting the aim. Immediately to his right was a single wheel. His hand closed around it as the metal sweat against his skin. He spun the wheel to the right, back to the left, over and over and under until the tube pointed directly at the soldiers at the bottom of the hill.

Paul placed his finger on the blinking, blinking, blinking switch. He swallowed the disgust, the fear, the hatred, the remorse, the suffering that gnawed at his heart. Once he pushed the button, men would die, and who he was would also be killed.

Theo. Please.

The soldiers were getting ready to charge up the hill. Hob's forces were down to a mere handful, and these cowered low behind their walls. Paul felt remorse sting his eyes. His beard itched, and he wanted to scratch it until he broke his skin. His weight shifted until it was heavy on the button—the light pulsed beneath his skin like blood.

So many would die.

But, if he didn't do it, innocent people would die.

Paul turned the wheel a little more and plunged the button-down with a rhythmic click. For a second, nothing happened. He unscrewed his eyes as his forehead furrowed.

The tank ruptured with a rolling, churning, spinning thunder. The manufactured monster breathed fire. Immediately a cloud of bubbling chaos erupted above the soldiers. The haze of drones became a dazzling shroud of burning metal and staggering machines. A dozen of them staggered out of the debris field, wearing garments of flame. The sky danced with beads of bobbling light.

Screams spewed from confused, terrified mouths as the soldiers spun around to face their new enemy. From their position, they witnessed, silhouetted by the glare of flames burning in a thousand ancient windows, a single adversary whose barrel still smoked from its previous attack.

Paul swallowed heavily. The drones reconfigured. The soldiers turned their weapons in his direction. Paul clicked the red button again with ease, but the tank didn't respond.

Paul needed to reload.

The soldiers spat retaliation. The tank rocked and shook as gunfire pelted its armored hide. Frantically, Paul grabbed the hatch and pulled his tomb closed. He returned to the goggles, his whole body becoming the tank's pounding heart.

The tank was surrounded. The air around Paul grew hot and clammy as sparks flew in all directions. Paul heard a grinding groan as drones landed on the tank's bulbous head. Soon, they'd be inside. The ugly machines would rip him out.

Theo. I'm coming.

Paul closed his eyes. He thought about his parents. He wished, so desperately that he could taste it, that he could run to them. He wanted his mother's arms around his neck. He wanted his father's reassuring hand on his arm.

Paul thought about Myra. She was the embodiment of both of their parents. She was their mother's kindness and father's smile. She wore them both like a garment of praise. The world did not deserve them.

But Paul would see them soon.

The tank groaned and protested. Sparks danced on his skin like warm reminders that he was alive. But, this was his end. This was the point in which all of his suffering became a lie—a memory blurring into legend. Paul was not afraid. He was ready. His heart, mind, body, and soul were all prepared for what was coming next.

An explosion shook through the tank and rolled up his legs. He heard screams squeeze through the metal. The barrage concentrated upon his position weaned until it was only a trickle. A second explosion followed the first, and now shock and anger were muffled conversations outside of his iron hull. Paul scrutinized the darkness around him until he found the goggles. He nestled in behind them until he could see the drama unfolding just outside his plated barricade.

A third detonation illuminated his vision and almost blinded him. Soldiers flew through the air and landed in the arms of death. Two tanks advanced down the hill towards the soldiers. Hob had taken advantage of Paul's surprise attack as he dealt uninhibited destruction upon Eberry's forces.

Triumph crept into Paul's chest.

But, Hob was not in the clear yet. Drones still clotted the gloom in one massive cloud of blackened humidity. Paul glanced back down at the red button and saw that it was blinking again. Was it primed and ready to fire? There was only one way of finding out. Frantically, he readjusted the wheel on his right until he had the right trajectory.

The drones were smarter than before and were no longer hovering in place. They moved in a shifting and shrinking haze. They were directly above Hob, now, and Paul could tell they were going to simultaneously dive at his remaining armored hulks and take them both out at the same time. He had one chance to take out as many as he could.

Paul held his breath, hoping it would help steady his aim as he made small adjustments on the wheel. As his chest ached and his head began to swim, he made one final calculation and stabbed at the button with his thumb.

The blast was instantaneous. Drones disappeared in an engulfing column of flame. The air rained down pieces and remnants as the remaining drones fanned out. Paul yelled triumphantly as he started to readjust his aim. The nose of the tank settled on another cluster of drones. All he had to do was wait for the red button to begin blinking again. Paul was so wrapped up in his victory that he heard the noise too late.

The hillside around him hummed with the sound of drones. Paul turned his eyes to the ceiling, knowing that though he could not see them, there were dozens of drones gathered just above his tank. Paul swallowed the lump in his throat.

The drones descended in a crescendo of detonations. Before Paul could react, darkness smothered his mind.

Chapter 44: Retirement

Sebastian, Retirement

Sebastian's mind reeled as the stench struck him across his chest. Nausea bubbled in his throat and steamed out his nostrils. The air reeked of death and the odor of decay, which grew stronger in waves as the boat entered an open waterway. Sebastian clutched the edge of the boat and willed his body to settle. His eyes scanned a lake of oily darkness.

"The bodies have been drifting towards this destination for many cycles," Stephen shouted in a whisper that broke the gloom. Even as he spoke, Sebastian could see pale, soggy objects bobbing in the water. "We've managed to prevent most of them from getting this far, but lately, more and more bodies have washed down here," he said glumly.

Sebastian barely registered his words. All he saw was the bloated face—too grotesquely distorted to be recognizable.

"So, someone's been dumping the bodies?" Damien inserted. His voice was even, steady. Death wasn't an anomaly to him. Sebastian was jealous of his steel, his resolve, as his legs quivered uncertainly.

"That's what we assumed, at first. But, we started to observe closer. We sent teams ahead to scope out the area, and we discovered that these bodies weren't here by accident. They're all heading towards one place," Stephen said ominously.

"What place?" Sebastian asked unsteadily. But he already knew. He could see the glow of a distant structure like a beacon. But, even as he wished and hoped that it provided safety, he could see it fluctuate and grow like something hungry and malnourished.

"Retirement. The bodies are heading to Retirement."

Sebastian couldn't hear. The intensity of the truth rang sharply in his mind as it bore down on his shoulders. He clutched the side of the boat and leaned on it until the edge dug into his hips.

"And not just the dead. The living are brought here, too. Sometimes, they're too weak to resist—they come in on stretchers and get dumped in a pile. Other times, they're brought in and marched into a chamber where they get gassed," Stephen said hollowly. Even in the gloom, Sebastian could see the horrors reflected in his eyes.

"What do they do with the bodies?" Damien wondered aloud. Sebastian didn't want to know. He didn't want to hear another word. It was too much. It was too sudden—too true.

The darkness lit up with a spasm of orange light that bathed the bodies floating on the water.

"They burn them. Sometimes alive."

Tears rushed down Sebastian's cheeks as a sob tumbled from his lips. But he wasn't crying for the dead. He wasn't sorrowful over the defenseless, the innocent. No, he wept over the truth. For years, he'd believed death was a lie. Life was guaranteed. All one had to do was trust and obey, and the Lord Protector would take care of the rest.

In the end, it was living that ended up being false. It was the façade. It was the lie. And he'd bought into it, and for this, Sebastian wept tears that did not heal.

Stephen's hand clasped Sebastian's shoulder. Sebastian jerked away and refused to be comforted. He was the fool. He was the manipulated. He was stupid. He did not deserve to be comforted for being misled.

The three of them stood in waves of silence that bumped up against the boat with each passing body. Sebastian slapped at his tears until his face stung.

"There aren't many Enforcers or drones around here. No need since most of the people who end up here are too weak or blind to see what's about to happen to them. It took us a while, but we managed to map out the area."

"I'm looking for an old man. Father O'Reilly. I was told he was being transferred to this location," Damien said with a hint of worry in his voice.

Sebastian turned to face the two of them. Stephen wore a look of lamentation.

"There's hope we can find him," Stephen offered.

Sebastian grew cold. How could he still have that light? There was no hope left in Axiom. Hope was dead, and death was the true victor. The Lord Protector was simply the gleaning.

He looked to Damien, whose grit and hardness surged like rapids. Sebastian envied Damien because he saw the world as it truly was. For Damien, death was not the anomaly.

Living was the exception.

"I'm leaving Axiom," Sebastian said despondently. The words were bittersweet on his lips. He longed to run from Axiom, to flee the prison that his ignorance had created around him. But, the words brought longing.

He longed to return to the day before the incident on the train—before Sam died. He wanted to return to the time when he was innocent, oblivious, naïve. Sebastian didn't want to know pain and suffering and hope because they were all the same. He wanted to return to when he was empty, but there was no going back, so he had to go forward.

Sebastian had to go away.

"We've found a way out…," Stephen started, "… it's where they dump the remains. It's not heavily guarded, and sometimes the passage is completely vacant."

An image crossed Sebastian's thoughts. He could see mountains of ash and bones—his first introduction to the Scar. So be it. At least he'd start off knowing the world as it truly was underneath—dust and decay.

"Then that's the way I'll go."

Stephen opened his mouth. "Sebastian, surely—"

"—That's the way I'll go," Sebastian interrupted. Stephen's mouth closed. His countenance fell, and Sebastian saw some of that hope leave his eyes. Good. The less he hoped in Sebastian, the better.

"Alright. We'll change directions." Sebastian did not respond, and Stephen took the hint. With a sigh, he turned away. Once the darkness swallowed him up, Sebastian rotated back around.

"You're making a mistake," Damien said pointedly. Sebastian ignored him. "Listen, if you run now, you'll never stop running. You have to face this."

"Face it!?" Sebastian shouted as he turned on Damien. Damien did not flinch as his eyes narrowed. "You don't get it, do you? I can't win. We can't win. This whole time I thought we were going to change things, but I never even knew what was needing to be changed."

"Well, now you know," Damien said bluntly.

"I can't change death! Look at all of this, Damien!" Sebastian exclaimed as he held his arms out. "None of this means anything, and nothing I can do will change it," he said breathlessly. Damien was silent for a couple of heartbeats.

"You're right. It's meaningless. All of this death, and despair, and darkness makes no sense and has no purpose. But, I believe that Theo can make something meaningful out of what is meaningless," Damien said assuredly. Sebastian snorted.

"No, Damien. Theo's not here. He wasn't there when Sam died. He wasn't there when the Lord Protector brought Hydra down. He wasn't there when my father stabbed me. He wasn't there because he isn't here. Period." Damien was silent as he received Sebastian's verbal blows.

"I get it, Sebastian. You're mad. You're betrayed. You've been beaten. But, that doesn't mean you should run," he said firmly. "Trust me—I just got to the place where I've stopped running," Damien urged.

"What else should I do? Nothing I do will make a difference," Sebastian said resignedly.

"No. Nothing you do *alone* will make a difference. Sebastian. Axiom doesn't need you to be its savior," Damien stated poignantly.

The words sunk into Sebastian like echoes.

"Then what does it need, Damien?"

"We need you to lead, Sebastian."

Sebastian didn't respond. He knew and felt Damien's statement as he remembered standing in front of his friends, his

275

fellow human beings, and stirring within them the desire for change still lingered in his bones like the ebb and flow of water.

It was the first time in his life Sebastian felt meaningful—purposeful. But, as Sebastian stared out over the water, he could still see the bloated remains of his guidance. No matter how passionate he was, Sebastian understood the truth.

Leadership was a watery grave.

Chapter 45: Omnipotence

Rais, Citadel, Fortitude

Rais fidgeted in his chair. He was not used to sitting, waiting, dawdling. He was a man of action—precise and lethal choices. Waiting for his prey to spring a trap wasn't the way he operated. No, he went out and found his enemy. He hunted.

"Are you certain this is the best way, my Lord?" Rais inquired to the man standing with his back turned. The Lord Protector did not move. He made no indication he heard Rais. Rather, he continued to stare out the vast window as the amber glow from the Star silhouetted his frame in a ruby sketch. The man was as immovable as time itself.

Rais wondered what went on in the man's mind. Had time created a man who was more genius, more of a god than he was human? Or had the centuries, the millennia, eroded him down into mania and paranoia?

Many hundreds of years ago—Rais had long since forgotten—he'd been afraid of the Lord Protector. Such a man was a giant—an epigraph of supremacy. When Rais was first introduced to the Lord Protector, he trembled. He felt small.

Now, Rais sat in a chair.

"All it would take is the utilization of some of my newest tech. Ever since you birthed violence, I have been very, very hard at work," Rais said with fever on his tongue.

"I created bombs that can vaporize a person down to their atoms. I created a weapon that turns a person inside out. I created a device that makes a person expand until their bones and muscles rupture. And I have so much more in the works. I am so close to creating a mindreading device!" Rais said enthusiastically as he rose to his feet. Still, the Lord Protector hadn't turned. A feeling of disgust and sickly rejection stabbed at Rais as his lip curled.

"Surely, you're proud of what I've accomplished!"

The Lord Protector didn't respond. His room pulsed with red veins of light that shimmered like a heartbeat. Rais held his breath as his temper flared. He wanted to lash out. He wanted to shake the man and snap him back into this reality. How many worlds did the man wander with each passing memory? It didn't matter. There were problems here, now, that Rais needed to address. Rais was used to the silence, used to the long stretches of inactivity, but now was not the time to delay.

"Is the next phase ready?" The Lord Protector asked in a low, soft tone. His voice was distant as if Rais and the Lord Protector weren't even in the same room.

"Yes. The assimilation is ready. Though it is relatively untested on human beings. There's no telling if it will work."

"It will work," the Lord Protector promised.

Why? Because the Lord Protector trusted Rais? Because he thought Rais was capable? Because Rais was intelligent and knew what he was doing? Or did he just know, like a human machine which ran the numbers and spat out a probability? Rais figured it was probably the latter.

"And what about Horrus? Should I remove him from the playing field?"

"No. Horrus is a pretentious, self-aggrandizing imbecile who is doing more harm to his cause than he does to human freedom. Removing him would benefit Byron more than it would hurt the Hajj. Besides, the rest of Byron's assets will be rounded up," the Lord Protector said humorously.

Rais drew inward. He wanted, needed blood. If not Horrus, then who could he attack?

"As for you, I need you at Radiant," the Lord Protector provided as if reading his thoughts.

"Radiant? What for?"

"It's going to be under siege soon," the Lord Protector said casually. Rais's attention piqued.

"By whom?"

"Soren's forces. And some of the slaves who managed to escape my brother's clutches."

Rais smiled. This situation was improving. Slaves possessed layers of pain and suffering that he could peel back and examine. He could practically taste their misery. How many horrors could he pull forth from their memories?

"You leave immediately. I should warn you, though, Damien will be there. He'll come after the girl," the Lord Protector assured. Rais didn't know what girl he referred to, but he didn't care. At the sound of Damien's name, his appetite capitulated into starvation. The boy managed to slip through his fingertips once, but it wouldn't happen again.

"And what about the boy—1C118? I assume Rick didn't have the spine to follow through."

"No. A father's love, no matter how distant and cold is predictable. The boy is still alive."

Rais was surprised. Lorenzo didn't make mistakes. How could it be that still breathed?

"Will he be a problem?" Rais inquired. The Lord Protector's shoulders stiffened a centimeter and gave away his disapproval. Rais felt his stomach drop.

"No. Sebastian is precisely where I need him to be."

Part III

Chapter 46: Amends

Paraclete, Industry Protectorate

"I have something for you," the Paraclete said as he approached the crude grave. He reached into his pocket and pulled out a round, pink object.

"I made it for you," he said whimsically as he turned it over in his hand.

He rotated a small peg that made a grating noise. After he winded the toy, he placed it on top of the makeshift grave. Once he let go, a miniature horse popped up from the middle and started to turn on an axis. As it spun, soft music played.

The Paraclete clasped his hands behind his back and stared down at the grave. Deep, unsettling emotions brew in his chest. He knew what lay ahead of him, his destiny, and he was afraid. But, above this fear was a sadness that gripped him—one that held him in place.

He remembered distinctly the moment Lucy was born, her soft, breathtaking screams erupting as she entered the world. He remembered Mary's weak but delighted smile as Lucy was laid on her chest. Richard remembered the joy, the happiness, now a distant, haunting memory.

"Let me hold her, Mary," he said in a voice wavering with emotion. He extended his arms, but just before Lucy was lifted into his arms, a door appeared, and Enforcers burst into the makeshift nursery. In a flurry of motion and chaotic noise, Richard felt his arms pulled behind him. He watched in horror as the Enforcers approached the bed.

"No, no! You can't have her!" Mary shouted. Rick struggled against the Enforcer as he watched Lucy get pulled out of Mary's arms.

"What are you doing? Do you know who I am?" Richard bellowed threateningly.

The Enforcers froze and glanced at each other. Lucy was wailing, and Richard's pulse was pounding in his ears. "I am Vice

Administrator for Industry. I demand to talk to whoever authorized this," he said through gritted teeth.

"You know the rules, Figure," a low voice said stiffly. Rick's eyes flew to the doorway where a young man stood, with arms folded across his chest. A wry smile played on his lips. He beckoned with a tilt of his head.

"Richard, please. Don't let them take my baby," Mary begged. Richard grabbed her hand and clasped it firmly.

"I'll talk to him and make sure he understands. I promise," he assured. Richard let go as Mary whimpered. He took a steadying, deep breath and approached the door. As he passed Lucy, he fought the urge to reach out to her, to hold her.

"You can't do this, Clauberg. Please," Richard implored as he rounded the corner of the door.

"Are you begging? Pathetic," Clauberg said as he rubbed his brow. "You know our policies, Richard."

"Yes! But, there has to be some exception for us!" Richard hissed.

"For us? You mean the woman you *love*, correct?"

A weight plummeted in Rick's chest. Love was forbidden. He glanced back inside at Mary, suddenly fully aware of how much danger he'd just put her in. His eyes flew back to Doctor Clauberg.

"Nobody needs to know about this," Richard suggested.

"By nobody, I assume you mean the Lord Protector. Trust me, he knows. In fact, you have been summoned to see him," Clauberg said with a wry smile.

Cold, prickly terror gripped his heart.

"For what reason?"

"What other reason is there?" Clauberg asked humorously. Richard was silent for a minute. Uncertainty beaded on his forehead in sticky drops. "You just couldn't be satisfied with the first Offspring, could you?" Clauberg provided with a malicious grin.

"You can't take her, Josef. At least let me talk to the Lord Protector, first," he demanded weakly.

283

"You don't get it, Richard. It was the Lord Protector who sent me. Your child is not wanted in Axiom," he stated firmly.

Out of the corner of his eye, Richard watched the Enforcers emerge. In the arms of one of them was a bundle of cloth that was wiggling and kicking. Richard's face turned pale as he turned back to Josef.

"Please, Josef," Richard begged as his voice broke.

"What happens next is your fault," Clauberg blamed with a shrug of his shoulders. Richard collapsed inwardly. He wanted to reach out, grab his daughter, and run. Everything in him screamed and demanded that he protect her from what was about to occur.

"Richard! Don't let them take her! Richard!"

Richard didn't move as they carried his daughter away.

Tears poured out of the Paraclete's eyes as the music box reached a faded end. The silence surrounded him in a choking embrace.

"I'll hold you soon," he promised as he rose. Richard took a deep, steadying breath. "I'll leave the music with you," he stated evenly as he regained his rigor and stoicism. He took one last look at the gravestone before he turned and walked away.

Chapter 47: A Broken History

Paul, Slave Compound

Paul stirred from layers of folded darkness. His body groaned as pain echoed through every fiber of his consciousness. His skin felt coated and caked as if wrapped in mud. His nostrils flared as he caught the whiff of a strong odor that stung his senses. The pungent smell cleared his mind and pulled his heavy eyelids open. Paul blinked back grit as tears defensively rolled down his cheeks.

Pieces of light illuminated his memory. He could see the battlefield exploding in front of his thoughts. He saw the bodies arch through the air, the drones flash and burst into fireballs, and felt the ground shake with resistance. He could remember, jaggedly, the world turning violently on its side as the drones assaulted his tank.

I'm alive.

Paul almost didn't believe it. The detonations still trembled in his bones. He tested his movements and cautiously encouraged his limbs. Each one responded painfully to his will.

"You're a fool," a low, rumbling voice crawled from the darkness. Paul's attention widened until he perceived a shadow sitting in the dark. The room was poorly lit, so it was hard for him to decipher who it was but, the ragged breathing brought volumes of wretched, broken air which gave Hob away.

"And why's that?" Paul grimaced as he sat upright in his bed. Bandages coated his arms as the skin beneath them ebbed and flowed with fire. Paul was used to fire. "Because I managed to get myself blown up?" Paul said with a soft, wheezy chuckle. His chest hurt with the motion, but he ignored the discomfort.

"You came back for me," Hob said almost too softly. Paul, expecting a verbal lashing, tilted his head in confusion.

"What do you mean? You were under attack."

"You could've gotten away. The tower fell. The enemy was decimated. All you had to do was run and never look back," Hob said with a hint of disappointment.

Paul remembered staring at the destroyed tower and bearing the knowledge of freedom. But how could he make that decision? How could Paul leave anyone, even Hob, to die? Paul knew he couldn't live with himself—live with the knowledge that he gave up someone's life for his own.

"You needed help," Paul said straightforwardly.

"You don't get it, do you?" Hob bit out as he emerged from the darkness. His face was bruised, and he had multiple cuts on his forearms. The man paced a few feet from Paul's bed. He wore a gaunt fever in his eyes.

"My brother wants me dead. And that means I'm going to die. He's planned this for centuries," he said emphatically. Paul found it hard to believe him. No matter how powerful or how much control he possessed, no one could influence reality in such a manner. "You don't believe me?" Hob asked as if reading Paul's mind.

Paul hesitated. "I don't doubt your brother's power, but no man can be more than a man. Theo alone is the protector of destiny," Paul offered as Hob came to a stop.

"Destiny bows to tyrants and time!" Hob hissed. The two of them were gravely silent. Hob's chest heaved.

"I came back for you because it was the right thing to do, Hob," Paul said softly. "It's what Theo would do. Whether you believe in him or not."

"Believe!? Ha! I used to serve him, Paul. My brother and I both." Paul's forehead wrinkled together. Nothing Hob was suggesting made sense. The man's face lit up with memories dragged from ancient history.

"Lorenzo and I worked together as we tried to fix the world's problems. Our goals were lofty, but our intentions were pure! We were going to change everything. We were going to help humanity," he said breathlessly. Paul digested the information carefully.

"What happened?"

A flash of sadness rolled across the man's face. "My brother became someone...something else. And I tried to stop the change. In the end, though, I became my brother's scythe—

his monster." Hob stopped as disdain staggered across his eyes. "There's no redemption for the things I've done."

"I don't believe that," Paul said emphatically. He opened his mouth to explain, but he could see Hob's strained grin. Hob knew what Paul was going to say. He knew the truth.

"A man has to want redemption, Paul," he said hollowly. Paul felt sad for him. Terribly, consummately sad. "But, none of this miserable, pathetic soap opera matters. Eberry's forces are amassing again. We pushed him back, but we'll be overrun on the next assault. We're facing the end."

"What are we supposed to do?"

"There's nothing you can do. Once my brother decides, fate aligns." Paul shook his head.

"I refuse to accept that. We have to resist. We have to stand our ground."

"We have no ground to stand upon. We're backed in a corner. All I have left are a handful of men who are too dumb enough to stop listening." Paul's heart dropped.

"The slaves?" Hob glanced at him.

"Your prized possession is safe. You saved them. Your plan worked," Hob said casually. Paul breathed a sigh of relief. "It was a good plan," Hob ceded. Paul glanced up at him, expecting a smirk, but could see Hob was serious. "Leadership comes naturally for you. Now I know why my brother wants to keep you alive," he said mysteriously.

"There's got to be enough of us to make a difference," Paul said. Hob shook his head.

"Why does it matter to you? I thought you were against spilling blood?" Hob suggested.

"I am," Paul began as he struggled through himself, "but sometimes a person has to wander into the darkness to be the light." Hob didn't respond immediately.

"Fine. But, we do it my way." Paul didn't like the sound of that, but he knew it was the only option they had left.

"Agreed."

Hob grinned.

Chapter 48: Mother Mary

Mary, Medical Protectorate, Radiant

Mary administered the dose into the line as the mixture of medicines snaked their way down the clear tubing and into the patient's arm. As she watched, whispers of vigor wandered through her body.

Mary felt alert, like every sense inside was tuned. She could still feel the fear and terror feasting at her courage from when she'd stood in front of the Head Mother. As Mary remembered, her words echoed in Mary's mind.

"We have the mother," The Head Mother said confidently. As soon as she spoke, Mother Cynthia disconnected the line and turned to Mary. In her hands were two of the vials Mary had attempted to use as replacements for the typical drugs the victims received hour after hour.

"Do you have any explanation for this?" The Head Mother's commanding voice penetrated Mary.

Mary remembered saliva glistening off of the woman's sharpened teeth. At that moment, Mary faced a choice. She could lie and pretend nothing ever happened. She could go back to being the obedient, dutiful Figure she'd always occupied. Mary could go back to being P31—a Role. Or, Mary could unleash the truth and let it carve out its path.

"I was switching out the medications," Mary said honestly. The Head Mother's eyes narrowed.

"I gathered as much. On whose authorization?" Her words pierced Mary and pinned her to the wall behind her.

"My own."

"I see, and what were you intending on administering to the patients?" Mary peered at the Head Mother. Was the woman truly a mother, or was it merely a twisted, corrupt use of the title? Did she care about the men and women strapped to their beds as they wasted away into nothingness?

Mary didn't know.

"Life. I was giving them life."

A razor-thin silence formed between them both as the Head Mother's face grew smoky and somber.

"And you understand what that would do? That it's never be done before and that waking the patients would destabilize all of Radiant and result in chaos and hysteria?"

It would result in anarchy.

"Yes."

"Why would you do this?"

So many answers tumbled throughout Mary's weary and worn heart. She'd given too much to Axiom, and she was tired of letting go of what was most valuable. She'd made that mistake with Sebastian. It was time for her to retaliate.

"Because Radiant must be destroyed," she said in a powerful whisper. Mary had nothing left to hide. She had nothing left to lose. As she stared at the Head Mother, she wondered what horrors lay ahead of her.

"And you understand that such an act will result in punishment?" Mary nodded. "And yet you care so deeply about these victims that you'd sacrifice your own life?"

"Yes," Mary said without hesitation. The Head Mother paused. Mary could feel her heavy gaze dissecting her. Every fiber in Mary's body tingled with anticipation. She prepared herself as the anxiety settled into her bones.

"Mary," the Head Mother began in a low voice, "have you ever heard of the Hajj?"

Mother Mary watched the liquids as they slipped into the patient's body. She looked at the young woman's face. Beneath relaxed muscles and matted hair, she looked at peace.

Soon, you will be, child.

At first, Mary was confused. She'd heard rumors, whispers, of an underground force which resisted the Lord Protector and his Enforcers, but she assumed it was mere propaganda—fearmongering.

"The Hajj? They're made up," Mary said evenly. She had no idea where the conversation was going but could see the Head Mother's shoulders relax a fraction.

"No, Mary, they are quite real. They have infiltrated almost every organization in Axiom, including Radiant." The Head Mother's words were grave. Mary's skin crawled as she understood the implications.

"I have nothing to do with them," Mary defended as paranoia settled into her mind. Though her crime was severe, being attached and affiliated with a rebel group would result in horrors that Mary didn't want to imagine.

"I know," The Head Mother said as she leaned up against the wall behind her. Mary's brow creased together in folds of bewilderment. "I know because I am the Hajj member in Radiant." Her words rang in Mary's ears. Was it a trick? Was the Head Mother trying to lure her in and ensnare her?

The look on her face was frank and firm.

"You're serious." The Head Mother nodded with a small tilt of her head. Mary was shocked. The whole time the Head Mother paraded around in a cloud of haunt, though she was working against Doctor Clauberg and his schemes. As Mary looked at her, she couldn't help but see a genuine warmth in her otherwise brooding demeanor.

"Your plan," the Head Mother started, "is brilliant. I never thought about incorporating the victims, but it makes so much sense." Mary found herself nodding, despite the relative shock still numbing her body. "But, what do we do once they're awake?" She asked thoughtfully. Through her aggressive character, Mary could see concern.

"Someone needs to lead them," Mary said softly. The Head Mother's lips formed a crisp line as they exchanged glances. The two of them were caregivers—not leaders. Mary especially had no desire to marshal the forces, rally the troops, nor lead the charge. "Is there anyone who can help? Anybody in the Hajj?" Mother Cynthia tilted her head as if thinking.

"Yes, actually. My contact, he's the Administrator over Agriculture. He will know if there are any units available," she said confidently. Mary nodded as a burst of excitement flared in her chest.

"Call him."

"I did. Are you sure you want to be a part of this?" The Head Mother invited.

Mary didn't hesitate.

"I am."

Mother Mary put the needle back on her cart. She looked at the woman in front of her with deep, stirring compassion. She hoped that when the girl awoke, she'd be willing to help overthrow Radiant. She hoped she awoke at all.

There was no telling what damage was going on inside the woman's mind. For all Mary knew, every single one of them could wake up combative, or out of their minds, or incapable of speech, or any number of possible side effects.

But Mary had to try. She had to bring them back to life. She had to save them. She felt this need inside of her chest. It gnawed. Every one of them was Sebastian.

They were children, at a distance.

"Mother Mary." The whisper lunged out of the darkness and made Mary jump. But, she recognized the voice.

"Head Mother?" The imposing woman melted out of the nothingness as she stepped into the light of Mary's cart. The single bulb cast a weak glow on the woman's skin. The look she threw at Mary made her blood grow cold.

"There's been a development," she said tersely.

"Of what sort?" Mary asked as confusion broke out in beads of sweat.

"A couple of Enforcers are here for you. You're being collected," she said ambiguously.

"Collected? You mean, Extracted, right?" Fear and trepidation were opposite beats of her heart.

"That...I do not know. It does not appear so. If that were the case, they'd already have you in restraints. Instead, they sent me to retrieve you. For what reason, I do not know." The two of them shared a pregnant silence.

"And what about all of them?" Mary asked as she extended her hands to the islands of low light.

"They will be saved. Because of you," the Head Mother said proudly. Mary bit her lip uncertainly. She wanted to be there for each of them when they rose from their enslavement. "Help is on the way," the Head Mother said confidently. Her words made Mary feel better. "I will buy you some time to get your things in order," the fixed woman said as she tilted her head and settled back into the ashen veil.

Mother Mary was alone. Her eyes roamed the faces of the victims. Each one she knew intimately. There were no strangers as they slept. But, she was being taken away. She was being removed. Why? Mary didn't know. Her attention went back to the IV line that was nearing emptiness. The last of her medicine was being administered.

Radiant was going to have an awakening.

Chapter 49: The Suffering

Sebastian, Industry Protectorate, Hydra

The wind stirred Sebastian's hair and stroked his face tenderly. He yearned for the caress to be real, to be human. He wanted the wind to take with it the doubts and fears and uncertainties weighing upon his thoughts. Sebastian stood at the front of the boat with his eyes closed.

Why didn't you leave?

Sebastian didn't know the answer. He desired freedom. He thirsted for it, even.

Like a deer pants for streams of water,
so I thirst for you.

But, what was freedom without justice? Could he live with himself knowing he abandoned so many to the tyranny of a monster? Sebastian didn't know how even to live yet, but he knew the voice inside of his mind wouldn't let him rest. The result of turning his back on Axiom would be a life unlivable.

The boat bobbed up and down on the water. The motion spun inside Sebastian's body. Still, he did not open his eyes. Sebastian knew what was approaching in the indiscernible dark. He knew what dreadful mirror would be reflected. He could feel the trepidation gather on his skin like oil.

"We're almost there," Stephen spoke from behind Sebastian. His voice was solemn, uncertain. "You know, we don't have to see it, Sebastian."

Sebastian didn't want to see. But he knew he needed to. There was too much in himself that was unresolved. Stephen took his silence as his answer as his footsteps receded. Sebastian returned his attention to the wind's hand running across his skin. Why couldn't he be like the wind—unseen, inscrutable, present.

Sebastian's musing was interrupted by laughter. Sebastian could hear Damien talking in a low voice to the old man from just over his shoulder. Sebastian hadn't yet faced Father O'Reilly. Truly, he didn't know what to say. A part of Sebastian wanted to blame the old man.

Yes, it was Sam's death that propelled Sebastian along this path, but it was the old man who'd given Sebastian the final push. By giving Sebastian the book, he'd sentenced Sebastian to a misery of understanding.

The air thinned. The canyon walls around the boat widened as the gorge opened up on both sides. Sebastian swallowed heavily as the boat slowed. His heart gorged upon his temples as the throbbing intensified. He fought the urge to dive back into the water—to satisfy the need to run.

But, Sebastian knew, there was no running from this.

Sebastian saw the monstrous memory every time he closed his eyes. It was sickly nostalgia bloated with watery despair. It infiltrated every breath. It was why drowning was so easy. Above the water, he couldn't breathe.

Even now, with eyes screwed shut, he could see his greatest fears unfolding like they were happening. Cold heat crawled up his spine and nuzzled into his courage.

He couldn't open them.

He couldn't open them.

He wouldn't open them!

Sam's smile filled Sebastian's mind. His words were clear as if they never left his ear.

We have a destiny.

The penstocks closed around his irregular heart, and calm returned. It wasn't permanent, Sebastian knew, but he invited it in hungrily. Sam's image faded from his mind. Resolve gathered like clouds. As the boat came to a halt, Sebastian knew he was at his destination. He knew he was where he needed to be—not hiding, or disappearing into the Scar, or drowning at the bottom of the river.

Sebastian took a deep breath. His eyes slid open.

Looming above the boat, silhouetted in the dark by blazing red lines, was Hydra. Sebastian could feel his heart plummet as his eyes traced the edges of the massive gap in the middle. Red lines collected on either side of the hole and gave the appearance of an enormous wound that was festered and aggravated. Pieces of Hydra fell off in chunks like bits of flame that splashed into the water coursing through the breach.

Sporadically, the red lines shot towards each other as if trying to reconnect Hydra's broken halves. They connected in a dazzling display of sparks and grandeur. But, the task was too much. The wound was too great—the pain too immense.

There was no restoring what was lost.

Sebastian could still see Hydra crumbling. He could still see whole industries get wiped away. He could feel every single person dying, like breathing in lungful after lungful of water. Tears rushed to his cheeks. This time, they weren't for him. They weren't for all the mistakes he'd made. They weren't even for his disappointments, anxieties, or fears.

The tears were for Axiom.

Sebastian sobbed, and sobbed, and sobbed. He sobbed through Sam's death. He poured himself out through being rejected by the Directors. He broke wide open as he closed himself inside knowing he could never be his mother's son. He screamed and raged in the quiet betrayal of his father attempting to kill him. He swam through the murky depths of despair as Hydra fell apart right before his eyes. Sebastian faced all of his pain, all of his suffering, all of his loss, and he wept.

Eventually, Sebastian acknowledged a presence amid his pain. He did not announce himself. He did not prod or intrude. Nor did Sebastian get the sense that he was there out of curiosity or pity. No, he was simply there. Waiting.

"Damien?" Sebastian said as he wiped away agony.

"Sebastian," Damien said confidently.

Sebastian stood and turned. Behind him, Hydra burned.

"Get me to the Hajj."

Chapter 50: Betrayal

Byron, Citadel, The Refuge

Byron seethed. His customarily controlled demeanor—a byproduct of years of hiding his true intentions—was unraveling. Like pins needling into his chest, the anger pricked his heart and set it thrusting back and forth.

The betrayal was fresh on his mind.

As he trudged up the steps and neared the Refuge, his anger didn't subside. Hastily, he cleared the wall in front of him and stepped inside the luminous room.

Abby wasn't present, and this brought a new wave of irritation. His skin felt hot and restless. Keenly aware of how close he was to losing his cool, Byron closed his eyes and took a steadying, calming breath. Maybe it was simply a misunderstanding—an error in the intel.

Byron heard footsteps approaching from the opposite side of the room—from Abby's Quarters. He could tell it was her by the soft pitter-patter of her gait. As she neared, he worked through his words until he found what he wanted to say. The wall in front of him dissipated as she entered.

"Oh. Hey, dad. I didn't know you were stopping by," Abby said as her voice broke away from the dialect of her mother, smooth and lush, to her tone, high-pitched and curious. As she spoke, Director Florence's face disappeared, and her daughter took her place.

Byron was used to the transition—he'd seen it hundreds of times—but he was beginning to see just how similar Abby was to her mother. Even with the transition, Byron could still see his deceased wife. Byron looked past his wife and glared at his daughter.

"What did you do?" He leveled. Her head tilted.

"What do you mean? I just made dinner, if that's what you're asking," she said sincerely.

Byron was prepared for her deflection and subtlety. After all, he'd raised her. He'd taught her how to step into the role of her mother. He'd taught her how to be diplomatic,

296

direct, authoritative. He'd taught her how to feign ignorance and attack with wisdom. Everything Abigail Florence represented was because he'd taught her. Yet, he didn't see this betrayal coming, and that's what hurt the most.

"Radiant," he said bitterly. With a single word, Byron brought his daughter up to speed with her father's fury. Her eyes narrowed, but she did not speak. Her lack of defense enticed him to rage, but he didn't take the bait. "I take it from your silence that you understand the gravity of your decision to go behind my back," he accused. Her face flashed disdain.

"I did no such thing, father," she said hollowly. Byron's temper flared, but he held it in check. This was not hide and seek. He would not let her pull him out into the open.

"According to the information I received, my assets are presently on the move towards Radiant. Is this true?"

"Some are already inside Radiant," Abby interrupted.

This new piece of information brought a new level of anger. Byron hid it, though, behind tact and guile. If he let Abby see just how perturbed and unfettered he was, she would have the upper hand.

"By whose authority?"

"Yours," Abby stated firmly.

"I did not permit nor grant any such thing," he began through gritted teeth.

"You did, father, when you trained me. When you raised me to understand how all of this," she indicated as she extended her hands, "works. You taught me that we could not stand idly by while powerful forces tried to push us down."

"Don't patronize to me, child," Byron started. His blood was boiling. "You willingly chose to go behind my back. You knew exactly what I would say if you brought these plans to me from the beginning," he accused. Abby nodded.

"Yes, father. You showed me that one must not always wait for those in authority to make the right call. You were distracted by Horrus and by Sebastian's whereabouts and by the massive machine that is the Hajj. If I brought my plans to you, your position would ultimately be biased and tainted by the

297

present threats and pressures. I was planning for the future, for the next three moves, so that you wouldn't have to."

"No," Byron said bluntly. "That is not your call to make, Abigail. I am in charge," he said pointedly.

"So, you know how to contact all of the Administrators? You know how to leverage Axiom's NOOM system—what's left of it—so that your assets will make it out alive?" Abby said with fire in the voice. Byron felt himself being backed into a corner as his lip curled.

"Tell me, father, where's Damien right now? Where's the Lord Protector? Is he right outside? Is he in this room? Are there barriers protecting us from being overheard, seen? Yes, and none of them are by your design. You may lead the Hajj, but I designed it. I built it," she said vehemently.

Byron could feel his pulse in his temple. He wanted to put his daughter in her place. He wanted to step forward and back her up against the wall as he explained to her all the death that he saw every day. He wanted her to understand why he made the decisions he made to protect them, save people, and prevent chaos. But, he remained rooted in place.

"You betrayed me, Abigail."

"I did the right thing, dad," Abby said staunchly. Byron shook his head. They'd reached an impasse.

"Rais is on his way to Radiant," he revealed. Byron watched the color drain from his daughter's face. He pitied her.

"Rais? Alone?"

"He has a substantial force with him. He'll arrive just as your forces will." Byron watched the fear accumulate behind his daughter's eyes.

"We have to send help," she pleaded.

"No, Abigail. There's no one to send."

"They'll be slaughtered, dad. Please." Tears were brimming in her eyes. Byron knew the argument was over, now. His heart felt heavy and clogged, but he knew he had to make this decision.

"Abigail, *you* sent them to the slaughter. You failed to account for all the variables, and now people are going to die."

Abby shook her head aggressively. "Now, I have to contact the rest of the Administrators. I can use your mistake to our advantage. While Rais is distracted, we can take out his stronghold in Technology," Byron reassured. Abby did not look consoled as she stared at him with angry, puffy eyes.

"Now, who's the one betrayed?" Abby accused. Byron felt the weight on her statement as his body stiffened. "All I needed was for you to trust me," she said sorrowfully. As she spoke, the wall behind Byron started to bleed as red veins rose out of the surface. Byron followed her wide-eyed gaze until he was staring at the intrusion. His heart suddenly grew sad, but he did not know why. Byron turned back to his daughter.

"You've proven that I can't," he said. Fresh tears rose to the surface of Abby's ache. With a flick of her wrist, Byron's daughter disappeared, and his wife's face returned. There were no tears on her rosy cheeks. Without a word, Director Florence departed the room and left Byron alone.

Chapter 51: Turning Tide

Sebastian, Location Unknown

Sebastian felt emptied. As the boat sped through the darkened landscape, a stillness gathered in his chest. His tears were dried, now. Hydra was behind them. He did not know what lay ahead, but Sebastian had already accepted that he couldn't avoid it any longer.

You can't avoid him, either.

Sebastian bit his cheek and turned. He could see the old man's silhouette. He sat alone, propped up against the stack of bodies smothered by the tarp like some kind of guardian.

Sebastian swallowed the lump in his throat.

He didn't want to go to him because Sebastian knew that the man had knowledge he did not want to know. Not everything the man was going to speak to him made sense, even if his words were real, and Sebastian found this hurdle almost insurmountable. But, he knew he needed to talk to him. His journey started with him, so perhaps his next step did too.

"Something you want to say, my boy?" The old man spoke from the darkness. His voice was like water. Somehow, Sebastian's feet had taken him across the deck.

"I...I need to know. Why me?" The question felt heavy as it left his tongue, but he didn't feel lighter.

"Ah. The age-old question. Take a seat, son," the old man indicated as he extended his hand to the space beside him. Sebastian felt weariness take over his body as his knees bowed, and he sat down next to him.

As the wind of his entrance settled, Sebastian could smell the old man—like the refreshing aroma of machinery in Hydra. For a few seconds, there was only a wakeful silence. Sebastian pushed forward.

"Was it an accident?"

"An accident? You mean a mistake, correct? Was it a mistake that I gave you the book and sent you on a journey in search of the truth?"

"Yes," Sebastian said softly. He didn't know what he wanted to hear.

"Son, all of life is a journey in pursuit of the truth. I simply gave you the tool that would help you arrive quicker than others," he said mystically. Sebastian didn't like the answer but knew it was true. "And when you got there, what did you find?" Sebastian peered into himself.

"A world I never knew existed."

"A kingdom, you'd say?"

"Yes. But what does it all mean? How can all of this—all of my emotions, and knowledge, and mystery, and information, and the unknown—how can it all exist together?"

"That is for you to figure out, Sebastian. I can paint the masterpiece that is living, but if you can only see in black and white, how can I describe the color of a sunrise?"

"I've never seen a sunrise," Sebastian deflected.

"Exactly."

Sebastian returned to the comfort of silence and thoughts. The old man hadn't yet answered his questions, but nor had Sebastian asked what he'd intended to ask. Their conversation had taken a life of its own.

"What do I do? With this world?"

"You take responsibility, Sebastian. You've become an administrator, a steward, of this kingdom within. It is up to you to lead others along the same journey." Bitterness coiled in Sebastian's heart.

"I tried that," he spat. "And it ended in suffering."

"Where were you leading them?" The question caught Sebastian off-guard.

"What do you mean?"

"A man can only follow another man if the one leading knows where they are going," the old man said cryptically. Sebastian chewed on his words until he tasted their meaning.

"I have to walk alone," he said resolutely.

"Before you can know where others must go, yes. You were created for a purpose, Sebastian. You are not a mistake,

but you must *become* to show others the way they must go."
Sebastian heard his words, but they'd lost their meaning.

"What if I don't want this? What if I don't want to lead? What if I just want to stay in the background and remain anonymous, uninvolved, compliant?" It was what he ached for—this normalcy.

"Then Hydra would not have fallen," the old man said. His words were poignant, real, and they tore into Sebastian with their ferocity. As if sensing the torrent of pain crashing upon him, the old man put his hand on Sebastian's shoulder. Sebastian felt the warmth of his touch settle into his skin.

"I have seen thousands of years, Sebastian. What's happening in Axiom was eventual. In some ways, it was unavoidable. But, what makes the inevitable meaningful is the one who gathers the pieces and puts everything back together."

The old man returned to silence. Sebastian's heart spun in his chest. He needed to be alone, but he could not leave the old man. Beyond this moment was loneliness.

Before he could respond, though, Sebastian felt the wood vibrate as heavy feet ran across the deck. He heard shouting, too, and rose to his feet.

Something was wrong.

A low, monotonous buzz filled the air above them as the drones clouded the darkness with bobbing, weaving red lights. Sebastian turned to the old man.

"They've found us!"

Chapter 52: The Grunge

Paraclete, Technology Protectorate, The Nest

The Paraclete walked with determined, purposeful steps as he exited the Train. The events that had unfolded in the last few cycles were all a blur, but his goal was steadfast in his thoughts. Nobody stopped him as he traversed the streets of Technology. They looked at his armor and saw the Paraclete. They looked at a man and saw a nightmare.

The Paraclete had numerous resources at his disposal. He could go outside of the laws to accomplish his tasks. In a way, it was the perfect punishment. For following the law, for hurting his son, shame was now his armor, and he carried out the desecration of the very laws he'd trusted for so very long. He was a willful adulterer of decree.

But, his willingness had come to its end.

Over the cycles, Rick had made numerous mistakes—mistakes that borrowed his attention daily. He'd learned to hide the shame—to masquerade it as authority and cynicism. It was easier to look outward and force others to bear the brunt of the one he distrusted the most—himself.

But, Axiom was unraveling.

The fabric of permanence was meeting its undoing. Despite his fear and trepidation, Rick was at an impasse. Axiom was going under, and he would go with it. Without knowing what was just anymore, he knew he was no longer on the side of righteousness.

He could no longer validate his actions. There was nothing he could do for this society as it broke into pieces. There was too much wrong for him to make anything right. No, now it was time to right his own wrongs.

Rick stood in front of a black door to The Nest. Once he opened it, there'd be no going back. But, what would he even go back to? The shadow behind him no longer matched the man inside the Paraclete's armor—a man suspended between time and consequence. No, the only way was forward. Rick scanned his manipulor on the door, and it opened with a hiss.

As soon as he entered, two men sitting before a wall of Coms snapped their heads around. The looks on their faces showed that they weren't expecting a visitor, let alone the Paraclete. Once they recognized his armor, they abruptly rose to their feet. They stiffened with sudden weariness and draining fear. Why was the Paraclete here? Did he suspect corruption from either of them? Were they going to be dragged in front of the Directors—what was left of them?

"At ease, gentlemen," Rick spoke as his voice filtered through the helmet. He sounded hollow and alone—just a man trapped in between metal walls. The two men relaxed, and the first stuttered out a response.

"How can we help you, Paraclete?"

Richard's words weighed on his mind. He glanced at both men, taking in the details of their drained faces. Both were clad in black with a single symbol on their chest—a red triangle denoting their position in a three-fold security system. The other two—the Observers and the Enforcers—were not as important as these two.

These men were the deadening blow that made subjugation possible. They were Communicators—in control of every message, every sound fed into Axiom. The window of success was slipping closed. The timing had to be perfect. If either of these men didn't comply, then he'd have to take extreme measures into his hands.

"I need for you to vacate your positions," Rick said in a gruff voice. He looked past their etched looks of bewilderment at the panel of screens. Each screen had a message, a video fed to different corners of Axiom.

"That's not possible, sir. We've received no orders from Administrator Rais."

"Rais is...indisposed. I was sent in his stead." The second man's eyes narrowed.

"Let me give him a call, Paraclete. That way, we can clear this all up," he suggested. Rick could feel the armor getting clammy with sweat and frustration. They weren't buying it.

"I wouldn't do that, Hank." At the sound of his name, the man froze. "Unless you want the truth to come out about all those visits to the Medical Protectorate." Hank's face drained.

"What's he going on about?" The first Communicator asked as his brow furrowed. Hank gave him a terrified gaze.

"Oh, I didn't forget about you, Lawrence." Lawrence turned his head slowly to Rick as terror glimmered black in his eyes. "Let's not talk about what you've said about the Lord Protector when no one was listening—that is when you thought no one was listening. You of all people should know nothing goes unheard in Axiom," Rick said bluntly.

Both men were against the wall, now.

"What are you going to do with this...information?" Hank asked softly.

"Nothing. If you leave now."

"Yes, sir," Lawrence offered as he led the way to the door. Hank followed, his head hanging low. The Paraclete didn't turn to watch them leave. Once the door closed with a hiss, Rick relaxed as his broad shoulders slumped into their natural position. He waited, listened, but aside from random chirps from the machines in front of him, silence befriended him.

Richard set his backpack on the ground carefully. His fingers went to his helmet as he lifted it off his face. Cool air settled on his sweaty skin as he licked perspiration off his lips. He set the helmet on the desk in front of him as his other hand removed his chest plate. It fell to the ground with a clang and revealed a chest heaving with calm anxiety.

The armor encasing his shoulders, his biceps, his forearms peeled away like paper. The day he didn't fight for his daughter fell off in a single, painful layer. Every day he trained Sebastian, doing everything to make him feel small and insignificant, broke up in his hands. The moment in the hospital when he saw his son on the hospital bed but didn't go to him— didn't strengthen him—this fell away with a clang. The feeling of betrayal in Sebastian's eyes when Rick plunged the sedative into his gut dripped from his chin.

Eventually, all the pieces were on the floor.

Rick could feel his heart pounding in his chest. He smelled of body odor and claustrophobia as he pulled his shirt over his head. He pushed his soaked pants down to his ankles and crawled out of his garments. Once unclothed, he reached for his bookbag and pulled out his change of clothes. They were simple Administrator clothes, but they were clean.

Rick glanced down at his manipulor and read the time. He was running out of the precious commodity. Phase two was already drawing to a close, and the third part of his plan wasn't even prepared. Rick immediately set to work as his hands went into the backpack again.

The object he pulled out was of his design. He'd read about this same device from numerous volumes in the Directory, and in the end, it was easy to create. In his haste, however, he'd failed to test the device to make sure it worked. He set this spike of fear aside as he continued setting it up for its purpose. Once it was in position, he double-checked his work before moving his attention to the displays in front of him.

The display that mattered to him was in the middle of the dozen screens. It was blank and appeared to be turned off, but Rick knew better. Unlike the other screens, this one didn't convey an image to the rest of Axiom. It was an audio relay.

He'd stumbled across its purpose when reading about the effect of sound on the brain and concentration. This screen controlled a single stretch of sound coined "the Grunge." It was a mixture of sounds emitted at a frequency that caused the brain to enter into a stage of cognitive paralysis. In essence, it numbed the brain until it became plastic, moldable, pliable.

It was the perfect system. Instead of trying to control thousands of wills all at once, the Lord Protector simply enslaved the minds of thousands all at once. The signal was powerful in Citadel, amongst the Prominent who felt the euphoria of being so invaluably close to the Lord Protector. In the end, it was all manipulation. They were puppets—unable to think for themselves.

Rick remembered the first time he felt the signal. He couldn't hear it, but his brain subconsciously registered the frequency. He remembered feeling nauseous and weak—like he couldn't think straight. It was the first time he put the pieces together and understood how loyal subjects so easily surrounded the Lord Protector.

And the Grunge was being fed by this console.

Richard keyed a few commands into the display as he prepared for what was approaching. Sweat dripped from his nose, and another wave of anxiety rolled over him. He wiped his brow as he typed, hoping that he remembered the sequence correctly. He cursed himself for not writing it down, but it was too late to regret his actions. With a final tap, the command was ready. Rick stepped back. A single emerald word blinked.

Execute?

A knock clapped against the metal door and caused Richard to jump. He glanced down at his manipulor. They were ahead of schedule.

Rick felt suddenly self-conscious as his hands smoothed out his skin-tight clothes. He dabbed at the sweat coating his arms as he moved towards the door. Another knock rapped against the metal. He put his hand up against the surface and took a deep, steadying breath. With a flick of his wrist, the door opened with a stirring hiss.

The woman was surprised to see him. A mixture of emotions rushed to Rick's skin, but he concealed them.

"P31 as you requested, Paraclete."

"Thank you, Preva. You may go," Rick said swiftly. With a nod, the man departed—taking with him his accusations. Rick's attention settled on the woman in front of him. A longing silence rose between them as Rick stared into her face.

"Please. Come in," he said in soft invitation.

Behind Mary's eyes was confusion, but she complied none the less as she entered and walked passed him. Once she was inside, Rick put his hand against the door and cycled through the commands on his manipulor until he found the override prompt. He pressed the order, and the door slid shut.

"Why am I here?" Mary asked with a hint of hardness. "I'm not something you pull around whenever you want, E64."

Rick floundered in the face of her anger. She blamed him. She probably even hated him. Suddenly, he wasn't sure this was a good idea anymore. What if she rejected him? What if she was too far gone?

He had to try.

"I asked you a question," she said tersely. Rick nodded and walked past her as he made his way to the monitor. He took one last look at the screen before hitting the single question blinking up at him from the dark. Immediately, he felt a sensation in his ears as goosebumps crawled across his scalp.

The Grunge was gone. The veil was lifted.

Rick took a deep breath and turned to face Mary. The warm sound of guitar strings entered the conversation. The tune was inviting, earnest. Rick took a step towards her.

"What's the reason for all of this, Richard?" Mary asked as fear entered her voice.

I don't want to set the world on fire.

The melancholy melody washed them both in shock and sorrow. The music curled around Richard and filled the room. The song broke open across Mary's face in peals of emotion. For the first time, they both heard music.

I just want to start a flame in your heart.

Richard extended his hand. His eyes shown with vulnerability and hope. His hand hung in the air for a painful second before Mary reached for it. Their fingers entwined.

In my heart, I have but one desire.

Rick pulled her close until he could breathe her in. She looked up at him with both fear and relief. Rick could see every speck of green in her blue eyes. He could count every wrinkle like they were memories displayed on her smooth, milky skin. He could see the waves of distrust get washed over by contentment.

"You do remember," she said breathlessly.

"Always," he whispered. He felt his body relax into Mary as he let go of the last of his armor. Mary placed her head on his chest, and for the first time in decades, Rick felt whole.

And that one is you.

Beyond the song, a dull pounding entered the melody as the door shuddered from blows. Rick didn't stop swaying in place, and Mary didn't lift her head as she spoke.

"They'll kill you for this, Richard."

"I know."

Mary squeezed him harder. For now, they were one. As the pounding continued, the two of them swayed. Years of distance, of avoidance, of trying to stop loving her melted away until what remained was a single strand of understanding.

Heat rushed to Rick's cheeks as the song lulled onward. He could feel decades of grief and regret welling up within. The weight of his pain almost made him choke as hot tears slipped down his cheeks and fell on Mary's shoulder.

"I'm sorry," he said finally. Mary looked up at him with wonder. "I let them take Lucy. I let them take our daughter," Rick said as he broke down. Rick had never forgiven himself, and without forgiveness, he could not love. There was no room for it amongst his hatred.

"I just want to hold her," Rick said through his anguish. "I didn't get to hold her, Mary. I didn't get to hold my baby girl."

Mary had no words for him. Nothing could heal his pain. She could only hug him tighter as the last note filled the room, and the pounding intensified.

Chapter 53: Change of Plans

Myra, Medical Protectorate, Radiant

The tension hung over Myra like an unlit cavern. The moistness of its presence made it hard for her to breathe as she watched Preva Adair. Adair inclined her helmet towards the building in front of them—a gray, featureless square without any defining characteristics. It was almost as if the building was designed not to stand out but instead hide in the shadows and remain unseen. Yet, the tension remained. Myra could see it in Preva Adair's rigid posture.

Two silent figures emerged from the side of the building with weapons displayed. Myra felt her adrenaline spike. Once she recognized their armor, she knew they were the two scouts sent ahead. The two of them drew near the Preva.

"Report," Preva Adair commanded tersely. Her gaze hadn't left the building.

"At least a dozen Enforcers stationed throughout the facility. Light weaponry."

"Infiltration?" Preva Adair continued.

"The place is a fortress. Heavy security measures including anti-admission measures. Only those with clearance can access and use the NOOM to open up the building," the second man provided. Myra listened with interest.

"Explains why there are so few guards. So, you found no way inside?" The two men hesitated. "Well, go on, gentlemen. What did you find?"

"Yes, Preva. We found a possible soft spot on the left side of the structure," the man said as his voice trailed off.

"And you didn't think this was worth providing? What did you find?" She commanded.

"A slim chute," the first soldier conveyed.

"A chute?"

"Yes. It's where they drop the bodies for collection," the second soldier said ominously. Preva Adair was silent.

"Then that's our way inside. We have people waiting for us and wounded who need help. Preva Scott, you will take two

310

men and go up through the chute. I will wait with the other half for you to open it up from the inside. Understood?" Both men snapped to attention and saluted.

"Yes, Preva."

"Dismissed."

Paul, Slave Compound, Hob's Mansion

Paul walked alongside the tank with his weapon held firmly in his hands. The metal felt cold and sticky in his grip. He readjusted and wiped the sweat off his palm. Nervous energy and trepidation churned his blood.

The hillside in front of Hob's mansion had been turned into a battlefield. Barricades and piles of rubble hid dozens of guards, and numerous slaves were hidden. Paul's eyes scanned the area, looking for weaknesses.

The tank came to a halt and quieted to a steady purr. The hatch popped open, and Hob pushed his head out. Even in the semidarkness, Paul could see the fear and worry enflamed upon his face. Hob knew, just as much as Paul did that they were about to be overrun. Hob had done the same calculations Paul had, and the result was always the same.

"Ready?" Hob asked from his perch.

Paul nodded as he propped his weapon on the side of the tank. Immediately, relief rushed into the pressure on his arms. He steadied himself and gazed down the barrel. The gun felt odd in his hands because he knew what he was about to do.

Yes, the first wave would be drones. Eberry was predictable in this regard. So far, his strategy hadn't changed. First, he sent a massive wave of expendable drones to soften up the enemy and waste ammunition. Then, Eberry attacked with his human forces.

Paul dreaded the idea of taking another human life. He knew that it would destroy him at the core of his being, but he had no other choice. He had to defend those he loved and cared for. So, no matter how torn Paul was, he would have to point his gun at another person and pull the trigger. Paul set that idea aside, though, until he would have to face it. Right now, it was going to be drones that received his bullets.

"Yeah," Paul said shallowly. How could anyone possibly be ready for what was about to happen?

"They'll attack us on the right side, first," Hob provided. Paul shook his head as his eyes scanned the groups of men.

"No. They'll go right up the middle. Divide our forces in half and then come from both sides," Paul said knowledgeably. It was plain to see. Hob, thankfully, did not argue.

Paul heard voices from behind him. He glanced backward at the remains of Hob's mansion. There, in the darkness, were those who could not fight. Most of them were slaves. His people. He would fight to the death to defend them.

A hum caught Paul's attention as his attention snapped to the landscape in front of him. A single, dazzling line of illumination carved the land in half. The light came from above them, from a crack that had appeared in the dome. The luminesce beam shimmered and flickered with life. It invited him to go and bathe in its glow. Even watching the light stirred in Paul a sense of longing—a yearning for a time that was simpler and less painful. The light, though, belonged to a world long forgotten.

I am the light of the world.

Whoever walks with me will not walk in darkness.

Paul hoped that was true. He'd gotten used to the dark. Accepted it, even. But as he watched the light pouring through the jagged scar in the ceiling, he knew the darkness fled.

"Here they come," Hob said in a low voice before he ducked back inside the tank. Paul tightened his grip as beady, red dots appeared just on the edge of the shadowed city. Paul tried to count but gave up. There had to be hundreds of them.

The air thundered with the sound of the drone army. Paul could see some of the men below growing agitated as fear took over. Some dropped their weapons and covered their ears.

"Steady!" Paul yelled. He peered down his barrel.

The drones swarmed.

Paul's finger went to the trigger, but he did not fire. He knew the machines were still out of range and didn't want to waste his ammunition. A couple of the guards and slaves below, however, started to fire aimlessly.

"Hold your fire!" Paul attempted.

The random gunshots abated at the sound of his voice. Paul's heart pounded in his ears as the red swarm drew nearer. The drone wave entered the shards of light pouring through the gap. Their blacked hulls gleamed in the creamy glow. Paul swallowed heavily as his eyes took in the magnitude of the attack. Paul's finger flew to the trigger.

"Fire!"

Bullets erupted as the men poked their heads over their barriers. The tank shook with power as it sent forth a blast. Almost halfway across the expanse, the air became a ball of fire as the shot detonated. Drones fell out of the air as bullets peppered their hulls. But, the mass of red eyes approached undeterred, unfettered.

Paul kept firing even as his hand cramped. Each discharge from the tank made his ears ring, and his body shake, but he did not lose his bearings as he stared down at the drone army. Now, the machines were falling even faster as their numbers thinned and the landscape became dotted with their broken and shattered carcasses. But it wasn't enough to stop a hundred drones from approaching the huddled army.

The drones fired. Red streaks struck guards and slaves squarely. Bodies flew through the air as detonations punctured the earth. Paul did not relent as his weapon poured forth retaliation. Hob continued to fire as the air just dozens of feet away from them exploded in flames and debris.

Paul watched as the drone army did as he had feared. The main column positioned itself down the middle and scattered the forces. The wedge prevented Hob from concentrating his fire on one area of the battlefield. Paul's eyes darted back and forth as his mind made up a tactical decision.

"Fire on the right!" Paul shouted, hoping Hob understood. He ran from his cover and headed to the left. The forces on the right were almost depleted and would need the most attention, which was why he'd told Hob to focus on the right. The left, though stronger, would need all the help it could get once the tank's aim prioritized to the right.

Paul fired as he ran, aiming at two drones descending upon a pair of fleeing guards. Reflexively, they ducked as Paul's shots flew over their heads. The drones disappeared in clouds of smoke and clanging metal.

"Let's go!" Paul shouted as he passed the two men. He did not wait to see if they were following as he continued his surge down the hillside. Below, drones had a group of men pinned down. Paul didn't grant them the opportunity to figure out the best angle to strike as he sent more gunfire down the hillside. One drone spun out of control and crashed to the ground as the remaining drones turned their attention to Paul.

Red oozed out of their underbellies as the air around Paul burned. He could feel their attacks splash all around him as the hillside turned to globs of fiery mud. He had no traction, no place to hide, as his feet carried him down towards the enemy.

Gunfire spat from behind Paul as the two men he'd rescued joined the attack. Three of the drones disappeared in balls of smoke and fire. Paul took out another two before he reached the bottom of the hill. He slowed as he approached.

"Thanks," one of them said breathlessly.

"Thank me later. We're not out of this, yet," he said stoically. Paul checked his weapon, looked each man in the face, and then together they charged.

Myra was tired of waiting. Her heart pulled at her because she knew they were running out of time. Even from a distance, she could hear the slaves crying for help, begging for a reprieve from their pain. Myra bit her lip until it bled as she approached Preva Adair. The woman was stillness.

"Must you be so loud?" Preva Adair said tersely. Myra stopped midstride but then continued.

"How much longer?" Myra pleaded. Preva Adair made no indication that she'd heard Myra. "Please, we need help, and we need it now. My people are dying," Myra stated firmly.

"This isn't a game. There's no set time limit to these things. We wait until we have a way inside. If that doesn't work for you, then, by all means, find somewhere else your people can find help," the Preva said concisely. Myra went to protest when they were both interrupted.

"Preva Adair. Come in! Preva Adair. Come in!" A voice chirped from inside Preva Adair's helmet. It was so loud that even Myra could hear the voice. Preva Adair didn't so much as flinch as her wrist flicked, and she spoke to her manipulor.

"Say again, Preva Scott. Do we have an opening?"

"Yes, ma'am. But, you're not going to believe this," Preva Scott said cryptically.

"Believe what, Preva?"

"Hard to describe, ma'am. Meet us on the right side of the building, and we can get you in," Preva Scott provided before the comm went silent. Myra looked at Preva Adair, wondering what she was thinking behind that opaque visor.

"Gather your people. It seems the opportunity to get them help has arrived," Preva Adair clipped as she turned to her forces. Myra watched her leave as an unsettled feeling collected in her chest.

The last of the drones fled as gunfire chased them into the darkness. Paul felt relief rush in, but this was short lived as he witnessed the death and destruction all around him. Numerous were dead, and many more were wounded. Groans and cries of pain filled their victory with gloom.

A haunting thought registered in Paul's head.

The fight wasn't over.

Eberry had yet to send his more lethal human forces. The drones were just the forward assault. The worst of it was yet to come. Paul stared out across the broken landscape towards the blackened city. He wondered how many were amassing there, in the shadows. He wondered how quickly they'd be overwhelmed. The idea drove a spike of fear in his heart. He'd stood before death numerous times, but never a death so brutal, so shallow.

"Slave," Hob spoke. Paul glanced back up the hill. Hob was standing at the top. With a nod of his head, he indicated that he wanted Paul to come up to him. Paul hated being summoned but knew it was futile to try and resist Hob.

"Jennings," Paul said to a guard crouched low. His hands were tightening a cloth wrapped around another guard's leg as he attempted to stop the bleeding. Once he had it fastened, Jennings stood. A fiery gash stretched across his brow, and blood was crusted on his cheek.

"Sir," Jennings said.

"We need to gather all the wounded and move them up the hill. Can you coordinate that?" Paul asked. Jennings nodded. "Good. I'll be right back to help," he said begrudgingly as Paul started up the hill.

Paul was breathless once he got to the top. His body felt tired and worn, and knowing there was still more fighting to do and blood to be spilled made him weary all over. Hob was waiting by his tank and straightened as Paul neared. .

"You called?" Paul said with a sigh. Hob was silent.

"You ran towards the battle," Hob reflected. Paul shrugged his shoulders.

"They needed help," he argued.

"Even after everything I said. You still were willing to risk your life for what? Strangers? Some of the very men who mistreated you?"

Paul nodded. Hob returned to his somber silence. Paul didn't wait for him to continue talking. He wasn't about to get lashed at because he did the right thing. He turned and started to walk away.

"There's a way out," Hob said evenly. Paul stopped and turned on his heel.

"What do you mean?"

"Behind my mansion. In the mountains. It's an old depot. The train used to get me to Axiom," Hob said.

Paul's ears burned.

"A way out? This whole time and you're just now telling me? Did it occur to you that it would be important to know?"

"Yes."

"Why? Why not before? Why not before more lives were lost? Why is it just now a useful piece of information?"

"It was going to be used," Hob said hollowly. Paul glared at Hob with a furnace raging in his chest.

"When I came to save you. You were trying to sneak away, weren't you?" Hob nodded. Paul clenched his jaw.

"But, I didn't go," Hob offered. "I had my chance when you were unconscious, but I didn't take it," Hob said with a hint of sorrow. Paul's eyes narrowed.

"Why not?"

"If I fled, where would I go?" Hob asked slowly. Paul felt pity tug at his chest. "I don't belong in Axiom," he said honestly. Paul joined in on his silence as they sat around this truth.

"What do we do now?" Paul asked.

"You have to go. Take your slaves, the guards, everyone who is able with you," Hob commanded.

"No. Eberry's forces will be here soon. Without my help, you'll be overrun. I'm staying."

"No, you aren't. I have blood on my hands, Paul, and you do not. Taking human life changes you—it turns you toward darkness. Once you start down this path, you don't leave it. I will hold them off and give you time to get away." Paul could tell there was no room for arguing.

"Thank you, David."

"You need to get moving," Hob deflected. Paul nodded as he turned to his people.

Chapter 54: Stranger Things

Byron, Citadel, The Refuge

Byron stood in front of the displays with arms clasped behind his back. He waited, with tension building in his shoulders, to hear from Theres. Theres's Industry Protectorate shared its western border with Technology, and for years Rais had been the thorn in her side. He constantly pilfered some of her best people and boldest ideas.

This encroachment made their relationship strained, but what stirred the greatest dislike in Theres was the fact Rais hardly, if at all, shared any of his inventions with Industry. While Technology advanced and prospered, Industry lagged. Machines became outdated. Productivity slowed. Thus, it didn't take much to motivate Theres to act swiftly.

Byron heard movement behind him but didn't turn. He knew it was Abby. She still wasn't talking to him. He could tell, though, by her silence that she had something to say.

"What do you need?" Byron asked without turning around. His words were short. His daughter needed to understand the gravity of her choices.

"I need to check on…"

"Your unit. That's what you call them. They're your unit, and their success and failure rest squarely on you, Abby." His words came off colder and harsher than he intended, but it got his point across. It was easy to call men to fight. It was much harder to see them be defeated.

"I know, dad. I just want to check in with them," she pushed. Byron glanced at the blank screens again.

"Fine. Make it quick. I should be receiving communication from Theres soon." Byron stepped aside and let his daughter take over the console. Her fingers flew over the keypad and struck multiple icons with swift ease.

"I encrypted the channel if you're wondering. It's why I'm taking so long," Abby said as her words searched for approval. Byron hadn't wondered but recognized the wisdom.

"Good thinking," he said briefly. Abby reached for a white button and pressed it.

"Blue Leader, this is Overwatch. Can you hear me?"

For a few agonizing seconds, there was silence. Byron watched Abby's face and saw the dread building up in her eyes.

"Overwatch, this is Blue Leader. Hear you loud and clear." A sigh escaped Abby's lips as crimson relief flooded her cheeks. Byron was happy for her, too.

"Good to hear from you, Blue Leader. What's your situation? Have you made contact?"

She let go of the button and stared at the screen in front of her with composure. Byron continued to stare at Abby, but he was seeing less and less of his daughter.

"We're about to enter the facility, Overwatch. We're dealing with at least a dozen Enforcers, but no contact as of yet," the voice clipped.

Byron didn't immediately recognize the female voice, which meant that whoever was on the other side was not from any of the internal Protectorates. This had to mean Soren was involved in this operation. He'd have to deal with him later. It was one thing for his daughter to act against his will, but another thing entirely when an Administrator planned and schemed behind his back.

"I understand. I'm patching into your helmet as we speak," Abby iterated as her hands traveled over the keyboard. The screen before them popped into life.

Byron was impressed. Helmets operated on a limited frequency that only allowed for certain transmissions to enter in and out, yet Abby had hacked into it without being hindered. He made a mental note to ask her later how she managed to do so without getting caught.

"I see what you see, Blue Leader. I must warn you. There's been a development," Abby said as her voice faltered.

"A development? Clarification, Overwatch."

Abby glanced at her father, and he dipped his head.

"Rais is on the way," Abby said hollowly.

"How many are accompanying him?" The woman asked undisturbed. The display in front of Abby bobbed as the woman—obviously a high ranking Preva—approached an outer wall to an unrecognizable building. Abby looked again to Byron. Byron took this opportunity to step to the console as his finger depressed the white button.

"Preva, this is Byron. Rais is on his way with at least twenty Enforcers, if not more. Your position is compromised. It's time for you to pull out," Byron commanded.

"No!" Abby hissed. "Why'd you say that? There's still a chance," she insisted.

"For people to die, Abby," Byron said as he turned to face his daughter. "Your plan didn't work, but you live to fight another day." Abby wore a look of fury and disbelief on her face, but Byron ignored her as he returned to the screen. "Acknowledge?" Byron clipped.

"No can do, sir. We have wounded who need immediate medical attention." Byron's brow furrowed.

"Wounded? You said you hadn't made contact?"

"We picked up a group of runaways. They're led by a girl named Myra," the Preva said frankly. Abby shot under Byron's arm and pressed the button.

"The slaves? You found them?" Byron looked into his daughter's face, which was mere inches from his own. The pieces were starting to fall together.

"Yes, Overwatch. We found them exactly where you said they'd be," Blue Leader said. Byron felt guilty. Abby hadn't tried to subvert his authority. She'd acted out of the best interest of others. "We're entering the facility, Overwatch. Hang tight," the Preva said directly.

Abby retreated from under Byron and stood just behind his shoulder. They both watched the screen in front of them as the wall dematerialized. Two Enforcers on the other side beckoned them forward. Byron held his breath, knowing that at any moment, the Enforcers protecting Radiant could engage Blue Leader and her team. But, after a dozen passing seconds of silence, Byron let go and breathed again.

"What do you see?" Byron asked in a hush.

"Report, Preva Scott," Blue Leader conveyed briefly.

"Yes, Preva. It's difficult to describe what we found."

"Do your best," Blue Leader said tersely.

"Well," the second Enforcer started, "we heard a commotion and loud noises, and then we came upon what looks like a vast holding room filled with people. It's just on the other side of this door," the man said as he pointed.

"How large is the force?" Blue Leader asked sharply.

"That's the thing, Preva. There is no force. The people—they've gone crazy."

For a second, there was an infinitude of silence.

"Show me."

Byron and Abby followed Blue Leader as she trailed after her two men. Abby flashed a confused look at Byron, who continued to watch the screen with a growing sense of dread. Neither of them spoke.

"Just beyond there," Preva Scott said as he pointed at a door. The door had a handle and looked like it turned on a hinge. It was older than most of Axiom. Blue Leader approached the door and grabbed the handle. It turned slowly with a sharp squeak as the Preva pushed the door open just enough to see into the room.

Byron tilted his head to the side as the image came into focus. For a second, all he could see was darkness and pinpricks of light. One of the lights was on the floor and illuminated a gurney lying on the ground in a disorganized heap. There was something else, though, on the tiled floor. It looked familiar—an outline Byron recognized. His heart stopped when he recognized footprints drawn by blood.

A shattering scream shot through the screen and struck them both like cold knives. Byron's skin crawled as his hand flew to the button.

"Blue Leader, get out of there!"

But it was too late. In front of them, the screen was consumed by a shadow laden figure who forced himself through the door with a grunt and snarl. The man--if he could be called

321

such—yanked the door open and ran straight at Blue Leader with arms flailing.

"Open fire!" Blue Leader bellowed.

The screen went blank. A sickening silence settled in the room as Byron stepped away from the display. His body tingled as words failed.

"What just happened?" Abby asked with fear hiding in her voice. Byron could only shake his head.

"Blue Leader, come in. Come in, Blue Leader."

The silence deepened into a chasm.

"Blue Leader, come in. I repeat, Blue Leader respond."

The screen remained mirrored with darkness.

"What do we do?" Abby spoke unevenly. Byron didn't know what to do. He had no idea what even happened, let alone how to fix it. Suddenly, the screen on his right flickered to life. Immediately, he recognized Theres's face. Relief flooded in as he moved in front of the display.

"Theres? Is that you? Please tell me some good news," he said breathlessly. Theres's gaze wavered.

"I regret to inform you, Byron, that I am no longer under your authority," Theres said hollowly. Byron watched her eyes flick to the right as if she was looking behind Byron. "I have sworn complete fealty to the Lord Protector and turned over all my forces to him." Byron was speechless. Theres's last words fell like a blow. Her eyes returned to Byron's as she stared across Axiom.

"They're coming for you, Byron," she said as her lip quivered. The screen went blank, and despair gripped Byron.

"Dad?"

Byron couldn't meet his daughter's gaze. He couldn't face this truth as it wore itself out on Abby's tears. He felt sick to his stomach and immensely tired.

"Did we just lose?"

There was nothing left. Lorenzo had won. They could run, but where would they go? Byron felt fear make its home in his mind. He was a dead man. And what was worse, he had shared with the other Heads that Abby was his daughter. Now, her life was in danger because of him.

A loud bang carried up the back stairwell leading down to the alley. Instinctively, Byron grabbed his daughter.

"Get behind me!" Abby obeyed. He felt her head pressed against his back. His hands balled into fists as he prepared to launch himself at whoever was stomping up the stairs.

"Abby?" A familiar voice spoke from the darkness as he approached the top of the stairs. Byron couldn't believe it, and for a second thought it was a trick.

"Damien?" Abby asked as she poked her head around his shoulder. A young man emerged from the darkened stairs. His face was dripping with sweat, and his hair concealed a fresh cut, but otherwise, he was immediately recognizable.

"Damien!" Abby shouted as she sprinted to his side. She embraced him in a tight hug as Byron dropped his fists.

"Good to see you, too, Abster," Damien said breathlessly as he eventually returned the hug.

"I'm just glad it's you and not somebody else," Abby said as she pulled away.

"And who exactly were you expecting?" Damien asked incredulously. He looked to Byron and read the grief still on Byron's face. "What happened, Byron?"

"We've been defeated," Byron said simply. Damien threw him a challenging look.

"You're kidding, right?" Byron shook his head. "Well, then you might need to explain that to them," Damien said as he tilted his head over his shoulder.

Byron stared into the darkness as more people emerged. Byron couldn't believe what he was seeing. Soon, the new arrivals filled the entire room. He didn't recognize any of them except the old man, Father O'Reilly, who slipped inside.

"How'd you find all of them? Who's their leader?" Abby asked over the multitude of voices.

323

"I am." The voice was strong and confident as a young man entered the room. All heads turned in his direction as he stared at them with eyes full of strength and determination.

"My name is Sebastian."

Chapter 55: A Turn of Events

Rick, Citadel, Fortitude

Rick stood in front of the doors, leading into Fortitude. He was surprised—surprised he wasn't dead. As soon as Enforcers ripped through the door, Richard was dragged away from Mary and a hood was placed over his head. When it was removed, Rick was shoved into an elevator that brought him up, up, up as his heart sank down, down, down.

"Come in, Richard," the Lord Protector beckoned. Rick steeled himself and pushed the door. Immediately, the aroma of knowledge and time encircled him.

Rick ignored the walls, which pulsed with red energy like a heart beating. He gravitated instead towards the center of the room, where a single light cast a circle of illumination. There, the Lord Protector sat with his leg across his knee.

Rick hesitated. What awaited him?

"Please, Richard. Take a seat," the Lord Protector invited. His casual demeanor unnerved Rick, but he complied as he sat in a chair opposite of the Lord Protector. A long, throbbing silence fell between them. Rick didn't meet the Lord Protector's gaze. He waited for what was to come—his sentence. The Lord Protector would cast his judgment, and then Rick would die.

"I want to play a game," the Lord Protector said nonchalantly. Richard looked at him, confused.

"A game, my Lord?"

"I am not your Lord, Richard. Not anymore. You made that abundantly clear when you acted on your own will," he said gravely. Richard heard sorrow.

"I'm sorry."

"No need to apologize. The game, though, it's simple. I tell you a story, and you have to figure out the missing pieces. You ask me questions, and I will tell you yes, no, or your question is irrelevant. Make sense?" It didn't. Rick nodded.

"Excellent," he replied with a quick smile. "Let me tell you the story, and we'll go from there."

"Yes, my L—."

"—Lorenzo will do just fine." Rick felt disoriented. He'd never seen the Lord Protector—Lorenzo—so vulnerable and open. The transition was jarring and uncomfortable.

"Yes, Lorenzo."

"Gracias. Let's begin. There once was a man who woke up, and all around him was an impenetrable darkness. He couldn't see anything at all, and in an act of desperation, the man went to take his own life. Then, he saw a light and stopped. Why?" Lorenzo asked as he put his fingers together under his chin. The abrupt end of the story caught Rick off-guard. He tried to compose himself as he cleared his throat.

"So, I...ask questions?"

"Yes," Lorenzo said with a wink. Rick felt unsettled, but he knew he had to go along with Lorenzo's desire to play.

"Okay. So, the man tried to kill himself."

"Is that a question?" Lorenzo chided.

"No. I apologize. Does it matter how he attempted it?"

"No. It's irrelevant."

Richard paused and tried to think through the details. "Was he traveling towards the light?" Lorenzo's eyes lit up.

"Yes."

"Was he on a train?"

"Yes! Astute observations, Richard. Very good." The comment put Rick at ease.

"Was he with anyone?"

"Irrelevant." Richard dropped into contemplative silence as he sat deeper into the chair.

"Was he always in the dark?"

"No, not always." Richard picked up on the hint, even if it wasn't intentional.

"Was he in a tunnel?"

"Si." Richard glanced at him. "It means yes," Lorenzo said as he chuckled.

"So, he was on a train, and he was asleep, but when he woke up, he was in a tunnel?"

"Yes."

Richard could see the outline of the truth, but he knew he was still missing some pieces.

"Was he afraid of the dark?" Lorenzo paused as if working the question over.

"No."

"Was he afraid of not being able to see in the dark?"

"Yes," Lorenzo said with intensity.

"Could he always see?"

"No!" Lorenzo shouted as he sat on the edge of his seat. Richard was close. He could feel it. Rick's mind worked feverishly. What was he missing!?

"Was he born able to see?"

"No."

"But, he could see when he got on the train?"

"Yes."

Richard could almost visualize it.

"But, when he woke up in the tunnel, he thought he was unable to see, and this drove him to take his own life?"

"Yes! Good job, Richard! Well done!" Lorenzo shouted as he slapped his knee. His eyes were giddy, and Richard felt elation roll over him. He even let himself smile at his success. The two of them sat in this reprieve for a couple of heartbeats.

"Why am I here?" Richard finally asked. Lorenzo smiled.

"Because you woke Axiom up, Richard," Lorenzo said solemnly. "I must admit it was very clever. Using music. But, I don't think you understand what you've done."

"I do understand," Richard said with a hint of defiance.

"You think you do," Lorenzo said sternly. "You think you're helping them, but really you are waking people up in the middle of a very long tunnel, Richard. Unlike the man on the train, the end of the tunnel is still very far off. Without that light, people will lose hope. They won't feel safe or secure, and they will dissolve into chaos and confusion. This will result in the very undoing of Axiom and the destruction of this civilization," Lorenzo said ominously.

Richard was silent as the truth settled into him. His intent wasn't to cause unrest and chaos. Instead, he wanted to lash out at Lorenzo for the things he'd made him do. He wanted Lorenzo to feel just as out of control as he did.

"Being a father is hard," Lorenzo said sympathetically. Richard looked in his face and saw sincerity. "I am Axiom's father, its padre, its old man. I see my sons and daughters get hurt, and I want to hurt whoever is to blame," Lorenzo said through gritted teeth and balled fists. He paused and composed himself. "And you, Richard, are the one to blame." The threat was apparent.

"I'm sorry," Richard began.

"I don't need your apologies, Richard," Lorenzo scolded. "I need you to fix this. You do want to fix this, correct?" Lorenzo's eyebrows arched as he stared into Richard. Rick nodded. "Good. I knew you'd see reason."

"What must I do?"

"Simple. I need you to reach out to Sebastian and convince him to shorten this tunnel." At the sound of Sebastian's name, Richard's heart dropped. He didn't want to take part in what Lorenzo had planned for Sebastian, which would be worse than death. But what other option did he have?

"What makes you think he will listen to me?"

"The son always listens to the father," Lorenzo said sagely. "So, are you ready to do this?"

Richard nodded.

Chapter 56: Harbinger

Sebastian, Citadel, The Refuge

"It's good to meet you, Sebastian," a man spoke heavily as he approached Sebastian. The man was towering and broad, with a thick, well-groomed beard. His watery eyes conveyed both defeat and hope as Sebastian met them with his own gaze.

"I'm Byron. We've heard a lot about you."

"I'm sure none of it was true," Sebastian said bluntly.

"We've learned to pick out what is," the man said staunchly. "This is my daughter, Abby. We're the leaders of the Hajj organization," he said as he indicated to a young woman. Her spiked hair gave her a youthful, carefree appearance, though Sebastian could see a fire in her eyes.

"We're more like the Hajj group at this point," she said lightly as she laughed. Sebastian forced a smile but didn't get what was funny. As an awkward silence commenced, Sebastian pushed forward.

"I hear you're trying to take down the Lord Protector."

"That is our goal, yes," Byron said plainly.

"Well, yes and no. We don't want just to remove him. We want to restore order, promote peace, and set people free to be human and not simply puppets controlled by the master of the strings," Abby said as she cut across her father. Sebastian watched her father fight the urge to roll his eyes. Her words, though, resonated with Sebastian.

"Good. How can I help?" Sebastian asked eagerly. Abby and Byron glanced at each other as they both moved their hands to their hips.

"Well...you kind of just jumped into a dramatic change of plans." Byron flashed her a look of warning. "It's okay, dad. Who's he going to run to with this information?" Byron didn't respond. "As I was saying. Presently, we have a unit in Medical under attack at Radiant," Abby offered.

"Radiant?"

"Yeah. It's a secret facility where they drain people of their life force, which is then used to give people like the Prominent, the Directors, and the Lord Protector eternal life. We have a unit over there with a group of slaves—"

"—Slaves? Did you say something about slaves?" Damien interjected as he pushed past Stephen. Abby nodded.

"Yes. Led by a girl named Myra."

"Myra!" Damien shouted as his face broke open with a wide grin. "She's alive! Did she ask about me? Is she here?" Damien asked as his eyes darted around. Abby frowned.

"No, Damien. She was rescued in the Agriculture Protectorate and is now in the company of one of our strike teams," Abby provided.

"Rescued? Is she hurt, Abby?" Damien asked as his exuberance faded to soberness.

"She's in good hands. One of the best we have."

"Is she hurt, Abby?" Damien persisted.

"We don't know, Damien," Byron interjected. "We were in communication with her, but something happened."

"What happened!?" Damien hissed. "Where is she?"

"She's in good hands—."

"—You've said that already! You aren't answering my question. What happened?"

"We don't know, Damien," Byron offered. "We think Rais might have gotten to Radiant." At the sound of Rais's name, Damien's face drained of color and took on the palate of fury. His eyes darkened, and his jaw worked furiously. Sebastian could feel the heat of his anger as his fists balled.

"I'm leaving. Now," Damien said resolutely.

"No, Damien. That wouldn't be wise," Abby stated.

"And why not?" Damien challenged.

"Because—." Abby stopped as her manipulor flashed a series of bright lights. She stared at it a second. Byron's also started to flash. Abby looked up at her father with concern. Suddenly, an image was projected from both of their manipulors. At first, Sebastian didn't understand what he was seeing. The image looked human—like someone's head.

"Put it on the screens," Byron ordered. Abby flicked her wrist, and the screens all transitioned at the same time. Immediately, a voice spoke from all directions as it filled the room and struck Sebastian across the chest.

"1C118, can you hear me? 1C118, please pay attention," E64 said emphatically as his eyes searched through the Coms. Sebastian's heart clambered to his throat. "1C118, I don't have much time. Please, listen to me," he said urgently. All eyes turned to Sebastian as numbness spread through his body. His father looked haggard and scared. His words were laced with worry.

"Can he hear me?" Sebastian asked hurriedly.

"No. I can try and patch you through."

"No! It could be a trap," Byron suggested as he cut across his daughter.

"1C118, can you hear me? 1C118, you need to listen to me," he said earnestly. Sebastian couldn't take it much longer. What was his father doing!?

"Is this broadcast to all of Axiom?" Byron asked.

Abby nodded.

"1C118, this is E64. You need to listen to me. Wherever you are, pay attention."

"Question is, how? I heard about him hacking into the auditory security, but a hack on this scale could only mean one thing," Byron suggested.

"That he's working with the Lord Protector," Sebastian said hollowly. He couldn't believe it. He didn't know if he was angry or heartbroken. The betrayal hit him in the gut like a knife. "Turn it off," Sebastian said through gritted teeth. Abby went to her manipulor.

"Sebastian," Richard said solemnly.

"Wait," Sebastian interjected.

"Please listen to me."

Sebastian approached the multitude of displays, each one portraying a man whose eyes searched in every direction. Sebastian stopped as the glow from the Coms warmed him. His attention focused on the screen in front of him. The man ended his roaming as his gaze rested on Sebastian's.

"I am proud to be your father."

The screen flashed with the discharge of a weapon as the red energy struck Richard in the gut. His face streamed with a thousand agonies as tears spilled from his eyes. Sebastian watched his lip tremble, and the color fade from his cheeks.

"Forgive me, son."

The screen turned to black.

Chapter 57: Rise

Preva Adair, Medical Protectorate, Radiant

Preva Adair's mind worked feverishly as she aimed down the barrel of her weapon. Her shoulder burned where the man had viciously attacked her. She'd never seen such mania—such ferocity. With eyes as black as an unlit room, the man had hardly seemed human.

Now, his body was full of holes. It took some convincing for her to get her men back in line, though. They were terrified. But, they had a mission to complete.

"Preva Scott, report," Preva Adair directed.

"We've made our way to the other side of the facility."

"Ping your location," Adair ordered. A single dot showed up in her visor. His route generated a map on her display. "Got it. Have you found the control room?"

"Affirmative. We've found the control room, but we hear noises on the other side of a door. Could be survivors. Could be more of those...things," he said gravely.

"Understood. Stay where you are. I'll stack up with you," Preva Adair offered.

"Copy," Preva Scott responded. She could hear the relief in his voice.

The line cut out, and Preva Adair stared briefly at the route she needed to take. She turned to her group, which was six strong. The other half of her assault team was outside, watching over the slaves and covering their exit should anything go awry. Judging by how things had already developed, Preva Adair was hopeful awry was the limit of how bad this operation was developing.

"We're moving out. Stay alert," she instructed. Preva Adair raised her weapon again and led the way.

Abby, Citadel, The Refuge

The room was quiet and still. The shock and disbelief weighed upon everyone and had brought Sebastian to a sitting position against the wall. Nobody looked at him, but everyone

333

could read the pain on his face. Some of the people Damien had brought with him had been moved downstairs, which was a risk, but Sebastian needed space to grieve and lament. Abby shifted from foot to foot as she spoke to her father in a hushed tone.

"What do you think, dad?" Abby inquired. The anguish on her father's face was deep and carved out a concrete frown. She could see all the variables spinning behind his eyes.

"We need to strike, now, and hit him decisively. How fast do you think Soren will take to muster the full strength of Agriculture?" Byron asked heavily. Abby shrugged.

"I don't know, dad. The people he trusts are tied up in Radiant. I don't know if he has anyone else," she responded.

"Then you need to ask. Since you guys are in league with one another." Abby couldn't tell if her father was stating an observation or if he was being cynical.

"And if he says no?"

"Then we use what we got," Byron said bluntly.

"You mean the people that will only follow Sebastian? I've already talked to them, and they don't exactly trust us," Abby said frankly. Byron shook his head in frustration.

"Then we ask him to join us."

Abby flashed him a cross look.

"He just lost his father," Abby said sternly.

"And we're about to lose Axiom," Byron hissed. "We can't wait around for him to mourn. That's just reality," he insisted. "We have to leverage every resource we have and take Lorenzo down by force. If we're going to act, the time is now." Abby was silent as she moved into her thoughts.

There had to be another way.

Preva Adair saw the lights on Preva Scott's helmet. They dipped in acknowledgment as she approached. He and his two men flanked a doorway with their weapons pointed down.

"Report," she whispered.

"The movement stopped. I think they know we're out here," Preva Scott offered. Preva Adair was relieved and unsettled at the same time. She was relieved it wasn't one of those nightmarish attackers, but on the other hand, it could be anyone who might fight against them.

"Have you made contact?" Preva Scott shook his head. "Well, there's only one way to figure this out," she offered. Preva Scott stepped aside and let Adair approach. With her gloved hand, she rapped against the door.

"This is Blue Leader. We've been sent to assess this facility. Is there anyone in there who I may speak to?" It was a lie, yes, but there was no need to tell whoever it was on the other side that they were an assault unit meant to take down and dismantle Radiant.

"Blue Leader? I am the Head Mother. Before I permit you entrance, I need to know if you have the password," a muffled voice insisted. Preva Adair tilted her head. Password? She didn't have time for games. The heat rose up her collar.

"Listen, you need to let me in. Something has gone wrong with this facility, and we're here to restore order." Her words were met with silence. Adair's impatience mounted, but a thought occurred to her. She was aware that there was a Hajj agent in Radiant. If the voice belonged to that person, then the password was a legitimate demand. Preva Adair stepped away from the door and accessed her manipulor.

Only one person could help her get inside.

Damien, Citadel, The Refuge

Damien entered the room as a palpable sorrow settled on his shoulders. His eyes flicked to Sebastian, who had his head concealed in his knees. He felt bad for Sebastian.

Damien intimately understood his suffering. He had lost a parent and had to carry that pain with him for years. It was something he still bore, though he didn't handle it alone. As much as Damien wanted to comfort him, Damien didn't have time to console Sebastian.

Damien's attention went to Abby, who huddled with Byron. He already knew what he was going to say and likewise knew what Byron would say. Abby looked up at him as he approached, but then her manipulor flashed repeatedly and pulled her gaze away from him. Abby withdrew from her father and went to the display screens.

"Blue Leader, this is Overwatch," Abby said confidently as her finger depressed a white button.

"Overwatch, this is Blue Leader. We may have found the control room, and possibly the asset, but they're asking for a password, over," a strong female voice responded.

"Understood. Try Ichthys," Abby provided.

"Copy." Abby glanced over at Damien. "Blue Leader, what's the status on the slaves you picked up?" Abby asked. Damien leaned into the conversation.

"They're secure outside the facility. We're waiting on more details about our present situation before we move them inside," Blue Leader answered. Damien's patience flared.

"Situation, Blue Leader? Is Rais at Radiant?"

"Uncertain. Something's wrong with the patients. They've gone crazy, for lack of a better term," Blue Leader said ambiguously. Abby threw a look at Damien, who was standing with his arms folded.

"Crazy? Care to elaborate?"

"One of them attacked us. He hardly seemed human. We're not sure if it's something Rais released upon them or if it's a separate incident. We'll know more when we get in the control room," Blue Leader said pointedly. Abby got the hint.

"Understood. Keep me updated," she said as she closed the channel. Abby looked up at Damien.

"I'm going," Damien said pointedly.

Abby's lips formed a thin line.

"I figured you would. What are you going to do?" Damien opened his mouth to speak but was interrupted as Byron stepped into their conversation.

"You're not going to do anything. We need your help assaulting Citadel," Byron commanded. Damien was aggressively shaking his head.

"No. I'm going to get Myra," Damien volleyed back. Abby's eyes bounced to her father.

336

"Radiant isn't the objective. We take Lorenzo down, now, while Rais is preoccupied," Byron stated firmly. Damien could feel the heat crawling up his neck.

"I don't care about your objective, Byron. Rais is preoccupied with somebody I care about," Damien said through clenched teeth.

"You should care, Damien. If we attack with a sizeable force, we can take down Lorenzo, and Rais will surrender, and you'll get...," Byron said as he trailed off.

"Myra. Her name is Myra," Damien said passionately.

"Of course. We take down Lorenzo, and you have my word that we'll save Myra."

"No." The word was spoken so softly that the three of them almost didn't hear it. Out of the corner of his eye, though, Damien saw Sebastian rise to his feet. Slowly, everyone's gaze moved over to the young man whose face was etched with tears and pain, but whose eyes resonated with purpose.

"I said no," Sebastian stated firmly.

"What do you mean?" Byron asked incredulously.

"We can't attack the Lord Protector," Sebastian responded knowledgeably. Byron scoffed.

"And why not?"

"Because it's what he wants," Sebastian said hauntingly. A converged silence carried between them. "Everything you've done thus far has played directly into his hands, correct?" Byron didn't respond. Abby stepped forward.

"Yes, Sebastian." Abby ignored the glare Byron threw at her as Sebastian nodded.

"He wants us to dissolve into violence. He wants us to take him on by force. When we do, we become the monsters, the tyrants, the madmen he wants us to become," Sebastian said sagely. Damien knew he was right, and judging by the way the fire abated in Byron's eyes, Damien knew Byron recognized this fact, too.

"What do you propose?" Abby asked. Sebastian's hand went to his chin.

"I have a plan."

Chapter 58: Breaking Open

Paul, Slave Compound, The Valley

As soon as the tank started to fire, panic settled into the people. It took everything Paul had to hold everyone together. The entrance into the mountains was just ahead, a deep valley carved into the darkness. Despite knowing freedom was near, fear was a much stronger motivator as the people stumbled over each other in desperation. The line of people—slaves and guards alike—were splintering into different factions.

"Jennings," Paul shouted.

"Sir!" The former Enforcer responded.

"I need you to lead them out of here. I'll fall back and make sure no one gets left behind." Paul said as his feet started to carry him away. Jennings threw an acknowledgment over his shoulder as he began to command organization from the group's front. Paul ran, desperate not to leave anyone behind.

"Keep going!" Paul yelled as he sprinted past ragged and worn individuals. "Almost there!"

A couple of minutes later, he'd reached the back of the procession. It consisted of a few of the older, more feeble people. Paul approached and offered his shoulder.

"You can do this," he whispered. The woman merely nodded as she put her weight on Paul.

Paul could see Hob's tank just on the top of the hill. Flashes of brilliant light erupted from the barrel, which was already burning red like iron melting in a fire. No amount of retaliation could stop what was coming, though. Paul could already see a large force preparing to charge the hill. A tremendous amount of trepidation gathered in his chest.

Paul felt like he was abandoning Hob to a dark and violent fate. Surely Hob knew there was no hope in fending off all of Eberry's forces. Yet, he didn't retreat. He didn't hide his tank behind the rubble to give him the advantage. No, he stayed atop the hill like a ruler making his final stand.

The first wave of soldiers charged Hob's tank. Paul watched as they got within firing distance and peppered the machine with gunfire. Hob retaliated with an earth-shattering blast that sent the group flying in multiple directions. Paul didn't have the stomach to watch their shattered bodies land. As the dust cleared, though, his eyes returned to the tank. The goliath machine emerged from the smoke and shadows like a beast defending its lair.

A cloud of drones drifted above the hill. Hob's attention rightly turned to these pestilent attackers, but as the tank lifted its barrel, two groups of soldiers approached from under his aim. Gunfire struck the tank from every angle.

Still, Hob did not move. For a second, the barrel hung suspended in the air, motionless, and Paul was afraid that Hob was dead. But, then the barrel inched upward until it was aiming high above the drones.

Hob was going to miss! What was he thinking? Paul's communicator gargled at his waistline.

"Paul?" Hob spoke hollowly. Paul snatched the box off his belt and brought it to his lips.

"David?" For a second, there was silence.

"The valley should protect you." Paul traced the trajectory of Hob's barrel and understood. "Your sister is alive," Hob whispered. Paul's mouth fell open in disbelief.

"Get out of Axiom. Both of you get as far away from my brother as you can," Hob said evenly as the sound of violence carried over the communicator. Paul waited for more to be said—waited for Hob to ask for forgiveness or absolution, or hope. But, no words came. Paul depressed the button slowly.

"Goodbye, David."

"Thank you, Paul."

"Everybody get down!" Paul shouted as his words clapped off the valley walls. He pushed the woman down.

The barrel, ablaze in the darkness, burst into flame. The shot went high, high, high as it arched. It entered into the light like a star crashing through the night before it detonated on the edge of the massive crack in the dome.

At first, nothing happened. After a few passing seconds, the gunfire resumed as Hob's tank shook and rolled with each act of violence. Paul watched, though, as a second sliver of light appeared. Then a third.

By the time the forces below noticed and started to scatter, it was too late. Chunks of the ceiling came crashing down as the ground seized and spat, and Hob's tank disappeared in a pile of rubble.

Paul's eyes danced upward.

Light spilled into the valley.

The Lord Protector, Citadel, Fortitude

The Lord Protector draped a sheet over the body on the table. He hadn't wanted to kill the Figure, but sometimes one had to sacrifice a pawn to move a more substantial piece in position. Before he covered Richard's face, the Lord Protector stopped and looked at the man. He could see every wrinkle, every gray hair, every concern now relaxed into permanence.

"Thank you for your help," the Lord Protector whispered. As he went to draw the cloth over his face, the Lord Protector felt the air shift as someone entered the room. The Lord Protector didn't turn.

"Impressive," he said. "Not many possess the will to project themselves across the system," the Lord Protector congratulated as he turned to face Sebastian. His eyes scanned the young man from top to bottom. Sebastian held nothing back as he approached. Neither of them spoke.

Sebastian walked past the Lord Protector and stood next to his father's body. Lorenzo could sense his pain as his head dipped closer to the Figure's pale, empty face. Lorenzo watched agony well up in Sebastian's eyes as tears formed.

The Lord Protector enjoyed the genuineness of Sebastian's emotions. Sebastian's hand moved to his father's face as he caressed a brow that had softened. It was like watching a sunset over a vast ocean. Or standing before mountains topped with fresh snow. Or silence before the rage and wrath of a waterfall. Moments in time and space that surpassed both.

340

A part of Lorenzo wanted to console Sebastian, to educate him on the futility of his pain. But, the Lord Protector knew he shouldn't intervene. This was a defining moment for Sebastian, which could turn his character in an entirely different direction if mishandled.

Lorenzo knew that Sebastian was in a state of transformation from the inside out. After all, this was the only change that ever lasted. Thus far, Lorenzo had worked diligently to guide and steer Sebastian in the right direction. However, like all human beings, Sebastian was fragile, brittle—metal that was still being pounded upon and shaped into something useful.

And Lorenzo had great use for him.

"Why do you want to kill me?" Sebastian asked as he rose from his stooped position. His voice was grave, sober, and belonged to a much older man than the boy in front of him. Lorenzo licked his lips and took a deep, steadying breath.

"You misunderstand, Sebastian. I have watched you grow up, develop, mature, and overcome hurdle after hurdle. I have analyzed every aspect of who you are—your will, your emotional capacity, your mental prowess. I know what amount of pressure causes you to be afraid. I know what circumstances make you courageous. I know what knowledge gives you hope. I know everything about you," Lorenzo said intimately. He felt relieved to bring the truth out into the open.

"I don't want to kill you, Sebastian. I want to create you. Every moment leading up to this has been by my design. You are who you are because of me."

The Lord Protector paused and allowed time for this truth to settle into Sebastian. A deep, fathomless valley inside the man wanted Sebastian to know how much he cared about the young man. But, such powerful emotions were meant to be metered out in doses.

"You're wrong, Lorenzo. That's your name, right? Lorenzo? After all, you are just a man."

"Yes, but the man who controls destiny. But entertain me. How is it that I am wrong?"

"Simple. I have something that you could never give."

341

"What is that, Sebastian?"

"Purpose."

A stealthy silence fell between them. Sebastian stood tall, upright, comfortable in the Lord Protector's presence.

"I see. And I suppose you came here to tell me to surrender? Do you have any idea what kind of authority would take my place? This kingdom is held upright by my power. Remove me, and protocols kick in that will bring it all tumbling down. It's laughable if you think that you are in control."

Sebastian gave a flash of a grin.

"Didn't you know?"

"Know what?"

"I am not in control," he said triumphantly.

Lorenzo felt uneasiness creep into his mind. His will searched out, scanning Citadel, just as a wave of coding breached the firewalls around the city. He tried to prevent the flow of a massive surge of information that he had been too distracted to see beforehand. No matter what he did to stop it, he was too late as the commands and prompts infiltrated Citadel's systems.

"What have you done?" Lorenzo asked softly. He was slightly impressed.

"I have set them free. Goodbye, Lorenzo." Sebastian's image dissolved, and then he was gone.

Chapter 59: The Broadcast

Sebastian, Citadel, The Refuge

"Just stare directly ahead. What you see is what they see," Abby instructed. Sebastian gazed into the screen, and a gaunt, worn face stared back at him.

"Is it ready?" Sebastian asked. His whole body tingled with anticipation. He was exhausted from the sheer amount of energy and concentration he'd needed to project himself into Fortitude, but this needed to be done.

"Almost. Give me ten seconds," Abby said feverishly. Sebastian was right in trusting her to do this task. It was she who'd made it possible for him to show up in Fortitude. It was Abby who'd breached Citadel's security system and whose signal was spreading throughout Axiom.

As incredible as these feats were, her role in the next phase was just as necessary and daunting. As Sebastian watched her, though, all he saw was confidence.

"You can start in three, two, one..."

Sebastian looked directly ahead as his words rose to his throat. Nothing came out, though, as his mind worked against him. What if his statements weren't enough? What if they weren't heard? Out of the corner of his eye, he could see Abby urging him to speak. Sebastian took a steadying breath as his first sentence fell from his lips.

"People of Axiom. My name is Sebastian," Sebastian said as he licked his lips. His mouth was dry, and his voice was hoarse, but he continued. "Many of you know who I am by another name—1C118. You know me as a dissenter, a rebel, the Diseased." His words felt forced and foolish.

Would anyone listen?

"But, I am neither of these. In fact, I want to show you the truth. I want to show you what really happened at Hydra." Sebastian looked over at Abby and nodded. She pressed a button on her manipulor, and immediately the screen in front of him transitioned to Hydra.

An alarm bellowed as Hydra thundered. Anxiety blossomed inside Sebastian's chest as the fear surged. He forced himself to watch, though, as the generator broke free from its mooring.

Sebastian's stomach churned as he watched the screen. He watched as Hydra shook and trembled as the generator raged. He watched as a lone figure ran into the room and placed his hand on the ground. Sebastian watched as he created walls that would mend the generator and hold it in place. Blue lines coursed from his fingertips and built around the generator until it slipped back into its correct position. The alarm faded, and a peaceful, unsettled silence fell.

Sebastian could hear the words before they were spoken. A chill ran down his spine.

"You are a fool, Sebastian."

The Lord Protector appeared in the center of the vast room. His image shimmered with power. Sebastian could no longer hear him as his pain spoke louder than words. Tears were already brimming in his eyes as he watched Hydra splinter.

As the water fell, tears slipped silently down his cheeks. The image faded, and the screen returned to a mirror of his agony. For a minute, he did not speak.

"Sebastian?" Abby whispered.

"You have seen the truth," he said solemnly. "I am not the person you've been taught to hate. Your teacher is a liar and a deceiver. It is he who must be faced. It is he who must be held accountable for bringing violence to Axiom."

"I don't want to fight. I don't want more people to die. But, this must end. The Lord Protector—Lorenzo—he must be stopped. I am coming to Citadel peacefully. Please, do not try to stop me," Sebastian cautioned.

Sebastian took a breath. He knew his hand revealed. He knew that it was likely he was going to die. But, he wanted his transparency to be the flame that ignited freedom.

"Citadel, I will see you soon," Sebastian promised as he stepped out of the frame.

Chapter 60: The Wrinkle

Preva Adair, Medical Protectorate, Radiant

Preva Adair entered the control room with her weapon lowered. She watched the four women stuffed inside. One stood directly in front of the other three. She was the leader.

"Head Mother?" Preva asked with a tilt of her head. The woman nodded.

"I'm Blue Leader. We're here to help."

"About time Citadel sent someone," one of the women behind her volleyed. Preva Adair ignored the comment. She didn't want to overcomplicate the situation. Once Rais arrived, it would be clear that the Lord Protector didn't send Preva Adair and her team.

"We need to get out of here. Now," Preva Adair insisted. "Is this everyone?" The Head Mother shook her head. Adair was afraid of this.

"How many more?" Adair asked tersely.

"We don't know. When it all happened, we were attacked. I'm not sure who got away and who didn't," the Head Mother said as a crestfallen memory ignited in her eyes.

"What happened?" Preva Adair inquired. "What's wrong with those people?"

"We don't know. They just woke up all of a sudden and started attacking," the woman behind the Head Mother offered. By the look on the Head Mother's face, Preva Adair knew the woman knew more than she was saying.

"Head Mother? What happened here?" Adair insisted. The Head Mother looked at her feet.

"We woke them up," she said softly. The women behind her looked at her with angry confusion. "Radiant was killing them—draining them of everything valuable. We wanted to set them free, but when they awoke they were already empty. Just husks of whatever else was left," the Head Mother said tearfully.

Preva Adair worked through her nightmarish statement. She'd always known Radiant existed, but the horrors the facility promoted were far worse than she'd imagined.

"How dare you!?" The woman behind the Head Mother spat. "You did this! You put us all in danger!" The woman shouted viciously. The other women joined in as the Head Mother took it without speaking.

"Enough!" Preva Adair shouted. Immediately, the women quieted. "What's done is done. What matters is what we do next. Head Mother, how can we locate any of the other survivors?" The Head Mother nodded, relieved, and turned towards the command console.

"We can cycle through all the feeds. So far, we've been focusing on the main room to make sure none of those things get out."

"Is that a possibility?" Preva Adair asked as she sauntered up beside the woman.

"The doors are locked. They can be opened from the outside, but not from inside the main room," she offered.

"So that none of the patients could escape," Preva Adair said in observation. The Head Mother didn't respond. "So, the main problem is contained. Did any of them slip out before you locked it down?" The Head Mother nodded.

"We think a handful got through. But, we're not sure. We lost power to over half the facility." Preva Adair groaned inwardly. This was getting worse the more they talked about it.

"Alright. Let's do a cursory sweep of all the feeds to see if we can put any of the pieces together," Adair directed.

The Head Mother's hands went to work on the console. The feeds in front of Adair started to transition from room to room, pausing just long enough for her to analyze and then nod for the next one to be displayed.

"Stop!" Adair hissed. The feed rested on a camera facing the outside of Radiant. Preva Adair cursed under her breath.

Rais had arrived. Almost fifty Enforcers were lined up, waiting to get inside.

Preva Adair found the channel which belonged to her men stationed on the outside.

"Perimeter, do you copy?" No response. "Perimeter, respond." A single figure stepped away from the massive group of Enforcers. Myra was in his arms, trying desperately to break free. Preva Adair felt her adrenaline spike in her armored shell.

"Ah, this must be Adair," Rais's oily voice spoke over the channel. "Glad I could join your little party," he grated. Preva Adair didn't respond as her mind worked relentlessly. "If you're trying to figure out how to prevent me from getting inside, know that the longer I have to wait, the more of your men I kill. Starting first, of course, with the ladies. This one," he said as he threw Myra to the ground. She let out a small whimper as she fell, "will go first."

Preva Adair's pulse pounded.

"Do not test me, Adair. You have until the count of three." Rais pointed his gun at the girl still sprawled on the floor. He rested the barrel against her head. "One."

"Don't!" Adair shouted immediately. She clenched her jaw tightly until she saw Rais remove his aim. "We'll let you in. Meet us in the main room so we can talk," she offered. Rais flashed a thumbs up in the direction of the camera. Preva Adair stepped away, fuming.

"The main room?" The Head Mother finally asked. Preva Adair looked at her as her heart pounded in her ears.

"Yes. How much control over the doors do you have from this position?"

"Complete. Why?" Preva Adair looked back at Rais as his unit started marching forward.

"Let them in. It's time they joined in on the fun," Preva Adair said as she grabbed her weapon and headed to the door.

Chapter 61: Departure

Sebastian, The Train

Sebastian felt Citadel pulling on him like gravity. No matter how hard he tried to resist it, the empty Train continued forward. Sebastian could barely feel it beneath his feet as it coursed through the gory darkness.

A red haze hung over his compartment as if the air was filled with a fine, blood dust. His chest felt heavy as he breathed Axiom into himself. Sebastian held on firmly to the pole. He was afraid that if he sat down, he wouldn't rise.

The Train entered a tunnel. The walls were afire with crimson as they flashed by in hues of radiance. He closed his eyes to block it out as adrenaline flooded his veins.

Vibrant orange rushed through his memories. The compartment rippled as energy ripped through every fiber. Glass shimmered in the air like drops of water. Sam was standing in front of him, his smile burning through the explosion wrapping around his body.

Sebastian. What makes us human?

Sebastian opened his eyes. The world hadn't gotten any less maroon, but he could face it, now. If his purpose was to die, then so be it. There was no fighting it.

"How are you feeling?" A soft, feminine voice consoled in his ear. Sebastian spoke, knowing only Abby was listening.

"I'm good, I suppose. All things considered," he offered. It felt like a hollow, pathetic answer, but he ignored it. What else was he supposed to say? That he was scared? That he knew the end was coming?

"I'm with you, Sebastian. No matter what happens."

Sebastian was silent. He wanted to be alone, to end quietly, but he also didn't want to die alone.

It was a strange irony.

"How much longer?" He inquired. Abby had complete control of the Train, which prevented them from getting disturbed or stopped ahead of schedule.

"Two more Stations," she said simply. Sebastian returned to the depths of silence. He sunk down, down, down within them until he touched bottom. And there he remained, with arms wrapped around his legs, holding his breath.

"Last Station."

Sebastian could feel his lungs burning. He was running out of borrowed air. The Train slowed as he neared his destination. The panic settled in as his body writhed and rebelled. The Train stopped and the doors broke the surface.

"This is as far as I can take you," Abby said. Sebastian stared outward at the empty Station. Without a word, he stepped off. His legs felt weak and insufficient, but they carried his weight none the less. His eyes went wide, searching for Enforcers, but none came out of the shadows. Instead, both entrances leading into Citadel were blocked.

"I can't get through," Sebastian provided.

"Lorenzo put these up after the Directory was attacked. They're meant to control all the access points. I'm almost finished breaking down the code. Give me a sec," she said distractedly. Sebastian knew she was hard at work as he stepped towards the entrance on his right. Immediately, the walls burst to life. He took a quick step backward as a figure filled the wall in front of him.

"Sebastian," Lorenzo spoke evenly.

"You won't stop me from getting past this wall," Sebastian said confidently.

"And once you step foot in Citadel?" Lorenzo asked as his eyebrow arched. Sebastian didn't respond. They both already knew the answer. "Do you think that by doing this, you won't fulfill your destiny, Sebastian?"

Sebastian knew that answer, too.

"I won't be your puppet," he provided. "Even if it means I lay down my life to prevent that from happening," Sebastian said bitterly. Lorenzo grinned.

"Good luck." His words were distorted midway through as the wall in front of Sebastian dissolved and retreated. Sebastian stared into a gaping doorway.

349

"That should do it," Abby urged. Sebastian breathed in deep. What would be on the other side? How many Enforcers would be waiting for him?

Before his mind could convince his body, Sebastian put his first foot forward, then the next, and then the next until he was moving through the doorway. As soon as he was through, the entrance closed behind him, and cool air settled on his skin. He looked to the end of the hallway, where it opened up into another room. That's where he'd get gunned down. That's where he was going to die.

"Thank you, Abby. Make sure everyone in Axiom sees," he said through his emotions. He walked forward, his hand trailing against the wall. He thought about the concrete surface and wondered how many people walked past it and never known it was there. As he reached the end of the hall—the end of his journey—his heart settled, and his resolve stiffened.

Sebastian stepped through into the next room and stared into a sea of Enforcers. Their visors glared at him. Their weapons stared at him. Sebastian took a steadying breath and waited for the pain to envelope.

Seconds passed, and still, no shot was fired. Sebastian swallowed heavily. Perhaps they were simply going to take him prisoner so that Lorenzo could do it himself.

"1C118?" One of them asked from the sea.

"My name is Sebastian," he said defiantly. The words hung in the air between rebellion and bloodshed. The same man stepped forward and held up his hand.

"Stand down, gentlemen. It's him," the man commanded. Immediately, the men all lowered their weapons as a weight fell off of Sebastian.

"I don't understand," Sebastian stammered. The man turned to him and took off his helmet.

"Name's Guyer. Don't be afraid, Sebastian. We're here to help," he said through seasoned eyes and gray hair.

"You want to help me? Why?" Sebastian was still in disbelief and didn't entirely trust the situation.

"We got your message. We all did. And there's more in the Citadel who are willing to join us. Even if some aren't," he offered. Reassurance was gathering in Sebastian.

"You want to take down Lorenzo?" Sebastian posed. He had to know these Enforcers understood the consequences.

"We want to remove him by force if necessary," Guyer clapped back. All of his men joined in with their own declarations. Sebastian couldn't believe it as excitement mounted in his chest.

"How many more of you are there?"

"We don't know. All communication was severed once you told us you were coming. Dozens, hopefully. Or it could be just us. Regardless, we'll follow you right up to his front door. So, what's the plan?" Sebastian bit his lip. He hadn't actually thought he was going to get much further than this.

"Give me a minute," Sebastian deflected.

"Might want to make it a quick minute. There are still plenty of Enforcers serving Lorenzo who are out looking for you," Guyer warned. Sebastian nodded as he pulled away.

"Abby? Did you get all of that?"

"Loud and clear, Sebastian. This is huge!" She quipped.

"I know. I know. So, what do I do now?"

"Glad you asked. While you were chatting it up with Guyer, I downloaded every live feed I could get my hands on. It looks like he's right—there's still plenty of Enforcers surrounding Fortitude. I can navigate you through the city, but it looks like you have a fight on your hands."

Sebastian didn't like the sound of that. He didn't want to come in as the conqueror. But, maybe if people saw the Enforcers who willingly defected, they might understand this wasn't about taking over.

"Alright. How will I know where to go?"

"Grab some armor from the Enforcers. Specifically, a helmet, though just running around in a helmet might make you look kind of stupid," Abby said with a soft laugh.

"Good point," Sebastian conceded.

"Once you have it all on, I'll be able to patch in," Abby pointed out. Sebastian broke off the conversation and approached Guyer, who was surveying his unit with steel.

"What's our heading?" Guyer said in a gravelly voice.

"I need armor," Sebastian responded. Guyer grinned.

"Wouldn't want you picked off as soon as it all started, eh? Cormack!" Guyer shouted as an Enforcer snapped to attention and hastily approached. "Get this...," Guyer looked him up and down, "man an outfit." In response, Cormack snapped a salute and then hurried away. Guyer continued to eye Sebastian.

"And make it fancy," Guyer ordered.

Chapter 62: Assault

Damien, Medical Protectorate, Radiant

Damien slid up alongside Radiant with his weapon loose in his grip. Across from him, he could see Soren—in his green outlined armor—approaching in the same manner. Damien entered the halo of light cast by a pair of floodlights positioned above the doors. He stopped and held up his hand. With a whisper, the men behind him came to a halt.

No one exited. No one came out to fend them off. The doors remained shut, and Radiant remained dormant and still. The tension was a pleasant aggravation in Damien's gut. He'd forgotten just how sweet it was to approach battle. The feeling swelled in his blood and throbbed in his temples.

Byron melted out of the darkness as he led the charge. His armor, a charcoal gray with white lines, gleamed dully in the light. He sauntered towards the doors with his weapon raised.

"Ready?" Byron clapped. Damien looked at Soren, who nodded in his direction.

"Ready," Damien said feverishly.

"Grab the doors," Byron commanded. In unison, Damien and Soren grabbed either door handle and pulled. Byron trained his weapon on the darkness emanating from within Radiant.

Damien let the door go and held it open with his foot. He pointed his weapon at the open doorway as he held his breath in anticipation. Soren was in a crouched position across from him as the man behind him held the door open.

The pulse pounded in Damien's head as he waited. Still, no one emerged to thwart their advance. Damien slid forward to get a better look inside the darkness.

Without warning, something slammed into Damien and thrust him off his feet. His weapon flew out of his grip as his head clapped against the ground, and stars danced in front of his eyes. Damien whipped his body into a roll and came up onto one knee as he prepared to retaliate.

Damien didn't understand what he was seeing. The person who'd run into him was standing in the middle of the arc of light projecting from Radiant. Judging from the length of hair and the slim build, Damien concluded it was a woman.

"Don't shoot!" Byron commanded. "She's unarmed." Soren lowered his weapon as Damien searched for his own. He could still feel where the woman had run into him. She certainly packed a punch.

"Let me talk to her," Byron suggested. Damien watched him press on his manipulor as his visor changed from black to clear. Damien could see his eyes just inside the helmet as he raised a gloved hand. "Figure, we aren't here to hurt you," Byron's voice projected.

The woman's head snapped to attention as if she saw him for the first time. Damien didn't like the look of her hands as they twisted into claws. His eyes went to his gun, which was a couple of feet away.

"Byron," Damien began, "something isn't right." The tension of battle had turned into trepidation.

"Figure, you're safe," Byron tried again.

The woman's head tilted in his direction. From her lips burst an unearthly screech just as she charged. Byron didn't even have time to react as the woman lunged at him.

Damien fired.

The shot hit her broadside as she collided with Byron. The two of them went down, though Damien knew only one of them would rise. Soren sprinted towards Byron and pulled the woman off of him.

"What was that!?" Soren shouted in Damien's ear. Damien watched him pull Byron to his feet.

Before Byron could respond, a low groan emitted from the darkness just inside Radiant. Byron and Soren both brought their weapons to bear. Damien aimed directly into the darkness, knowing that whatever came out was not going to be friendly.

Another screech emanated from within as Damien pulled the trigger.

354

Sebastian, Citadel

Sebastian felt stiff inside of his armor. It wrapped around him like water and clung to his skin like vapor. He felt comfortable discomfort as the armor closed in around his vital organs and shielded his vulnerable areas. He moved his arms to test his range of motion and did likewise with his legs.

"She the right fit?" Guyer asked as he approached. He had his weapon in both hands.

"It's a little..."

"Tight. Rides up in the crotch, doesn't it?" Sebastian glanced up into the visor and couldn't tell if the man was being serious or not.

"A little," Sebastian finally revealed.

"Happens to the best of us. You'll get used to it," Guyer provided as he turned his head to look over Sebastian's shoulder. "Once we open up that wall, we're stepping into the worst-case scenario. It's a one-way shot to Fortitude, but there's plenty of vantage points for our enemy to fire from. We'll be taking shots from above and in front of us," he said seriously. Sebastian followed his words as the image coagulated in his mind. The situation was bleak, to say the least. "But, you have assured me that your..."

"Abby."

"Yes, you're Abby will be able to help us out. If that's the case, we won't be completely slaughtered from the get-go," Guyer stated with a chuckle.

Sebastian didn't know whether to join in or be horrified. Every ounce of reasoning in his body was telling him to run, to flee, to retreat. But, he knew there was nowhere for him to run. The way was forward, even if the journey was short. Sebastian looked into Guyer's visor and wondered what was running through the man's mind.

"Are you sure you want to do this?" Sebastian asked. Guyer nodded immediately.

"The man brought death to Axiom. He must be removed," Guyer said simply. Sebastian glanced over his soldier at Guyer's men. "Don't worry about them. They know what

355

they're up against. They'll follow you anywhere," Guyer spoke into Sebastian's thoughts.

Sebastian's focus returned to Guyer. He followed the visor's gaze to the wall they would be opening soon. Sebastian picked up his helmet and slid it over his head.

"Okay. I'm ready," Sebastian said as a display appeared in front of his eyes.

"Excellent," Guyer answered. He let out a shrill whistle, and immediately his men stopped what they were doing and stacked up on either side of the wall. Sebastian felt his legs moving but didn't know what he was doing.

"Can you hear me?" Abby asked into his ear.

"Yeah. You ready for this?" Sebastian said uneasily.

"I'm with you," Abby stated firmly. Sebastian stopped walking as he fell alongside Guyer. He felt small next to the man. The wall in front of them glared back at Sebastian.

"Sure, you don't want a weapon?" Guyer asked without turning his helmet. Sebastian nodded vigorously, not completely sure if he agreed with his principles. "Alright," Guyer said with a lift of his voice. "Gentlemen, keep your eyes up and your weapons level. And give 'em all you got!" Guyer barked. There was a cHorrus of agreement. "Clear it," Guyer said evenly.

Without warning, the wall in front of Sebastian disappeared. Immediately, gunfire erupted.

Damien's shot connected as a man went spiraling. Both with wild looks in their eyes, two other people peeled off of the leading group and sprinted towards Damien.

"Open fire!" Byron shouted.

Way behind old man!

Damien squeezed the trigger as the first of the two fell to the ground. The man behind Damien shot the second just as the attacker got too close to Damien. The body collapsed in front of Damien as he put another shot into the back of its head. He rose and scanned his targets, but there was none.

"Can someone please tell me what is going on!?" Soren shouted. Byron didn't respond, and Damien knew it was because he had no idea.

A sound bounced out of the darkness, and everyone's weapon rose sharply. Bloodlust surged through Damien's veins. Whatever was about to come out was going to receive the same swift treatment as the last wave. His finger toyed with the trigger as he took a deep breath.

"Hold your fire! Hold your fire," a gargled voice spoke in his ear. "This is Blue Leader. Hold your fire. We're coming out."

"Forward!" Guyer shouted.

Without hesitation, his men moved through the door and into oppressive gunfire. Sebastian watched the first two collapse as the shots cut through their bodies. Two more moved into position, and one managed to get through the door as the second fell backward in a heap of lifeless armor.

"Move!" Guyer bellowed as he shoved Sebastian shoved forward. Sebastian stumbled but stayed on his feet as gunfire sizzled through the air around him. He felt himself moving but couldn't feel his thoughts commanding any of his actions.

Guyer pushed him again, and this time it was behind a pile of dead Enforcers that provided him with cover. Sebastian's mind was locked in place. Guyer's men retaliated with their own gunfire, but they were struck down from above as soon as they broke from cover.

Think.

"Get behind cover!" Guyer shouted as he waved his men forward.

Think.

The second wave of Enforcers emerged from the wall and was met with unrelenting violence. The air smelled of fear and death as the entrance became clogged with bodies.

Think!

Sebastian glanced over his makeshift cover as his eyes scanned the street in front of him. In the distance was Fortitude, and hanging above it was the Star, which burned like

357

a massive red eye. Gunfire was coming from all angles, especially above.

"Abby!" Sebastian shouted.

"Here!"

"We need our heads cleared!"

"Got it!"

Above them, lines appeared from both sides of the street and connected in the middle. The gunfire from above was immediately extinguished as a transparent wall shimmered with the shots from the Enforcers in the buildings.

"We got cover! Move! Move! Move!" Guyer commanded as he surged forward.

"I need you to be faster," Sebastian said to Abby.

"I know, I know. I'll be better next time," Abby promised. Sebastian stood, shakily, and followed Guyer.

"Blue Leader!" Byron shouted. "Please tell us what's going on," he commanded. An Enforcer emerged from the darkness, though Damien's finger did not leave the trigger. Her blue-lined armor was dented, and some of it was missing. A large crack ran up and down her visor.

"We set up a trap for Rais using the husks, but it all went sideways," she said vaguely. Damien could tell she was a little dazed as she stumbled in her gait.

"What's a husk?" Soren asked as he caught the woman.

"Those things. They aren't human," Blue Leader said distantly. An ominous silence enveloped them.

"You said it went sideways? Elaborate." Byron said.

"We trapped Rais inside the main with the husks, but not before he dragged the rest of my people in there with him. We've been fighting our way back in," Blue Leader said shakily. Damien's attention prickled.

"You say he dragged your people in there. Did he also take the slaves?" Damien asked as he approached the woman. He still had his weapon trained on her.

"Lower your weapon, Damien," Soren suggested lowly. The woman didn't respond.

"I asked you a question!" Damien shouted.

"I don't know. I don't know. It all fell apart. We got hit by those things as soon as we tried to get inside," Blue Leader said as her emotions broke into her words.

"Does he have Myra!?" Damien roared.

The look Damien received was enough of an answer. Without consideration, Damien charged into the darkness as Byron shouted after him.

Sebastian lunged over a broken wall. Ahead of him, gunfire clacked and spat, though he couldn't tell who was shooting. The initial fear and paralysis were gone. Now, he had an objective. He had to keep as many of Guyer's men alive so they could reach Fortitude together.

"Useless!" A voice shouted from every surface. "You cannot stop me!" Lorenzo bellowed. Sebastian could feel his voice on his skin, but he didn't stop running.

"I am inevitable! I am destiny!"

Sebastian approached the front line of the battle. His eyes scanned the street frantically. He could see walls appearing out of the ground just as bolts of gunfire were about to strike Guyer's men, and Sebastian knew Abby was hard at work protecting them.

"Abby! I need to go up!" Sebastian voiced as he quickened his speed. He was coming up on the fight, but he couldn't slow down. He watched as red streams of death surged towards him.

"Jump!" Abby shouted.

Sebastian leaped just as a step appeared beneath his feet. The shots punched the ground where he stood, but he didn't stop as each step collided with another invisible ledge. Up, up, up he climbed until he was above the raging battle.

"Make sure you stay with them," Sebastian said stoically. He ran through the air until the sound of gunfire started to fade.

"But what about you?" Sebastian's jaw clenched.

"This was always a one-way trip," he said bluntly. "Give me a clear path to Lorenzo. That's all I need," he said somberly. Abby was quiet for a moment.

"I'll lead you down," she said in resolution. Sebastian felt his steps begin to approach the empty street beneath him.

"Thank you," Sebastian said with words that meant a thousand meanings.

"Of course. Good luck, Sebastian." Sebastian heard the line close as his feet slapped against the gilded street.

The street was eerily quiet. The battle was behind him like a memory that was still fresh. Sebastian hesitated as his eyes roamed the empty street.

"What will they think when they realize you left them behind?" Lorenzo spoke as his image materialized on the walls. Sebastian ignored him as his pace quickened. He could see Fortitude just ahead. The light from the Star warmed his skin with beads of bloody light.

"They'll be just another casualty in your crusade, Sebastian. Just like your friends in Hydra. Just like your father. Just like Sam," Lorenzo said coldly. Sebastian felt each word as they stabbed into him.

"I'm giving you a chance to surrender," Sebastian said softly. Lorenzo laughed as his teeth flashed across every surface. The cacophony of amusement rolled through Citadel.

"Surrender!? No, Sebastian. I cannot give away what I am," Lorenzo said.

Ahead of Sebastian, three drones entered the street and rained fire down upon him. Before the red balls of energy could connect with him, walls appeared to protect him.

"Keep going!" Abby yelled. "I'll do the best I can," she said breathlessly. Just as her words left her, spikes shot out of the walls and impaled the drones in midair.

To his right, Sebastian could see numerous drones racing down an alley. He quickened his pace but knew that there was no way he could outrun them. Just as they were about to enter the street, an intricately woven net appeared made out of pale, white light. The drones collided with the net and instantly burst into a ball of fiery debris.

Sebastian's gaze returned to the street in front of him. His mind registered too late what he saw as his body came to a stumbling stop.

The street was blocked. Dozens of people, all clad in gold, stood in the way.

It was the Prominent.

Darkness wrapped around Damien like an embrace as he entered Radiant. A light flickered ahead of him as his breath came in ragged huffs. He could see pools of blood on the ground and heard his feet spatter in the gore as he tread through the dark. His eyes, accustomed to the night, searched for the door and found it directly ahead of him.

"Don't go in there!" Blue Leader shouted. Damien's hand grasped the handle. He stopped long enough to listen. He could hear muffled shouting and gunfire. He heard screaming— a girl's scream.

Myra was inside.

Damien opened the door.

Sebastian's breath came in fear dripped gasps. His eyes went to the towering structure just beyond. Fortitude was so close, but he'd come to the end of his journey. He could hear drones approaching from behind. The path in front of him was barred by the Prominent.

This was the end.

At least he was going to die at the hands of the people, and not those of Lorenzo. His blood would be remembered that way. His death would be stained on the streets forever.

Sebastian could feel the drones beating the air. He heard the sound of Enforcers marching towards him.

A man separated himself from the others and approached Sebastian. In his hand was a long piece of metal. Sebastian did his best not to think about what the first blow would feel like. The man stopped just feet away, but Sebastian didn't retreat. They looked at each other for a long second.

"For Axiom," the man said softly.

With a rumble, the man held his weapon in the air as the Prominent behind him did the same. The mass surged forward as they ripped past Sebastian. As a new battle raged behind him, Sebastian stared at the black tower looming over the street—over him.

Fortitude was within reach.

Damien entered the room with his gun level. He saw movement but couldn't make out if it was friend or foe. Before he could decide, he felt his body get slammed backward into the door as the wind rushed out of his chest. The hulking body that had charged him—a husk—threw him to the ground like he was made of feathers.

Damien landed with a thud as fire burned through his bones. He didn't wait for another round as he rolled into a fighting stance. The beast charged again, but this time Damien was ready as his fist struck against flesh.

A promising crack responded as his fist connected with cartilage. A humanlike groan escaped from the monster, but Damien didn't let it deceive him as he struck again with a punch that knocked the thing off its feet.

Damien turned swiftly as his eyes scanned the darkness. He could see, in the distance, gunfire. A scream echoed across the room and struck him in the chest.

"I'm coming, Myra!" Damien bellowed.

Another husk bolted towards him, and Damien ducked under its arms. Behind it, a second screeched but succumbed to silence when Damien struck it with an uppercut under the chin.

A third roared from the darkness just a few feet after the second, but Damien met it with a kick that hit it squarely in the chest. The first husk attacked from behind as Damien felt a thrust that sent him reeling forward into the third husk. He used the momentum change to his advantage as he brought his knee up into its face with a sickening crunch.

"I'm coming, Myra!" Damien promised as he spun around. The husk shrieked at Damien as it charged.

Behind Sebastian, a battle was unfolding as the Prominent combated the Enforcers and drones. In front of him was a still, eerie vacancy. He could see the steps leading up to the demolished and burned Directory. A low, smoky fog wreathed the ruins as if it was still smoldering. Behind the Directory was Fortitude, which the Star bathed in a red glow.

Standing in front of the Directory was a lone figure. Sebastian immediately recognized the stature of a man who wore time like a garment.

Lorenzo.

The man stood alone, waiting. Sebastian approached cautiously, knowing he was walking into an ambush. But, he had to face him. He had to face Lorenzo and let him know he wasn't afraid. He needed Axiom to see that even a tyrant like Lorenzo could be met as a man.

"Welcome, Sebastian," the voice boomed from all directions. Behind Sebastian, the city projected Lorenzo on every surface until his image was magnified a million times. Sebastian could feel the heat of his stare as he approached. "Welcome to your rightful place," the face whispered thunderously.

"Welcome home."

An Enforcer reached for Damien out of the darkness and struck him with his weapon. The blow dazed him as pain exploded along his jaw. Damien put up his arms just as a second blow descended. His forearms received the brunt of the attack and granted him enough time to wrench the weapon out of the Enforcer's grip.

Damien turned the weapon around and pulled the trigger, but it merely clicked, and clicked, and clicked. Knowing it was empty, the Enforcer charged. Damien sidestepped just as a husk approached from behind. The Enforcer and the husk collided and went spiraling into the snarling darkness.

Myra screamed. Damien's eyes flew to the pool of light, where she writhed and moaned.

"Hold on, Myra!" Damien screamed as anguish and fear curdled in his voice. He sprinted towards the light. He deflected a blow that struck his rib cage.

Suddenly, he was yanked backward.

Damien reached with his arms towards Myra but was quickly losing ground. Something had him by the waist and was aggressively pulling him into the dark. He felt the grip in his bones as his waist exploded in pain.

A gunshot burst from the darkness as the husk's grip released and Damien fell to the floor.

"Go, Damien! Go!" Soren shouted as he shot again.

Damien's feet slapped against desperation. An Enforcer stepped in the way, and Damien went airborne. His elbow came crashing down on the Enforcer's faceplate, and the two of them rolled into the light. Only one of them rose as Damien landed in front of Myra.

"Myra?" Damien said hurriedly. Myra moaned in response. Her hair was matted to her forehead, and her face was pale. Damien watched her eyes roam irregularly as if she were dreaming. "Myra, it's me Damien. Please, Myra. Say something," Damien begged. Her breath was shallow, and vomit coated her chin.

"Predictable," Rais said coolly. Damien spun around and moved into a defensive stance between Myra and Rais. "She was the bait, and the prey came so willingly," Rais said as he emerged from the gloom. Behind him, three Enforcers stood with their backs to him, protecting him from the monsters lurking in the darkness.

"What did you do to her?" Damien hissed.

"Gave her a little medicine," Rais said as he extended a needle. Rage twisted in Damien's gut. "She won't last long. Definitely not as long as you," Rais said as his eyes narrowed. His grip wrapped around the needle. "You ready to die, boy?" Damien's lip curled into a snarl as his fists formed balls of wrath.

Damien charged.

"See what you've done," Lorenzo said mockingly. Sebastian was mere feet away from the man. So close, he could smell Lorenzo's antiquity—the aroma of time.

"I didn't do this. You did," Sebastian accused. "And now the world sees you for who you are," Sebastian said in a low voice. Lorenzo smirked.

"Not the world, Sebastian. Not yet. As for you, you were exactly what I foresaw. Which is why," Lorenzo paused as Enforcers emerged from the smoke-laden darkness, "you have reached the end of your journey." Sebastian's eyes remained on Lorenzo. He knew he was surrounded.

"I have done what I needed to do," Sebastian said defiantly. Lorenzo laughed, and the laughter rolled across Citadel like a storm. Sebastian could feel it stir his body like the wind. The Enforcers raised their weapons.

"Where is your purpose now!?" Lorenzo roared. His voice carried across all of Axiom, filling every quiet corner. It permeated every surface and seeped from every crack. It bubbled over itself, building, building, building into a violent crescendo which did not abate or cease.

Silence didn't return as Axiom groaned from within.

Damien aimed at Rais's ribcage, but just as his fist made contact, Rais struck him from behind. The blow sent Damien sprawling as shock and confusion brought him to his knees. Damien shot back up and spun to face his adversary. Rais was standing behind him, now, but he had no idea how Rais got there so quickly.

"Confused?" Rais inquired with a sly grin. "Just a little modification I made. I am faster, stronger, smarter than you will ever be, Damien," Rais said as he twirled the needle.

Damien bolted towards him, but Rais nimbly sidestepped his attack. Damien felt an explosion of pain in his shoulder, which sent him to his knees. He caught himself before he hit the ground. Myra was a few feet away—so close that

Damien could see the golden strands of her hair and smell her sweet, earthy scent.

The pain radiated in Damien's shoulder. He reached up and felt the needle as he pulled it out. Only half of the toxin had entered into his body, but he knew it was enough.

"Ready to face your darkness, boy?" Rais cackled. Already Damien could feel the poison entering his bloodstream. The agony was spreading across his mind like shards of fire.

Myra moaned as her eyes focused on Damien.

"You came for me," Myra said weakly.

Damien grunted and rose to his feet. His legs felt unsteady, and fatigue punched every muscle, but he had enough to turn around and face Rais.

"I have already faced my darkness, and I am not afraid," Damien said defiantly as his hand closed around the needle. Damien raced forward, but this time he was ready for Rais to sidestep him to the left. Damien spun the needle around and felt it sink into the man's chest.

Rais faltered as shock and confusion rolled across his face. He reached weakly for the needle protruding from his chest. Damien scooped Myra in his arms and turned to face Rais. Damien watched the fear and pain shimmer in Rais's eyes.

"Have you faced yours?" Damien said nastily as he kicked Rais into the waiting arms of a pair of husks.

Sebastian heard the sound before he understood what it meant. Lorenzo's gaze moved over Sebastian and looked towards Citadel as the sound of metal and concrete ripping in half filled the air. For the first time, fear appeared on the face that had seen thousands of years.

"I don't know where my purpose is, Lorenzo," Sebastian said lowly. The Enforcers watched in horror just long enough to know they were in danger. As they abandoned their positions and fled, Lorenzo's eyes frantically scanned the dome ceiling. Behind Sebastian, Guyer and his men charged up the hill.

"But, I know it isn't with you," Sebastian said as light spilled into Axiom.

Chapter 63: Integration

Sebastian

Sebastian walked through the building with a sense of disbelief. He wasn't sure if what had taken place in the last few cycles was true. Had the Lord Protector finally been usurped? Was a new dawn breaking forth over Axiom?

As light, beautiful, transient light spilled into the very bones of Axiom, he couldn't help but trust and hope that something had changed. A shift had occurred, which was moving the gears of history towards a better day. People—no longer Figures—were awakening.

A new order was being established, one that was breaking in with force and fire. One that was pouring into the wound that the Lord Protector had ruptured. Yes, Axiom was different, now.

It was better.

And yet, his feet were carrying Sebastian towards a cell. He didn't know why, but Sebastian had to see him. He had to talk to him. It was a longing, like a distant echo he wanted to hear. It beat in his veins until his heart pointed him towards this direction, down a hallway poorly lit as if time itself had eaten away at the luminous bulbs hanging in dirty casings. As he approached, Sebastian tried to work out what he was going to say. What would his words be?

"Halt!" A deep voice conveyed as Sebastian turned a final corner. Two guards stood in front of a gray, lifeless door.

"State your business," the second guard said firmly as his hand went to the weapon in his holster. Sebastian felt a pinprick of anxiety burst in his chest. He'd only worked out words for the man beyond the door and not the two men barring his way.

"Wait just a minute...," the first guard started as his eyes narrowed, "Are you ?" A giddy sense of acknowledgment triumphed over the tension in his gut.

"I am Sebastian."

The two men shared looks of excitement and concealed nervousness. Sebastian had a distinct impression—one he'd felt more than once over the last few cycles—that he was an important figure.

He'd once read about an idea, in a book he'd been forced to read during his retraining, about a certain type of people who were esteemed and considered set apart from the rest. These people were idolized and regarded highly. They were *celebrities*, and Sebastian belonged to them, now.

"What is your name?" Sebastian asked candidly.

"M25," the first guard conveyed.

"No. What is your name?"

The look that splashed across his face was one that Sebastian had also gotten used to seeing. Sebastian knew that inside the guard was a struggle, a war, between the old manner of doing things and the new. One was binding and stringent, and it demanded allegiance and subjugation. The latter offered freedom and encouraged self-expression. Sebastian would know, for he'd ushered in this age of self-awareness.

"It's okay," Sebastian soothed. "You're safe, now. You both are. You are free to tell me who you are." Some habits were hard to tear down. The first guard, a thick-necked man who stood a head taller than Sebastian, swallowed heavily as he choked on the words rising to his lips.

"It's Roger," he said as if relieved.

"Pleased to meet you, Roger." Sebastian looked to the second guard, but his lips were firmly shut. Sebastian wasn't shocked, though.

For some, they'd carry with them the old regime for the rest of their lives. There would always be the fear in Axiom that the Lord Protector's influence would rise back up into a position of power. Indeed, even Sebastian lost sleep over this idea. But, he hoped that the momentum of change would build a new foundation over the old, brittle bones of the past.

"The pleasure is our own, 1C—I mean Sebastian. You're a hero." The mysticism was in his eyes. Sebastian enjoyed it just long enough to see it begin to fade.

"I'm just a man like yourself. But, I have come here on official business," Sebastian related. This was a lie, but it rolled off his tongue easily enough.

"Of course! What can we do?"

Sebastian bit the inside of his cheek.

"I need to see him."

A cloaked silence enshrouded them. Sebastian knew that what he was asking was dangerous, but he had to enter the cell. He had to see Lorenzo face to face. He had to feel the weight of his voice as it filled the room. He had to smell the grandeur and enormity of a man who'd stood the test of time. He had to see whom he defeated.

Above all, Sebastian needed to know.

"I can't, sir. We've been told to keep this door closed to everyone. The Lord Protector is extremely dangerous. They say he can see into your mind and read your thoughts," Roger said with a shudder. Sebastian didn't doubt many legends were floating around about the man beyond the door. You didn't live as long as he did without creating myths.

"He's only a man, Roger. There's nothing to be afraid of," Sebastian assured. He could see, though, he wasn't getting anywhere with Roger. Superstition and fear prevented logic from ever finding fertile ground. Sebastian glanced at the second guard, whose lips had turned into thin lines. His eyes were worn, and deep shadows adorned his face.

"How about you? Do you believe the stories?" Sebastian inquired. The man slowly and subtlety shook his head. "Good. Then tell me why I shouldn't go in there and see him?" Sebastian challenged. The second guard looked him in the eye.

"The man killed my whole family. Wiped out both my Figureheads when he destroyed Hydra. I didn't find out until later that I was related to them," the guard said flatly.

It was a reoccurring story that Sebastian had heard many times. Once people were awakened, they started to seek out the comfort of kinship and companionship. For some, they only found a watery grave. Sebastian could see, though, loathing and hatred seething beneath his skin.

"He took my Figurehead, too." Sebastian paused and allowed the guard to share the moment of animosity with him. When the guard nodded, he continued. "Let me in, and I will get answers. I won't be able to bring them back, but I can make him feel the weight of their deaths," Sebastian promised. The guard swallowed heavily, nodded, and then fished in his pocket.

"What are you doing?" Roger asked incredulously as he threw up his hands. The second guard didn't answer as he slipped a key into the lock. With a sharp clang, the lock rattled open. The guard turned to Sebastian.

"Make him pay for what he did. Make him understand," the man said mournfully. Sebastian nodded as the door opened with a languished groan. Sebastian stepped inside.

The room was poorly lit. Other than a single bulb illuminating a chair and a table, inky blackness resided in the rest of the space. As the cool settled on Sebastian's skin, the aroma of mildew and sterility filled his nostrils. The door clanged shut behind him, and ridges erupted up and down his arms as a trickle of tension crawled up his neck.

Sebastian did not move. He listened. He knew that Lorenzo was just beyond the light, watching him. But he wasn't afraid. No, it was he who had his back up against the door.

"Sebastian," a voice rattled from the depths of time itself. "How very good to see you." Sebastian heard chains clink together from inside the gloom. Still, the darkness had not revealed the Lord Protector.

"May I sit?" Sebastian asked.

"By all means. You've earned it, after all." Sebastian caught the hint of humor in his voice but ignored it. He pulled the chair out from under the table and sat down. Still, the man in chains hadn't entered the light.

"I've come to ask you a few questions, Lorenzo. That's your name, right? It's alright if I call you that?" Sebastian goaded. He heard a soft chuckle from the darkness.

"Absolutely. If you believe we are equals, of course."

"That would mean I'd have to see you as human, Lorenzo. And I don't think you are human. I think you lost your humanity a long time ago," Sebastian offered.

He'd thought long and hard about the man he was talking to, now. He'd approached this conversation from every angle—every vantage point as he sought to understand what made Lorenzo the Lord Protector he'd claimed for millennia. After exhausting every ounce of deduction he contained, he'd concluded that time itself had eroded the man who entered a Role and replaced it with an idea—a living symbol. Somewhere along the way, Lorenzo had bought into his image and became a breathing statue.

"You're right about that, Sebastian. But that is not why you are here. You, my dear, have questions," he said softly. Sebastian was annoyed. Lorenzo was trying to control the conversation. He wasn't about to let him do so.

"You killed thousands of people. Do you not understand what you've done?" Sebastian accused emptily.

"Don't do that, Sebastian. Don't bow to the anxieties that others have heaped upon you. You are not their martyr. It's pathetic that you'd buy into that kind of melodrama and to see you pander is revolting. Don't pretend. Don't wear their clothes. This is not about the people I killed—people I killed hundreds of years ago when I set all of these events in motion."

Sebastian laughed hollowly as he leaned into the table. "Hundreds of years ago? Are you insane, Lorenzo? You pretend that you are some sort of god."

"I am a god!" Lorenzo bellowed as he burst from the darkness. The chains went taught as the man's face came within inches of Sebastian's own.

Sebastian flinched and recoiled backward as he stared into the wild eyes of the Lord Protector. His hair was matted to his forehead and sticking up in tufts on the top of his scalp. Shadows buried into his eyelids, and a row of stubble had erupted across his chin. Spittle coated his lips and showered onto the table.

As Sebastian gathered himself, Lorenzo disappeared back into the darkness. A steady, angry pulsing stillness resumed. "I apologize. I still haven't answered your question," Lorenzo said evenly as if nothing had happened. Sebastian could feel his heart languishing in his throat.

"I didn't ask one," he whispered.

"Oh, but you did. When you walked in, I could see it in your eyes," he chided.

"See what?" Sebastian asked tersely.

"The why. Why me? Why now? Why? Why? Why? It's exhausting, isn't it? Not knowing. Not having all the answers to all the puzzles," Lorenzo said sympathetically.
Sebastian was silent. Lorenzo was toying with him, trying to get in his head again. Sebastian chewed on words that he'd wanted to regurgitate for a while.

"You once stated that this was for me," he began in a low tone. "When you brought down Hydra. You said it was for me. At first, I thought you merely meant the dam."

"But, you don't assume that anymore?"

"No."

"Very good, Sebastian. As usual, your logic and reasoning prevail. Nicely done," he said coolly. Sebastian's head was buzzing with frustration and revelation. "Which brings us to the why, correct?"

"Yes," Sebastian said resignedly. He felt the rigid, ironclad walls inside of him starting to crumble. He no longer had the upper hand in this conversation. He'd entered into territory that he was ill-prepared to wander, for he was venturing into the will of the Lord Protector.

"Mind if I join you?" Lorenzo asked softly.

Sebastian nodded as the sound of chains unraveling rebounded off the walls. A figure emerged from the darkness and pulled a chair to the table. The Lord Protector sat down and folded one leg across the other. His gaze was casual, even, and measured. Even here, Sebastian could sense that the man was in control of himself.

The two sat in mutual, borrowed silence for a couple of breaths. Sebastian stared at him, trying to decide if he hated Lorenzo or not. In a sense, he felt betrayed. Here was someone he'd idolized, worshipped his whole life. There was an intimacy that Sebastian had built up through the years that was now a raw, open wound.

"It started on the Train, didn't it? The day it blew up. That was you?" The memory breached his walls and came crashing into him. He was there, like he always was, sitting down as Sam shielded him from the blast. Sebastian wondered if he'd ever leave that place—the one of fire and death, of Sam's sacrifice and his complicity. He didn't know.

"Yes." Lorenzo offered no further explanation, and Sebastian didn't press. He was dealing with a man who'd organized his words long before Sebastian asked.

"And then Hydra on the day I prevented the power station from rupturing. That was also you. Were you testing me? Trying to figure me out?" Sebastian felt the spite gather on his tongue as he spoke. He felt used and manipulated. A part of him desperately wanted Lorenzo to admit that he didn't have a plan—that he was merely guessing and testing different ideas.

"Very good. But, too easy, don't you think? These are all rudimentary details. Any blind man can follow the bread crumbs, Sebastian. Try harder."

"You wanted me to succeed," Sebastian admitted. Lorenzo nodded, and immediately Sebastian started to feel defeat creep into his chest. "Why?"

"The ultimate question. Do you believe you truly have a purpose, dear boy?" Sebastian reflected on his question. He remembered the conversation they'd had when he stood in front of his father's body. It was meant to be a diversion, a means of distraction, but the words still meant something regardless of why they'd been spoken.

"Sometimes," he offered. It was the best truth he could tell. Lorenzo smiled at his response.

"Axiom is not just a structure—nor is it simply a society. It's an organism. It breathes. It devours. And unless it is fed over and over again, it will die." Sebastian had no idea where the conversation was suddenly going, but Lorenzo continued to speak. "I have nurtured Axiom for millennia, but it has come time for Axiom to become something else—to evolve. Without change, it will perish. Like a fledgling bird, Axiom will end up devouring itself if it doesn't leave the nest."

"What do I have to do with that? Why did you choose me?" Sebastian asked without hiding his irritation. He was wasting his time talking to a madman who had bought into his own grandeur.

"Everything, my dear boy. Everything I have done has led to this point. You think you have freedom, but really you are fulfilling my purpose. Every victory you have ever claimed has been given by my hand. Every word you've ever spoken was whispered in your ear by my wisdom. I am in this jail cell because I choose to be here. You think you are in control, Sebastian. But, truly, I am still guiding you."

Sebastian could feel the heat rising up his neck. Was Lorenzo speaking the truth? Or was this more feigning and mental assault? Sebastian didn't know.

"There's no way you planned all of this. It's not possible. Even for you," Sebastian challenged. He hoped he was right.

"We'll see. Even now, mechanisms are in motion that will unfold in the most unimaginable ways. Like a plague, chaos is bursting forth with rage. Forces are aligning against Axiom, ready to tear it down. Axiom is calling forth a new regime—a new order—"

"—A new leader." Sebastian spoke the words just as stunned silence filled his throat. Could it be true? The darkness seemed to swirl around him as it listened in to their conversation. Lorenzo sat back into his chair until only the edge of his face was still illuminated.

"Precisely, Sebastian." A lump rose, and Sebastian swallowed heavily.

"No."

"No?"

"I won't do it. I won't be a puppet for you. I won't be Axiom's Lord Protector," Sebastian said with quiet defiance. Lorenzo chuckled.

"Sebastian, you already are." Fear and frustration made Sebastian rise to his feet. The air around him quivered with this knowledge. "And you aren't going to be able to stop what's coming," Lorenzo promised. His face wore satisfaction.

"We stopped you, Lorenzo. That's why you're in a cell." Lorenzo chuckled. "What's so funny?" Sebastian asked angrily.

"You forget the most important truth, Sebastian," Lorenzo said coolly.

"Let me guess—you've seen thousands of years, and you saw this coming?" Lorenzo's lips curled into a grin.

"No. You forget that I...," his words distorted and filled with a rasping undertone. Sebastian watched in shock as his skin oozed with scarlet. Red lines traced their way across his body until he was a million pieces held together by blood.

"Am Axiom."

Lorenzo dissolved into a thousand strands of shimmering ruby. Sebastian stared numbly at the empty chair as the Lord Protector filled Axiom.

Acknowledgements

A story is a journey, and along the way I have met many people who have made the process enjoyable and easier. I want to thank my wife, Kristie, for her unrelenting support. I want to thank those who read advanced copies of Citadel and provided important critique and insight into making it a better story. I want to thank Lucas Miles, who gave me incredible insight into how to successfully launch a story—your knowledge is tremendously appreciated! A tremendous thank you to Brady Killingsworth whose red pen saved me from embarrassment. I want to thank my dad for checking in on my progress, and encouraging me to build my network. I want to thank God, for giving me the capabilities and drive to write good stories. And lastly, I want to thank you, the reader. You took a shot by reading this novel. I'm hardly a name you'd recognize, and yet you picked up my work. Thank you. You make all of the agonizing nights, the third and fourth cups of coffee, and the feelings of desperation worth it. I'd love to connect with you on social media and discuss what you thought about my book.

Kristofor Hellmeister

Made in the USA
Columbia, SC
17 March 2023